Alex G

The Helsinki Pact

The Chesil Press, Dorset

First published June 2015
by The Chesil Press, Dorset, UK
www.chesilpress.com

British Library Cataloguing in Publication Data. A catalogue record for this book is available from the British Library.

ISBN: 978-0-9933024-0-4

All rights reserved
No part of this publication may be reproduced or transmitted in any form or by any means, electronic or mechanical, including photocopy, recording, or any information storage or retrieval system without the written permission of the publisher

This book is a work of fiction

© Copyright Alex Cugia
The moral rights of the author have been asserted

Prologue
March 1989

It was a strange setting in which to discuss the future of a nation.

Alfred Herren rubbed his gloved hand over the room window to clear it and watched as the dark grey Tupolev jet rebounded twice on the icy air field and ground to a halt. The Soviet officials were fifty minutes late. "In all likelihood deliberately," he thought "a crude negotiating tactic." But calling this meeting on Soviet ground, in an abandoned military base on the Finnish border, was at least an admission of interest. Chancellor Kohl had confided to him that his overture to President Gorbachev had struck a chord. Now it was time to lay all the cards on the table. If the information he had received on the economic situation in the Soviet Union was correct then the deck was stacked in his favour.

Herren removed a glove, blew on his numbed fingers and pondered the potential outcomes. As CEO of Deutsche Bank he had lived through countless business negotiations and had generally been able to pull off the expected result. But businessmen were by definition rational beings, even if they didn't always act that way. Seen from the Soviet side, where it would be viewed as a political move, his proposal could seem a provocation, an insult to a ruling superpower. The meeting could last a few minutes and officially would never have taken place. No trace would exist in the records. Or the lives of millions of people and the very shape of Europe would later change forever as a result of the processes started by their discussions.

Through the whirlwind of snow and ice fragments raised by the jet's exhausts he could make out the silhouettes of two men leaving the plane. Herren immediately identified the first, tall, well-built and in military uniform, as General Lushev, Commander of the Warsaw Pact forces. "The man behind him is probably a political emissary." he thought. He glanced through the dossier prepared by the German Interior Ministry. "Ah. Undersecretary Pershev." he realised as the men came closer. Pershev was a rising star, educated in the United States and young to have reached the eminence he had. A little younger than Herren at just over forty he was the former head of one of the country's largest conglomerates and now one of Gorbachev's most influential advisors.

Herren shut the report with a wry smile. "They mean business," he mused to himself "if they're sending a Herren clone to negotiate."

The door at the far end of the now abandoned training room opened loudly and the noise of General Lushev's boots on the cement floor resonated across the bare walls. He looked considerably older than the picture in Herren's file but no less imposing. He was over six feet tall with vivid green eyes that betrayed intelligence and suspicion and that contrasted with his grey-white hair. Herren sensed their intensity as the eyes scanned him, searching for a weak spot. A massive hand took his a moment later and gripped hard.

Lushev broke off, turned to Pershev and spoke a long sentence in Russian. There was a long, awkward silence before Pershev nodded, taking three chairs from a stack in the corner and gesturing to everyone to sit down.

"Mr Herren, please take a seat." he said in fluent English. His tone was pleasant yet firm. "I hope you'll forgive us the discomfort of this deserted air base as a meeting place, but we understood that confidentiality was of the utmost importance." He was dressed elegantly: and with his dark grey suit, starched white shirt and yellow tie he could have easily passed as a successful Western European businessman. "Now, we understood from President Gorbachev that your Chancellor has a proposal aimed at enhancing German-Soviet cooperation. I'm afraid we've only been given a very sketchy outline but I'm sure you won't mind expanding."

Herren looked at him and then at Lushev. "If you'll forgive my lack of diplomacy I'll go straight to the point. We each have something the other needs. The Soviet Union is on the verge of economic collapse. Gorbachev's *perestroika* reforms so far have had a disastrous effect on the economy. Trying to keep up with President Reagan's increase in military spending, his so-called Star Wars Program, has caused your engine to melt down. The queues for food have never been longer. Social unrest is mounting."

He paused for effect, as Pershev translated. He tried to read some form of reaction in General Lushev's eyes, but could see no trace of agreement or denial.

"A mounting wave of nationalism is being used by local politicians to snatch power for themselves. Requests for independence are cropping up everywhere: Hungary, Georgia, Lithuania, now Kazakhstan. The USSR is ready to explode. To hold it together you only have two options: repressive military action or money."

Herren waited, but still no reaction. There was no doubt that the picture he had painted was correct− the Soviet Union was close to the brink. In all likelihood this was the main reason Gorbachev had been incessantly visiting the Western capitals in the last few months. The biggest threat to the USSR was coming not from its historical enemies but from within itself.

"Military intervention against the provinces would go against all of Gorbachev's tenets and compromise his credibility worldwide." Herren continued. "The rouble is non-convertible, and the internal savings rate abysmal. So you need foreign capital. But no Western government believes in your reforms enough to risk their own money. None except ours, that is. We are ready to put fifty billion Deutsche Marks on the table immediately. At a price, of course."

"What price?" Lushev intervened, in a thick Russian accent.

Herren moved toward the whiteboard to draw a rough sketch. "You have a vast empire, the biggest in the world in land area. The USSR stretches from Asia and the Pacific Ocean in the east, here, just across the Bering Straits from the US, and west to Europe, over 10,000 kilometres in distance. But the DDR, the German Democratic Republic, East Germany, call it as you will, is a Soviet creation. A puppet country. It should return to being part of Germany. We want you to cut the strings and let history take its natural course."

Pershev shot up from his chair. "You have the nerve to propose we sell you the DDR for fifty billion Deutsche Marks?" he shouted. He seized the cloth and wiped Herren's drawing in one swift move. "And this is what your Chancellor meant by enhancing the Soviet-German relationship?"

"Gentlemen, please." Herren said, noticing that Lushev was still sitting motionless in his chair. "We're all men of the political world here and we know how these things work. A proposal of financial assistance scandalizes you? Just over a hundred years ago, you sold Alaska to the United States. What is the lesser evil? You need our money desperately. And we can accomplish our mission with an invisible hand, so the Soviet Union will not lose face. In fact it will gain further in credibility. There is only one German nation, not two. Sooner or later, they will reunite. But if you hold on for too long it will be too late for the Soviet Union."

Two hours later, the snow cut slantingly through the freezing wind as Alfred Herren hurried back toward his private jet. Part of him was elated, another extremely worried. How long could negotiations be kept hidden from the DDR informants? East Germany's despotic ruling elite would use every means in its power to avoid being wiped away. The road to a new Europe was likely to be paved with dead bodies. Would his be among the first, he wondered, and he sat on the plane and took from his wallet a picture of his wife and their new born baby. The serene bliss of that moment during the summer holidays seemed ages away and he felt a chilling premonition about what his own future might be.

But first he had to report to Kohl. Lushev and Pershev would report in turn to Gorbachev. Assuming all went well, and he was certain that it would knowing how desperate the USSR was for hard currency, they would all meet again in a week, this time in Finland, neutral territory. He pulled out a pad from his briefcase, wrote *The Helsinki Pact* neatly at the top of a sheet, and began to make notes for his meeting with Kohl first thing in the morning.

Chapter 1
Friday 1 September 1989

Always when Thomas crossed he felt adrift in a time he couldn't quite grasp. Deceptively similar to his own, this country was one where he was no longer able to understand intuitively how things worked. "Make a simple mistake here," he thought "even from ignorance, and you could find yourself in jail."

He had been entering through the Friedrichstrasse crossing for months now but invariably he would feel apprehensive and uneasy until he was safely through. Even when he'd escaped to the city streets this feeling of wariness as to what might happen persisted for at least an hour, often longer. Each time the city's drabness struck him, marking the contrast with the determined jollity of the western sector. The brutalist architecture of the new buildings casually thrown down, it seemed, among the elegant constructions of the past didn't help, but there was also a general strangeness to the country, something at the same time familiar but also quite foreign to him.

Twice already he had stopped suddenly, wheeled round and walked rapidly back in the direction he'd come, scanning carefully the people on all sides, convinced that he was being followed. He'd been on edge from the moment he'd woken up, and the slow shuffle to the immigration desk had made things worse. He wished he hadn't learned of the soundproofed room deep in the building. Kai had joked about it but Thomas couldn't get it out of his mind, wondering if he'd end up there, wondering how he would cope if he did.

He'd been making regular crossings for months now but previously he'd had nothing more incriminating with him than some excess currency. This crossing was different.

Convinced he'd overlooked some detail which would have him suspected and given a full body search, his nerves at breaking point as a result of the stuttering movements of the queue and the menace brought by the armed guards round the stuffy hall, he'd nearly abandoned the attempt in order to return to the safety of his apartment. And then he'd thought that his risk was nothing to that of Kai, who was risking his life. He'd breathed slowly and deeply to steady his nerves, tried not to think of the soundproofed room, had shuffled forward with the rest trying to look a bit bored, a bit annoyed with the delays, and then suddenly he was through, out in the open.

Now on the streets of East Berlin, hurrying towards Kai's apartment, he couldn't shake off the feeling that something would go wrong, that he'd be stopped and invited - that was the word they used, although it was no use declining – to visit a drab, anonymous office hidden away somewhere where he would have to explain to the police or Stasi officers just what he'd been up to.

This time when he wheeled round and walked back he'd stopped on the corner, looked ostentatiously at his watch and exaggerated his gesture of annoyance as if whoever he was due to meet there was very late. He then spent several minutes scrutinising the passers-by, checking to see if there were any faces he'd seen recently or if anyone seemed to be paying him particular attention. There were two men in identical belted raincoats approaching him on the crossing who had looked at him and said something to each other. As he idly turned he saw one glancing back.

"Damn this!" he thought. "I'm getting paranoid!" He took a final scan of the streets, turned, and set off on the last few hundred metres towards Kai's apartment.

He crossed the wide Alexanderplatz, next to the towering TV antenna which had become the world recognised symbol of East Berlin. A closed subway station, now unused, faced him on the right. He recognised the landmarks and remembered that Kai's apartment block was just round the corner.

Visiting East Germans at home was not actually prohibited but it was strongly discouraged. Thomas had visited Kai only once before, shortly after he'd moved in, and he wondered if he was pushing his luck. People trying to escape were usually shot, if caught in the attempt, and anyone helping escapees could expect pretty much an indefinite jail sentence.

The building was old, unlovely, and not especially well maintained but its location, close to the now abandoned subway station, was exactly what Kai had been seeking for some time. Kai's apartment was right at the top but had a private utility room in the basement. This was the last of a row of such rooms, separated from the others by a noisy boiler room which the caretaker rarely visited, and on the closest side of the building to the Alexanderplatz.

The street door was unlocked and as Thomas entered he felt rather than saw a movement to his left and noticed the door to the only apartment on the ground floor, presumably that of the caretaker, standing very slightly ajar and then clicking shut as he crossed the hall to the stairs.

He climbed slowly to Kai's apartment, thinking of the woman who managed the cleaning and collected the rents and who, Kai was certain, was one of East Germany's multitude of Stasi informers. He was annoyed at being seen but realised that one could hardly avoid that in East Germany where, so some said, at least one in ten people were informers under Stasi control. At least it was gloomy in the hallway and he'd instinctively turned away as soon as he'd realised he was being watched. Kai had said he'd sometimes come across the woman unexpectedly, including once when he'd stormed out of the apartment following a furious quarrel with Ulrike and surprised her apparently tying her shoelaces right outside his door.

Thomas knocked and the door opened immediately, bringing with it the sounds of Strauss's Horn Concerto No 1. Thomas spoke formally and in a voice firm enough to carry downstairs rather than merely to the young man facing him.

"Good morning, Mr Schulz, I'd hoped to learn more about music in East Berlin. Is this a convenient time? And isn't that Baumann with the Leipzig orchestra, with Masur?"

Kai had raised a sardonic eyebrow, bringing a tremor to Thomas's voice which he'd had difficulty controlling.

"Of course, Mr Schmidt, of course. I've been looking forward to your visit. I thought that today we might look at going below the surface, exploring some of the hidden depths of the art for which we're so renowned."

He ushered Thomas in with a flourish, kicked the door shut, switched tracks on the tape deck and turned up the volume, filling the apartment with the full punk rock blast of *God Save the Queen*.

"Great guy Masur, especially the way he's moving now, but this is more like it." He moved to the music for a moment or two then turned to embrace Thomas.

"God, Kai, you do push things. My nerves are already shot bringing this stuff over." They hugged each other.

"You have to. It's the only way to remain sane. Anything else and you become one of them, or give up, stop living. They've hauled me in a couple of times, complained about my choice of music, but I just play dumb and they shout at me and nothing happens. They think I'm a half-wit. I guess you found what you were looking for. That's great! Let's see. Let's see!"

Thomas cut away the false lining of his jacket, removed the papers hidden there and spread them out on the table. Kai pored over them, tracing the lines with a finger and reading the station names with pure pleasure, a smile creasing his face.

"This is wonderful! Wonderful. Far more detailed than I'd ever hoped possible. This is going to make all the difference to us. Just wonderful!" He hugged Thomas hard again.

Thomas unfolded the construction plans of the now closed Alexanderplatz station and he and Kai pored over them, identifying the apartment block, measuring distances and checking angles. One of the documents was a blueprint on translucent paper showing the area's geology on the same scale as the construction plans and this confirmed what Kai had earlier been able to establish through talking casually to engineers and builders. The project was audacious but realistic, they could both see that now. Kai became serious. "I really think you've saved our lives with this."

Later at Kai's door they again shook hands formally. The album had come round to *Anarchy in the UK* for the second time, the volume now less of a full throated roar.

"Thank you again, Mr Schulz. That was very helpful and informative."

"My pleasure Mr Schmidt. I believe I learned from you in turn. I look forward to our next meeting, perhaps in a week or two if things go to plan." There was the slightest of smiles on Kai's face as he shut the door.

As Thomas clattered downstairs and crossed the hallway there was again a slight click from the door on his right. He scowled at it then opened the street door and walked away from the building. He should get something to eat, he felt, but decided first to make a business visit to the Ephraim Palais, an old French restaurant which many considered among the best in East Berlin. Perhaps Axel Gutwein, the restaurant manager he'd come to know well, would feed him.

Like most students in West Berlin Thomas lived hand to mouth. After his father had died relations with his mother had deteriorated. He'd finally had enough and, partly on account of following a girlfriend, partly because of its reputation as a party city, he'd moved from his family home in Frankfurt to Berlin and found a flat. He'd enrolled in the university to study economics, a course chosen less through a love of the subject than as a calculated assessment that an economics degree might help if he ever decided to return to Frankfurt and join the Bundesbank in the shadow of his illustrious father. His real love was opera and although he couldn't afford it he'd found ways of hustling money for occasional singing lessons even if that too often meant dodging his landlord.

Opera in East Berlin had a good reputation, he'd remembered. Visitors to West Berlin liked to visit the East, gawking at the Wall, shivering slightly from being in a communist country, asking how people set about escaping, and even, a few of them, admiring and curious about the history of that now separate part of the region. His eye for the main chance had alerted him to the opportunities that existed when a country's exchange rate was held at a wholly artificial level.

His venture had started slowly but was now going well and bringing him enough money to take more regular singing lessons and generally to enjoy life more. He focussed particularly on opera lovers, of whom there were many. He could put them at ease through his enthusiasm, knowledge and upbringing and by letting them deduce that his own voice was well regarded and that he was being encouraged to perform. He would hint at La Scala but modestly refuse to elaborate when pressed. His character of impoverished student from a good family and with a burning desire to succeed on the stage went down particularly well with visiting wealthy widows and divorcees from the US eager to spend their money on deliciously alarming excursions they could describe later at home to their less adventurous, or simply less rich, friends. Later each one would dwell nostalgically on the special relationship they, and only they, had developed with their handsome, well bred and attentive young guide. They sighed. If only they had been half a century younger.

His clients understood that an evening at the opera was incomplete without dinner in one or other of what passed as fine restaurants in the East. He would settle up in Ost Marks but charged his clients in DM at the official rate of 1:1 less a small discount he offered. This discount sweetened the deals and bound his clients more tightly to him both because they took pleasure in their cleverness in getting Ost Marks at a preferential rate and because the implied minor illegality heightened the thrill of visiting this curious and alarming country. He was entirely transparent as to his costs, showing openly restaurant bills and ticket prices, explaining that he got a small commission for bringing custom. He accepted tips only after an elaborate show of refusing, but did so graciously, bringing an additional glow to the giver. That he bought his Ost Marks at between 12 and 15 to the DM gave him sufficient room for generosity.

Only rarely did it cross his mind, still less trouble him, that some of his clients might not be what they seemed.

The Ephraim Palais was his favourite restaurant for this. He enjoyed the atmosphere and though it had lost some of its former glory he liked bringing clients there and watching them marvel at its faded opulence.

Axel was in his office, more baroque salon than modern business powerhouse and complete with ornate mirrors and overstuffed easy chairs in dull green velvet. Thomas took a long draught of the *pils* Axel offered, set it down on a mat on the Empire side table, and approached his mission obliquely.

"Axel, you know I bring tourists here and how much they enjoy it. And you make out separate bills for everyone at the end."

Axel nodded. He liked Thomas but wondered what scam he was going to suggest now.

"Suppose we offer them a fixed price menu? That would make things easier, wouldn't it? And suppose I paid in advance? You set up a kind of reverse tab and I'll preload it, maybe four or five thousand marks. You charge whatever number of meals it is against it and let me know how the balance is going and when it needs more. It would save time, make life easier for everyone."

Axel thought. There was something odd here but he couldn't work out what it was and the idea of cash up front was attractive. If Thomas kept a credit balance with him that meant he'd keep coming back to spend it. And if anything went wrong he could simply pocket what was left.

"Hmm. Maybe 50 to 60 marks a head would work." said Axel. "That's about the average spend, I guess."

"You could give me a discount on the menu prices." added Thomas. "What? 25% perhaps?"

Axel laughed. One of the things he liked about Thomas was that he was always on the make but had no embarrassment about it and didn't let a refusal dent his good nature or stop future attempts.

"OK! Let's do it – 55 Ost Marks a head for dinner on the menu with one glass of wine and anything more to drink to be paid for. Some of your clients drink like fish and the wines cost me enough as it is. Once you've set the tab up I'll charge the meals against it at 50 marks each and the wine at menu prices."

They shook hands. Axel waved his hand at the door. "Now finish your beer, I've work to get on with." He laughed again.

Thomas sauntered down the street, pleased with the good start to the evening. Now he'd get paid in the West as usual but by banking his East German cash at the restaurant would avoid the risk of bringing currency out of the country illegally.

He'd become hungrier and so decided to eat and have another beer or two. Setting off for a nearby *kneipe* he liked he noticed four young women approaching from a side street, one of them slightly apart from and trailing her companions as if disdaining their evident good spirits. He slowed down, ostensibly looking at the Parliament building ahead, to let them catch him up. As the first ones overtook him the young blonde trailing the group stopped and asked him for a light.

"I'm sorry, but I don't smoke."

"Oh, well, it can wait. I only smoke very occasionally." She pushed the pack into the breast pocket of her denim jacket, tured to leave then glanced back.

"Wait! Uh, would you like to go for a beer?" he said.

She stared levelly at him, holding his gaze until he dropped his eyes.

"I don't know my way around here and I don't know anyone so I just thought, well, I suppose thought there might be somewhere lively we could have a drink."

Again she stared at him, saying nothing.

"So you thought you'd try your luck. You're from the West. Whereabouts?"

"Frankfurt. But I live in West Berlin now. I'm Thomas, Thomas Wundart. How did you guess I'm not from here?"

"Your clothes, your accent, your air of superiority, the way you said 'There might be somewhere lively' as in 'Yeah, there's surely a decent bar somewhere even in a dump like the DDR', your general cocky manner … What else would you like me to say? Doesn't take much, does it?"

She again looked steadily at him, this time with the slightest of smiles on her face.

Women in the West didn't talk to Thomas that way and this woman's manner and confidence made him suddenly very interested in her. He'd already been attracted by her shape and the lights on her hair when he first saw her and although he still wanted her physically there was now something more that he'd rarely experienced, part irritation, part excitement, a sense that he was being tested to see if he was more than his surface, was worth getting to know, was at least her equal. But he sensed interest beyond the lightly hidden contempt and he had to build on that, not seem vacuous, boring or a typically materialist Westerner.

There was a silence while he struggled to think what to say and then she spoke again.

"Look, Thomas, I'm sick of tourists from the West patronising us. Maybe you didn't mean it in that way, though. I won't go for a beer with you, not now anyway, but you can come to this gig we're all off to if you want. That's if you've any interest in music." She nodded toward the Parliament building where her friends had gone and where three young men in jeans that moment pulled open the orange doors and disappeared inside. "I'm Bettina." she added.

She set off without waiting for an answer and Thomas hurried after her. There was no one in the long corridor just inside the door but as they walked to the end Thomas heard faint music getting louder. They descended some stairs and as Bettina pulled open a door marked *Freie Deutsche Jugend* he was hit by a crude cover blast of OMD's *Enola Gay*. The room had couples dancing energetically under strobe lights and Thomas smiled, thinking that even when partying members of the communist Free German Youth were making political statements about nuclear war and the perfidious USA.

"Who's the band?" he shouted.

"*Ficken den Westen*. They're from round here, student group, mainly do warm-ups, play covers. Then there's a DJ for a bit and the main band comes on at midnight. Shame you'll miss that – they're from Leipzig. Really, really good. But – if you will live in the West … " Again there was the hint of a smile.

"Well, I know you had Bruce Springsteen here, last year wasn't it?"

"July. Quarter of a million at the concert, maybe more. It was OK, but I'm more interested in what we do ourselves."

She shrugged and her eyes flickered down his body, lingered briefly, then returned to his face, the pupils widening almost imperceptibly. Thomas ached to hold her but, uncharacteristically, decided not to risk suggesting dancing. That, and perhaps more, would come later.

They stood at the bar, looking out over the crowd, saying nothing. He bought a couple of beers and placed one carefully by her hand and then, testing, lifted his own bottle and held it out to her, pleased when she took her own and clinked the two briefly.

"So, Thomas, what do you do? And why are you in East Berlin tonight?"

"I'm a student, economics, but what I really want to do is become an opera singer. I'm taking lessons. What about you? What do you do?"

"Interesting mix! Me? I study history, here at the Free University. Modern European stuff mainly. And I work part-time at the History Museum." She slid her empty bottle along the counter. "Ever been there? Maybe you should visit it if you haven't seen it."

"Once, but perhaps I need to visit it again. I could do with understanding more about different views on recent events, what others think happened during this century."

Again there was that long level look denoting an awareness of the gap between what he'd said and what he really meant but this time it was she who glanced away first. She hooded her eyes, opened her mouth and tapped it lightly twice with the opened fingers of her right hand, and then looked straight back at him. Again that hint of a smile.

His face felt warm and he glanced at his feet. "When do you work there? Every day, regularly or just sometimes?"

"Wednesday to Friday afternoons, usually. I get in about three, stay for a bit, usually till it closes. Mostly it's indexing and sometimes moving books up from the stacks."

A figure in torn jeans and tee shirt, a cigarette hanging from a wispily bearded mouth lurched from the crowd and stopped in front of them, swaying slightly as he tried to focus on Thomas. "I need a light, man."

Irritated, Thomas was curt. "I don't smoke." He turned, shutting out the figure and trying to rekindle the feeling growing between them which the student had interrupted. He glanced at his watch.

"I need to go." he said "But I would like to look round the Museum again, perhaps next week, Thursday probably."

"Well, ask at the desk in case I'm there. My surname is List."

They left the room together and as he walked up the stairs away from her he saw that she'd lifted the handset of a public phone along the downstairs corridor in the other direction.

"Colonel Dieter, please." she said and after a moment added "Yes, I've found him." and then spoke quietly for a short period.

Chapter 2
Friday 1 and Saturday 2 September 1989

When Ulrike returned from work about seven in the evening Kai fetched out from their hiding place under the kitchen floor the documents Thomas had brought. Not even giving her time to remove her coat, let alone eat, he turned on the ghetto blaster to drown out any conversation, sat her down at the table and spread the documents out with a flourish.

"Just look at this! Look at what Thomas has found for us. Isn't it wonderful? Look – here's our apartment block, right here, and here's Alexanderplatz and here ... "

She stared at the finely drawn diagrams and at the blueprint, wanting to match Kai's enthusiasm but unable to share what he was saying. Well, they'd finally got her, she reflected bitterly. That's what came of refusing the shop manager's advances. Not that it was unexpected. Ever since she'd slapped him hard in the storeroom after it became clear that merely wriggling away from his grasp and saying 'no' wasn't enough she'd realised that it was only a matter of time. Herr Wagner was known to be capricious and to become mean and vindictive when thwarted. It had been a month ago now but when she saw her name entered as item 8 on the agenda for the works council meeting she knew what was coming.

He'd been clever, she conceded, very clever, but then he always was. He spoke in sorrow, told the meeting how he'd tried frequently to give friendly advice to her about her work, her timekeeping on breaks, even - and here he hesitated but finally spoke with the air of someone pained by having to do what he knew was his duty to the organisation and to his country – even her *attitude*. Had it not been for that, he'd said, there might have been a way back, a way for her to learn to become a trusted and valuable employee. But everyone was in it together and the state depended on proper support from its people. He'd shaken his head slightly in despair at his own failure, saw to it that the meeting understood how hurt *he* was and left it to others to propose her dismissal. She couldn't help but notice the glance of triumph that flashed between Wagner and the pretty new trainee who, she understood immediately, was to be her replacement in a week's time. It was then she'd slipped out to oil the squeaky hinges of the outer door to the storeroom, a small revolt which gave her a flare of amusement and satisfaction as she thought about how Wagner had relied on its warning.

" ... and then we're there. No distance at all. Isn't that wonderful? ... Ulrike? Ulrike!"

She blinked as Kai waved a hand in front of her face, looked at the plans uncomprehendingly for a moment, and then smiled up at him. "Yes, wonderful. But maybe if you just explain some of that again to me ... "

He laughed. "I'll get you some coffee and then we can eat and I'll tell you all about it later. Bernhard and Klaus said they were coming over, didn't they? We'll talk about it then."

Just after eight the doorbell rang and Kai opened it to Bernhard who motioned downwards with his finger and raised his eyebrows as he stepped into the apartment. Kai banged the door shut, keeping the catch open, and then immediately opened it silently and leaned over the rail to catch sight of Frau Schwinewitz scuttling back to her ground floor apartment. Moments later the street door opened and as Klaus made for the stairs Kai noticed Frau Schwinewitz's door opening a crack. "At least I give her plenty of exercise!" Kai thought with amusement as he waited for Klaus to arrive.

Dropping the catch and locking the door fully they all shook hands. Kai again spread out the papers on the table and turned up the volume of the music.

"Look, guys. See what Thomas brought me today. Look at these. This confirms everything I've been telling you about. Look at the detail!"

"Remind me how this idea of breaking into the subway tunnel came up." Bernhard asked.

"Thomas's idea. He's at university in West Berlin and he uses this line regularly. He saw the ghost stations in East Berlin because the train ran through them although they never stopped. They were a kind of preserved bit of the past he said, unchanged since before the war, but closed since the Wall was put up. He wondered if it might be a way of getting out of East Berlin. Most of the digging had been done so it was just a case of finding a way to break into the subway itself and then following the tunnel to a station in the West. And then I found this apartment, about as close as you can get to the line itself, and with that utility room in the basement."

"Great idea! I like it." said Bernhard. "How far away are we here?"

"I've been working it out from the plans and it's about twenty metres from the edge of the building here to the wall of the tunnel as it enters the station. It looks further from the street but that's because we're looking at the building itself and the tunnel's on this side, luckily."

"How deep is it?"

Kai squinted at some figures on the edge of the plan. "The base, that's the rails I suppose, seems to be at 28m. Our basement's underground but only just and so that means the floor's maybe, what, five metres at most underground, less probably. God! We can't dig down that much." They stared at each other in dismay.

"That's not right, though, surely?" Bernhard said. "Sometimes when you walk along the street at the back of the station you can hear the trains right underneath. It can't be 28m, it just can't be."

He spun round the plan and ran a finger down the columns of numbers at the edge, then smiled.

"No, look. 28m is the foundation, the bedrock. The tunnel floor is ten metres here and, look, it rises in this direction so it's just under eight metres at this edge, maybe nine or so in the middle of the plan. And the tunnel roof's five metres above the tunnel floor so that's pretty much the same level as the basement floor. We'll have to dig down a bit from the basement floor anyway, maybe a metre, couple of metres at most, and if we keep things level we should hit the tunnel wall somewhere in the middle, maybe two to three metres above the tracks anyway."

Kai slapped his forehead and rested his head on his cupped hands for a moment then beamed shamefacedly at Bernhard. "I was worried there, thought we were so close and it was turning out all wrong. OK, let's get going. It's not even nine, we can get started straight away, do a couple of hours at least tonight." Kai swallowed his coffee, grabbed his coat and stood waiting expectantly for Bernhard and Klaus who sat calmly looking over the plans together, occasionally sipping coffee.

"Come on!" he urged. "We're wasting time!"

"Sit down Kai! Have some more coffee." Bernhard leaned back in his chair and smiled at Kai's impetuosity. "You know the story of the two bulls? One day, as an old bull stood munching grass the young bull sharing his field came thundering up to him. 'Grand-dad! Grand-dad!' he bellowed 'There must be thirty new heifers just brought into that field up there. Let's rush up the hill and shag one or two. Come on! Come on! We're wasting time.' And the old bull looked placidly him, glanced up the hill at the young cows, bent and took another mouthful of grass and chewed it reflectively while the young bull stamped and snorted and foamed with excitement. 'Hmm.' he said 'OK, but let's just amble up the hill instead when we want to, save our energy, and then we can shag the lot.'"

Kai laughed. "OK, granddad! But why not get started? Why wait?"

"We have to break through the floor to make a start. That's concrete and however we do it that's going to be noisy. You told me Saturday's when Schwinewitz goes to Normannenstrasse for her weekly debriefing. She'll be away with her handlers all morning like the good snitch she is. That's when we have to break through. Now where's that beer you promised me?"

"Can you get sacks?" Kai asked Klaus. "And how do we dump the soil we dig out? What about taking to your site and adding it to the stuff being dug out there. Any problems with that?"

"Shouldn't think so. There's a dozen sacks in the van already and I can get more on Monday. That should be plenty. They're all marked 'Kugia Konstruction' so that won't be suspicious if anyone sees them. You might have to help me sometimes, Bernhard. Got some wood too, struts and planks for the tunnel supports. Let's fetch these in later and get them to the basement when your woman downstairs has gone to bed."

*

By nine on the Saturday Bernhard and Klaus were again in the apartment, drinking coffee as Kai leaned over the rail watching for Frau Schwinewitz to leave. Minutes later the three men, accompanied by a protesting Ulrike, slipped down the stairs carrying a pickaxe, a stout spade and other tools, including a small electrically driven pneumatic drill, face mask and ear muffs which Bernhard had removed temporarily when the construction site had closed down for the weekend.

"Why do I have to be there? I can't dig. I've got stuff to do this morning."

"Sorry Ulrike" said Bernhard "but we need you. Old Schwinehag may be out for the morning but we can't risk alerting anyone at all. Someone might come down and if they do you need to warn us to keep quiet."

He handed her a small piece of wood wrapped around with wire, a push button on one side and the other with a small plastic box covering part of the electronics. "I need you to stand in the corridor and if you hear someone coming just press that button firmly for a second or so. Then when it's all clear again, press it quickly three times."

In the basement room the three men stood looking at the floor, working out where to break through. The building was old but also had been put up during a period of cost cutting and shoddy construction and the floor carried the characteristic crack pattern of a poorly controlled initial mix, perhaps worsened through frost damage during some of the severe winters when the basement was largely unused.

"Come on! Come on! We gotta train to catch and it won't wait. WhooooHoooo! WhooooHoooo! Let's get this baby goin'!" Kai sang. He pointed to a spot close to the west wall of the room, facing towards Alexanderplatz, where the cracks were more numerous and deeper and where a few small plugs of concrete had pulled out and left conical dips two or three centimetres across running in a rough arc. "What about here?"

"Sure. Seems good as anywhere." Bernhard propped up the alarm box where he could see it, pulled on the ear muffs and mouth mask, plugged in the jack drill and switched on the power at the socket. "Better put your fingers in your ears if you plan to stay. This is loud!"

He held the cross bar firmly in his left hand, grasped the other handle with his right, pushed the bit into a small cavity in the floor and pulled the trigger.

Despite the warning the volume of noise in the small room shocked Kai. The roar of the powerful motor combined with the harsh thumping screech of the bit pounding and turning on the concrete blasted off the room's hard surfaces, bouncing and echoing around them, defeating his fingers in his ears and setting his teeth on edge. "Jesus Christ!"

Almost immediately the red light on the alarm box glowed and went off. Bernhard switched off the drill and the three stood listening.

"You two wait here till I find out what's going on. Maybe that woman's back early. Best I go and check with Ulrike."

The corridor was empty as Kai left the room and he found Ulrike half way up the stairs looking worried. "God! Kai. What was all that noise? It sounded like you were demolishing the building."

"That's a bit awkward if it's so noisy. Let's see what it's like in the hall."

They walked up the stairs, opened the door at the top and stood in the empty hall. Frau Schwinewitz's apartment door was firmly closed and they had to assume she was still out being debriefed. Ulrike pressed the button on the alarm device three times in quick succession and in a moment the dull roar of the drill began again, reduced by the distance and the closed doors but still clearly audible.

"Music! That might help. You stay here in the hall Ulrike. They might as well get on with it but watch out for anyone coming. Send the signal if any of the doors open."

Kai ran up to the apartment and returned quickly with the ghetto blaster, taking it down to the basement. The drilling noise stopped, replaced by the first track of *Never Mind the Bollocks* played at full volume, the sound penetrating the hall, somewhat muffled but still powerful, then stopped.

"Klaus complained! Said that racket was worse than the drill." Kai laughed as he reappeared. "I told him he could stand in the corridor if he didn't appreciate great music. Let's hear it with the drill. Bernhard's going to run it more slowly to try to cut the noise down." He pressed the button on the alarm device three times and the shoe stamping of *Holidays in the Sun* broke out, overlaid with what might have been mistaken for an eccentric and rapid boot stamping variant, a crazed cover version, had it not gone on insistently through the following tracks. Kai stood listening for several minutes, walking about the hall and up to the first floor.

"Hmm. It'll do, I suppose. Have to. At least it hides it a bit and maybe it won't take too long to break through the floor. You'd best stay up here. I bet it'll be Braun from the first floor who'll come nosing around, though, complaining about 'that racket' if he hears anything. You know the one I mean, him always going on about decadent youth listening to pop music and always making too much noise." He mimicked a sour face, moved his head around and whined. "'Wasn't like that in our day!' Pillock!"

He returned to the basement. Klaus was standing outside the door, coughing. Kai entered quickly and found Bernhard still hunched over the drill pounding away at the floor, a hazy smoke of cement dust now filling the room and an irregular trench connecting the pits, a little over half a circle of about a metre wide. Bernhard grinned at him and continued working, starting on the second half, poking into and enlarging cracks in order to join up with the existing trench. Sometimes the work went well, the drill blade cracking and ripping the concrete easily and then slowing and jumping off harder elements in the aggregate. Absorbed in his task Bernhard failed to notice the warning light come on and Kai had to punch his arm to get him to stop. They turned down the volume of the music and stood trying to hear.

"Someone going out or coming in, I guess. It's getting on for half past ten, now, so we should have at least a couple of hours before Schwinewitz gets back. How much longer do you reckon, Bernhard?"

"Not long. Ten minutes maybe to complete the circle I guess. Then we need to break that bit of concrete away – we'll use the sledgehammer for that, less noise, less continuous noise anyway."

In reality it took much longer, the concrete being much more irregular in thickness than Bernhard had realised. Smashing at it with the hammer or the pickaxe had little effect other than sending chips flying and occasionally running a crack. Ulrike had become angry at the enforced waiting, insisted on returning to the apartment and Kai had taken her place in the hall. It was now approaching midday. Bernhard had returned to using the hammer drill and Kai was getting tired of hearing the same Sex Pistols' songs over and over. He was beginning to worry whether Frau Schwinewitz would return before they'd finished. As she hardly left the building otherwise that was potentially serious. In any case, the hammer drill had to be back in the tool store at the construction site by 7.30 on Monday morning.

Suddenly, the background thumping of the drill over the raucous music stopped and was replaced by erratic dull thuds. The music stopped as well and shortly afterwards Klaus appeared through the basement door.

"We've done it! Bernhard cut through nearly all of it – it was over half a metre thick at one point. I think they'd just tipped concrete in here and there to fill up holes they'd left, real cheapjack building. Anyway, there's a big hole in the floor now so we're OK."

The three of them worked in pairs in half hour shifts during the afternoon and late into the evening, camouflaged for sound by a variety of bands, one person digging and another filling the sacks with excavated soil and rubble. At first it was easy. They dug down a metre below the floor and then started a horizontal, slightly sloping tunnel west towards Alexanderplatz.

As Kai ended a digging shift he stretched and casually tried to lift one of the filled bags.

"God! That's heavy!" He lifted it again, raising it from the floor with difficulty, and walked a few paces round the room before it slipped from his hands. "Do we have to fill them so much? That's not going to be easy moving them up stairs and out to the van. And if Schwinewitch is around ... "

"But we're also running out of bags. Look, we've already filled ten out of the ones I brought over and that's before we've even really started on the proper tunnel. I'd no idea the earth was going to be so heavy or so bulky, once we'd dug it out. This isn't going to work is it? We've got ten, twenty times as much to dig out, how can we carry all that out without being seen? And if we don't do that where can we put it all? Maybe we should just forget the whole idea." Klaus sat down gloomily on one of the filled bags.

"Bugger that! I'm not forgetting it." said Kai furiously. "I've had enough of this country and I'm getting out. And this tunnel is how we're going to do it."

"I don't like it here either but there's just too many things that could go wrong. " Klaus objected. "It's not just shifting the earth. Alexanderplatz is still used for the other lines isn't it? There'll be people around, passengers, police,

Stasi, everyone you don't want, till midnight anyway, probably later. I bet there are guards patrolling when it's closed as well."

"I've been into all this with Thomas and we've checked things out. Yes, the station's still used but it's an entirely different part, different lines. The bit we're breaking into is really another station completely. No one's going to be around in that part, not even maintenance. No one's been there for years. It's completely shut off, deserted."

"I still don't like it." said Klaus. "The more I think of it now the more crackpot it seems. Someone's going to hear us or see or we'll get run over by a train or step on the life rail or something. And you know what happens if we get caught. If we're lucky not to get shot trying to escape we'll be in jail for ever. The foreman was complaining about shortage of bags this morning and fussing about the drill not being where he'd left it. And this thing about getting rid of the earth has tipped it for me. It's just too risky."

"I'm with Kai." said Bernard. "Everything's risky but I'm getting out, whatever it takes. I'll eat the fucking earth myself if that's the only way we can get rid of it, just to get out of this shitty country. We'll work something out tomorrow. Come on, Klaus. Let's get these tools back to the van and you can give me a lift home."

Chapter 3
Sunday 3 September through to Saturday 9 September 1989

Bernhard and Klaus returned together the following day, Sunday. Klaus was reluctant, nervous and anxious about getting caught and ending up either shot or imprisoned but Bernhard had insisted Klaus drive him over.

"Think about what you can do when you get there!" said Kai. "Think of the freedom. None of this looking over your shoulder all the time. None of this thinking twice before you say anything. And you're a skilled carpenter, you'll be able to pick up a job in no time. Think of the money you'll make! Think of all the rubbish you'll be able to buy, stuff which you just can't get here!"

"True. And I do think of that. I want that. But I also think how really risky it is. And then there's Ingrid. You know Ingrid, Bernhard, she's in accounts. Well, we've got together and sometimes she stays over. I don't want to lose her."

"Well, you certainly can't take her, not right now anyway!" Bernhard looked startled. He'd known vaguely of Klaus's interest but hadn't taken it very seriously. "You've not said anything to her, have you? No hints, no pillow talk?"

"I've said nothing. What do you take me for?" Klaus was indignant. He sat down. "Why are you looking at me like that. Anyway, why would it matter? Ulrike knows all about it and she's coming with us. You've not got a girlfriend, Bernhard, but Ingrid and I are getting close. Maybe I'd like to take her. Maybe she'd want to come. What would be wrong with that?"

Bernhard glanced at Kai. "You know where her father works, don't you? Normannenstrasse. He's head of the division that controls this sector." He walked over and stood directly in front of Klaus, leaned close as Klaus stood up. "I like you, Klaus, I do, but if I find out you've said a word to Ingrid, dropped a hint, anything, anything at all, I'll break your fucking neck. Don't think I won't. That heavy machinery I work can cause accidents if I get a bit careless. And if Kai and I get picked up first, well, I've some pretty good mates on the site." He laughed. "We're the Stasi of the heavy plant operators, we know exactly what's going on and how to deal with it."

He made a shudder at Klaus and growled theatrically in his face. "We're ruthless!"

He threw an arm around Klaus's shoulder. "Look Klaus, no cunt's worth it. Send for her later if you want. OK, let's get working. I'll start digging and you fill the bags. How about getting us some coffee, Kai?"

Working in shifts as before they made good progress, opening up over a metre of the tunnel by late Sunday evening. Kai, smaller and slighter than the others and with a desk job, found it harder. By the time they stopped his muscles were aching, he was drenched with sweat and it was with difficulty that he was able to stand upright. He groaned and tried to stretch.

"Ugh! I don't think I can survive another fortnight, maybe more even, of this! You'll have to carry me through the tunnel when we finish, I think. But, seriously, guys, I'm excited about it. We've only got evenings now till next weekend but I'm going to take a day off, maybe Wednesday, say I'm sick or something. How about one of you doing the same?"

"I guess I could." said Bernhard. "Not Wednesday, though. Maybe Friday when we're less busy, or Thursday. I'll sort something out, get one of my mates to cover. I'll let you know tomorrow."

All the bags had been filled by midday and they'd been forced to start building a spoil heap of excavated earth in a corner of the room. Bernhard walked over and looked at the mound, then dropped into the hole and looked over the tunnel start.

"I don't like this, though. We're going to run out of space well before the end. We can reduce the tunnel dimensions a bit, maybe. A metre 75 height is nice but we could get away with a metre, I think, maybe a metre 20, and, what, maybe three quarters wide, less if we can stand it. Can't avoid the shoring up either. I don't fancy being buried by a roof fall."

"Well, we've tried carrying the stuff out to the van and that's hopeless." said Klaus. "That woman caretaker was watching me when I carried the bags out and when I did the second lot she was on to me, asking what I was up to. Told her I was helping you clear out old junk, Kai, but she's not going to believe that, day after day. Something will go wrong and we'll be caught."

"Room nine is empty." said Kai suddenly. "I'm sure of it. That's three doors down the corridor from this one. It's the old couple on the floor below me. They find it hard enough getting up three flights to their apartment so they almost never go out, let alone down here. I know them a bit and they're OK so I'll find out what the score is. That one's got a padlock, not a mortice, so that's good. Bernhard, can you get some bolt cutters and a new padlock and we'll start moving the stuff in there."

They dug on through the following week starting each evening at seven and putting in four and sometime even five or more hours. On the Friday they'd hit the ten metre mark. They had been forced to change direction twice, once because of a water pipe exactly in their path which forced them downwards another half metre, and then because of a huge slab of rock too big and hard to break through and which seemed endless as they dug round it. Kai and Bernhard had bickered about whether to go left or right.

They'd tossed a coin, dug to their right for a couple of metres without success, bickered again, and Bernhard had finally broken through by going a metre to the left. At least, the consoled themselves, they now had a large, roomy chamber about half way along, useful for storing tools and bags.

But now it was getting increasingly difficult. There was little air in the tunnel and hardly any room to manoeuvre. Wary about Frau Schwinewitz's snooping they'd decided to wait to the Saturday morning to shift as much soil as they could into the neighbouring room. Till then they had no option but to pile up the excavated earth in the room and they'd already filled over half the cellar, floor to ceiling. Klaus had stolen a further twenty bags and the forty remaining, filled to bursting, sat in one corner, piled high on themselves in a shaky edifice which made everyone near it wary and which they resented because of the time spent juggling earth and bags around to fit in the small space.

On one occasion Kai had grown dizzy and collapsed as he'd crawled back and might well have suffocated had Bernhard, alarmed that he'd missed his shift change, not gone looking for him and dragged him out. They'd discussed trying to buy breathing equipment but in the end settled for installing a long plastic pipe back to the cellar which they could grab and get fairly fresh air through it if they began to feel faint.

One evening they returned to find that there had been a minor fall as part of the roof had collapsed and they'd then had to waste more time and space shoring up better the sides and building roof supports for a three metre stretch. Kai tried not to think about the many tonnes of material directly overhead and about what would happened if the roof gave way while anyone was under it.. Most of the time they'd had to work in the dark or using a small lantern battery torch as the heat from the electric lamp they'd brought quickly became intolerable.

Klaus had been becoming more and more withdrawn as he worked, grunting in response to comments and ignoring the banter of the others as they dealt with the various problems that kept occurring. On Saturday Kai repeated his monitoring of a fortnight earlier, looking down from the top floor to watch for Frau Schwinewitz's departure to her debriefing meeting. Ten minutes after she'd left Bernhard snapped off the existing padlock on the room three doors away and hung on the staple a second hand lock resembling the original. They crowded into the room, relieved to find it empty.

"Hey, it's just like mine. A few trips shifting that earth over and it'll be even more like mine! I'm going to paint the floor with a drawing of a jagged concrete hole and a tunnel entrance. Make me feel at home. What do you think, guys?"

Klaus grunted and returned a few moments later, dragging one of the sacks behind him, then emptied it in the far corner. Bernhard carried one from one room to the other and did the same but when Kai attempted it he could only drag the sack, spilling earth on to the corridor floor as he went and treading and scuffing it into the surface.

"Kai, get a brush and a cloth, maybe some water too, to clean all this up. Your snooping caretaker's going to go apeshit if she finds all this earth around. She'll suspect something and start watching you closely. We can't risk that. Go on. Klaus and I'll carry the bags over and empty them. You can stay in the room and fill them up for us."

At midday, their limbs aching and their faces and hands streaked with dirt, they took a break, looking with satisfaction at the greatly reduced pile of dirt in the tunnel room. Kai brought down coffee, a pail of water and some old cloths to clean themselves up when they'd finished.

"When does Schwinesnitch usually get back?" Bernhard asked.

"Half two, two maybe, something like that. Once she got back at one but mostly it's been later. We're safe for another half hour at least, I'd say, maybe another half hour after that. We should just about clear it completely in that time. I'll go up to the hall with the alarm device at one, though, to be safe."

Klaus stood, drained his coffee, dragged a bag over the floor, hoisted it on to his shoulder as he opened the door, stepped into the corridor and moments later burst back in and slid the bolt across.

"She's back! I saw her walking down that side corridor across from the other room. A few seconds earlier and I'd have bumped into her. Jesus! Or she might have seen me going in there with the dirt. Shit! We left it unlocked, didn't we? What if she notices that? Opens the door? We're finished!"

"That corridor's where her own basement room is." Kai said. "She's just putting something away or collecting something. I'll sneak out and if she's not about I'll fix the padlock And if she is, well, she knows me anyway, knows I do stuff down here, maybe I can ask her about something, get her upstairs again and one of you guys can lock it."

He slid back the bolt but just as he was about to ease open the door he heard soft footsteps approaching so he tapped the bolt silently back into place instead. Scarcely breathing the three men stood in the intense silence as the footsteps halted outside. The door handle turned and the door flexed slightly and gave a creak before the handle moved back again. After another period of silence the footsteps moved away and became fainter. In a moment there was the familiar creak of the door at the foot of the basement stairs opening and then closing again. They looked at each other and Kai shook his head slightly and put his finger to his mouth. Five minutes later the stair door creaked again, this time with a longer pause before the closing creak and the slight noise of footsteps followed.

"That's what she does, opens the door and then closes it again and if you go out you'll find her still snooping around." He shivered. "But I think she's really gone up now. I'd better go and check." He put his finger to his lips. "Not a sound."

In a few moments he returned. "She's gone. I put the other padlock back on. Let's hope she didn't notice anything. There's a fair bit of dirt in the corridor, though. She'll wonder about that so I'd better think up some story in case she says anything. Best stop for today."

"Look, guys. I can't take this any more." Klaus looked at Kai and then at Bernhard. "I'm sorry, I just can't. You know I've been leery about it for the past week or so. And then I keep thinking of Ingrid and how I'll feel if she's still here and I'm over there. I want to get out. Of course I do. But I want it to be with her. I want to be with her and with all this stuff going on we're going to get caught, I'm sure of it. If that happens I'll be dead or in jail and I'll never see her again. I'm sorry to let you down, guys, but I'm out of here." He looked warily at Bernhard. "And I promise, I'm going to forget everything we've done or you're doing. Don't worry about that. I promise you. I wish I could come with you - but I just can't." He held out his hand and after a moment's hesitation Bernhard took it and they embraced, Kai following.

Chapter 4
Thursday 14 September 1989

On the next Thursday Thomas crossed early and got to the German History Museum well before it closed for the day. He'd no intention of looking round - he'd visited it once, shortly after arriving in Berlin, and once was more than enough for these sorts of turgid fairytales, he thought - but he wanted to make sure that Bettina didn't leave early before he arrived. He sat on a low wall across the street where he could keep both the main entrance, and more particularly the side entrance, in view.

The weather had changed and an icy cold wind blew in from the east. A dense blanket of cloud covered the sky. In a nearby garden someone had lit a bonfire and the smell of apple wood and leaves reminded him of his parents' house in Frankfurt in autumn weekends when his father was alive. Although he was well wrapped up in a thick coat and scarf the wind still got to him and periodically he rose to stamp his feet and walk about a little on the pavement. Since they'd met nearly a week earlier he hadn't been able to get Bettina out of his mind. He'd spent the wait till he could see her again in thinking about her and rehearsing clever things to say when they met, things he knew he would nevertheless probably never say. He felt almost as edgy and apprehensive as when he'd crossed the previous week although then the penalties for failing would have been far more severe. He pictured her lying next to him, smiling up at him as he leant on his elbow, pulling him down to kiss him.

Then suddenly she was there. The museum had not long closed and staff were streaming out of the side door and there she was, on her own and among the stragglers. She looked beautiful and stylish, wearing a well fitting black leather jacket which set off her figure and complemented her blonde hair, her appearance bringing him to an ache of longing. He got up and moved towards her, waving a little self-consciously when he got closer.

"Oh, you. Thomas isn't it?, Thomas something or other. Can't you afford phones in the West now?"

"Wundart." He was pleased she'd recognised and remembered him.

"I tried calling ... " he said, embarrassed. "Well, actually, no, I didn't. I was afraid you might tell me not to show up, that you were busy or something. Shall we get some hot chocolate or coffee somewhere? It's freezing, total brass monkey weather."

They walked down a nearby side street and entered a small, nondescript shop with a sawdust strewn floor. The walls were plain and bare. A large black dog was dozing in a corner, close to the single tiny radiator. Wafts of aromatic steam, rich and chocolaty, came from behind a door to the left. The old woman behind the counter greeted Bettina with evident pleasure and broke into a flood of comment in a broad Sachsen accent which Thomas had difficulty in following. He thought he picked up a query about Bettina's 'new young man, handsome, eh?' and then something like 'But what about where it matters?' with the lascivious cackle which followed drowning Bettina's reply. They sat at one of the two tables in the back room.

"I used to spend a lot of time here" Bettina said "reading, but also just talking, discussing things with other students, arguing. Setting the world to rights." She smiled and looked round the room.

"So how was your visit to the museum?" she asked. "What did you think of the new exhibit? I mean the space given over to the history of our glorious leader. Right there in the entrance hall. How remarkable that he joined the Spartacus League when he was ten, the full Party at 17 and that he was one of the first members of the SED when it was formed? What commitment! What deep understanding of the proletarian struggle!"

There was a long silence while Thomas thought frantically of what comment he might make. Was she serious? Should he praise the exhibition, laugh at it, say he'd missed it? But how he could he miss something apparently so obvious? He caught her eye and that decided him.

"An exhibition devoted to Honecker's history could put the story of the DDR into proper perspective." he said, leaning back in his chair, waiting.

She laughed. "So you didn't visit the museum! Well, in your position I don't suppose I would have done either." She laughed again and then, suddenly, was serious. "But if you'd pretended, said what a fine exhibition it was perhaps, we'd have had our chocolate but we would never have met again." She looked down at the table and then looked levelly at him. "I'm glad that's not the case."

"Are you from Berlin?"

"Dresden. Have you been there?"

"Never. You'd need a special permit and I've never arranged one. I hear it's very beautiful."

"It was. Still is in parts. It was a wonderful, beautiful, old city, with narrow streets and some marvellous Baroque and Renaissance architecture. But you need to look at paintings and old photographs to get a proper understanding of what it was like, how wonderful it was."

Her tone was bitter and Thomas nodded silently. Almost the entire historic centre of what had been known as the Florence of Germany had vanished in February 1945, destroyed in the firestorm which the Allied bombing had intentionally created, a raid which aroused strong emotions on all sides.

"Is your family still there? How many are you?"

"My mother moved to Leipzig and there's now only her and Paul, that's my younger brother. He's 22, lives about half way between Dresden and Berlin. He's had some troubles and life isn't easy for him right now. But what about you? Tell me ... "

She was interrupted by the arrival of two steaming cups of hot chocolate, 'molten lava' as they were popularly named in the shop. Bettina insisted on paying.

"Thank you. But that means dinner's on me. I hope that's OK, that you're free. I know of a place not far from here. It's maybe not as, umm, distinctive, as this one but the food's very good and I've got to know them a bit there, business reasons, and, well, I'd like ... " He trailed off and they drank their chocolate in silence.

Thirty minutes later they were at the Ephraim Palais, its entrance decorated with stucco angels and gilded leaves lit by the ornate chandeliers and reflected in the huge Baroque mirrors framed in red and gold gesso which lined the hallway. The dominant dull red of the large oriental carpet subtly complemented the dark green marble which it partially hid.

"Good evening Madame. It's a pleasure to see you again Mr Wundart. The table in the alcove is ready for you."

As the waiter took their coats, led the way and helped them to their seats Thomas sensed Bettina's resistance and mounting anger. He looked warily at her over the spotless linen tablecloth as the waiter, having signalled someone across the room, turned back to them.

"Something to drink before you eat? We've been fortunate to get a few more cases of that Elbthal Weissburgunder you liked so much, Mr Wundart. Perhaps a bottle of that?"

Bettina's chair crashed to the floor she stood up in fury. Ignoring the startled glances from other diners she dashed the contents of her water glass in Thomas's face and would have upended everything from the table in his lap had he not managed to stop her fierce movements.

"Student? Student! You bastard! Your favourite wine! Your favourite table at East Berlin's most expensive restaurant! Is that how you try to impress the girls you pick up? Booking this before you even turned up at the Museum is so fucking sordid. How do you think that makes me feel? I'd begun to think you were different but you're just the same as the others – think all you need do is flash your money and the knickers fall off. Well, fuck you!"

As she stormed past Thomas grabbed her arm.

"Bettina, please. Please sit down. I swear you're the only girl I've ever brought into this place." He lowered his voice. "They know me because of the tours."

Bettina glared at him and shook her arm furiously in his grip. "Let me go! You're hurting me! Tours? What are you talking about? What tours?"

"I show people round East Berlin, show them the sights. I get them seats at the opera with dinner beforehand – that's usually here and that's why they know me. I'm not rich. I need money and this helps me pay for my studies and my singing lessons. They treat me well here because I bring them customers. That's all. Believe me, it's the first time I've ever come privately. And I wasn't trying to be smart or show off or anything like that. I just thought, well, I suppose I thought we'd both like it, the food and the atmosphere. And I wanted to be here with you." There was a pause. "And, yes, well, yes, I guess maybe a little bit I did want to impress you."

Thomas had released his grip and during this disjointed appeal Bettina had righted her chair and slowly sunk down on it, movements which gave Thomas some hope. "God, let me not screw it up again, don't let me say the wrong thing now." he thought. He took off his jacket, pushed back into the side pocket a handkerchief and packet of cigarettes which had fallen out during the struggle, and hung the garment over his chair. He sat down again and looked warily at her.

"I can't stand rich Wessies looking down on us, trying to buy their way into everything and everyone."

He looked at her again, trying to work out if there was something more behind her violent reaction. Her otherwise perfectly straight nose curled slightly at the tip and her clear, smooth skin had acquired a healthy pink tinge, slightly flushed with red. He thought how beautiful she looked and how desirable her anger had made her to him. If he'd dared he might have told her so but her reaction just then had awed him with its vehemence. She was clearly still prickly and suspicious and he was afraid that an incautious remark would sent her storming off into the night, out of his reach for ever.

She rearranged the cutlery in front of her, lining up the bases of the knives and forks in a straight line, adjusting them minutely. "So what do you show these people in your tours? How we survive despite our bad choice in being here in the first place?" She pulled a face and spoke in a pantomime voice. "Look, Commies can be almost human! Just fancy!"

"They're interested in places connected to escapes from East Berlin. Checkpoint Charlie, Spy's bridge, the Wall, obviously – that kind of thing. But I hardly do any general tours now, it's nearly all opera or opera and dinner, maybe sometimes a gallery or a museum. This way I not only get to hear opera most weeks, twice a week often, but I get paid for it."

"And I sometimes get to eat in restaurants like this one which I could never afford otherwise, even at special prices." he added cautiously, just as Axel arrived to welcome them. He introduced them.

"I was telling Bettina about the tours, Axel, and how they love eating here before going on to the opera. It's a beautiful building and great food and, well, I suppose ... " he ploughed on, realising that he was risking another outburst from Bettina " ... I suppose they're sometimes a bit surprised at how good it all is, not what they've been led to expect the East is like."

Bettina laughed, glanced at Axel who was opening a bottle of Elbthaler Weissburgunder which he'd brought as a gift, and said "Ah, the decadent, ignorant West. They think it's all queues, food shortages, old clothes and nothing but black bread to eat and thin beer to drink, eh Axel?"

Thomas relaxed and under the influence of the wine became expansive, amusing Bettina with some highlights of the tours but then finding himself telling her more than he'd intended, almost boasting about his success and realising at one point that the figures didn't add up at the official exchange rates, hurrying on so that she wouldn't notice the slip. Bettina drank very little, he noticed, even asking for water at one point. She also congratulated him on the wine, commenting on his apparent knowledge of the wine industry in Saxony and for a while they ate in companionable silence or made small talk, sometimes even eating from each other's plates.

"Santé, to a decadent, capitalistic evening! Now tell me more about yourself. What are your dreams, apart from becoming a millionaire, of course?"

"I'm an economics student, as I told you, but opera's my real passion and I intend to become a professional singer. I've had real battles with my parents over this. Both of them said that musicians never made any money, that music was fine as a hobby but that was all. They insisted I study economics and be as successful as my father had been. I resisted that for a while but in the end I thought that economics was maybe OK as a kind of security blanket thing, something I could always fall back on. So right now I'm trying to do both, which is difficult, but it's music that I really love."

"Is your family supporting you?"

"That would require a long answer, but the short one is no. My father's dead now and my mother and I don't really get on that well. I guess I escaped to Berlin and I have to make my own way."

The more the conversation flowed the easier it seemed and the more brilliant it appeared to become to Thomas. They found they shared a passion for music, for Russian literature and for more besides. Thomas was becoming obsessed with Bettina but unsure just how she felt about him as he sensed a wariness, a kind of 'this far but no further' tension in her. She refused a brandy and as he glanced at his watch he realised that it was nearly time to meet Mark.

"Bettina, I'm sorry, but it's getting kind of late and I have to go. I have to meet a friend, just someone who sometimes helps me get the opera tickets. Excuse me for a minute while I settle the bill at the desk."

She got up as he returned.

"I must ring my mother. She sometimes gets a little worried if she knows I'm out and it's getting late. Is there a telephone here, do you know?" He indicated the booth down a corridor.

Some minutes later they met near the door, Thomas with her leather jacket draped over his arm. The streets had been washed by a sudden shower, and the lights reflected off the asphalt. There was a smell of damp earth as they walked along the river bank, the Spree gliding blackly on the other side of the low wall, and when Thomas took Bettina's hand he found the warmth and slight pressure returned. They linked fingers. They crossed the Mühlendamm Bridge in silence and Bettina said softly, almost to herself, "Perhaps I shouldn't admit it but it's been a wonderful evening. Thank you."

"For me too. I loved being with you and I'm so sorry I have to leave early like this. But I'd like to see you again. Will you come to the opera with me? I have an old friend from Frankfurt and his girlfriend coming for the weekend tomorrow and we're all going to see *Fidelio*. We could go then, perhaps."

"That would be ... , yes ... , yes, that would be good. I'd like that. I'll meet you outside at, what, 7.15 tomorrow evening?"

Thomas reached his hand behind her neck and gently pulled her towards him, meeting little resistance. Nuzzling her neck he inhaled the light jasmine perfume of her skin. She leant into his shoulder for a moment and they stood in silence, pressing together, before she straightened and pushed him gently away.

"No, Thomas ... I mustn't. Not now. Let's, let's just wait until, well, for a bit. I should go." She looked at him, serious for a moment, started to say something but looked down and away. "Be careful."

She kissed him lightly and walked quickly in the direction of the museum. Thomas watched her disappear then hurried off for the Nikolaikirche, conscious that he would be late.

It was drizzling slightly and the streets were deserted. Thomas found Mark pacing in front of the church, puffing nervously on an imported cigarette which he was just lighting from the end of his last one. He threw the butt down and ground it out with his shoe. Thomas walked towards him, discreetly giving the sign that he intended exchanging 300 DM into Ost Marks at the current black market rate of 15:1 and received acknowledgement from Mark.

He took a pack of cigarettes from pocket, put one to his lips and, as stranger to stranger, asked Mark for a light. As he bowed his head to the match and inhaled he felt the acid rising from his stomach into his throat. Mark dropped his cigarette packet and Thomas courteously picked it up, palming and offering instead his own one with the Deutsche Marks inside and putting Mark's identical package into his own pocket.

"We need to talk." Mark whispered. "Ten minutes. Sit on the bench behind the church."

Thomas walked on, glancing carefully around, scouting the surroundings for suspicious faces or followers. Most people seemed to be Western tourists admiring the buildings, the quaint houses rebuilt along the original mediaeval perimeter. There was a fog drifting in from the Spree and it felt clammy and cold. He reached the end of the street, threw away the cigarette in his hand, looked at a building as if admiring its design then turned and retraced his steps.

Passing the bronze statue at the side of the double-domed church he found a bench, partly hidden in the shadows, where he checked the contents of his exchanged cigarette packet and found it short, 3,000 Ost Marks against the 4,500 he was expecting. In a moment Mark sat down and Thomas turned angrily to him. "What ... "

"Listen, Thomas." Mark interrupted, his broad Sachsen accent thickening as Thomas had noticed it did at times of stress. "You're a smart guy. That opera tickets and dinner deal you run is clever. But you can do a lot better ... "

"I've never told you what I do." Thomas stood up, furious but also apprehensive. "You've been spying on me! And I want the rest of my money. That packet was 1,500 short."

"Look, this is the East. It's a police state. I take precautions. I have to. I need to know who I'm dealing with.

Stasi agents play at being Western tourists exchanging currency like you do, black market currency. They reassure you and then when the sums get big enough they report you, have you arrested and make off with your money as well. That means five years in jail and I just don't like to be fucked over."

Thomas sat down.

"Look, Thomas, now that I know you're OK I'll trust you with a new deal. We can make a lot more money together."

The acid returned and Thomas felt naked and insecure. Someone had followed him closely enough to learn all about his opera tours and he hadn't noticed. What else did he not know about?

"Next time, bring your car in. I'll show you where to hide stuff in it. Light drugs, nothing serious. Maryjane, hash, maybe some coke. People are depressed here and there's a huge potential market."

"You're out of your mind. And if I get caught? You'll be clear but I'll be thrown in jail here. No way am I risking that!"

"It won't happen. They're not concerned about what comes in, only what goes out. They won't search your car coming in, only when you leave but that's to check you're not helping any Ossies to escape. People do it all the time, even with heavier stuff. The KoKo supplies the upper crust and I'm targeting the middle classes."

"What are you talking about?"

"Schalck-Golodkowski and his cronies. Kommerzielle Koordinierung, KoKo. They control everything that comes in, legal and otherwise. Anyway, that's my problem. Get it in here and I'll pay you ten times your costs. We'll both do well out of it."

For a moment he was tempted. Perhaps Mark was right. Perhaps the risk was minimal and worth taking. The opera tours were good but this would solve any financial problems at a stroke, give him even more money for expensive singing lessons. He could finally sign up at the conservatory, perhaps even afford some advanced classes with Maestro Rufini. Or he could most likely rot in an East German jail for a decade or more.

"Sorry Mark, that's not me. I'm not getting into that racket. I won't do it."

Mark stared at him for a few moments.

"You're a wimp. And a fool. I should turn you in – at least that would get me some credit. But I thought you might say that so that's why I changed the rate today. If you'd agreed it would have been 15:1 but from now on it's 10:1.

"We agreed fifteen. I could have got fourteen from Dresdner Bank when I left West Berlin today. Now give me the fifteen we agreed. I gave you DM300 and I want my four and half thousand Ost Marks. Stop pissing about."

"3,000. Take it or leave it."

"Forty five hundred, nothing less. I could turn *you* in just as easily. Don't think I won't."

"It would really be very, very stupid if you tried that. OK. Just this once I'll do it at twelve and a half. I've got the other seven fifty in the car over at Melchiorplatz. But remember, ten to one is the deal for everything now. I'm not interested at anything higher."

He set off and Thomas followed, still arguing. He was furious but knew that he had little choice but to accept the reduced rate, at least for now. He had to get over to the Ephraim Palais again to bank this latest lot of money and it was getting late. Oh, well, he thought, he knew where he could get better rates so he was probably well rid of Mark.

Just as Mark opened the car door two men jumped out of an old grey Trabant parked slightly down the street on the opposite side and ran towards them shouting something which Thomas couldn't properly understand.

"Come on! Get in!" Mark glanced over, gesticulated at Thomas and jumped into the driver's seat starting the engine instantly.

The car took off and swung round with a roar of the engine and a squeal of tyres, the force throwing Thomas back in his seat and almost tumbling him out of the still open door which swung madly before he caught and closed it. He looked back over his shoulder. One of the men had kneeled and was aiming a rifle towards them. Thomas ducked instinctively as he heard the gunshots in quick succession and the car swerved suddenly. He looked up to see Mark slumped over the wheel and as the engine roared again and the car plunged forward it smashed into a wall, jerking him hard against the windscreen, and he lost consciousness.

Chapter 5
Thursday 14 and Friday 15 September 1989

Stephan struggled up the stairs as fast as he could in the teeming subway crowd, fretting at those in his way, muttering apologies on his frequent collisions, darting into fortuitous spaces as they opened up. Bursting on to Frankfurt's Opernplatz he dodged past a phalanx of uniformed men, pin stripe suited and swinging identical briefcases in unison, men who walked briskly looking straight ahead to reassure themselves they had important tasks in hand. He sprinted through the Taunusanlage Park, closing on the twin towers of the Deutsche Bank. It was already 8.30.

At the bank headquarters he pushed the revolving door hard, stumbled into the spacious entrance hall with its internal fountains and hanging crystal decorations, waved at the guard who nodded in recognition, and rushed for the mirrored wall hiding the lifts to the boardroom floors. A panel slid open as he arrived and he squeezed into the first cage just as its doors were closing. He greeted the others as usual but his glasses were fogged and he had no idea who was present. He felt hot and sticky, out of control, and cursed the subway company and its unreliability. There again, he thought wryly, perhaps he should have resisted taking that extra fifteen minutes in bed with Camille.

He whirled into his office on the 30th floor, hurled his coat at a chair and tugged papers from his briefcase, ordering these quickly and handing them to his secretary to type. He rushed to his inner office and went over the contract documents once more in preparation for the imminent meeting with his boss, Alfred Herren, CEO of Deutsche Bank.

At five to nine Stephan sank into a soft, dark leather armchair by Herren's desk. He clutched the papers for the Board meeting which Lise had completed from his handwritten notes moments earlier. He'd had no time to review them, something he would ordinarily have done as Herren had an uncanny eye for detail and would pounce on any error. Fortunately Lise was one of the best secretaries in the company and he was confident she would have typed everything up correctly and laid it out neatly.

"Good morning, Mr Fischer. Where are we on the Morgan Grenfell acquisition process? Any major changes since the last contract revision?"

"I've summarised them here." He handed a set of papers to Herren. "The two main changes relate to the guaranteed bonus payments, which have been reduced substantially, and the request that the CEO of Morgan Grenfell, Mr Ryan, take a board seat here in Frankfurt."

Stephan paused to watch Herren's reaction to this apparent provocation. Since its founding in 1870 Deutsche Bank had never once admitted a foreigner to its board. The idea was unthinkable—Deutsche Bank was far more than simply a commercial bank but was intimately enmeshed with German industry, through mutual and interlocking directorships, and also with the German political establishment. No important economic decision was ever taken by the government without at least informal prior consultation with the bank, typically with the CEO himself.

Herren looked unperturbed. "I see that Mr Ryan has followed my suggestion. Giving Ryan a seat will reassure Morgan Grenfell employees that this is an integration, not a takeover. And if Morgan doesn't get the results we expect they won't be able to put the blame on us."

Herren's cunning and skill in reaching his objectives again impressed Stephan. Had Herren proposed bringing Ryan on to the board the other members would almost certainly have blocked it. But by having Ryan present it as a fundamental point in the acquisition negotiations he ensured that the proposal would be accepted, albeit reluctantly, by his co-directors.

Herren glanced quickly over the papers. "Yes, everything seems to be here. If I have any questions I'll call you. We need to complete within a week but I feel that Mr Ryan is ready to sign." he said, with the calm confidence which could still surprise Stephan. The competing bid from the French Societé Générale didn't seem to worry him in the least.

"But there's another matter I want to tell you about, a new project I want you to start working on immediately. It's extremely confidential. Extremely confidential." He paused and looked intently at Stephan. "We are about to launch our first Euroloan programme for the Soviet Union. Fifteen billion Deutsche Marks."

"Fifteen billion!" Stephan could hardly contain his amazement. "The Soviet Union?"

"Exactly."

"Have they done deals of this kind before? Any documentation I can go through to find ... "

"There have been some small issues, in the millions, through some agency but this will be their first time accessing Western capital markets at anything like this level. That's what makes this project so interesting. You'll learn a lot from it, I'm sure of that." The board meeting was about to start and Herren got up to leave.

"But do you think the markets would take that kind of credit without some form of guarantee?" Stephan tried his best to sound positive as he rose and walked to the door. He knew from experience that Herren hated to be contradicted. But the idea made no sense whatsoever unless some entity like the World Bank or the IFC guaranteed the loan. The risk of a country like the USSR defaulting on the loan was too high to attract investors, whatever the interest rate put on the paper.

"You're right. Soviet paper would be unsellable without some guarantee. That's why the Federal Republic of West Germany has agreed to provide that reassurance."

Herren was looking at him calmly, the hint of a smile about to break out, enjoying Stephan's astonishment and discomfiture.

"You will be working on the documentation with senior members of the Ministry of Finance. The first meeting is scheduled for tomorrow at nine. You should ... "

The phone ringing interrupted him.

"We'll speak further after the board meeting." He waved Stephan out of the office, turning on the speaker phone. Stephan heard "The Chancellor is on the line for you, Mr Herren." as he closed the door with care.

Stephan slowly returned to his office, collecting coffee on the way. He'd been working non-stop for the past five months on the Morgan Grenfell acquisition and had been looking forward to some breathing space and time for a social life. Camille would be furious at this new load on him. And the first meeting was tomorrow. God, let it not interfere with this coming weekend in Berlin with Thomas, he thought. Even at the speed that Stephan drove it was still a five hour trip and he'd arranged to collect Camille from their apartment at midday. Well, she wouldn't like it, but at least she was used to his being late. Surely the meeting would be over by half past twelve at the latest.

Not that he was wild about listening to opera – he took some pride in describing himself as having Van Gogh's ear for music—but he desperately wanted time away from work and he knew how much Camille was looking forward to the trip as she'd never been to Berlin. He and Thomas had spoken yesterday to finalise details and he'd learned of some feisty new woman that Thomas had just met and was hoping to get to know better. As for the opera - "Best seats in the house!" Thomas had said – it might turn out better than he feared and in any case he knew how much music meant to his friend. They deserved this weekend, he thought, and he was looking forward to it.

*

Anxious about being punctual the following day Stephan had set two alarm clocks, placing the more insistent one on top of his wardrobe, out of easy reach. Of course he'd then slept badly, his mind racing with thoughts about what he might have overlooked in his preparations or what might go wrong during the meeting itself or how long it would go on for. After tossing and turning and peering blearily at the time every hour or so, desperately afraid he was now going to sleep through when he needed to be up, he finally abandoned his futile attempts and rose at 6.15, a good half hour before he needed to. It was always the same when he started a new deal or had an important meeting, he thought crossly, as he yawned and made himself some strong coffee.

Herren dealt only with the top echelon of business and political figures and that meant that Stephan, as his assistant, had to work hard to be respected. He was conscious that that he didn't always make a strong enough first impression, that these powerful men disdained him to some extent. Perhaps I need to be more arrogant, more opinionated, he thought; I may come to be less liked but they'll listen to me and what's more important they'll remember me. He struck a pose and growled at his reflection in the bathroom mirror. At least his teeth and his skin were good, he thought.

The meeting was to be held at the offices of Gottlieb Chance, the law firm founded in Frankfurt fifty years earlier and which had risen to become immensely powerful in its work within the financial sector. It was hardly known outside this specialist area and its partners worked hard to ensure that that situation continued. Its discretion was legendary and it was that, coupled with its reputation for reliability and a wide ranging understanding of law and finance, which had brought it to its current dominant position. If you were unsure about legal precedents and perhaps consequent implications relating to some arcane financial instrument or transaction or policy you could be certain that a Gottlieb Chance partner would know the answer.

The receptionist summoned an assistant who accompanied Stephan in the lift and showed him to the large meeting room at the very top of the building. The entire outer wall of this room was lightly smoked glass and gave Stephan, from his position on the forty fifth floor, a breathtaking view of Frankfurt. To his left he could see the Main curving away in both directions and an old building he decided must be St Bartholomew's Cathedral, a large 18th century etching of which hung on the wall to his right. Hanging beside it was a Merian engraving of Frankfurt with the same church centrally placed while several other engravings or etchings of Hesse and old urban or village views of the Main and the Rhein decorated the other walls.

Stephan was the first to arrive and as the assistant left him he tried the door through which they'd entered, the only one in the room, finding without surprise that it was locked. Gottlieb Chance deserved its reputation as a consummately professional firm, he thought. Sitting down at the massive oval mahogany table which dominated the room he skimmed through some documents on earlier Euroloan deals he'd found in the Deutsche Bank library. As he'd expected there was almost nothing there of much interest; there were no useful Soviet economic figures, nothing on the USSR Central Bank's currency or gold reserves. He'd have to be very alert during this meeting and learn as it progressed.

The door opened and Weigel, the German Finance Minister, closely followed by Herren and six other formally suited men entered. Everyone was in their late fifties or older, Stephan noted apprehensively.

"Weigel looks even more impressive than he does on television!" Stephan thought noting that even his enormous black eyebrows, looking almost like moustaches transplanted to above his eyes, appeared different and gave him additional gravity. Herren greeted Stephan, shook hands, introduced him to Weigel, and then to the others. Apart from two Finance Ministry officials there were a couple of senior Bundesbank officials and two Gottlieb Chance partners - Erich von Hesswald, the senior partner, and a colleague, a specialist in Eastern and Central European finance.

Weigel briskly called the meeting to order, surprising Stephan who had expected representatives of the Soviet government to be present. They were, after all, the party seeking the loan and so responsible for repaying it.

"Gentlemen, you will all be aware that this is the first time that the Soviet Union has sought to access Western capital markets in any significant manner. We therefore thought it important to be here today to underline our government's commitment to this project. The Central Committee of the USSR has been implementing radical reforms, *perestroika*, in response to the policy of *glasnost* introduced by Mr Gorbachev. We believe these reforms are desirable and will bring about dramatic changes, changes which will be evident not only in the Soviet Union itself but also in its relations with other countries, including our own. There is still internal resistance to Mr Gorbachev's reforms, however, and Chancellor Kohl believes that Mr Gorbachev is risking a great deal and should be supported in facilitating a structural shift towards a more democratic and more open Soviet Union. This demands finance and as German Finance Minister I am in complete agreement with the Chancellor on these various matters."

He paused, took a long sip of water from the glass on his left, and looked slowly round the room at all those present. Feeling out of place in the company in which he now found himself Stephan felt a powerful urge to look down as Weigel paused and looked at him curiously. Meeting and holding the Minister's gaze with an effort of will Stephan recognised the authority others spoke of and with which he dominated the Bundestag during discussions on finance and the economy. Weigel nodded slightly and moved his gaze to the next man and resumed his comment.

"It's for these reasons that Chancellor Kohl has decided that we must provide a guarantee on these loans. I repeat, I am in entire agreement with the Chancellor on this point. The close personal friendship and mutual trust which has developed between Chancellor Kohl and Secretary Gorbachev is shown by their request that we negotiate the terms and conditions of this financing on their behalf. Dr Herren, would you kindly expand on this."

"Thank you." said Herren, barely glancing at Weigel but focusing on a document he had placed in front of him. "The Ministry of Finance and the Bundesbank will in this instance be representing both the issuer, the USSR, and the guarantor of the loans, the West German government. This is largely because the Soviet Central Bank officials lack experience in such matters."

Stephan listened attentively to Herren's words but his mind kept buzzing with questions. There was a structural conflict between the issuer and the guarantor. Each wanted the other's responsibilities under the loan to be as great as possible, to minimise their own. It made no conventional sense whatsoever that the German authorities were covering both roles.

"In total we expect to finance something of the order of fifty billion Deutsche Marks." Herren continued. "We will break up the financing into a series of smaller elements, placed through different instruments and having different maturities. We would like our group here to draw up a munster, a complete set of documentation which will then be adapted for each issue. We will present the credit initially through a Euroloan for fifteen billion DM, wholly underwritten by Deutsche Bank, and we would expect to close this first deal by the end of October."

The oldest person in the room was clearly von Hesswald and although he looked frail, his white hair shining brightly in the cone of light from one of the halogen lamps, Stephan saw that his eyes were attentive and alert.

"Dr Herren, forgive me, but I have a question on the structure of the transactions. I'm not sure whether this is a question for you or rather for the Finance Minister. I believe a difficulty in presenting this opportunity to investors will derive from the fact that the Soviet Union is essentially a self-contained economic system. There is very limited financial interface with the West and therefore the USSR has in turn very limited access to foreign currency and very few reserves so denominated. This will make it difficult for them to repay a loan denominated in a hard currency – unless, perhaps, we have title to some suitably valuable and accessible asset, their oil or gas reserves, for example. Are you thinking of securing privileged access to some valuable assets, or are we looking at a very strong guarantee from the West German government? I believe these can be the only alternatives if we want to get the deal placed successfully."

Herren and Weigel glanced at each other. The Finance Minister looked around the room for some seconds before answering. Stephan thought he detected uneasiness and a hint of tension behind the conversational tone in which Weigel replied. "No, there will be no form of privileged access to Soviet assets. At the request of the lead manager, Deutsche Bank, the German government will provide investors with a pass-through guarantee."

Von Hesswald nodded his head slowly in assent. "Then I guess that potential problem is solved."

Stephan looked at Herren and then at Weigel, trying to make sense of what had just been said. A pass-through guarantee was the strongest form of loan guarantee possible and meant that investors would have immediate and total recourse to the guarantor in the event of any failure. For all practical purposes it was as if the loan liability were being issued by the German government itself. No wonder no Soviet Union officials were at the meeting – their presence was completely irrelevant.

Chapter 6
Friday 15 September 1989

Thomas slowly drifted into consciousness from some deep pit, struggling painfully out so that he increasingly came to regret leaving his former stupor. A fierce, throbbing pain towards the back of his head grew and pulsated as his senses returned. His forehead ached and as he gingerly explored he found a large bump and what he took to be dried blood just above his right eye. His nose felt tender and swollen and he could breathe only through his mouth which was now dry and rancid, his lips cracked.

He was in darkness, lying on what seemed to be a concrete floor, his left leg twisted under him and his right at an odd and uncomfortable angle. The air felt damp, stagnant and heavy. There was a sour, musty smell overlaid with a sharp, ammonia tang. His ears buzzed with the oppressive silence. He screamed in frustration but all he could manage was a moaning croak and when the meagre echoes had died the silence was worse.

He tried to stand up but his right knee gave way with a stab of pain and he lay on the stone while he recovered. The skin below his knee felt raw and tender and the leg of his jeans was stiff and crusted with something. His right shoulder down to the middle of his chest felt bruised and painful. Half hopping on his left knee and his arms, dragging his right leg behind him and shuddering when that knee took inadvertent weight, he explored his surroundings.

There was a smooth, solid metal door with a small rectangular flap near the base but with no sign of any keyhole or catch. The fit with the metal frame was complete and only by sliding a fingernail could he detect any crack. He pushed at the flap and although it gave slightly it seemed to be blocked, presumably capable of being opened only from outside.

The wall was rough, apparently made of breeze blocks, and the ceiling, which he could just brush with his fingers when he'd hauled himself painfully upright, seemed to be of similar construction. Above the door there was a small grill and later on he discovered a second on the facing wall, this one carrying a slightly cooler, faint, waft of sweeter air. On that wall he also found a small basin with one tap, cold, and beside it a steel lavatory pan with no seat. He splashed his face with water and drank some from his cupped hands, wincing at the cold and at how the water stung bits of raw flesh.

Feeling his way to the fourth wall he swore as he banged into something angular and hard and jarred his right leg in recoil, sending a Roman candle of pain flashing behind his eyes. This was an iron bed frame, bolted to the wall, covered with a thin mattress and a coarse wool blanket, a lumpy pillow at the end. Shivering, he dragged himself under the blanket and tried to make sense of what had happened. Where the hell was he? And why was he there anyway?

At first he got nowhere. He'd clearly lost consciousness, but how and when? He had a vague memory of a car but if he'd been injured then why was he not in some hospital? Why was he not being cared for properly? Why had he been flung into this place, with no regard for his injuries, like some expendable animal? He tried hard to remember what had happened but could make little sense of the confused and disjointed memories. There was something about someone shooting, but that made no sense. By habit he glanced at his wrist but saw no familiar phosphorus gleam and when he felt for his watch found nothing.

Then with a jolt of pleasure he remembered his dinner with Bettina. He remembered their tender parting by the bridge and for a few moments almost forgot his pain and his surroundings as he relived the experience. Disconnected scenes started to drift into his mind, coalescing into some sort of order - the sullen walk to the car, his earlier argument with Mark, the attempted escape, the men who had shouted. He remembered Mark's lunatic driving as they took off but then nothing, hard as he tried. They must have crashed, he thought, and quite badly judging by his injuries.

This must be a cell, and the people who had challenged and pursued them must have been Vopo agents or, worse, from the Stasi, the secret police. Had he exchanged money with Mark? He couldn't remember exactly but whether he had or hadn't didn't really matter given the amount of currency he'd had. That it was DM or Ost Marks was irrelevant - it would be obvious what he and Mark been doing. There was no way he could pretend that he was an innocent tourist. He was clearly facing a lengthy prison sentence. But why was he not in an ordinary police cell? Why was no one around? And what time was it?

He got up, limped over and started pounding weakly on the metal door but he might as well have tried to push down the Berlin Wall on his own for all the effect it had. He tried to shout but again there was only a harsh croak, the effort tearing painfully at his throat. He felt immensely tired, groped his way back and sank on the bed in despair and exhaustion, falling deeply asleep in seconds.

Woken later by the grating noise made by the opening cell door, Thomas struggled into consciousness and turned on his elbow, blinking in the strong light from the unshaded fitting in the ceiling. He saw in front of him dark brown shoes and matching socks, a pair of dark brown trousers surmounted by a light brown sweater covering a white shirt. The man looked about fifty, ramrod straight with closely cropped grizzled hair, neatly trimmed, and with penetrating blue eyes which stared hard at Thomas for a long moment.

He seemed to be waiting. Thomas felt impelled to struggle off the bed and stand up half upright, his left hand on the wall for support, although he dearly longed to be left alone to sleep off his pain and his injuries.

"Mr Wundart, I expect you realise why you are here and what you will be charged with." The man's deep voice had a slight edge, but the tone was friendly. There was almost no trace of an East German accent. "You and your colleague, Mark Schmidt, were caught with drugs and with an excessive amount of West German currency. You tried to escape arrest. Your companion is dead. You may have survived but you face a substantial prison sentence."

Thomas stared at him. The loose memories fitted together better and he remembered Mark's invitation to smuggle drugs into East Berlin. But he'd refused, surely? He'd had nothing to do with that.

"Drugs? What drugs? What are you talking about?"

"Your car had more than two kilos of heroin and cocaine packed in the wheel well of the boot. We have reliable witnesses to its discovery and we have pictures of the cargo in place. I see you have not earlier come to our attention for infractions and so you may be unaware of how efficient justice is in East Berlin. You will be tried in two days' time. Given the clear evidence against you the trial will be swift, an hour or two at most. We will provide you with a lawyer, of course."

"I had nothing to do with any of that. That wasn't my car. Who are you? And why are you telling me all this?"

"My name is Colonel Dieter but you're in no position to ask questions, Mr Wundart. You are in serious trouble. Do not think that your West German passport will allow you to escape the consequences of your criminal behaviour."

His voice took on a sharper, more aggressive tone. "However, we don't particularly enjoy sending young people like you to jail. I see that you're a student and you appear to be well educated and from a good family. This, uh, escapade, will certainly destroy whatever career you had in mind. No doubt you've already taken risks - the question now is what are you ready to risk in return for getting out of here?"

"I'm ready to pay a fine. I had four thou ... "

"Pffftt!" Dieter stared at Thomas with contempt and shook his head slightly. "You Westerners think that any problem can be fixed with the right amount of money! You think anyone can be bought. Not here. In any case, the money you smuggled has been impounded."

He paused, letting his words sink in, staring at Thomas. He leaned closer, and Thomas could feel his breath on his face and picked up the faint scent of a cigar. His voice became friendlier, avuncular. "You have your whole life ahead of you." Dieter said softly. "Don't throw it away." He seemed saddened at the idea that anyone should make such a foolish mistake. "Don't throw your life away." For an eerie moment Thomas saw his father standing in front of him using just those phrases when he'd pressed Thomas to give up the idea of becoming a professional musician.

He stepped back, straightened, jabbed his forefinger as he spoke. "The world is changing, political relationships are much more fluid, they change daily. We need to keep in the flow, keep up to date, but the most important bits of history are never written down. And politicians are very well versed in the arts of deceit. Therefore we believe that using people who keep their ears and eyes open, reporters you could call them, is the best way to gain information."

There was silence and Thomas thought over what Dieter had said and what he seemed to want.

"I don't see how I can help you. Why would you think I'm close to any information like that? I'm only a student, for Christ's sake."

"It's our business to know a great deal of trivial information about many different matters which could become useful. For instance, you will remember that your first visit to East Berlin occurred on 14 November 1988. You crossed in the morning, just before 11am, and returned to West Berlin almost exactly twelve hours later. You have made fifteen visits since that first one – I'm pleased to know that you enjoy so much visiting our city."

"Yes." thought Thomas. "But that's hardly impressive, that's just collating standard immigration information." If he was careful he could get out of this more easily than he'd feared.

Dieter smiled thinly, waiting until Thomas had begun to relax, and continued gently. "It's a shame you don't get on better with your widowed mother, though, isn't it? Your brother Will seems to – or maybe that's because he doesn't have your independence and arrogance, do you think? But then it was your father you were particularly close to wasn't it? Perhaps more to the point, your father was a senior director of the Bundesbank. He would probably have become the next Governor had he lived. You undoubtedly have access to many very influential people there, perhaps old friends or colleagues of your well-respected father, people like Hans Schacht, for instance, or Joachim Zimmerman, would you say?, people who may already know you or who would be happy to talk to his son, people whose information could be useful to us."

Thomas stared at Dieter in horror, then looked away, unable to stand the penetrating examination, so much at variance with the calm and reasonable voice.

"Unconsidered trifles can be valuable when connected to other information we have. We're skilled at making these connections. You can become our Autolycus, snapping up careless morsels from the West. All this unpleasantness will vanish." Dieter clicked his fingers. "Your life will continue much as before."

Dieter's voice suddenly lost its soothing tone, became brisk as if he'd suddenly become bored talking to someone who couldn't see where his best interests clearly lay. He glanced at this watch. "But the choice is yours. You have two days before the trial. Think about your future. Remember, the choice is yours."

He turned on his heel and slammed the door shut, the dull clang overlaid, Thomas noticed despite himself, with dying harmonics. The switch outside clicked and the steps echoed down the corridor leaving Thomas in darkness. A faint glow came through the flap in the door but as the footsteps finally faded even that vanished and Thomas was left with the absolute darkness again singing in his ears.

Chapter 7
Friday 15 September 1989

Dieter's footsteps had died away and the now total silence made the darkness heavy and oppressive. Thomas glanced by habit at his wrist then remembered that his watch had gone. He felt for the bed and sat down. The darkness waved and swirled in front of his eyes and took on a solidity, seeming to press down on him, force him back against the wall. He suddenly relived the terror when, as a child, he'd dived at high tide deep into an underwater cave in a cliff and became disorientated, unable to sense the way to the surface, desperate to breathe, scrabbling deeper and panicking as he struggled to escape. He clutched and pulled up with all his strength on the hard, sharp edge of the bed frame, searing pain into his hands but returning him to reality and halting for the moment the mad drumming in his ears and the feelings of nausea. He heard his heart hammering as Dieter's words, insisting that it was up to him to choose, kept pace in his head.

Whether Thomas faced trial or not was entirely under Dieter's control, he realised. Dieter could certainly also influence the trial as he wished, ensuring a long sentence of perhaps twenty years or more, if he felt so inclined. Lawyer there might be for him but that was mere gloss and would make no difference to the result.

He'd already been stitched up on a drugs-related charge, Thomas thought, and although he was innocent of that he knew that getting off would be almost impossible if Dieter chose to press his case. Conditions might be better than what he was enduring now but whatever the improvement he just couldn't face twenty years in a Stasi jail.

He remembered the contempt Dieter had shown when he'd offered to pay a fine. Money worked in the West but here it didn't, or at least not in the same way. He thought back to how often money had bought him out of trouble. That new housemaid when he got back from university at Christmas; their child would have been about three now. He remembered how exasperated his father had been as he'd paid for the clinic and given the girl a generous amount to forget the careless indiscretion and to start again in another town. But here it was a matter of principle, not price. This was unfamiliar to him and Thomas was unsure how to handle it. The mantra started up again loudly in his head. It was his choice, certainly, but even that freedom to choose, he realised, was illusory.

But what was Dieter seeking to achieve? Yes, Thomas knew, even if only casually, many important people in Frankfurt through his family's connections. Frankfurt was Germany's financial powerhouse but all the political power was in Bonn and it was Bonn that called the shots. He knew very few people there and certainly no one of high political status or power. Why was Frankfurt so important? Why was the Stasi so interested in him? Why him?

Thomas heard steps outside and then a harsh screech ripped his ears as the panel in the door opened. In the rectangle of light which followed he saw a tray and at the same time, out of the corner of his eye, he sensed the rapid scurry of something small along the floor by the far wall. He reached for the tray and the panel snapped shut, the footsteps dying away and leaving the darkness as oppressive as before. He felt for a fork or a spoon but there was nothing of that kind, merely some hard bread, a bowl of mushy mixture that might have been old potato salad and a tin mug of flat water.

His anger flared up but he stopped himself in time from hurling the tray into the darkness. That would disturb no one other than himself. He laughed suddenly, remembering the care with which he and Stephan had examined the menu and the expensive wine list when they'd last met. Well, nor was he now at the Ephraim Palais but he was hungry and had no way of knowing when his next meal would come. He'd better accept what was offered.

He dozed fitfully, waking with a start, his limbs and chest still painful, fully alert and again conscious of the decision he had to make although still refusing to acknowledge that the choice offered was no choice at all. Perhaps Dieter wasn't so powerful as he seemed. Perhaps he could get a fair trial after all. Perhaps he could get friends in the West to pull strings to get him out. He tried to sleep but as this list of hopeful possibilities churned in his mind, growing wilder as time passed, he realised that he was trudging down a corridor with only one exit. "But if I don't do it, someone else will. If I don't collaborate, they'll find other ways to get what they need anyway." he thought. "And it's not as if I'll have access to any important secrets." He looked into the blackness. "I just need my life back. Is that so bad?"

The tray and the mug were each too flimsy to make much noise on the door but he found that by hitting the panel with the side of his clenched hand at a certain spot he could make it flex slightly and generate an additional faint booming which faded down the corridor. The slight scrabbling in the far corner that occasionally he heard and which he linked to the scurrying flash he'd caught earlier when the tray arrived gave him strength and after many minutes he head footsteps dragging towards his cell. The panel scraped open once more and Thomas briefly basked in the light.

"I need to speak to Colonel Dieter!"

The man laughed. "Go back to sleep. It's the middle of the night! He gets in later at weekends and doesn't stay long. When he gets here in a few hours we'll tell him you want an audience. Perhaps he'll be able to fit you in today. If not, you'll have to wait till Monday."

It must already be Saturday morning, he thought. His flatmate, John, wouldn't be concerned because they each would go off suddenly if something came up. But then he remembered Stephan and the planned visit to the opera. Shit! There was Bettina as well. They'd agreed to meet on Friday evening outside the opera house. After their difficult start standing her up was the last thing he needed. Well, being locked up in a Stasi dungeon was a pretty good excuse, he thought bitterly as he again fell asleep.

The light being switched on from outside and then the noise made by the door opening woke Thomas. His neck and his arm felt stiff and cramped, his leg ached, and he shivered slightly in the cell's dampness. Dieter, this time in uniform, stood in the doorway his face in shadow so that it took Thomas a moment to realize that it was the man he'd met earlier.

"What have you decided?"

Some of Thomas's earlier confidence drained away as he looked at Dieter, the crisp, full military uniform reinforcing his stern bearing and reminding Thomas of the vast difference in the power of each of them.

"I'll do what you want – but only on certain conditions."

Dieter smiled coldly.

"Do you really think you're in any position to dictate anything?" He made a small gesture with his fingers. "But, well, go on."

"I'll help, but you need to let me get on with my life. I'm a student. I've got a life ahead of me. I can't give that up."

"We want you to be successful. We will even help you because that will make your job easier. All we need is that you get for us information from certain people. Provided you do that to our satisfaction we'll make sure that your life continues pretty much as before."

"Who do I have to inform on? Are you going to tell me that just now?" Thomas felt some of his earlier confidence returning. How would they know that he reported things correctly and completely. If anything was too secret or too dangerous to West Germany he could easily forget about it or subtly misrepresent what he'd learned.

"Let's see." said Dieter. "Frankfurt. We know your family is well connected, particularly in banking circles through your late father. Who do you know who might interest us?"

"I have an uncle in Essen who heads a major pharmaceutical plant and who obviously knows many important industrialists. I'm sure he could be someone worth following more closely, also as ... "

The slap of Dieter's gloves on Thomas's face echoed in the cell. It had been more done out of irritation and warning than real anger but his cheek stung and he sensed again the menace behind Dieter's urbane and sophisticated manner.

"Why would we care about industrial espionage when our factories produce all that the DDR needs? I'm interested only in anyone close to the levers of power. Who do you know, or who can you contact, high up in the Bundesbank or maybe one of the important ministries such as Finance?"

A guard entered and handed a note to Dieter who scanned it quickly.

"Good!" he said "You haven't been missed. I had one of our female agents call up your apartment to say you were spending a couple of nights with her. Your flatmate, John he said his name was, took that as quite normal. He said there were several calls from a Stephan Fischer, calling from Frankfurt – I have his number here so you can call him back. Who is Fischer? Tell me about him."

Thomas's mind raced, wondering what he could say and hold back about Stephan. What did Dieter already know? Would he guess if Thomas lied?

"I'm waiting, Mr Wundart. Who is Fischer? ."

"He's an old friend. We're the same age. We were at school together, grew up together. We meet every few months either here or in Frankfurt. He and his girlfriend were coming to visit this weekend."

"And what does he do? The office number is in the Deutsche Bank headquarters. Where does he work? What is his position? What other friends of his do you know?"

"He's an assistant there. He's been there for perhaps a year but I'm not sure exactly what he does. I've met some of his friends but apart from his girlfriend, Camille, I don't really know them."

This was dangerous ground, Thomas realised, but he hoped that his feigned candour and apparent willingness to cooperate would satisfy Dieter. The slap of the gloves, harder this time, jolted him.

"He's an old friend, you say. My patience is limited. You will know *exactly* what he does! You said he's an assistant, not a trainee. Which department? Who does he work for? You know, Mr Wundart, we expect far more cooperation from our agents. I'm not a dentist, I shouldn't have to pull stuff out bit by bit!"

Thomas looked down and as he again glanced up saw that Dieter was staring steadily at him, waiting, dominating Thomas.

"I, I believe he's Alfred Herren's personal assistant."

Dieter's eyes gleamed and opened slightly and a flicker of excitement lit his face before he resumed his usual manner and tone of voice.

"Ah! The CEO of Deutsche Bank. You say he was due to visit you for the weekend ... "

"And now I've missed him through being stuck here. We shan't get a chance again for a month or two, I expect." This was a small victory, he thought.

Dieter ignored the comment.

"Where were you going to meet them? And when?"

"Stephan had booked a room in a West Berlin hotel near my apartment but we thought it best to meet at the Opera House here. On Friday evening, yesterday evening, maybe half past seven. He was going to telephone to let me know when he could get away. We were going to see *Fidelio*. He'll be concerned about why I didn't appear, about what's happened to me."

Dieter's face was immobile.

"OK!" he said "I think we have a deal. I'll get the charge against you dropped and your trial cancelled. In return you'll intensify your contacts with Mr Fischer, see him more frequently in Frankfurt, find interesting things to bring him to Berlin. You'll find out from him all you can about Herren and what's going on in his office. There are other people in Deutsche Bank we'll want to know about as well and we'll tell you about these. Perhaps we'll even transfer you back to Frankfurt for a while. I'll have someone bring you to my office one hour from now."

"What time is it now?"

Dieter smiled as he closed the door and the darkness returned.

Approaching forty minutes later Thomas stepped into sunlight and a fresh breeze, a welcome change to his dank and gloomy cell. He looked back at the featureless block of concrete, a single storey high with no windows and only the heavily fortified door at the side. There was no one around. No signs or writing identified the building, apparently abandoned in a field. From a casual glance it looked like a partially derelict industrial or agricultural unit. Kai had once told Thomas that there were a dozen such buildings scattered around the perimeter of the city and in out of the way places. Officially they didn't exist.

The young escorting officer led him to a grey Trabant. As he settled in his seat Thomas discreetly tried to open the door but found the handle had no effect. He tried to talk to the driver who ignored him and drove precisely and with care. In about fifteen minutes Thomas began to recognise where they were and realised they'd entered from the north and were approaching the city centre. The sun broke from the clouds on to his face through the windows and he basked in the warmth, closing his eyes and listening to the drumming of the tyres.

He woke with a start. This must be Saturday, he thought again, judging by the daylight and the slope of the sun's rays. Yet that was difficult to understand. How could he have slept, or been unconscious, for so long? Then he remembered recently reading of an experiment where volunteers had been kept deep underground in limestone caves to check the effect on circadian rhythms and how initially the absolute blackness and lack of ordinary sensation had disorientated them.

His own experience made no real sense but then the time in the cell had seemed to have had a life of its own, stretching and contracting without properly matching what he'd felt of time passing. He felt weak, unsure of what he wanted, unsure even ... and with an effort he decided not to follow where his thoughts seemed to be leading.

I am Thomas Wundart, West German citizen, economics student in West Berlin but going to become an opera singer, he told himself at speed, over and over. He closed his eyes and breathed deliberately and slowly.

As he was repeating the mantra they stopped by a solid door beside which was a metal plaque on which Thomas read *Ministerium für Staatssicherheit*, the Ministry for State Security and the most feared address in East Berlin. The Stasi HQ was where regime opponents, and too often ordinary citizens picked up in the wrong place, often vanished without trace, held in what was almost a state within a state. Senior Stasi members largely made their own rules, acted with extreme secrecy and ignored the law with impunity when necessary. With its capillary network of agents spread throughout the country and abroad, it was a formidable power base.

The officer led Thomas through a network of corridors into a large room with spacious windows overlooking Normannenstrasse. A huge and ornate desk dominated the well furnished room with, behind it, a large nineteenth century oil painting of a battle scene, apparently commemorating a victory in the Franco Prussian War. A marble statue of Dzerzhinsky, the founder of the Cheka, precursor of the KGB, stood on the right. Dieter entered and sat down at his desk, ignoring the two standing in front of him. Pulling out a file from a drawer, he placed a series of papers on the desk and gestured to the officer to leave.

"You will sign these documents. You needn't read them. However, the first paper says that you are collaborating with us of your own free will. If you play any tricks on us we'll release that to the press in the West and to the West German secret service, the BND. The second document is your confession to your crime and the charges laid against you. If we set you free and you try to change your mind we will find you and return you here – make no mistake about that – and that sheet will mean your trial will take only a few minutes, the result a foregone conclusion."

Thomas signed both papers quickly without reading them. Dieter took his left hand, pressed the thumb on an ink pad and further marked each paper with the print.

"Despite what you might think you have no way of leaving West Berlin without our permission and you will only leave with my prior agreement and approval. Your name will be on the checklists used by the border guards. In case you think that false travel documents might work let me assure you that they will also have several photographs of you and that they are extremely efficient in their work.

They have been well trained in psychological profiling and analysis, for instance. You might be surprised to learn how well even West Berlin's Tegel Airport is covered by us and the extent of our agent network in the West. If you try anything foolish and survive the attempt you'll find our prison impossible to escape from, even with twenty years of trying."

Despite the sun and the pleasant warmth in the room Thomas felt chilled. Dieter poured some mineral water into an elaborately decorated beer stein.

"Our department's operational offices are in Alexanderstrasse, number 12. You will report there and receive further instructions weekly, sometimes more frequently if necessary. You will report there on Monday morning at 9.00am, for your first briefing. You will ultimately report to me but most of your contact will be with a junior agent who will take responsibility for you. In exceptional cases you may be brought also to my operational office."

He lit a cigar, leaned back in his chair, smiled thinly, pressed the record button on the machine standing on his desk, and said "Now tell me all about yourself."

The interrogation continued for some two hours, Dieter looking steadily at him and occasionally making notes. From time to time he revisited Thomas's answers, sometimes asking the same question in different ways, sometimes pretending to have misunderstood or remembered wrongly, constantly checking the truth of what Thomas was saying, right down to intimate details of his life, his friends and his sexual habits and experiences. He got increasingly confused and even began to doubt his own answers, to worry whether what he was saying was sufficiently accurate and true. Only in one area, which took all his strength to hide, was he anything other than fully open with Dieter but he felt that Kai had risked enough already without being incriminated and probably spied on as one of his East German friends.

"Initially, I want to know everything you can tell me about Alfred Herren and what he's working on. We know he has the ear of Chancellor Kohl and that the government listens to his advice on many financial and policy matters. Perhaps you will need to halt your studies for the moment and become an intern at the bank. That should be easy with your connections and your friendship with Fischer. I shall decide that later. If you are there you will meet daily with Fischer and report everything by telephone to your contact at an agreed hour each day."

"Obviously no one must know about your connection with us. If there is any leak then not only your life but that of anyone who knows this about you will be at risk. Your contact will brief you in detail at your meeting in just over a week's time. Do you want to ask anything?"

"Who is my contact?"

Dieter turned toward him with a smile, the more unexpected because of its apparently genuine warmth. It was the kind of smile his father used to give him when he returned from one of his many work trips abroad. He pressed a button on his desk and Thomas heard a buzzer next door. "I would introduce you ... " he waited for a moment "But then I have the impression you may already have met."

The connecting door opened and a figure walked in slowly. Thomas started from his chair, his initial horror changing to anger.

"Miss List is one of our best young agents." said Dieter, formally introducing Bettina, a slight smile flickering on his face.

"You bitch! You goddamn, lying, treacherous bitch."

Thomas sank back into his chair, then swung sideways to avoid looking at Bettina as she sat in the chair next to his.

A faint trace of her perfume reached his nostrils, transporting him back to the moments by the river, where he'd inhaled it so fully, nuzzling her neck and her face, now feeling sick with the recollection, an idiot for having believed there was something there between them.

"You goddamn lying bitch." he thought. "It was to have me trust you, keep me around until everything was ready. Just what the Stasi would require. How much further would you have gone if necessary?"

He felt anger, tried to glare at her but couldn't as a deep sadness and despair suddenly welled up and choked him.

"I'm afraid we weren't entirely straight with you earlier, Mr Wundart." Dieter opened a drawer in his desk and handed Thomas his watch. "It's now nearly four in the afternoon, but *Friday*, not Saturday as the guard may have implied earlier. So of course you will all go the opera as planned tonight. I think your friend Stephan and" – Dieter glanced at his notes – "his friend Camille will be excited to meet your beautiful new girlfriend. And as a Berliner now" - he marked the ambiguity with an emphasis on the noun - "she'll know the good places to go to eat afterwards. Forget business - that can wait till later. This is pleasure. Enjoy your evening. I'm sure you'll all have a wonderful time."

Chapter 8
Friday 15 September 1989

"That's a bugger Klaus leaving like that." said Bernhard.

The work became harder with only two working but also because of the distance they'd reached. The confined space was too small for both and so they developed a routine where one would dig but also fill the bag and the other would fetch and stack it up in the corner. Then the bags had to be moved periodically to the other room, risky because Frau Schwinewitz was a lurking menace, suddenly appearing. Although it was almost impossible for her to be completely silent coming down the stairs they became tense and snappy with each other during these periods.

In between times they built the roof supports and the wall cladding. All this slowed down their progress considerably and because neither dared to call in sick for the second week running they had to do what they could in the evenings only.

By the Friday evening, nearly a week after Klaus had left, they measured the tunnel at just under 19 metres of travel. They stood in the room, looking morosely into the tunnel mouth.

"I guess that's about sixteen, maybe a little more, in a straight line." said Kai. "Allowing for the pipe first of all, then that bloody great rock we had work round. Three quarters there, about. So maybe another three or four to go, till we hit the wall. Sunday? Monday? Weekend at very latest, I guess. What do you think?"

"Depends if we hit another big rock or more of that stuff with lots of little stones. Oh, god, that bit – you just couldn't drive the spade in, use the pickaxe to loosen it, scoop it, same again, over and over. But, yeah, mid week probably."

"I have nightmares about this tunnel. The dirt and the work. I wake up thrashing about thinking it's falling in on me. How much longer? Are we ever going to make it? Surely we're nearly there." He stretched and yawned again, luxuriously. "We're close, though, I'm sure of that. Look, your plans showed it about 20 metres in a straight line and we're well over that now. OK, it's not straight but it must be approaching that. I reckon we'll hit the wall tomorrow." He straightened, beamed at Kai and clapped his hands sharply "OK. Last shift tonight. In you go, Kai and see what you can do."

For twenty minutes Kai dug with renewed energy. The thought of coming close to the finish had fired him up and he'd forgotten his tiredness and aching limbs. He filled one bag in record time and summoned Bernhard to collect it, returning to attack the surface with enthusiasm. Suddenly Bernhard was back in the tunnel.

"It's that Schwinewitz woman outside the door. She's banging on the door, shouting and saying she wants to talk to you. She says she knows you're in here. Go and talk to her now before she goes and calls the Stasi or the police."

"Oh shit." They scuttled back quickly. Bernhard moved to the tunnel mouth as Kai stood by the door, listening.

"I can hear you moving in there. Now open this door right now!" Frau Schwinewitz shouted, banging on the door. "You've been avoiding me for weeks and your rent is well overdue. Come out of there at once. If you don't come out I'm going to get the police and have you kicked out of your flat."

Kai and Bernhard stood silently, looking at each other.

"OK, that's it. I know you can hear me. I'm going to call the police now, and they'll sort you out. We'll see how this story ends, Herr Rumpel."

There was a further long silence and then they heard her footsteps echoing down the long corridor.

"Go and stop her." whispered Bernhard, throwing Kai a clean sweater to cover his muddy shirt. "Comb your hair and wipe that smudge off your forehead, yes, just there. Tell her she'll have the rent Monday at latest, maybe even tomorrow. You're getting it from a friend and you don't think he's around. Make up some story anyway."

He opened the door silently and pushed Kai into the corridor where he chased after the woman.

"Frau Schwinewitz! Frau Schwinewitz!"

He caught up with her just as she reached her apartment door.

"I'm sorry Frau Schwinewitz. I think I heard you shouting but I'd fallen asleep. I've been working extra hours, cutting out some designs down in the basement to make a bit more money. Look, is it about my rent? I called round a couple of time to pay you but we never seemed to meet and I didn't want to just push it under the door."

She stared at him for a moment. "Really, Herr Rumpel? How strange. And I'd somehow had got the impression you were trying to avoid me. But that's OK. I can take the money now." She held out her hand.

"I'm sorry. I don't have it right now. I left it with a friend for safekeeping – you remember Klaus, he was helping me move some things a couple of weeks ago. I need to get it back from him and when I do I'll bring it straight round. You'll have it Monday, Monday evening, I promise. I'll go and see him after work, on my way home."

"You know, Herr Rumpel, I don't think I believe you. What's wrong with tomorrow? Or Sunday?"

"He's away. He's gone to, to Leipzig. To see, to see a friend. A girlfriend. Driving. In his van. He'll drive back just in time for work on Monday morning, early. But I'll catch him on Monday evening. He'll be home by seven. Or maybe half past. I promise. And I'll bring it to your flat. Will that be alright?"

She narrowed her eyes and stared at him.

"I'll expect you absolutely not later than nine." she said. "And let me warn you - make sure this is the last time you're late. I've had enough. I'll make sure you're evicted if you're as much as a day late in future. Do you understand?"

"Thank you, Frau Schwinewitz. It will be the very last time. I promise you that. Yes, I can most certainly promise you that."

Chapter 9
Friday 15 September 1989

The Deutsche Staats Oper, the East Berlin opera house, was brilliantly lit and streams of people, some in fine overcoats and expensive furs, were flowing towards it from both directions along Unter den Linden. As Thomas approached he saw Bettina standing by the main entrance. She was wearing a deceptively simple and very elegant black dress with a discreet pattern of small white flowers and over it a slim grey coat, falling open in front. Her blonde hair, loosely tied and cascading over her shoulders, caught and reflected the light as if burnished. Despite his new detestation of her he found himself imagining the pleasures of lifting and running her hair through his fingers as she smiled up at him. He acknowledged her style and beauty and how marvellous she looked and saw from the lingering glances of others that he was not alone in his appreciation.

"Hi there!"

Ordinarily Thomas would have revelled in being the man accompanying someone so beautiful and elegant but now he barely acknowledged her greeting, looking around for Stephan and Camille. He thought back to his visit with Bettina to the Ephraim Palais and felt ridiculous and ashamed. He should never have taken her to such an expensive restaurant so soon after meeting her and he should certainly not have drunk so much that he'd become expansive and indiscreet about what he was doing. That he'd been strongly attracted to her, wanted to impress her, was no excuse for such juvenile behaviour. He'd been like the worst kind of amateur, playing at being in the black market money big league but being caught by the oldest kind of trap there was. He felt sick at the realisation that she'd been using him. He felt pain at the thought that the scene by the river, the memory of which he'd relied on to keep him going in jail, had been a mere act on her part, counterfeit and fake. Despite this he realised, seeing her standing there, that he still wanted her. That was going to be difficult.

"Perhaps by force." he thought with a savage flash of emotion. "She's not the only one who can betray trust. Pay back time!" Then he returned to his senses and acknowledged how much he was now in her power and how much worse it could still get for him if she chose.

The first bell rang but there was still no sign of Stephan and Camille.

"We should go in. I'll leave their tickets at the box office and they can find us when they get here."

Their seats were close to the stage and as Thomas led the way, brusquely and deliberately preceding Bettina, he realised too late that that meant she would be sitting next to Stephan or Camille, a closeness he'd wanted to avoid. He tried to change seats but she simply smiled sweetly and remained where she was. As the lights dimmed his friends arrived, slipping into their seats as the orchestra began playing the Overture to *Fidelio*. To his irritation and growing resentment, Thomas realised that Bettina was spending a good deal of time talking animatedly with Camille next to her and often also with Stephan, both of whom appeared to be enjoying themselves immensely. He felt morose and out of place, unable even to lose himself as he ordinarily would in the opera, and at one point felt a surge of conflicting emotions as Camille laughed delightedly at something Bettina had said and Bettina turned to Thomas, placing her hand with apparent fondness over his for a moment and smiling up at him.

"Fantastic!" Stephan said as they exited, the crowd slowly dispersing in the nearby streets. "It's the first time I didn't fall asleep in one of these opera thingies!"

"Probably because you didn't listen." Thomas snapped. "You seemed to spend the whole time talking. Didn't you notice the people behind you? They'd have killed you gladly, given the chance."

Bettina and Camille were chatting animatedly but as the men followed them Stephan, surprised by Thomas's mood, glanced over and stopped in astonishment.

"Jesus! What's happened to your face?" Thomas, initially resisting, let Stephan turn him round so that the light fell better on his lacerated forehead and swollen nose while Camille and Bettina strolled ahead. "You look like Jimmy Durante – Schnoz Wundart, that's what we'll call you now." He laughed and lowered his voice. "Look, I know how you like to get right into things with a new girlfriend but ... " he opened his eyes wide in mock surprise, sucked in his breath noisily, and spoke in a stagy whisper " ... did you really turn her on that much? Wow!"

Thomas jerked Stephan's hands from his hunched shoulders with a brusque shrug. "Well, funny you should say that, because ... " he started, then, "Oh, just leave it, will you? It was a stupid acquaintance of mine who crashed his car when I was in it."

"I couldn't work out why Fidelio seemed to be a woman until Bettina told me it was really Larana, I think that was her name, pretending to be a man to get her husband out of jail. Imagine that!" said Camille as Thomas and Stephan caught up with them. "And she made all these snarky comments about how all these big ideas like freedom and liberty get spoilt when some people have too much power and that really brought it all to life for me."

She turned to Bettina. "And I loved that story you told me about the swan."

"What story?" Stephan asked. "I didn't hear that."

Bettina smiled. "Something that happened in a performance of *Lohengrin*. The tenor had just finished his aria and was supposed to be spirited away by this mechanical swan. But the swan wasn't there. By mistake it had been moved during the aria and had disappeared off stage. No sign of it! So there he was, standing around, meant to leave the stage but not knowing how to manage it. Finally he turns to the soprano and asks 'Excuse me, but when's the next swan?'"

Stephan and Camille roared with laughter and even Thomas chuckled despite himself.

"So, where next?" Stephan asked, wiping his eyes. "I think we should avoid Thomas's nouveau riche traps and head for a real local place. Bettina, any ideas?"

"Sure. I know a good place. But we'll be better accepted if you two take your ties and jackets off." She caught Thomas's eye. "Your face won't be out of place anyway."

"Oh, and before I forget, Thomas, I've talked to the personnel department." Stephan added.

"It's called Unter den Linden because of the lime trees lining each side of the street." Thomas broke in wildly, gesturing around him. "They were planted sometime in the 17th century. Look how regular and even they are. People walk under them, you see." He walked over and smacked the trunk of one a couple of times proprietorially and gazed up into the crown. "Come and look at this Stephan."

"I do know that, Thomas! We learned it in school, for heaven's sake. Anyway, there's a couple of dates available for your interviews, though not immediately I'm afraid – either a fortnight today, Friday 29 it must be, or the following Monday, 2 October."

"Great!" said Thomas, trying to sound enthusiastic, as he noticed Bettina's interested gaze and slight smile. "Thanks very much. I'll, I'll let you know soon. As I can."

Stephan's new BMW 7 looked increasingly out of place as they left the town centre and headed north through the generally unlit streets. Ruined buildings stood next to others which had been rebuilt carefully after the war. There was very little traffic and the roads were a mix of potholed streets with broken pavements and stretches of sometimes irregular asphalt. Thomas realized they were in Prenzlauer Berg, formerly an elegant residential area of the city. Eventually Bettina told Stephan to pull in and park.

"It's maybe half a kilometre away from here but it's probably better not to park too close. Generally people here are alright, but sometimes they resent seeing a West German luxury car and things can happen. Especially if they've had one beer too many!"

The building was old, built of stone and with a raked roof of thick grey tiles. The sign on the wall above the door read 'Restauration 1900'. The room they entered was stiflingly hot and packed with people and Thomas's eyes stung in the pall of smoke which hit them. There was a strong smell of beer and sauerkraut laced with occasional sharp aromas of fruit schnapps.

Bettina eased their way through the crowd, stopping every few paces to greet one person or another, people of all ages and sizes. "Heinz, Ingrid, good to see you." She smiled and shook hands, sometimes introducing the others. "Klaus, these are my friends Camille and Stephen, from Frankfurt, and Thomas is a student in West Berlin. Klaus was an economics student as well, Leipzig wasn't it, Klaus?" The hubbub of chatter and the background music made it difficult to make any sense of the conversations and Thomas stared gloomily around as they jolted their way through. They squeezed into a second and larger room which was somewhat emptier.

"This is the restaurant part. There's another room downstairs which is usually quieter. Used to be a bomb shelter so it's maybe a bit bleak, though. Best stay here, I think."

The smell of beer and the vinegary tang of sauerkraut remained but were now muted, overlaid by the scent of roasted meat and baked potatoes which made Thomas realise how hungry he was.

"I hope no one's vegetarian – this place is noted for its pork." Bettina said as she managed to find some unoccupied space at one of the long refectory tables with their plain wooden benches.

"Just so long as the pigs don't come in." Thomas muttered morosely. "I've had it up to here with that lot."

The waitress brought them beers and returned shortly with steaming plates of roast pork and crackling and for a time no one spoke, being too occupied in eating heartily.

Stephan turned to Bettina. "So, are you from East Berlin?"

"No, I moved here about four years ago. My dad was from a small town near Dresden, so that's where we lived. And you're from Frankfurt, aren't you? Like Thomas." She snapped off a piece of crackling, dipped it in apple sauce and crunched a bite.

"That's right. We were at school together. Known each other since this high." He held his hand maybe half a metre above the table surface. "Our families were good friends and lived fairly close so that's how we got to know each other. Are your parents still in Dresden? And what does your dad do?"

"He was in the export business, electronics, and he had to travel a lot, including in the West, the Ruhr mainly I think it was. That got more difficult when the Wall went up, 1961, but because of his work he could still get permits. Then after one trip in 1970, I'd just turned five, he was away for a long time and almost immediately he came back he went off again. That was the last we saw of him. He wrote to my mother on different occasions saying each time he had to stay a bit longer and then a few months later told her that he'd decided to settle in Essen and that he'd find a way to get us there. What is Essen like anyway? It's close to Frankfurt, I think, isn't that right?"

"Not too far. Industrial, coal and steel. Not really my kind of town though there are parts that are OK. I sometimes have to go there to visit one or other corporation to discuss things. So, what happened? Didn't your dad send for you? Could you not get out? Have you ever been there at all?"

Stephan thought for a long moment that Bettina hadn't heard what he'd said, that the noise of the restaurant was too much. But then she spoke, quietly and looking away, so that they all had to strain to hear.

"After a bit the letters stopped. My mother heard he'd moved in with someone else. I guess that having to choose between his family and his money he just couldn't part with his money, that's all." She took a long pull of her beer.

There was silence. Thomas and Stephan stared into their beers and Camille reached out a hand and briefly touched Bettina's. Despite his continuing fury with her Thomas remembered Bettina's reaction at the Ephraim Palais and now understood it better. He could see better why she was so strongly contemptuous of that kind of selfish consumption and thirst for luxury. The Western world placed money and consumption above everything else, in her view, and it was the lure of this that she blamed for her father's betrayal of his family.

Perhaps it wasn't quite as simple as that, thought Thomas, but as he thought of the five year old Bettina wearying her mother with questions as to her daddy's return, today?, tomorrow?, soon?, then growing progressively more puzzled and sad, more silent, until she came to accept that he'd gone for good, came to understand later that he'd chosen living in the West against his wife and children, he saw how hurt she'd been by someone she'd relied on unquestioningly. He was silent as the mood changed and the others started chattering and ordering more beers.

Bettina drained her beer and looked at her watch. "We need to get going – we've got to get back to the car and it will take you at least another fifteen minutes to get to the closest border crossing from there. And you'll need to allow some extra time in case you get a bit lost."

Stephan called the waitress and paid for everyone, with both Thomas and Bettina protesting that they should divide evenly. They fought their way back through the now even more crowded outer room to the street and, shivering and pulling their coats tighter round them, set off for the car.

Bettina pointed across what had presumably earlier been an apartment block but was now a surrealist urban garden with small trees growing on tops of ruined walls and others showing behind shattered window openings, the ground covered with now dying down rose bay willow herb and other vegetation. "There, look, that apartment block is where I live, third floor at the back."

Even at a hundred metres or so away it was easy to see that the building looked run down though not as derelict as some others nearby. At first they'd been walking abreast, Camille's arm in Stephan's and tucked closely to his side, but as the streets narrowed Stephan dropped back to walk with Thomas who was slouching along behind them, as Bettina and Camille went ahead, talking animatedly.

"What's the matter with you? You've been obnoxious all evening. Bettina is simply fantastic. Camille and I both think that. She's intelligent, lively, caring, beautiful ... we like her a lot. She seems to really like you too but if you don't watch out you'll lose her. I don't understand why you were ignoring her so completely." He stopped and looked at him as Thomas grunted and shrugged. "Have you had a fight or something? It really wasn't her that hit you, was it?

I can't believe that. But you've just been blocking her out all evening."

Thomas sighed. "It's a long story, Stephan. Let's just say there are reasons. And, no, she didn't hit me, that was really a car crash, like I said." He swallowed. "She had nothing to do with my face."

He felt guilty. He was going to betray Stephan to get his liberty back. And he had no idea what price he ultimately might have to pay. He had a dread that his involvement with the Stasi could even ruin his best friend's life. And now he was forced into close contact with someone he detested and feared but couldn't helping wanting as well. Then there was Kai. The Stasi almost certainly knew of his visits to Kai's apartment and perhaps even their meetings elsewhere. Would they would think it worth checking further on why Thomas and Kai had become friends, whether there was some hidden secret there that needed investigating? Perhaps they already knew about Kai's escape plans and would just pick him up when they felt like it.

What a fucking mess! He wished he could just say that he'd had enough, that he wasn't going ahead with what he'd agreed, that he'd take what would be coming to him. But he knew that he simply couldn't face jail in the East and there was no way he would avoid that if he refused to cooperate. Let others be heroes. He lashed out at a stone in his path, connecting and sending it flying wonderfully, swooping down and narrowly missing Stephan's car in its trajectory, and felt better.

Chapter 10
Saturday 16 September 1989 through Sunday 17 September

"I'm so sick of this place!" said Kai as they bolted themselves into the basement room on the Saturday morning. "Nothing but backbreaking digging and humping damp earth around every night, every weekend. And it's clammy in here and stinks. Look, there's mould on that wall over there. You'd think old Schwineschwein would notice the smell even in the corridor but I guess it's all those fags she smokes, probably can't smell much." He laughed. "Not even herself, obviously, or she'd do something about that!"

"We'll be out soon. In the West. Think of that! Then you can lie around and do nothing all day, drink, go to clubs, whatever you want, without worrying about someone snooping all the time."

"If only! And you're not the one she's chasing for rent, Bernhard. You know I promised to get it to her Monday evening. I can't give her the money by then, obviously, and if I don't she'll have the police on to me straight away and I'll be turfed out." He laughed again. "But I'd just love to see their faces when they open the door to check the cellar's empty!"

"OK. So we'll just have to finish it before then and get out of here then, won't we? We've got the whole weekend, Monday too if we need it. Tell Ulrike to get her stuff ready and we can go as soon as we break through."

They dug and shifted earth steadily throughout the day and by late evening had added just over a metre to the tunnel length. The next morning, Sunday, they began early and again made good progress until just after midday during one of Kai's shifts. He crawled out of the tunnel, frustrated and angry.

"It was going fine and then I hit what I thought was another big rock. It's not a rock but I don't know what it is and how big and what we can do about it. At the start it was just on the floor and so I thought I could get over it but it seems to be getting higher and higher as I dig. Have a look. Come and see what you think. Fuck! Just what we need!" He kicked one of the lowest bags of soil hard, dislodging a couple stacked on top which fell and tipped earth over the floor. "Shit!"

Bernhard crawled to the end of the tunnel, followed by Kai, and probed and scraped at the object in their way, digging experimentally in different directions. He motioned Kai back and shortly both of them sat on the floor, legs dangling into the hole in the floor.

"That's concrete, not rock. Did you see how it continued out on each side of our tunnel and how it seems to curve up in front. We've hit the tunnel roof . We've made it! We're almost there!" He beamed at Kai and they embraced.

"But, and it's a big one." Bernhard continued. "Looks like we've hit the tunnel at the wrong position. We're too high up. That's the curved roof. We can check this but I remember from looking at the plans that the walls were brick, rendered in the tunnels and faced with tiles in the stations, and that the roof was reinforced concrete, thick concrete at that. I can't remember if it was just curved rebar or steel mesh but either way we can't get through that, not in the time we have anyway and using these hand tools. And even if we could we'd be something like four and a half, five metres above the ground and without a rope and something to tie it to one of us is going to break a leg dropping down."

"Shit! So what do we do?"

"We'll have to backtrack a bit and down to find where this curve ends and then goes straight down, that's the brick wall. We can break through that. It really depends on where we've hit the roof as to how far back and down we'll need to go. I think the wall was maybe three metres, three metres something anyway, when the roof started so maybe it's not far back. Let's go and see what we can find out."

They crawled back into the tunnel and Bernhard began poking experimentally with the pickaxe in the floor of the tunnel. Initially there was resistance as he investigated every ten centimetres or so, the point going in deeper each time. Just short of a metre from where the slope of the roof emerged from the tunnel floor the pointed blade went in up to its shaft without meeting anything.

"I don't know. Maybe that's the end of it or maybe it's just lower than I can reach now. Anyway, it's got to be back to at least here so let's dig a bit and find out. I'll do that, Kai, you fill the bags and move them."

For nearly an hour, twice the length of an ordinary shift, Bernhard shovelled and probed with the pickaxe, caught up in fury at the misjudgement and working as if the tunnel were a malign force intentionally checking them and he fighting to defeat it. Kai didn't dare speak, filling and carrying bags silently and standing around unsure of what he could do to help. He returned to find Bernhard standing in an excavated sump about a metre and a half from the blocked end of the tunnel, beckoning him and waving the torch, shining it towards his own feet.

"This is the point. Look. Here's the end of the roof and the top row of bricks. I reckon we'll need to go down another metre and that should do it, expose enough of the wall to make a big enough entrance. We'll need to cut the hole back a bit too to give working room. The earth here isn't bad, hardly any stones, so it's doable quite soon I think. Your turn, Kai!"

He grinned and in a complicated dance in the now slightly enlarged space they changed places. It was two thirty in the afternoon and by shortly after six in the evening a panel of brick wall, a metre high by half a metre wide, was exposed.

Bernhard crawled out and handed Kai the hand drill he'd filched unnoticed from his employer's construction site. Kai took a last long breath of fresh air and crawled down the tunnel.

Working in the now dim light of the lantern torch and exploring the surface of the wall with his fingers Kai found a gap in the mortar between the bricks, held the drill firmly against it with the chest pad, and started turning the handle. After a few attempts when the bit skittered off it made a dent and started digging in solidly. He pushed further, hoping the wall wasn't too thick, that there was only a single layer of bricks. Suddenly, while still chewing out mortar, the resistance vanished and the drill pushed forward into a void. Kai poked and prodded at the mortar round the hole but couldn't get the brick to budge. He set about feverishly making another hole in the mortar above the same brick so that he could look through one and flash the light into the space beyond through the other.

His head was thumping with pain and he felt weak and dizzy with the reduction of oxygen, reminding him of his near earlier fainting. He was dripping with sweat and felt as if he was breathing in a furnace. He put the breathing tube to his mouth and sucked hard. He had to get out of there. He drew the smaller torch from his pocket and placed it over the wider opening, then put his eye to the one above. Nothing! There was not even a trace of light. His heart sank as the sweat poured down his face. He tried again, this time moving the torch to the hole where his eye had been. This time he thought he could vaguely see something. As his eyes got accustomed to the dimness, it looked more and more like dark tiles on a wall. He scraped away and widened the hole further. He stared at a patch of slanting black on pale green, unable to make any sense of what he could see, until he suddenly released he was looking at the end of the letter A. That it was in the old script had confused him but yes, there was no doubt — they had made it! As he crawled back, elated, he could hear Bernhard hissing his name, urging him back. They met halfway along the track in the chamber where there was just room to stand.

"There's something going on out there but I don't know what it is. The door creaked and the handle turned again so I guess it's old Schwineschwanzlutscher rooting around again. She's getting suspicious."

They listened at the door but there was silence. They opened it cautiously but there was nothing and no sign of anyone hanging around.

"I don't like this." Bernhard said. "You should tell Ulrike to get ready and both come back down here. Damn! I forgot my rucksack so I'll need to go back for that. I'll be as quick as I can. See you back here in a few minutes."

Kai raced up the stairs and burst into the flat. Ulrike was standing by the mirror, admiring her nose from different angles. She glanced at him, startled by the look on his face as he stood recovering his breath.

"Get your things." he said, panting hard. "Now! We've got to leave. Immediately."

"But ... I thought ... Have you broken through?" Her face lit up, then fell. "Or is there something wrong? What's happened?"

"Don't worry. We're through. It's fine, but there's no time to waste. Please, Ulrike, get your things. Now!"

Kai's voice had an edge she had never heard before and frightened by his tone she obeyed silently, hurrying into the bedroom to look for the few scattered objects she wanted to take.

Kai kept glancing at his watch. At least he'd bought some time by agreeing to deliver his rent on the Monday evening but there was no knowing how long it would take to break through the last bit to make a hole large enough to get through. Worse, Frau Schwinewitz was clearly suspicious and nosing around the basement corridor. Oh, well, she'd just have to make of it what she would and they'd have to hope she didn't call the police to break into the room.

There was no real choice. They had to go now. They had to risk it. Actually, he thought, they had to *do* it, they had to succeed now or it really was the finish of them all.

"By tomorrow I'll be in West Berlin!" he thought. "Or I'll be dead and won't care."

He traced for a few moments with his fingers the intricate leather patterning of the cowboy boots which had cost him a fortune, stroked and sniffed deeply the supple tan leather, remembering how he'd felt when he'd first worn them only a few months ago and how Ulrike, enchanted by his style, had struck up a conversation with him and they'd got together. He blinked, shook his head and returned to the present, grabbed his Swiss Army knife, a gift from Thomas, and moved on, filling his small rucksack rapidly.

As they moved carefully down the stairs Kai's mind raced, trying to cover all the angles, wondering if he'd overlooked anything important. They were particularly careful approaching the ground floor. He listened and the faint sound of a radio from Frau Schwinewitz's apartment, the door firmly closed, reassured him. They opened the door carefully then filed softly down the basement stairs without putting the lights on, hearts pounding.

In the darkness they felt their way along the familiar corridor and as Kai turned the key gently in the lock and began to ease the door open the corridor light snapped on, flooding the corners and blinding him for an instant. Frau Schwinewitz stepped out from the side corridor a few metres away, her gun pointing steadily at Kai.

"Well, well. Look what we have here!" she said, a slight tremor in her high pitched voice "Were you planning to go somewhere? I'd been wondering why the basement corridor kept getting dirty even though I cleaned it regularly. So I thought I'd wait for you." she said, smug at outwitting them. Her voice harshened. "Face the door, both of you."

Her voice echoed down the empty corridor. Kai turned to face the blank wall and Ulrike moved next to him in front of the door and felt for his hand.

"Now open the door. I want to see what you've been up to, before I call the police." She gestured with the gun to Ulrike.

Ulrike gave the door a light push.

The room was dark but the smell of damp earth reached to where they stood. Frau Schwinewitz squinted, stepping forward, peering into the darkness, sniffing the air, her gun carefully ready.

"Wider. Open it fully. And turn the light on."

Kai laughed. "Why would we use lights?" he jeered. "Knowing how you creep around, spying on everyone, looking for lights under doors, we'd as well have told you everything."

"You have a torch, then. Use that."

"It's in my rucksack."

"Get it out. Don't try anything or I'll shoot you, then her."

Kai slowly eased the rucksack off his back to the floor in front of him. Holding Frau Schwinewitz's gaze he squatted down, eased up the flap, pulled the drawstring and felt around with both hands, digging deep, then pulled the torch out and switched it on with his left hand, his right now hidden in his pocket, his thumbnail easing open the blade of his Swiss Army knife.

"Show me the room. Move it around. I want to see what you've been up to."

Kai lit up the centre of the far wall then moved the beam of light slowly down and to the right. Frau Schwinewitz moved closer. Her gun drooped, now pointing just beyond Ulrike's feet. She was almost in reach and Kai could hear her breathing quickening as he watched closely out of the corner of his eye. He ran the circle of light closer to the hole, picking out the edge and then flicked it back and up to the ceiling.

"Back! Bring it back down. What was that? Show me that again."

Kai moved the light slowly down until it shone into the hole in the floor of the room. The soil was piled high beside and around it and the supporting struts stretched faintly into the blackness like an early mine shaft. She moved closer to look. He tensed his foot and sprang awkwardly sideways, striking at Frau Schwinewitz and feeling the blade miss her arm and enter under one of her lower ribs as she staggered and fell away from him. The sharp crack of a shot shattered the relative silence in the corridor as the echoes bounced around the hard walls and the bullet passed through the door no more than a centimetre from where Ulrike was standing.

Frau Schwinewitz was lying on the floor, her left hand pressing the bleeding wound in her side the right firmly holding the pistol now pointing again straight at him as he stood by Ulrike.

"You bastard! You bloody, devious, bloody bastard! Escaping's bad enough. But attempted murder – they'll never let you out now."

Hampered by holding the gun trained on Kai she moved to a kneeling position then struggled to her feet and shuffled back a few steps, kicking the Swiss army knife well out of Kai's reach as she did so.

"You there, bitch, lock the door. Then throw me the keys."

Ulrike turned and locked the basement door, weighed the keys in her hand and threw them clumsily so that they landed short of Frau Schwinewitz and close to the far wall. Furious, Schwinewitz let off a warning shot which smacked into the wall between them, jolting them back in fright and making Ulrike fear she'd gone too far.

Frau Schwinewitz glared at them, raised her pistol and pointed it direct at Kai's chest. Ulrike could see the index finger tensing on the trigger and despite herself closed her eyes in terror and waited for the shot and the sound of Kai falling. When she looked up Frau Schwinewitz had edged forward and, supported by the wall, was beginning to crouch and feel for the keys, her gun still trained on Kai's chest. At the edge of her vision Ulrike glimpsed a slight movement.

Just as Frau Schwinewitz's hand grasped the bunch Bernhard jumped on her from behind, bouncing her head from the wall on to the concrete floor with a sharp crack echoing her involuntary shot a microsecond earlier, the bullet tugging at Kai's jacket but leaving him unharmed. She lay motionless on the floor, a trickle of blood now staining the concrete. After a few moments when it was clear that she was no danger to them Bernhard stepped forward, pocketed the gun and the keys, felt her wrist and lifted her head from the floor.

"She's alive but the skull seems cracked. And there's a narrow cut, but deep. I guess she fell hard on a key or something."

"We can't just leave her to die here." Ulrike was almost in tears.

"Tough shit!" said Kai. "We've got to get out straight away. If anyone's heard the shots the police will be here any moment."

"We're four or five metres underground" said Bernhard "and these walls are really solid. You said she was the only person living on the ground floor. No one will have heard anything."

"But we just can't leave her here. If she dies that's murder! They'll know what's happened. It's murder! The GDR will ask for us back and the West won't just ignore that, not for murder." Ulrike was becoming hysterical, tears streaming down her face, and Kai put his arms round her and stroked her hair. "I hated her but I didn't want to kill her. Damn! Damn! Damn! We've got to take her to hospital."

"No, Ulrike" he said. "We can't. They'll want to know what happened, probably get the police in to question us, maybe even hold us until she wakes up and can give her version. We can't do that. We don't have the time." He held her tightly for a moment then looked at her at forearm's length. "We don't have a choice. It's her or us. All we can do is maybe drag her to the stairs and leave her there. Someone will find her. We've got to go."

Chapter 11
Sunday 17 September 1989

"Do you have an alarm clock?" Bernhard asked suddenly, staring at the inert figure lying on the cellar floor.

"What the fuck has that got to do with anything?" Kai shouted. "Let's get out of here and stop pissing around."

Bernhard ignored him. Ulrike pulled out a small, old clock from her rucksack.

"We'll carry her to her apartment and make it seem that she fell and cracked her head there. It's just gone nine now. We'll leave the door ajar and set the alarm for ten. Someone should hear that, find the door open and rush her to hospital. Kai, scatter some dirt on the blood on the floor and move it around. We don't want anyone getting curious about things if they come down here."

They carried Frau Schwinewitz up the stairs, Ulrike pressing a cloth to the head wound to minimise the blood flow and scuffing with her shoe at odd drops which escaped. As they neared the hallway Ulrike listened at the street door then crossed quickly to the apartment, opening the door with keys taken from Frau Schwinewitz's pocket and urging them over quickly. Despite Frau Schwinewitz's slight frame the inert body was heavy and Bernhard and Kai were bathed in sweat as they laid her down, arranging her in mimicry of her earlier fall, placing her bloodied keys by her head wound, rucking up the thin carpet and positioning it so that it looked as if her outstretched right foot had caught it and brought her down.

"Where's the carpet fitter when you need him?" remarked Kai and the three burst into stifled giggles, clutching each other for a moment in relief, while Ulrike cautiously slid open the door and left it ajar.

The alarm clock, fully wound and set for 10pm, sat on the small table. No one was around and they darted back across the hall. Moments later they were again in the basement room.

Kai crawled to the end of the tunnel and started attacking the wall with all his strength, hammering in a stone chisel and sometimes trying to fracture bricks where there were apparent faults. He was sweating profusely but fear gave him impetus and new strength. The muscles of his arms ached but he pushed himself past the pain. The mortar was old but still hard and often difficult to break. Occasionally it crumbled and he was able to push chunks out and into the void beyond and on those occasions his hopes and his mood lurched in response. By now he'd removed a section of six bricks and he could see clearly into the tunnel. The sight of the pale green tiles lit up by the torch beam delighted him and spurred him on. There was a cool and welcoming draught coming from the hole, refreshing him.

It was now approaching nine thirty and as the hole was enlarged it began to get easier. He'd now removed nine bricks in three rows. It was wide enough to squeeze through, he thought, but it really needed to be at least another three or four rows, more if they had time. He worried about pushing Ulrike's stuffed rucksack through. Well, if it came to it they might have to abandon it, maybe empty it and repack it on the other side if there was time. He worried whether Frau Schwinewitz might have come back to consciousness early, that even now the police were about to storm down the stairs. Exhausted, he wormed his way back to the basement room to change places with Bernhard. Ulrike was standing there, her rucksack on the floor, pacing around in the small area of floor free of the mounds of soil, desperate to move out of the limbo where they found themselves. She smiled wanly as Kai emerged, dripping with sweat and caked with streaks of red clay.

"It's going well. We're nearly through. Bernhard will finish it." They embraced silently, clinging to and resting on each other.

At ten to ten Bernhard emerged from the tunnel, coughing and staggering as he came.

"We're almost there. A couple more bricks. I was going to finish it but I started getting dizzy and nauseous."

Before Kai could move Ulrike had ducked into the tunnel.

"I'll do it. I can't stand around here any more. I need to do this. I have to help."

Some minutes after ten they heard a whistle from Ulrike and they set off to join her, Kai dragging Ulrike's rucksack and his own awkwardly behind him. They left the rucksacks in the half way chamber and crowded together by the wall. Ulrike was crouching there, hot and dirty but flushed with the success of knocking out the last bricks. There was a single row left at floor level and above it a gaping, jagged hole seven bricks deep. Kai shone the torch into the darkness, the beam picking out a flat, gravel-strewn surface immediately below and beyond it the glint of rails and a tiled wall.

"It looks a bit over three metres. I'll go first to check there's no problems down there. Push the rucksacks through after I'm down and I'll catch them. You come next Kai, copy what I do and then we'll catch Ulrike when she drops. Ulrike, shine the light down below me."

As Kai returned with the rucksacks Bernhard turned his back to the hole, pushed his legs through and wriggled till he was hanging down, his hands gripping the row of bricks. Glancing down he judged his landing spot and dropped, falling lightly on bending knees. Kai pushed the three rucksacks through and followed, landing safely. Grinning at each other they high-fived and turned to help Ulrike. Dropping the torch into Bernhard's hands she turned and wriggled through feet first, dangling awkwardly half through the hole, resting on one elbow, her other hand scrabbling for the row of bricks. Her legs suddenly waved wildly.

"Oh God! I'm stuck! Something's caught! I can't move. Oh God! Help me."

The legs waved wildly again but fell closer so that Kai could now just touch them with stretched arms and guide them. Ulrike was clinging on with both hands to the row of bricks when one suddenly gave way and with a rip of cloth from her shirt she fell awkwardly sending Kai staggering away from her as he broke her fall. She lay there, winded and they heard a sharp intake of breath as Kai got to his feet. She saw him wince as he stood.

"What's wrong?"

"Ankle. Twisted I think, I hope, rather than broken. Hurts like hell though." He winced again as he put weight on left foot. "C'mon guys, let's move. It's nearly half past ten. They could have found Schwinehexe by now and be after us any minute."

They were nearly opposite the far end of a platform and behind them they could hear the rumbling of a train, the wheels singing on the rails and the lights approaching from round the bend, lighting up the brickwork of the tunnel. They moved into an alcove and watched as the train ran slowly through the gloom of the closed station, watching the faces of the strangers sitting there incuriously, minding their own business. Kai noticed a couple peering out at the eerie beauty, relic of an earlier era.

"Ghost train! WhooooHoooo!" sang Kai.

"Ghost station!" replied Bernhard. "And we're the ghost travellers." He was grinning widely.

They edged closer to the rails as the last two last carriages were moving past. Searching desperately for a handhold, somewhere to grasp and cling to, they quickly realized how impossible to it would be to jump on. Seconds later the train vanished, its tail light tracking the tunnel and disappearing in the distance. The faint sound faded away. The station returned to absolute darkness, absolute silence.

"Did you see where the train was headed?" Ulrike asked.

"Yeah, Leinestraße" said Bernhard. "That's the direction we need to go, I think. I wonder how often it runs, every fifteen minutes at this time, I guess, though maybe even less frequently Sunday evening."

"We've got to time it well." Kai's voice was tense. "There are three main stations on this side. We'll run to the first and wait there for the next train to pass. Then we'll start running again immediately. We can't wait in case the woman wakes up and talks. Let's go."

They set off in a row, Kai limping in front and Bernhard at the rear. Almost immediately there was the rattle and whine of another train. Kai flashed the torch beam along the tunnel walls, trying desperately to find somewhere to take refuge but there was nothing, no openings in the blank tunnel walls. The growl of steel on steel grew louder and they could feel the ground shaking. Kai finally saw a narrow niche, space only for one. Grabbing Ulrike's hand he pushed her to the gap.

"Get in there and squeeze as far back as you can. Keep your head in or you'll lose it." he shouted.

Turning he saw Bernhard lying on the ground between the rails. He quickly followed, praying that all those films he'd seen had got it right and that he'd avoid the live rail. The tunnel filled with thunder, the sound now was almost over them, the train moving at speed, the roar drumming off the walls, amplified by and echoing across the empty galleries. They held their breaths, waiting for the impact. The sound climaxed in a tumbling, screaming clatter and rushed into the distance. Kai didn't dare lift his head but lay where he was immersed in the silence until it was broken by

Ulrike's shrill, manic laughter. Bernhard went to her, shook her and finally she calmed down, sobbing slightly in relief.

"It was going the other way." Her voice squeaked. "It wasn't in this tunnel. It was the other one." She began laughing again, hysterically, then suddenly became quiet.

The set off again, loping along, running in short bursts, Bernhard now leading. Kai's limping got worse and he began falling behind. They finally reached Jannowitzbrücke station and hauled themselves up on to the platform. As they sat down, Bernhard checked his watch.

"Listen guys. It's nearly a quarter to so it's taken us twelve, thirteen minutes to get here. OK, that includes the stop we had to make but these first two stations are close and so that's slower than we need to be."

They sat on the station platform, catching their breaths, Kai resting his now aching ankle.

The next train arrived six minutes later. This time they saw it appear, its white front light illuminating the station, turning darkness into daylight for a moment. Ulrike began to jump about on the platform waving her arms and shining the torch wildly but no one in the carriages reacted. She slumped back on the platform as the train disappeared and as Bernhard got up from checking as well as he could how low the train ran on the tracks.

"Looks like there's just about enough space under it but it'll be very, very tight. Misjudge it, and ... " He shrugged and pulled a face. "Let's go. There's two more stops. And there's no certainty they'll always be running every eighteen minutes. They might be more frequent for the late evening crowds."

As they ran, Kai limping, it was clear they were slowing. Kai and Ulrike were finding it hard to match Bernhard's pace and he slowed down every so often to let them catch up. Both were panting and Kai was finding putting any weight on his ankle excruciating.

"We're running for our lives now." Bernhard said. "We've taken fourteen minutes to here and the train could come any second. Put all your energy into this last bit. We'll rest when we get there."

He set Kai and Ulrike running ahead, urging them on from behind, mixing encouragement with warning of the grave dangers they faced. Their pace increased although Kai could do little more than lurch along, putting his left foot down only for brief instants, virtually having to hop along for periods. It seemed a long three minutes before they rounded the bend and saw the Heinrich Heinestraße station just ahead. Bernhard leapt on to the platform and pulled up Kai and Ulrike who lay down on the floor, cheeks pressed on the concrete, exhausted. A couple of minutes later trains approached from both directions and they were bathed in lights and colours from each side, the effect beautiful but cruel in the reminder of risk.

In the silence after the trains had passed their breathing sounded unnaturally loud. Kai thought he heard distant footsteps but said nothing.

As they rested, waiting for another train to come and go, Kai started probing his ankle, shaking his head as he did so. He had studied the map a number of times, and knew the worst bit was still to come. And it was too risky waiting for the subway to shut down. If Frau Schwinewitz had been found and was conscious they'd already be after them. And with fugitives the policy was simple - no escape, shoot to kill.

"Look guys … There's no way you can make this next stop with me limping and holding you back. You two go ahead and I'll wait here until this circus shuts down and I can move safely. I'm pretty sure this subway line had a couple of minor stops that got closed down even before the wall came up and I think one might be just along here. Let's meet tomorrow morning at the Moritzplatz station for a coffee. 10.30?" He tried to laugh but didn't quite manage it.

"Let's not get dramatic here. We're not leaving you." Bernhard said, although he realised that what Kai proposed made objective sense. "We've made it so far, and we're going to make it the whole way. All of us. I promise."

They had to get moving before anyone started on their tracks. If they still hadn't reached the station after twenty minutes, they would try to hide in an alcove. Not on the tracks, though, he thought. There might be space but the risk of touching the live rail was too high.

At the distant and now familiar rumble he prodded Kai with his foot. "Up, up, up!" he said "We're off!"

Another train marked 'Leinestraße' trundled through the station and as soon as it had passed they set off. Bernhard was now carrying everyone's bags, Ulrike's on his back and the others crooked one on each elbow, and was running ahead, illuminating erratically the sides of the gallery to see how often there were crannies where they could shelter if trains came, but finding only minor openings, mostly too small to squeeze into.

As the minutes went by Bernhard worked at keeping up everyone's spirits. There was nothing but this never-ending tunnel. Eighteen minutes had now gone by but there was no sign of the Moritzplatz station. Nor was there any hiding place. Kai's breathing was becoming laboured and he kept cursing and groaning quietly. Nineteen minutes. Bernhard was getting frantic, looking for places to shelter. Twenty minutes. He saw a tiny alcove ahead and pushed Ulrike into it while he and Kai went on. Twenty-one minutes. They were at the end of a straight stretch, a couple of hundred metres or more in length, when they heard the singing and rumbling of the train and in a moment it came round the far corner.

Waving madly, Bernhard jumping up and down and Kai lurching and flashing the torch, they tried to attract attention, ready to press themselves against the tunnel walls or lie in between the rails in what would probably be a vain hope if the train didn't stop in time. There was no hiss of emergency brakes and as far as they could judge no change in speed. In another ten or twelve seconds at most the train would be on them.

As he drove the train automatically Franz Holderling was leafing through the pages of a girlie magazine he'd brought, admiring the female curves and the provocative poses on display, occasionally dragging his eyes away to glance briefly at the track rushing into the beam of the headlight. They would be approaching Moritzplatz station in about a minute, he reckoned, so there was still time before he needed to slow. He returned to the more important matter of staring at ZsaZsa's improbable cleavage and dreaming that he was gazing into her eyes while running a finger down the gulley. He turned his wrist and sensed the feel of a warm, soft weight on the palm of his hand. He looked up dreamily.

Suddenly there was a sharp crack, merging with an explosive bang, and the front light on the train shattered, leaving the tunnel in a darkness all the more complete in contrast to its earlier brilliant illumination. For a moment the train hurtled on then Holderling instinctively jerked his foot from the drive pedal and released the dead man's handle, bringing a sound of hissing brakes and the squeal of locked wheels on steel rails. As the train slid and then came to a shuddering stop he grabbed the emergency torch and pushed open the door in one movement. He dropped to the tracks, staggering back and sinking to his knees as the the powerful beam of the torch picked out the scene immediately in front of him.

"Oh God! Oh my God! Jesus!"

Chapter 12
Monday September 18 1989

On the Monday Thomas arrived for his first briefing with Bettina, scheduled for 9.00 sharp. It was now just after twenty past. He sauntered upstairs and ambled down the corridors towards the door the guard had indicated. Every so often he would stop and spend time looking at the pictures on the wall, almost persuading himself that they were of interest to him. When he finally arrived at the small office Bettina was standing at the far side of the room staring out of the window, her body rigid with contained anger. She swung round to confront him.

"Just what are you trying to prove, Thomas? You're thirty minutes late." Her voice was hard.

"Oh, am I late? I'm so sorry." He sat down without being invited, crossed his legs and examined his nails with care, one hand after the other. "It took me some time to find this place. I couldn't go around asking just anyone on the street now, could I?" He glanced around the office. "Pretty tacky building too, isn't it, no style, no style whatever – you'd think the Stasi could afford something better, wouldn't you? I mean, the BND building in Frankfurt has real class. Have you seen it? Wonderful architecture. Excellent decorative style."

Although he had no idea what the necessarily discreet BND building was like he guessed Bettina had no idea either.

"I got distracted by other things too, I guess, as it's the first time I've been around here." he said. "Do you know, just beyond the end of this street there's this old building with a small courtyard closed off by an elaborate iron gate – I just had to spend some time admiring that. Have you seen it?"

Although Bettina said nothing Thomas noted with satisfaction that her knuckles whitened visibly.

"And then, I also figured you were probably busy telling people convenient lies and getting others stuck in jail." he added. "You're good at that. You know the thing about you I hate the most?"

She looked at him coolly. She said nothing, waiting. There was a slight curve at the edges of her mouth which infuriated Thomas, driving him further than he'd initially intended.

"You don't? Let me tell you anyway. Hypocrisy. Your goddamned hypocrisy. All that bullshit you kept feeding Stephan and Camille about your life so you could win them over. All those hard luck tales, while looking oh so sincere. No wonder your dad pissed off out of it when he had a chance. You even fooled me again for a short while, and I already knew what you were like. That's what I find really disturbing. It was exactly like that first evening with me." He smiled sweetly at her. "You're the greatest lying, hypocritical, untrustworthy, devious bitch I think I've ever met."

She flushed but looked straight at him, holding his gaze until Thomas found himself glancing away despite his bravado. "Better now? Nobody forced you to take me to dinner that evening. You invited me. You persuaded me. You wanted me, remember. I noticed the cigarettes when they fell out of your jacket and wondered why, as you'd said you didn't smoke. So I checked them when you went to pay the bill. Nosiness, maybe, but that's how it is. Then I realised you were into black-market currency and I didn't have any choice. I liked you, enjoyed our evening, but personal feelings couldn't come into it. This is my country and once I knew you were a criminal my duty was clear."

"Your duty! Your duty!" Thomas shouted. "Your duty, as you choose to call it, means ruining other people's lives.

Do you realize that? I'm being asked to spy on my friends and to spy on and betray people I hardly know. And your duty, as you dignify this shitty behaviour, led to someone's death because you had your thugs follow me. It could as easily have led to mine."

"You were not the main object of our interest and I had no idea it was that particular bastard you were meeting later, the one you knew as Mark. His real name was Hans-Jörg Romer and he was much more than a black market currency dealer." She looked steadily at him again. "Much, much more. He used the Deutsche Marks you changed with him to import drugs and arms. Last week alone three people died from using badly-cut heroin, heroin he'd brought in and adulterated to increase his profits. And a month ago one of my friends died, shot by a gun your friend Mark had sold. Great business partner, Thomas."

Thomas said nothing. He thought back to how Mark had surprised him with details of his tour activities but also how, in the euphoria of meeting Bettina and taking her to dinner, he hadn't checked that he wasn't being followed to his meeting with Mark. He dropped his head into his hands and sat there, remembering Mark's proposal to smuggle drugs and his reassurance "it's been done before". At least he'd refused that offer – where would he be now if he'd got into that earlier with Mark? He remained silent and stared at the floor.

"We really, really wanted him alive. We'd been after him for months. We knew pretty much what he was up to but he was too clever at avoiding us. He changed his associates frequently, changed his appearance too, and he was very difficult to track. It was pure chance that you guided us to him. If it hadn't been for the cigarettes you wouldn't have been followed. And if it had been a commonplace transaction with almost anyone else, nothing much would have happened. You'd have been picked up probably, scared a bit, maybe pushed around to see if there was anything interesting you were hiding, but that would have been it." She got up and walked to the window and looked out.

"Once we saw who you were meeting we had no choice. We had to act. Our agents shot to stop the car and arrest you both, or at least him, but it seems one of the bullets hit him in the head – that's why the car crashed, why you were knocked out and your face mashed up a bit. We rushed him to hospital, St Hedwig's, but it was too late. But don't blame yourself for any of that part – if he hadn't made a run for it he'd be alive now. " Her voice had softened but now took on again its hard edge. "Your mistake was dealing with him in the first place, helping to fund his drug peddling and his arms trading, basically bringing him the hard currency which made him a fortune by destroying other people's lives. I wish he were still alive so that we could interrogate him fully, close off some loose ends, but at least now there's going to be a few who'll have more years of life than his antics would have allowed them otherwise."

Thomas sat silent again, digesting this information. He supposed it was true but perhaps it was exaggerated, further evidence of Bettina's duplicity.

"Then why am I here? You've got what you wanted."

"Yes, we were going to let you go, once it seemed clear that your connection with Romer wasn't that of an equal. Westerners get caught all the time smuggling currency, even if it's usually for less than the impressive amounts you were dealing in. As I said, we would have scared you, maybe stuck you in prison for a bit to get the point across and warned you not to try it again."

"Then why didn't you?"

"Because of Romer Dieter joined the case. That was your bad luck. Dieter saw your documents, thought your unusual surname was familiar, decided it was worth investigating you further. That's what he's good at, having hunches, joining things together. He checked up and realised that you were Albert Wundart's elder son. It was obvious then that your family would have good connections in the Western financial and political worlds and that you could be really useful to us. That was too good a chance to pass over. I did try to dissuade him, asked him just to let you go like anyone else." She was quiet for a moment. "Maybe I felt kind of responsible, I guess."

Thomas laughed angrily.

"Fuck off! Don't give me that shit about trying to help me. Maybe you can fool Camille, maybe even Stephan, but not me. I know you now. You're a cynical liar. I expect you enjoy hurting others and seeing them suffer."

"Think what you want, Thomas. We don't have to be friends. You don't have to believe what I tell you. But you don't know me at all, so you're really in no position to judge. And just for the record, I really didn't plan to harm you, and nothing I told Camille or Stephan on Friday was a lie. Maybe I shouldn't have said what I did but I kind of took time off from being an agent. I actually liked your friends. I had a good evening then. And everything I said to them was true."

She picked up a briefcase and put it on the desk in the centre of the room, then opened it and took out some documents.

"Now, if you've finished your insults and accusations, let's get on with the briefing."

She crossed her arms, leant forward and waited for Thomas to move his chair to the other side of the desk.

"Screw you!" Thomas retorted. "Goddamn it, Bettina, you're ruining my life and you act as if this is of no concern at all to you. As if it just happened of itself. As if you had nothing to do with it. You talk about 'duty' as if that excuses all this, as if that gives you a right to make me a spy for this shitty country against my own."

Bettina unfolded her arms, passed her open right hand over her eyes and then down across her mouth, stared up for a moment at the ceiling and then back, hard, at Thomas. Her face turned livid in a flash of anger, her nostrils flared and her mouth tightened as she breathed in hard, and Thomas dropped his gaze, unable to meet the force of her fury.

"*You* were the one doing something illegal. *You* were the one acting criminally. You seem to have forgotten that black-market currency trading is a serious crime. You were facing a good period in jail for that alone. And if we'd shown a connection with Romer's wider activities, tied you in with his drug dealing for example, you'd have been ten years older at least, fifteen or twenty maybe, before you saw the West again. What would that have done to your life, your career, your reputation?"

She paused to take a drink of water from the tumbler on the desk but Thomas was unable to say anything. "You knew very well what you were up to. *You* were the one funding those heroin deaths. Think about that. *You* killed my friend by funding the gun that shot him. Think about that. You believe you have a God-given right, because you're from the West, to take advantage of these poor idiots from the East, right? And you blame *me* for doing *my* duty. Your interest was in nothing but your own selfish needs, what you could get out of it, what you could get away with, just how much you could make stealing from others. You weren't a student funding his studies through harmless misdemeanours - you were nothing but a squalid little thief and your activities helped to kill people, to destroy them and their families. Think about *that.*" She paused for breath.

"But I didn't mean any harm. I didn't. Those deaths would have happened anyway. They weren't my fault." said Thomas. He'd tried to sound assertive but faced with

Bettina's now blazing blue eyes had merely felt defensive and even ashamed, his tone plaintive.

"By your black market antics, selling DMs at an Ost Mark rate high above the official one, you were stealing money from the country. That was money coming from our people's pockets to line yours, Thomas. You're a thief, Thomas, nothing but a shitty little thief. You were stealing from people who already had very little, who were a lot poorer than you, even as a student. Was that moral? You were funding criminals, facilitating those heroin deaths, the murder of my friend. Not your fault, you say, can't blame me!" she laughed harshly. "Didn't mean any harm!" She shook her head about in parody. "Given the consequences, is that something to feel proud of? Go on, tell me what a big man it makes you feel now. They're dead, Thomas, dead." She turned her head suddenly away from him, looked down and away and put her hand over her face.

There was silence and Thomas could think of no adequate response. Bettina was breathing heavily. Despite himself, he was impressed with her fury and the strength behind it and now starting to feel ashamed. She turned sharply round again.

"You haven't changed a tiny bit. Now you're out of prison, you're the same arrogant, egocentric, selfish Westerner you were when I first met you. And to think I even tried convincing Dieter to let you go. Where you are now, you've no one but yourself to blame. Step out of line again and, trust me, you'll see how bad it can really get."

Bettina turned abruptly and stared out of the window again, leaving Thomas dumbfounded, his emotions in turmoil. He noticed that her eyes were glistening and in a moment she scrunched them hard and wiped them with a handkerchief. Now truly ashamed, he sat on the chair and for a long time neither of them spoke. She stared out of the window.

"Look. Ummm, maybe, I guess, umm, maybe I overreacted a bit. It's just, it's just that I ... , I ... "

"I know. It's not a great position to be in. That I understand. But you've made the right choice. Dieter would have let you rot in jail."

Thomas could think of nothing more to say.

"I know you still feel sore about what's happened." she continued. "I don't like it much either but it's where we are. We can't change that. We're going to be together a great deal - we can either fight each other all the time or work out a way of engaging professionally. Even if we can't again become friends maybe we can at least work together civilly." She started to stretch out her hand then dropped it and for a period looked at him.

Eventually he nodded slightly, saying nothing, then sighed. "Maybe. OK. Maybe."

"What do you want to discuss?" he asked.

"Let's go over the information we'd like you to get from Stephan. And from anyone else there who might be helpful." She handed him a sheet of paper with a list of questions. "You need to memorise these - not by rote but to be clear about what you have to find out. Leave these papers behind when you go. And I have to remind you again not to give the slightest hint of what you're doing. Dieter has told you what will happen if anyone discovers what you're up to. And it will happen, believe me, Dieter is someone who keeps his word. You have to understand that."

They talked for nearly an hour, some of it role playing with Bettina as Stephan, which Thomas had disliked and handled mostly in a surly manner. Towards the end Dieter came in. "It's in both our interests that you succeed." he said. "The better you help us the quicker you'll be left to get on with your own life." He smiled and handed Thomas a stylish and expensive looking black leather briefcase with, Thomas was touched to see, the initials 'T W' discreetly blocked in gold on the front. "And as you're going to the hub of West German commerce I thought it might be good for you to look the part of a rising young banker." Inside was a return ticket on the morning flight to Frankfurt from Berlin's Tegel airport in exactly a week's time, together with the essential letter of exit authorisation.

*

Thomas left the meeting with Bettina depressed and with his emotions in a turmoil. He hadn't particularly liked or trusted Mark but it was indirectly through him that he'd got killed. Next week he had to spy on his best friend, Stephan. He'd thought at the restaurant with Bettina that things would develop, that they were going somewhere together, that life was beginning to smile on him, but now this. Suddenly everything had changed and he'd become a puppet controlled by others. By the time he'd reached his building back in West Berlin his mood had darkened again further and he started to trudge up stairs, thinking furiously and again pitying himself, seeing himself as a victim unjustly dealt with.

"Such a bitch!" he thought. "Leading me on, getting me to take her to dinner in a smart restaurant and then setting me up like this to be caught. How could they do this to me? All I've done is go out to earn the money I needed for living, using my brains rather than sitting around moaning. Ridiculous to say I was stealing from them, like she said. Fucking idle peasants in this shitty country and she's the worst. And she's a lying hypocrite, just like I told her."

Suddenly he stopped and listened. There were familiar voices on his floor above and, newly energised, his despair forgotten he rushed upwards, leaping two or three steps at a time, to the group lying around outside his apartment door.

Hurling himself on Kai he tried to lift him and whirl him round in joy.

"Kai! You're here! You did it! You've made it!"

He broke off at Kai's yelp of pain and looked down. "But what's happened to your foot?"

"I sprained it. Badly. But yes, we're here. We're here! We're in West Berlin! We got out! How about letting us in and making us some food? We've been here for hours and we're starving."

Thomas embraced Ulrike and Bernhard excitedly, opened the door and led them to the kitchen.

"How did it go? God, I'm so excited you made it. Look, here's the bathroom and here's some towels – Ulrike, have a shower and get cleaned up and then you two can do the same. Kai, tell me how you got on. I want to know everything." He began making coffee.

"Well, we caught the train, just like you said." Kai went over the whole story reaching the climax just as Bernhard returned washed and changed into clean clothes. There was absolute silence in the room.

"So there we were, about to be run over and with nowhere to go. The train was roaring towards us. I was in a panic. At least Ulrike was safe, out of the way." he said, caressing her short, recently bleached blonde hair. "Then I saw Bernhard pull out the gun and start shooting. I thought he was crazy – you can't stop a train like that. Was he trying to kill the driver for some reason? But when I heard the emergency brake come on I realized what he was doing."

"I guess we have Frau Schwinewitz to thank after all." Kai went on. "Without her gun, the train would have run us over. But it was Bernhard that saved our lives. The driver jumped down from the cab, waving around a torch, and then collapsed on his knees, thinking he'd hit us, I guess. That's when Ulrike squeezed past to the front, crying like crazy, throwing up because she was terrified about what she'd find and as he was talking to her we got up from beside the rails and Bernhard tapped him on the shoulder. The guy nearly had a heart attack, spun round and Bernhard said "Hey, we need a ride to the West. Didn't have time to buy tickets but could you take us anyway?"

Everyone laughed. Bernhard grinned, thinking back on the man's face, remembering that the driver had seemed more relieved that they were alive than scared of what they might do.

Kai sipped his coffee and took a bite of his cheese omelette. "Mmmm, Affen Titten geilen, man."

"The driver, Franz his name was, was a nice guy." Bernhard said. "We got in the cab with him and when we explained our story, he was really friendly. He kept on saying 'Just you wait until I tell my wife!' He told us his wife's friends teased her because of his boring job. 'They'll all be jealous as hell!' he said. It was his last shift so he insisted in taking us to Leinestraße and bringing us back to his place to get some sleep. We didn't want to wake you up in the middle of the night, so that's what we did. And his wife was a nurse so she strapped up Kai's ankle. They wanted to take him to the hospital but we couldn't risk that, him having to give all his details."

"From what I hear, Stasi agents are in West Berlin all the time." Kai added. "And with the Frau Schwinewitz thing it's going to be too risky to stay here so we need to leave very soon. Bernhard's going to Munich tomorrow to his cousin. Ulrike and I are still deciding where to go, maybe to Cologne for a bit as we've both got relatives there. And I wondered, Thomas, you going to the East as often as you do, if I give you the keys could you pick some things up from the flat, bring them over here. I'd really like my cowboy boots if you could get those and I know there's some things that Ulrike wasn't able to bring with her which she'd really like if you could manage that."

Chapter 13
Monday October 2 1989

Thomas came through immigration to the Frankfurt Airport international arrivals area and glanced around the waiting crowd. Some waiting there were eager with anticipation, children sitting aloft on shoulders and waving excitedly at real or imagined grandparents or shouting at fathers back from business trips. A thin, elderly woman with loose, straggly grey hair hanging well past her shoulders stood slightly apart, starting forward every time a young man appeared but then falling back again, her shoulders drooping. Others stood waiting, bored, their duty done by being there and careless as to whether their visitors arrived or not. He'd let his mother know his arrival time but he wasn't surprised not to see any sign of her. No doubt she was still harbouring some unknown grudge or other against him. For a moment the thought saddened him.

He took the subway, exiting at Taunusanlage. It was a clear day, warm and bright with slight, scudding clouds, although it was already well into autumn. He was very early and decided to walk the long way round, through the park and past the Mövenpick ice cream café.

Among the drug addicts shivering in the sun and the homeless soaking up the warmth until it was time for the soup kitchens to open he was surprised to see some clean but shabbily dressed young people. One of them, a man of about twenty, was holding up a placard with the request: "Refugee from East Germany – please help." Disturbed, Thomas rummaged through his pocket and dropped a 2DM coin into the cap in front of the man. It bothered him that this might now be the fate of Kai and Ulrike. Frankfurt was particularly expensive as a German city but any city, Cologne for instance, was going to be expensive compared with West Berlin and vastly more so than East Berlin. He'd asked Kai how much money he'd got but Kai had simply said in his casual, careless style "Oh, plenty, man! More than enough." which Thomas was certain was untrue.

He entered the Deutsche Bank building and stood for a while gazing round at the interior. He knew the twin towers well from the street but had never before been inside. Everything from the unpolished granite floor to the small fountain and pond was in typical Deutsche Bank style, understated but denoting power. People in suits were hurrying around, criss-crossing the lobby and constantly entering or leaving the elevators positioned at the sides.

Thomas glanced at his watch and approached the reception desk, disdained the stiff smile offered, and asked for Stephan. Moments later, as he was standing looking idly at the lifts, waiting for Stephan to emerge from one of them, he felt himself enveloped in a bear hug from behind and lifted slightly before a beaming Stephan released him.

"One of the perks!" he said, pointing back across the entrance hall. "Express lifts from the Board floors reserved for the privileged few. That's me now. Left hoi polloi behind, I have! It's great to see you again, though. It must be at least a year since you first promised to visit here. Great night at the opera, though. How's Bettina? Still beating you up!" He laughed and punched Thomas lightly on the shoulder. "Come on, let's look around before we have lunch."

The various floors appeared identical to Thomas, differing only in the particular modern artist chosen to decorate the walls of each. Thomas's knowledge of the modern art world was hazy but he recognised some of the paintings from his visits to Kassel's *documenta* and was impressed with works on the executive floor where Stephan worked. He looked closely at an installation set in an alcove. "Ah, Joseph Beuys. Now that he's dead I guess it's politically OK to bring him in to this temple to capitalism. Or maybe it's an ironic comment on where the bank's business funding ends up. What do you think, Stephan?"

"Nothing to do with the beauty of art!" Stephan laughed. "It's purely utilitarian. Someone getting out of the lift and seeing a Gerhard Richter knows he's on the wrong floor – he'd better get out of there fast and back to his own grubby area with Damien Hirsts on view!"

Leaving the lift on the first floor they walked along the suspended path which overlooked the main entrance and led towards the cafeteria. Below him Thomas could see the revolving doors and the hanging sculpture made of myriad crystal rods.

"This is one of the best things about working here." said Stephan, taking in the whole place with a proprietorial wave of his arm. "They call it the cafeteria but it's really a high level restaurant with its own kitchens run by a really great chef. None of this fast food rubbish for us! It's probably the most important place in the whole bank. It's where careers are made or lost."

"Of the cooks or the staff?" asked Thomas as they sat down by a window overlooking the trees and the park and Stephan poured each of them a glass of Riesling.

"Cooks don't have careers, they have jobs. If you come here make sure you use your lunchtimes efficiently. It's one of the best ways to get to know people and to exchange information and it's information that's our lifeblood. For me it's easy – people know I can't say much about what I do because it's mostly reserved information, confidential, but everyone tells me what they're up to, maybe hoping I'll pass it on to Herren. It's fascinating, really interesting."

They were silent for a while as they ate. Thomas glanced round and listened to the hubbub and clatter, open eyed and somewhat astonished at what he took to be the casual sophistication of the diners. "It's like my first day at secondary school! All these people. Everything so new and unfamiliar. I feel a bit overawed, like I was twelve again."

"Well, at least you can keep secrets." Stephan looked at him, smiling slightly.

Thomas was startled, thinking that Stephan had learned of his Stasi role. A sense of sudden shame and embarrassment welled up as he thought again about having to spy on his best friend. He reddened.

"I've got to hand it to you. Nobody ever found out about me and Suzie Bausch after you caught us that day in the sports pavilion."

Thomas laughed, relaxing. "Yeah, that was hard not dropping hints, what with her being the headmaster's daughter and her reputation for being so prim and untouchable. You were lucky it was me – you were at it so hard that I doubt even Bausch himself could have separated you."

"That was a great summer. What were we, fifteen I think. First times for each of us. She might have seemed prim but, well, believe me ... " He sighed. "My ma was best friends with Susie's and they'd have killed me if they'd known what was going on. She went to Mainz in September and we lost touch. I wonder where she is now. God, those were the days."

He sat up, reached into his briefcase and handed Thomas a sheet of paper.

"OK, business first. Here's your interview schedule. Today you'll be meeting people from corporate finance. The first two work together in the German top corporate team, mainly following the Daimler conglomerate companies. Be wary of Hans Paris, the MD, who's a shark. He'll probably try to intimidate you to see how you react under pressure. Give him back as good as he gives, particularly if he's rude – he just loves arrogant arseholes. The other three are from the international team: Herbert

Sheidt heads Italy, and you'll have a great time with him, I'm certain. The last two are technocrats. Likely to ask you theoretical questions on DCFs or IRRs, that kind of thing."

"Thanks for that advice. I'll try not to blow the interview." He thought back to his recent briefing with Bettina and the list of questions she'd prepared. "What are you working on now yourself?"

"I've not had a life for weeks. Camille is going nuts. I hardly see her these days. Berlin has been the only weekend I managed to take off work this month, two months even." He dug into his plate of salmon fusilli. "I've been saddled with this crazy project. Luckily Herren's off on Monday morning next and is going to be out for most of the week so maybe I'll get a chance to breathe."

As Stephan was talking a tall, silver haired man, conservatively dressed in a finely tailored suit walked up behind Stephan, parting and quieting with his presence the noisy hubbub as he approached. He laid a hand on Stephan's shoulder and as Stephan glanced up and then scrambled to his feet asked "Does your contract specify time to breathe Mr Fischer? Perhaps I should have Personnel look into that, eh?"

"Mr Herren! Is there something you need? I can be back in the office straight away if you require me."

"I just need a brief word in a moment Mr Fischer." Thomas began to stand and Herren turned to him courteously. "Are you a new recruit?"

"This is my very old friend Thomas Wundart, Mr Herren. He's interviewing with us today. Perhaps later he will ... "

"Wundart? Wundart. Hmm, an unusual name. Are you from Frankfurt?"

"His father was Albrecht Wundart." Stephan added.

"Really? Ah, yes. I knew him well, though not socially. We've sat together in many meetings in the past and I was very sorry to learn of his premature death. I'm pleased to have met his son. Please give my regards to your mother. Now, will you excuse us for a moment, Mr Wundart?"

He motioned to Thomas to sit down and took Stephan away a short distance for a brief discussion then turned, waved cordially to Thomas and strode away.

"So that's Herren!" Thomas said when Stephan returned and they resumed their meal. "He's got a real air of authority, hasn't he?"

"Too right. He's very shrewd, very smart and he gets results. Sometimes he just faces people down to get his own way. Sometimes he does it in such a roundabout manner that I can't keep up with him. I think, what's he playing at? why is he doing that? and then the next thing I know it all falls into place, exactly as he wanted."

"Well, I'm glad I met him. Brief though it was."

"He'll remember you. Make no mistake about that. Partly it's on account of your father, of course, but if you do come here the next time you see him he'll remember exactly who you are and where you met. Play that right and it'll stand you in good stead."

"I hope so. Maybe I'll throw something into my interview later – 'Interesting you should mention that aspect. I was discussing it with Mr Herren only today, at lunch.'" He laughed and took a sip of Riesling. "But you were about to tell me why you were so busy. Some crazy project, you said. What was that?"

Stephan looked at him for a moment, and hesitated. It was over a fortnight since he'd met the Finance Minister and it would be a relief to tell someone about it, maybe, if he was honest, even boast a little bit about how well he was getting on in his career. After all, Thomas had no links with competing banks or with the press and if he couldn't trust his oldest friend just who could he trust?

"You absolutely must say nothing to anyone. Nothing in the interviews or anywhere else."

Thomas nodded.

"It's a huge loan to the Soviet Union." Stephan smiled as he saw Thomas's eyes widen. "I was really surprised too, but in a way it makes sense. Gorbachev's reforms are producing great results politically but the country isn't doing that well economically so they need to raise money abroad. The West German government is prepared to help and Deutsche Bank has been brought in to manage the deal. I was at a meeting with the Finance Minister recently when it was discussed and agreed."

Thomas whistled and sat back.

"Whoah! That's cool. How large?"

"It's huge, really huge. I'm working on the first tranche and that's likely to be around fifteen billion DM. We're underwriting that but for the later tranches, maybe coming to twice as much again, we'll syndicate parts out to other German banks."

"Fifteen billion! God, that is huge, isn't it? And what, 45 in total you say. How can you take that kind of risk on a country like the USSR? What if it all goes wrong?"

Stephan looked around nervously and leaned closer to Thomas.

"Shhh! But you're right. I raised that point myself. No bank, including ours, will give them money unless some other rated entity guarantees the loan."

"So who's doing that? The World Bank?"

"Not the World Bank, though that could make sense." Stephan thought how much he missed being able to confide in someone who was at least his intellectual equal. He glanced around again and lowered his voice. "It's actually the West German government. I've only been involved in discussions on the technical aspects so I'm not clear about the background details, and that's extremely confidential anyway. All the documentation is in the hands of the Ministry of Finance and the Bundesbank and I don't get to see it. Not even the Russians are at the meetings. You're the first person I've mentioned this to. And you absolutely must, must, must, keep it completely secret."

"But why would the German government be doing this? Isn't that kind of odd?"

"I've tried asking Herren but he was always vague although he did mention similar examples. The US has been funding Israel for years, for instance, and it's poured money into areas to buy influence or control countries to their own benefit all over the place - Nicaragua, El Salvador, funding the coup against Allende in Chile, Egypt, other places in the Middle East, working with the Brits to get rid of Mossadegh in Iran way back in the '50s, and plenty more. Maybe no one's quite as bad as the US but they're all at it, the Brits, the French, us, the USSR, most countries. The thing is, though, that West Germany and the USSR are really on opposite sides of the political spectrum even though we're not as paranoid as the US – you'll remember that Reagan called the USSR 'the Empire of Evil' a few years ago. That's the bit I don't really understand. Why is the government prepared to guarantee this? What's the payoff?"

"Well, Reagan always was a bit loopy about these things but even allowing for that West Germany and the USSR really are on opposite sides, as you say, economically anyway, and it does seem very odd."

"My guess is there's some deal going on. West Germany's getting something in return. There's been little bits here and there I've picked up, overheard, whatever. For instance, some months ago, Herren came into my office, something he rarely does, and asked me whether I knew anything about the Louisiana Purchase."

"That was when the United States bought a large chunk of French colonial territory in eighteen something?"

"Yes, exactly. We discussed it for around ten minutes, agreeing on how intelligent Jefferson had been to buy from the French when Napoleon was at war and needed the money. What was it Rothschild used to say 'Buy on the sound of cannon, sell on the sound of trumpets.' After the Napoleonic wars the French would never have sold anyway, most likely. But think of it. Imagine a quarter of present US territory, even a bit more, right down the middle from the Canadian border to the Mexican Gulf, being French. Instead of the US we'd have had three countries there, maybe, a couple of Anglophone ones sandwiching a Francophone one."

"Who cares about the Dakotas, Oklahoma, Montana, all that dismal lot? Nothing but grain growing prairies worked by inbreds. Oh, and a few mountains. The really important question is what about New Orleans? That music, those sounds, that jazz, the atmosphere, Mardi Gras, the food, the women, best place in the whole damn US of A!"

Stephan laughed. "Might have become even better!"

Thomas nodded, perhaps thinking of a Creole Paris. "Well, my guess is that the Americans would have bought it, so to speak, some time later anyway, just like they did with Texas and California – bring in plenty of soldiers with plenty of fire power and make the Mexicans an offer they just couldn't refuse!"

"Possibly, but remember that the French were US allies in the Revolution. But anyway, the point is that after this conversation, Herren asked me if there were any lessons to be learned from that event. I answered that certainly one lesson was that it paid to propose a deal when the other side is at its weakest. He agreed with me, smiled and walked back into his office. At the time I was a bit puzzled about what all of this meant, but now it's starting to make sense."

"Wait a minute. You're not telling me you think West Germany has struck a deal to … "

"Shhh. Not so loud." Stephan admonished him, coming closer and looking around behind him.

"Yes, that's exactly what I think. I know it sounds absurd, but that's politics. It hasn't changed in the last hundred years as much as we sometimes think it has. It's only that the smoke screen has got thicker. Why do you think the East German government is tolerating all the demonstrations that are going on now against it? Only a year ago, they would have sent the tanks against the people without thinking twice. Now they're being stopped by the Russians. And it's only a question of time before the whole house of cards falls. Without the Russians, the DDR makes no sense whatsoever."

"You're right about that. But how can you be so sure of what's planned?"

"There's something else. Something I overheard last week, waiting to see Herren. His secretary had let me through but I stopped in front of his private door because I heard him pick up the phone and realised he was talking with the Chancellor. I only heard one side, obviously, and so only snippets, but it was quite extraordinary. They were talking about the East and Herren asked Kohl whether the issue of the military bases had been solved and whether a larger amount of money would have changed matters. He said that sixty or even seventy billion could be raised if necessary. Then he made a comment that things needed to happen in East Germany first and so Kohl should wait before telling the Western European allies. That was all I heard, though. His secretary came to tell me that he was taking an important call and that I should return later."

Thomas, his meal forgotten, had been sitting with his fork in the air, arrested on the way to his mouth. He ate the mouthful absently, leaned closer, whistled again softly, and put his fork down.

"So this huge loan has something to do with East Germany?"

"I'm certain of it. The impression I got was that Bonn will back the loan if they get Gorbachev's support on a pan-German solution of some kind. It probably doesn't mean reunification, but maybe a gradual liberalisation and a common economic market, something like that. German governments have been after that sort of thing since the fifties, a way to work towards the former unity. The problem has always been the USSR."

Thomas took a gulp of his Riesling. "Incredible! So, the Berlin Purchase, eh?"

"Look, Thomas, please, please don't breathe a word about this. If anything leaks to the press, you'll find my balls at the *boulette* shop."

Chapter 14
Tuesday 3 October 1989

"So, tell us what happened in Frankfurt yesterday. Everything. Leave nothing out, no matter how trivial you think it is. I'll decide what's important."

Dieter's voice was soft but clear in the large, empty room furnished only with a few scattered chairs and the solid table at which he was sitting. There were no windows, Thomas saw, no pictures or other decorations, and the walls looked irregular and slightly wavy, as if they were padded or insulated with some soft, grey plastic. Bettina sat in a corner, fidgeting with a pencil. Every so often she looked at Thomas as if willing him to understand something she was trying to convey.

Thomas had flown in that morning to West Berlin's airport, Tegel, from Frankfurt. As he'd entered the arrivals hall he'd noticed two men in dark glasses standing slightly to one side, watching the stream of passengers. He'd made for the exit, intending to get the airport bus to the centre and return to his apartment for a few hours before crossing to East Berlin for his meeting with Dieter late afternoon, but the men had fallen into step beside him, one on each side. The larger one had gripped his left biceps firmly and steered him to a car with darkened windows.

"Colonel Dieter would like to see you straight away, if that's convenient." he had said, stroking his moustache lightly on each side with his free hand as he spoke. Despite the apparent courtesy Thomas recognised it as the order it was. Ushered into the front seat he'd surreptitiously tried the handle as the driver was getting in finding, exactly as he'd expected, that he could open neither the door nor the window.

It had been a long drive and the nondescript, semi-abandoned building in East Berlin's suburbs reminded Thomas ominously of his prison cell. Dieter had greeted him briefly then pointed to a chair and as he'd sat down the two men had taken up positions by the only door.

"Start from your arrival at the Deutsche Bank building."

"As soon as I arrived, I met with Stephan. He showed me around the building, then we had lunch."

"Did you visit his office?"

"No, we didn't. That would have required extra security procedures, because it's on the Board members' floor. He only showed me around the other parts of the twin towers. At lunch, we discussed the people I'd be meeting for the interviews. He told me a little about what they did, and what they were likely to ask."

As Thomas spoke, he kept looking at the faces around the room. The bigger man was again stroking his moustache and there appeared to be a slight upward curl to his lips. Dieter remained as impassive as ever. Bettina seemed to be growing more and more nervous.

"Did he say anything interesting about them?" Dieter asked nonchalantly.

"No, not really. They were all from corporate finance, and mainly worked on corporate Eurobonds for German and international clients. I can tell you later about the interviews themselves."

Thomas had rehearsed carefully what he would say to Dieter when they met, although doing so had cost him a sleepless night. He'd worked out what to say to suggest that Stephan had been slightly indiscreet but without giving any hint of what's he'd actually learned at lunch.

"How long was your lunch with Stephan? Did you meet anyone else in the restaurant or while you were touring the building?"

"I guess it was about forty minutes. And, no, it was just Stephan and me. He greeted some colleagues during our tour but didn't introduce me. We reminisced a bit over lunch, school days, things like that, and then Stephan told me a little about the bank and what he was doing but said he couldn't really go into much detail."

"Tell us about Mr Herren. Did Stephan tell you at all what Herren was doing, or what his travel plans were, perhaps what business meetings he was attending?"

Dieter steepled his fingers, placed them on his mouth and looked steadily over them at Thomas. Thomas's felt his heart starting to thump and he glanced away and took a couple of breaths to steady himself. Bettina caught his eye, fidgeted on her chair, screwed her eyes up suddenly and looked down at her feet. Thomas to a breath to try to calm himself.

"I tried to bring Herren up in conversation a couple of times, like we had agreed. All Stephan said was that Herren had been busy with the acquisition of a UK merchant bank, and that he kept travelling a lot. He did say he'd had a meeting recently with Chancellor Kohl but he said he didn't know what it was about. He wouldn't go into more details, however, and I didn't want to make him suspicious by pressing him too much."

"Where was Herren travelling?"

"He only mentioned that he was leaving again next Monday morning, but didn't say where. He said he'd be away for a few days and that he, Stephan, was looking forward to a bit less pressure in the office."

"And that's all he said."

Thomas hesitated.

"Basically, yes."

"You're quite sure of that, Mr Wundart? Nothing you want to add?"

"This is easier than I expected." thought Thomas, pleased with his deception.

"Yes. There was one thing I forgot. Sorry. Stephan said that Herren had gone to Mainz suddenly last week. He said that he'd telephoned first thing in the morning to cancel a meeting and returned in the early evening, saying only that he'd gone to watch a golf match."

As Dieter stared at him Thomas wondered if he'd gone too far with that rococo extra touch.

"Hmmm. A golf match! Really? A *golf* match? And I'd thought that he found golf boring, that Herren's game was tennis." Dieter said, pronouncing the sentences slowly and carefully as if watching such an event showed Herren in a surprising but quite admirable light which he wanted to savour fully. "Well, well. It's as I feared." He paused for a long moment, continuing to look at Thomas. He shook his head almost imperceptibly and exhaled and Thomas was reminded suddenly of his headmaster expressing disappointment at some behaviour in which he'd been caught out. Bettina was now very still, tense, staring at the floor, refusing to meet his eye.

"Certain things just take time and learning can be a gradual process. I'm sure you're a quick learner, though, Thomas, and our friends here may help to teach you just how useful a good memory can be. Perhaps when we return to continue this conversation you'll have some more interesting things to tell us. Things that, on reflection, you may earlier have thought so trivial as to be scarcely worth mentioning."

He got up from his chair and as he reached the door turned to the larger man. "Spare his face." he said. "Come, Bettina."

Fifteen minutes later they returned. Thomas was crumpled in a corner, barely conscious, his face streaked with blood from a wound on his scalp and his right arm at an unnatural angle below his bruised and aching body. Angrily ordering the smaller man to bring some water, Bettina cradled Thomas's head and tidied up the blood streaks and the cut at the back. As she sprinkled water on his face Thomas could make out her voice, sounding a million miles distant as he swirled in and out of consciousness, whispering to him not to hide anything because Dieter already knew everything about his meeting with Stephan.

It took another ten minutes before Thomas fully regained consciousness. He could feel a sharp pain as he sucked in air to his lungs with difficulty. His right arm refused to move as he willed it and he saw that the upper part was at an odd angle and stuck in front of his chest. Bettina gently helped him drag his body up along the wall till he sat leaning back on it and his left arm for support.

"Your arm's dislocated, not broken." she said. "We'll get you a doctor shortly. Now tell us the truth, Thomas. All of it."

It was useless to play games. That much was now painfully clear. He had tried twice with Dieter but somehow this man was always one step ahead of him. He recounted the day in the twin towers and the discussion over lunch. He revealed that he'd met Herren briefly when he'd come to the restaurant to speak with Stephan. They asked him the same things a hundred times it seemed, in different ways. It felt as if they had the puzzle and only a few small pieces were missing. Then they asked him about his interviews and about whom he'd seen after he left the bank. Thomas briefly went over the evening with his brother and his mother.

"Did you tell your brother anything about why you were in Frankfurt or who'd sent you?"

"I mentioned meeting Stephan and my interview but nothing more. Please. He's just a kid. Keep him out of this."

"He's out of it as long as you keep him out. And everyone else. If you talk, your life is in danger but so is theirs. Do I make myself understood?"

It was late afternoon when he finally reached home. His shoulder, strapped into place by the doctor who seemed to consider his injuries as routine, was painful and his body ached. He climbed the stairs with difficulty wondering what explanation he could give to John but found a note to say he'd left for a few day holiday at a girlfriend's house at Wannsee, with a party of university friends, and that Thomas was welcome to join them.

He lay down on the bed without bothering to undress or wash. He drifted in and out of a troubled sleep and when he woke fully it was well into the following morning. His shoulder throbbed. He felt sick and profoundly depressed.

Chapter 15
Sunday 8 October 1989

Sunday October 8 was a bright, clear day, one of those where both the past warmth of summer and the coming bleakness of winter coexist in autumn. There was a crispness to the air, hinting at later snow from the vast plains to the east, but in the bright sunshine it was warm. It was approaching eleven and the three men – East Germany's elderly leader Erich Honecker, 82 year old Stasi head Erich Mielke, and Honecker's deputy Egon Krenz, a mere youth of 52 - now nervously pacing the garden of Honecker's villa just outside Berlin had spent most of the past hour inside the house in heated debate over the disturbing reports of growing unrest throughout the country and how best to contain it. Dresden had recently been turbulent and in Leipzig a pastor was openly mocking the government and calling into question its moral right to govern. The Stasi and KGB were unanimous in expecting a huge popular demonstration in that city the following day, a demonstration anticipated to be the largest in post-war history.

The automatic but strongly fortified gates flicked open and two official cars crunched over the gravel and swung round in front of the house.

"Time to start the meeting. Let's go in." said Honecker, opening the door and ushering Krenz and Mielke into the spotless hall. "There's Sindermann with Willi Stoph. Still giving himself airs, still thinking that being President of the Volkskammer has some status, still not realising he's no one. Bloody fool. Still, he had to be invited."

Leading the way to the large meeting room at the back of the house Honecker sat down at the head of the heavy, polished oak table. Krenz sat immediately to his left and

Mielke took his accustomed position at the corner of the far short end where he could most easily observe everyone present yet still see through the windows on both walls to observe anyone who might approach the room.

Within a few minutes the last of the vehicles arrived and their passengers hurried in to sit round the table, the more established members looking curiously at some newcomers. On the marble mantelpiece a large ormolu clock struck eleven and Honecker rapped the table for attention as the last stroke died away.

"Comrades! We are facing uprisings of counter-revolutionary unrest in parts of the Democratic Republic and we therefore need to take action urgently to contain and eliminate this treasonous behaviour. I have accordingly invited to this meeting not only those experienced in leading the socialist Republic but also others who may usefully contribute specialist information."

He glanced round the table and indicated a man of about sixty with unruly hair turning white, a keen, intelligent face sitting half way down on his left. "You will know Comrade Hans Modrow, Secretary of our Socialist Unity Party in Dresden and therefore responsible for guiding our citizenry there, a guidance which, if I may say so, perhaps needs some closer attention. On his left is Comrade General Horst Böhm, head of the Ministry of State Security in Dresden. He is, I know, someone who is assiduous in and fully committed to this vitally important work."

He looked with some distaste at a thin-faced man in his late thirties sitting beyond Böhm but although courtesy to others was not part of his character decided to treat the newcomer with at least minimal respect, aware that there was some tension between Putin and Modrow and thinking it prudent to cultivate possible allies.

"On Comrade Böhm's left is Comrade Major Vladimir Vladimirovich Putin. Comrade Putin is from Leningrad and is an officer within the Soviet Committee for State Security. His training has been in monitoring counter-revolutionary activities and in countering political dissent and his particular focus is on helping foreigners to understand how they might prove useful to us. It is true that the KGB might well learn from our own Ministry how best to manage matters of State security but I nevertheless thought it might be helpful to hear whether Comrade Putin could contribute anything helpful."

He looked round the table fixing each person with a direct gaze, relishing the authority which had kept him in power since the very beginning of the East German state, initially as the protégé of Walter Ulbricht, the country's first leader, and then as his successor. He gestured to his right.

"On the advice of Comrade Mielke, I have asked two others to attend. Comrade General Gerhard Neiber is the head of the State Security directorate charged with preventing escapes from the country. Sitting beside him is Comrade Colonel General Markus Wolf, deputy to and close ally of Comrade Mielke for 34 years."

"Here in our Democratic Republic the freedom and quality of life enjoyed by our citizens makes us the envy not just of our brothers and sisters in our socialist neighbours to the east, including even those in Moscow, but also in the west, now suffering from the excesses of capitalism and the corruption inevitably attendant on it, exactly as predicted over a century ago by Comrade Marx. Nevertheless, there remain in our State a number of citizens affected by the false consciousness which can arise from being exposed to the pernicious influence of wrong ideas coming from abroad, sadly even on occasion from other socialist states." He glanced pointedly at Putin as he said this. "This unrest has recently been fomented by assorted criminals and other treasonous anti-social elements and has to be stopped. Comrade Mielke?"

Mielke, the state's leading secret policeman through his career almost from the founding of the DDR and head of the Stasi from 1957, arranged the papers before him.

"As Comrade Honecker has explained, anti-social elements have been stirring up trouble, much of it criminal. We therefore need to deal promptly and firmly with this challenge to the authority of the State and the well-being of our citizens. Our elite unit, staffed by carefully selected members of the counter-terrorism and counter-espionage directorates, is intentionally small, rapidly reactive, and ruthless in action. Under my direction it will have no hesitation in challenging and destroying the hostile opposing forces and groups which are seeking to use what methods they can to bring about changes in power." He raised his hand and brought it down hard on the table as he spoke. "There must be zero tolerance of any illegality whatever. We will use whatever force is necessary to ensure the submission of counter-revolutionary elements."

Honecker and Mielke's three Stasi colleagues nodded in approval of Mielke's blunt approach. Egon Krenz, carefully eyeing Honecker, had started to do the same, even beginning to congratulate Mielke but suddenly stopped as he realised the embarrassed reactions of the majority. Horst Sindermann looked at Mielke with open contempt.

"These demonstrations have been peaceful." he said. "There is little evidence of the criminality you mention. Certainly those demonstrating show false consciousness and we must ensure that the virus does not spread and infect more of our citizens. But in my view to use force would be counter productive. Our citizens are echoing Comrade Secretary Gorbachev and are calling for openness, for *glasnost,* and for restructuring, *perestroika.* There is no sign that they wish to give up the advantages brought to them by socialism, merely that they wish to contribute positively to a discussion about its future. Comrade Mielke's proposed solution borders on illegality."

"I must agree, though reluctantly." said Putin. "Comrade Mielke is of course right in much of his analysis but we are living in difficult times. It is not that crushing an insect of insurrection is in itself wrong but whether that insect or its fellows can then sting badly the hand concerned." He paused for a moment and looked round. "Or even its keepers." he added, almost to himself. "Some may think the approach of Secretary Gorbachev mistaken - that's not for me to remark on - but he guides the Soviet Union and we must all both respect that and understand the position of Russia and the fraternal relationship there."

Honecker looked at Putin briefly then turned to Sinderman.

"Do you forget, Comrade, that although the ultimate public determiner of what is legal may well be the Supreme Court it is important that the Court gives its advice only having first determined the position of the Party? It is the Party which understands fully the Marxist-Leninist principles which guide our State. It is therefore the Party, and the Party alone, which is in the best position to understand the finer distinctions of the law where relevant to socialism. If the Party determines that prompt and decisive action needs to be taken in defence of socialism then it will advise the Court accordingly and expect the Court to play its full part in advancing the truth of that position to the citizens through its interpretation of our laws."

"Of course, Comrade Secretary. I fully understand that the ultimate position of the Party is critical and that you, as General Secretary, are uniquely positioned to interpret this for those of us who do not have your experience and command of socialist understanding."

There was something in Sinderman's tone of voice which caused Honecker to stare hard at him for a full minute but the President of the Leigislature remained impassive, a public picture of contrition. The room became very still.

"Let me now address your comments, Comrade Putin. Here in the German Democratic Republic we have done our *perestroika.* We have nothing to restructure. As for the openness of which Comrade Secretary Gorbachev speaks, we in the Politburo here share the views of Comrade Ceaucescu of the Socialist Republic of Romania and Comrade Zhikov of the People's Republic of Bulgaria that until false consciousness has been eradicated in our citizenry it is the duty of the Party to lead and not to be seduced to follow an empty form of democracy. The Party is helped strongly in this by the Ministry of State Security and it would therefore be wise to listen carefully to and then heed the advice of Comrade Mielke."

Mielke caught Honecker's eye and continued.

"Let me remind you further, Comrades. In 1953 there was a treasonous uprising by disaffected counter revolutionaries, something which threatened the very foundation of our new State and of the forward march of socialism. Then we called fraternally on the Soviet Occupation Forces to help us in this struggle and quickly succeeded in overcoming the enemies of the State. Comrade Secretary Gorbachev, however, has made it clear that the Brehznev doctrine of mutual support no longer holds. We can therefore no longer call on other fraternal forces to help us quash any rebellion but must do it ourselves."

"The people have forfeited the confidence of the government." thought Sindermann to himself, and smiled, as Mielke paused. "Would it not be easier for the government simply to dissolve the people and elect another?"

"I believe therefore that the correct approach is that of our wise comrades in China." Mielke continued." Only a few months ago in Tianamen Square they quickly took firm action to smother counter-revolutionary protests before they could take hold in the country. Our situation is comparable. We must, therefore, similarly be ready to smash forces hostile to our State and to the Party through all the means and methods at our disposal. We cannot flinch. We cannot be weak." He brushed the spittle away from the right side of his mouth. "History will honour our memory and the decisive action that we are now obliged to take. Ultimately the people will thank us."

Honecker nodded. "The Party is grateful to you, Comrade Mielke, for the way you guard and protect it. There is, however, another important matter which has come to our attention which I'd like Comrade Wolf to explain to us."

Wolf, son of a Jewish communist father and educated in Russia because his family had fled Germany following Hitler's rise to power, was the former head of the Stasi department concerned with foreign intelligence and widely regarded as a consummately skilled spymaster who had built up an extensive network of agents deep inside the West German establishment. He was now in his mid sixties, sophisticated and highly intelligent, still urbane and strikingly handsome, and unrivalled in his experience and knowledge of the intelligence world.

"My former department and its current head, Comrade Grossmann, came to learn hints of a curious proposal apparently involving the West German government making a substantial loan to the Soviet government. There were possible links with our country and I was therefore asked to help. We discussed matters with a number of people but there were important elements missing which made it difficult to establish exactly what was going on." He stopped, looked round the table, and took a sip of water.

"The man behind this is the managing director of Deutsche Bank, Alfred Herren. The loan proposed is significant, somewhere around 50 billion Deutsche Marks, and we understand that it's to be underwritten by the West German government. What is also clear is that our future as a country is intimately tied up with this proposal and this is currently being negotiated between the governments of the Soviet Union and of West Germany. We are not being consulted."

For a long moment there was silence and then everyone began talking at once. Despite Honecker's increasingly irritated banging on the table the noise continued until finally Wolf could again make himself heard.

"Comrades, I heard some of you just now suggest firm action to deal with the forces behind this plan. I agree with that view but we must be very careful in what action we take. This is a delicate situation which involves not just West Germany but also our comrades in the Soviet Union, as Comrade Putin has reminded us. If elimination is necessary in order to achieve our needs then no hint of complicity must attach to us."

"Of course!" said Mielke dryly. "You know, perhaps better than anyone, that we have always acted on that principle and will continue to do so. We are not responsible, however, for the antics of groups such as the Red Army Faction or such others operating in the West whose aims may on occasion coincide exactly with our own."

The meeting broke up. Honecker, usually deeply suspicious and alert to any deviant behaviour, failed to notice how Egon Krenz spoke briefly, alone or in small groups, to every member who had appeared concerned at Mielke's hardline stance. Mielke did notice but didn't care.

As far as he was concerned the individual was irrelevant, it was the Party alone that mattered.

And as Modrow drifted out, following Putin deep in converation with Böhm, he heard the Russian complain that in his view Gorbachev was weak and misguided; what was needed was someone of the stature, vision and force of a Mielke. "I am a specialist in communicating with people" Putin said "and I know the importance to that of knowing incriminating information." Insurrection could not be tolerated and so it was necessary to infiltrate and to set the state's opponents one against the other and break up any strength they might have from being united. Only by acting ruthlessly against enemies threatening the integrity of the state, could necessary order and control be maintained.

"Se vogliamo che tutto rimanga come è, bisogna che tutto cambi." Modrow murmured to himself and smiled at Putin in response to his hostile and suspicious glance. "*Il Gattopardo.*" he added. "Tancredi." He smiled again and walked on.

Chapter 16
Thursday 12 October 1989

Thomas thought back to his last visit to Frankfurt as Stephan guided him through the small Chinese restaurant. Dieter had somehow found a way to listen in on their conversation but he couldn't work out how that had happened. Impossible that he would have bugged the building, surely. Thomas wouldn't put it past the Stasi to attempt even that but if they'd somehow had the opportunity in the restaurant they couldn't possibly cover all the spaces where people sat. In any case, he was certain that Deutsche Bank would regularly sweep all their rooms for bugs.

They handed over their coats and Thomas added his briefcase, deciding he'd no need of it at lunch. An idea had flashed into his mind but he'd then lost it and he was still puzzling over the issue, the answer tantalisingly just out of his consciousness as they sat down at a corner table in the small, empty back room. A petite Chinese woman in an azure silk robe came over, took their orders and left.

"I know I said that you should take every chance of using the Deutsche Bank restaurant, of being seen there and chatting with people, learning what's going on. But this time it's better here as the place is always half empty and I wanted to make sure no one eavesdrops. The food's OK as well – not brilliant but perfectly good. I'd recommend the Peking duck."

"So, Stephan. What's up?"

"You remember the conversation we had last time you were here?"

"Sure."

The waitress arrived with a number of small dishes, one of them with the shredded duck meat, warm and aromatic and inviting. Thomas inhaled deeply then followed Stephan's example, laying a thin pancake on his plate and spreading it lightly with sauce from one of the dishes. They each added thinly sliced spring onions and other matchstick vegetables, sprinkled on the meat and fragments of crispy skin, rolled up their pancakes and ate in silence for some moments.

Stephen, still chewing, looked at Thomas who nodded in response to the eyebrows raised in query. "I'm now fully convinced, Thomas, that my suspicions were accurate and that what we spoke about that day is correct, it's what's actually happening. Among other things, Herren spent the whole day in Bonn when the Soviet delegation headed by Gorbachev came over last June."

"MmmHhh." Thomas rolled up another pancake and nodded again but said nothing, waiting for Stephan to go on.

"We've closed that financing deal I told you about. Between the Euroloan, the bonds and the medium term note program, the total financing is now set at fifty billion Deutsche Marks. That's a huge amount of money to lend to a country like Russia. Just huge! Now put it into context. The West German government has been the biggest sponsor of Russian *perestroika* anywhere in Europe, anywhere at all in fact. But why is it lending all this money? What is it getting out of it?"

"Maybe it thinks that these changes in the Soviet Union are going to open up things up massively and it's just getting on the ground floor, grabbing the chance to become a favoured partner, poking Britain in the eye when it comes to financial dealing."

"Possible, but I don't think that's it. Kohl's deeply conservative and traditional and he's a hawk as far as Eastern Europe's concerned. He'll do business with the Soviets if he has to and if it's good for the country but he won't like it and I'd doubt he thinks it's necessary. No, what he really wants is a greater Germany, German unification. I think he sees a way to work with Gorbachev to get that."

"Listen," Stephan continued. "Gorbachev was in East Germany just the other day and everyone could see how tense the relations were between him and Honecker. East Germany wants nothing to do with *perestroika* and the more liberal Gorbachev tries to make the Soviet Union, the more he pushes his *glasnost,* the more hostile and hard-line Honecker and the DDR politburo becomes. They see themselves as the remaining guardians of socialist purity but in addition they've either learned that Gorbachev has done some deal with the West and is hanging the Ossies out to dry in the process, or they strongly suspect that's what's going to happen, just like I do. They don't like it one little bit but it's entirely consistent with what I've been hearing and finding out."

"Consistent, yes, and persuasive." said Thomas slowly. "You think this is what Herren's been setting up, getting ready for the Berlin Purchase, as you called it. Gorbachev gets the money he needs and he works behind the scenes for German unification or, at least, does nothing to stop it."

"Well, it's pure speculation, obviously, but, yes, I think that's probably it. The facts back it up but nobody's ever going to find proof of it anywhere. Herren is now sending me over to East Germany to scout for potential banking acquisitions, to start building a banking network for us there. That also points in the same direction."

"You say the financing deal's been closed, the loans are in place. What happens next?"

"What do you think this opens the door to? Suppose all this is actually true, that it's going to happen soon, next year I'd guess. What's going to follow from that?"

Stephan sat back with an air of satisfaction and took a long pull of the Tsingtao beer they'd each ordered to complement the richness of the duck. For a short while there was silence. Stephan leaned forward again, closer to Thomas. "Isn't this going to be the biggest economic shock wave ever to hit the West European economies, at least in times of peace? And think of the opportunities if you know in advance what's going to happen! Just what could you do if you were in that privileged position?"

Thomas nodded.

"You're right about that. There's hardly anything would compare in terms of impact. And the opportunities for investment and speculation ... You could make a killing on practically anything you got involved in."

"Exactly! But how?" He look closely at Thomas. "What would you do, for instance?"

"Land values are dramatically lower there so I would buy land in Dresden or Leipzig, even Berlin. They've some good production and manufacturing plants in specialist areas like optics but most of it is all over the place, lurching from famine to glut and back again at the whim of the Party it seems. Anything to do with infrastructure would be worth investing in. Machinery. Communications. Some factories. And the government would be paying for it all so there would be no credit risk. I can see the West German companies having a field day and their stock values would soar."

"You're right. The government would be paying and interest rates would rise to hold off inflation. Bond prices would fall. So would the Deutsche Mark. That's another thing. There has to be a common currency but how are the two Marks going to be valued? I know there's an official exchange rate of parity but that's just absurd. Then there's the black market rates, which are astronomical, well, you probably know that anyway. My guess is that the DDR will push for as near parity as they can, that really helps them, while we'll want to keep as high a multiplier as we can get away with as otherwise it's just going to cost too much. And Kohl really wants unification so he's going to use his political muscle to make sure nothing derails that. Either way, though, there should be pretty good returns. Safe returns too! Absolutely gold plated safe, guaranteed by the Bundesbank."

Thomas whistled slowly, his food forgotten. "Yes, I suppose you could expect all the financial variables to be turned on their heads."

"Absolutely! It's the financial opportunity of a lifetime." Stephan checked his watch and signalled the waitress for the bill. "Hey, we need to head back to the bank for your meetings otherwise in the meantime you might miss out on the job opportunity of a lifetime. Let's talk more about this later. You're staying over tonight, aren't you?"

Chapter 17
Thursday 9 November 1989

Thomas's last two economics exams were scheduled for January. With the option of joining Deutsche Bank for an internship in February, passing them became critical, complementing the earlier ones which he'd passed brilliantly. Now that the Stasi was paying him a regular stipend his economic troubles were greatly reduced and he was able to focus more on his work. Latterly he'd been attending classes regularly and had spent the past weeks studying, sometimes even for up to fourteen hours a day, driven and taking time off only for the concession to himself of singing lessons.

He'd spoken to Bettina with increasing frequency, at least daily during the past week. These calls were supposedly on account of their roles as informer and monitor but in the past few days neither of them had mentioned anything to do with his work for the organisation. Most of the talk had been about developments in the DDR and where the country was headed.

Honecker had been deposed three weeks earlier but this had done nothing to stem the rising tide of protests. If anything their intensity had grown. On the previous Saturday a demonstration in Alexanderplatz initiated by actors and theatre employees and grudgingly permitted by the authorities had brought out well over half a million people, some said a million or even more, now the largest demonstration ever in East German history.

People were now protesting openly, careless of Stasi or police retribution, and their numbers and their demands were growing. Two days earlier the man who *was* the Stasi, Mielke, had resigned, tearfully protesting his love for the people and his desire to protect them. To his apparently genuine surprise and distress these claims made in parliament had been met with ridicule and derision.

The government itself had fallen on the same day although Egon Krenz, Honecker's replacement, had remained as Party leader. "He'll be gone by Christmas if this keeps up." Dieter had said.

People went about their usual business, mostly ignoring the fractured and conflicting news reports from the radio or television, particularly when the gap between the report and what could be seen happening not only in Dresden or Leipzig but in smaller towns and cities throughout the country, even in Berlin itself, was evident. There was a feeling of imminent change, of pressure building up which would be impossible to contain, yet few ordinary people, even the most vigorous protesters, could have said with certainty what would happen. There was optimism but simultaneously a sense of fear and gloomy foreboding.

"What's that quotation?" Thomas had said to Bettina one day "Something about things falling apart and the centre no longer holding."

"I don't know" she'd replied "but things certainly are falling apart. And perhaps the worst is the passion so many of us blindly have for what's going to destroy us. They don't understand what they'll get with this freedom they're chasing so hard. These coming changes terrify me."

He'd thought of this conversation again. How could she be so pessimistic about the future when all this ferment was happening? It could mean the end of his nightmare and surely she would welcome that for him. It was now almost ten in the evening and he had a sudden longing to hear her voice, to talk with her. He raced down the stairs and on to Gneisenaustrasse but no phones were free and two people were already waiting. He headed over to the Museumskneipe, one of his favourite haunts close to the

Europacenter, deciding to have a few drinks and call from there.

Thomas loved the kneipe for its absurd decoration: all sorts of old objects hung down from the ceiling, old tubas and trumpets through to life-sized pieces of an old warplane. The kneipe's seats had come from a 1920s train. He was sitting underneath an early industrial spinning machine and had just finished his second beer when he decided to try calling Bettina again. Again the line was engaged. He waited, tried again, waited, tried again, then after several more attempts gave up. A queue had formed behind him and people had started making barbed comments.

It was a cold, early November evening. He left the kneipe and was wandering aimlessly when he began noticing more and more people running as if fleeing for their lives, focused but distracted as if concentrating on saving themselves or watching some extraordinary, dramatic spectacle. Cars, forced to slow down or stop suddenly to avoid hitting people in the swirling crowds streaming on to the roads, were honking angrily, their brakes squealing and the drivers leaning out and shouting in fury. Thomas caught up with a young couple on Budapesterstrasse and asked them where everyone was heading, and just what was happening.

"The Wall! It's the Wall!" the girl answered, panting, trying to catch her breath and then bursting into tears. Thomas looked at her, puzzled by the tears flowing down her cheeks and the wide smile on her face. She grabbed him suddenly, kissed him exuberantly, and ran off, shouting something that Thomas couldn't understand, briefly deafened as he was by the desperate honking of a car about to run him over. He thought he heard something like "It's finished!"

Despite himself he found that he was running with the growing crowd towards the Brandenburg Gate, still a good fifteen minutes' away. People poured in from the side streets and the houses, the rivers of people becoming a turbulent flood of humanity. Traffic on the 17 Juni Strasse was practically at a standstill, unable to part the crowd. Thomas kept running until he was in full view of the Gate, part of the mass of people filling the Pariser Platz and pressing up against the eastern section of the Wall.

Thousands were now gathered on the western side of the Wall, on the other side of the Brandenburg Gate, shouting and chanting. Word had spread that Günther Schabowsky, the East Berlin Party Secretary, had announced on television the lifting of the travel ban and the immediate opening of the Wall. Thomas squeezed up on an observation turret together with four others and could see that nobody was yet risking crossing over. However, a growing mass of people was pressing the VoPos, the East German police, to be let through. An elderly woman was shouting and gesticulating close to a young officer's face though Thomas couldn't hear over the noise of the nearby West Berliners.

The crowd swelled and got noisier on both sides of the Wall. The VoPo officers in their sludgy green uniforms were half-heartedly holding back the crowd, sometimes shouting and displaying flashes of anger but usually exhibiting a kind of passive acceptance of what was happening, something very different from their usual arrogant behaviour. No one raised a machine gun or threatened the increasingly restive and daring crowd on the eastern side. A few from the west had clambered up and were sitting on the Wall itself, cheered on by those in the east. A VoPo raised a rifle towards the group but the eastern crowd howled with rage and surged towards him knocking the weapon out of his hands.

This broke the dam. Scores of East Berliners stormed the first barrier, then ran through the Gate and climbed up as best they could on the second part, reaching for the hands of the westerners sitting on top, some of whom were now even letting down ropes. With shouts and tears of joy they landed on the other side, hugging everyone in sight. In the controls turrets of the East the guards were standing impotently by, watching this dramatic shift in the ordered scheme of things, doing nothing.

Thomas felt an immense surge of pure joy and the thought that this could be the start of Germany unification flashed into his mind. The Stasi would disappear. Life would return to normal. Any hold that Dieter had over him would vanish. He'd wake up, the bad dream realised for what it was, and forgotten.

Thomas managed to negotiate his way through the maelstrom of people and get closer to the Western part of the Wall. A young man landed almost on top of him, then sank his face on his shoulder, crying. There was a confusion of sounds, of laughter, shouting, crying, singing, all merged into a single confused roaring as of a sea, excited at having covered hundreds of miles of open ocean to now pound on a promised beach. A small group of Easterners was whirling in a complex dance, buffeted by the crowd, approaching closer to the turrets and then whirling away before returning again like a dust storm and shouting insults at the guards, one of whom reached for his gun and then dejectedly put it down and looked elsewhere, diminished. On the western side, Easterners started running as if any moment they'd be pursued and hauled back. Some collapsed with exhaustion and lay sobbing on the ground.

Some Westerners had arrived with sacks of hammers and Thomas grabbed one, pounding at the Wall until some chips came away. With the help of others he climbed to the top of the structure, eager hands helping him up.

Although the former crossing here remained firmly closed, as it had been since mid-August, thousands were massing on the eastern side shouting for it to be opened, old and young and middle aged, men and women, children and even some still in uniform and with others pushing small carts or prams filled with sad possessions. Some were trying to force open the check point or attempting to climb up and over the barriers. Hundreds more were constantly running from Unter den Linden and the other side streets. Many of the guards were now abandoning their turrets and mingling with the raucous crowd.

Thomas now desperately wanted to see Bettina, to be with her and celebrate the happiness and euphoria which must surely now be gripping the whole country. He had a vague idea of how to reach her and thought he could manage it in less than an hour. Judging from the mass of people on both sides, this unprecedented spectacle of joy and brotherhood would go on for the whole night.

It seemed as if the whole of East Berlin was on the move towards the West and Thomas had difficulty making way in the other direction. Every so often the flood of people was so great he was forced back along Unter den Linden towards the Brandenburg Gate despite himself. Then the crowd would thin slightly and he'd make headway, dodging the constant stream coming towards him. There was a carnival atmosphere. Total strangers caught his eye and embraced him, beaming with joy. His mood changed. He remained euphoric but now he resented these constant contacts and felt jaundiced towards the people and their simple happiness. The tide of humanity and the waves of anonymous affection were obstacles in the way of his reaching Bettina quickly, something he needed desperately to do.

He dodged down some side streets and made progress and at Alexanderplatz found a phone booth to try calling

Bettina again. Her line was again engaged. Here the crowds were thinner and he ran for ten or fifteen minutes, asking directions a couple of times, finally finding the kneipe where they'd been on the evening Stephan had visited. He recognised the apartment block she'd pointed out on their return to the car and found the main door open. He climbed the stairs until, on the fourth floor, he saw her name on a door. For a few moments he stood there looking at it, catching his breath. Suddenly wondering why he'd come, fearing anger at this unannounced intrusion, he panicked and walked blindly down the flight of stairs, his steps slowing as he came to the second floor. He stood there for several minutes, arguing silently with himself, willing himself to act to see her, then turned, strode back to her door and pressed the bell before the next wave of doubt could hit him.

There was silence. After several minutes he put his ear to the door but heard nothing. The silence in the building was complete and he felt desperately sad and lost that she was not in. He turned to descend then changed his mind and sat on the top step, leant against the wall and closed his eyes to wait for her return. Behind him the door opened silently. Bettina looked at him, put her hand to her mouth and retreated but as she closed the door carefully the latch clicked.

"Bettina! Bettina! Please. Let me in. The Wall. You must know about the Wall and what's happening. Please. I want to see you and talk with you."

He knocked on the door but there was no response. He rested his forehead on the panels, willing her to open to him, and then slid to a crumpled heap. He turned and sat there, leaning angled against the wood. The sudden silent sliding open of the door took him by surprise and he tumbled backwards into her apartment.

She laughed, looking down at him as he scrambled to his feet but he saw that her face was red and swollen. They embraced, saying nothing. He tried to hold her longer but she pushed him gently away and, taking his hand, led him along the corridor and into a room on the right, dim, lit only by a nearby street lamp. She sat on a chair and motioned Thomas to sit on the bed, facing her. She sat, crouching forward on the chair, her head on her knees, for a long moment. Her body shuddered in a slow rhythm, shaking. Thomas started towards her, then sank back on the bed.

When she lifted her head briefly, Thomas could see tears streaming down her face. He got up and moved towards her, half kneeling, awkward for the moment at her level. He caressed her hair then gently pressed her head towards him. She resisted at first then leant against his shoulder, her face kept hidden. It was the first time he'd seen her fragility, and it moved him deeply. He bent down and gently kissed her hair, turned her face upwards to let him kiss her forehead, to brush his lips over hers, and then hold her, his cheek pressed to hers, the scent of her skin surrounding him and reminding him of how much he'd missed her. The swell of her breast on the inner crook of his elbow, rising and falling with her breathing and interrupted with an occasional shudder and gulp, excited him and he stroked her back then trailed his fingers down and again lightly up, now on top now under her loose shirt, the soft and warm skin exciting him further yet troubling him with her lack of response as if she was indifferent to anything he might do.

Her arms were round his neck but suddenly she sat upright and dropped them to her sides inside the ring of his own, pulling away and sweeping out with her movement his questing hand. She looked steadily at him, her mouth trembling.

"I'm sorry about weeping. I couldn't help myself."

Thomas felt ashamed of what had seemed natural comforting. "I'm sorry, I couldn't help myself either, seeing you like this. Maybe you wanted to be left alone and I barged in on you. I tried calling but your line was always engaged. I just ... " He searched for the right words. "I just really wanted to see you. That's all." He got up. "I can go now."

She looked at him in silence, face sad and eyes wet. She gave him a half smile. "I'd left the phone off the hook. I couldn't face talking, seeing anyone. But I'm glad now that you came." she said, and Thomas believed her. "I missed talking to you too. Would you like something to drink?" She got up.

Thomas nodded. "Whatever you've got."

She left the room and came back a minute later with a bottle and two ornate glasses, long stemmed, the bowls decorated with green glass and gold.

"Hungarian." she said, her voice still shaky. "I've had it for a while, for a special occasion. And, well ... I guess today is pretty historic."

They sat back down, and Thomas poured them wine. They clinked glasses but Bettina seemed miles away, her gaze vacantly on the wall behind him. They drank in silence, separate, alone.

Finally, with a slight start, she returned, her attempt at a smile showing the depth of her despair. "I'm sorry, I'm really not great company today. You know, I'm just not feeling all that well."

"You don't need to excuse yourself." He looked in her eyes. "Do you feel like talking?"

She looked at him for a while without changing expression. Then she gave a nod that was almost not there.

"It's because of what's happened today?"

She nodded quickly, and tears again started flowing down her face. "This is only the beginning." She caught her breath. "But it's the end of life as we know it. Nothing will ever be the same again. Nothing. Nothing. Nothing. Nothing. Everything will change."

The phrases came from between her tears, despairing. With difficulty Thomas restrained himself from taking her in his arms and kissing her, comforting her by his embrace.

"But why should you be so sad?" he asked gently. "All the people I've met while coming here were ecstatic. From today they're free to come and go wherever they please. They're free, Bettina, free. Surely that can't be a bad thing."

He paused to see what effect his words were having on her. She was still crying, shaking her head ever more wildly as he spoke. When she finally spoke, her voice was darker, controlling a bleak, desolate fury.

"But they're not free." she said. "Freedom is a state of mind, Thomas. Those climbing over the Wall have grown up with so very little. They had so very little but they had culture and they had things to believe in. And everybody had the same amount of whatever little there was. Everyone was treated the same. Now everything will change. It will never be like that again. Today it's started, Thomas. We'll all become like you Westerners, always longing for what we haven't got, forever trying to reach the next rung of the ladder by stepping on someone below. We'll become selfish, looking out for ourselves and what we want, not part of a community looking after each other. We'll become enslaved to Western desires for consumer goods, to buying stuff we don't want and don't need. I want to have time to think, to experience life and people, not be hit constantly with your advertising, your marketing to buy, buy, buy, get the latest, get the best, get the newest, spend money you haven't got for things you don't really want to keep up with others you don't really know and probably don't like anyway. You don't understand: the Wall was to keep all that out, keep your lifestyle out, not to keep us in."

Thomas thought for a moment over what she'd said. Some things rang true, too true for him to accept. But her reaction felt too strong for it to be purely theoretical. He thought back on what she'd said about her family. Her father was in the West. Now there was the possibility of meeting him, or making the conscious choice to ignore his existence.

"But walls are symbols, Bettina," he said gently "and any country which builds a wall to keep others out, to try to keep themselves secure, has already failed."

He poured them each another glass of wine.

"It's human nature, Bettina. People long for a better life. You can't just try to fence people in and tell them to try to be happy. Or tell them what they should believe in. OK," he conceded "Maybe not that last part. It's not what you should do but it's something we do all the time in the West as well."

"You're right, maybe it is human nature. Maybe greed, envy and violence are just a part of us. But I've been over to the West, and I can tell you I've seen more happy people in our poor villages than I've seen in your rich cities. Just give it time. You'll make them feel poor, slowly convincing them that their lives were inadequate without some of your useless products. The real tragedy is that we'll lose the little we've got and gain nothing worthwhile in return."

"What do you mean?"

"The majority of our people don't realize they're poor by your standards. East Germany is considered the jewel of the Warsaw Pact. But when they come over and get absorbed into your cities, they'll feel poor. And nothing you can do or give them will make them feel better. The real, black market exchange rate is what, ten to one? They won't be able to afford your lifestyle. Do you understand this?"

Thomas nodded in silence. Bettina got up and put an Eterna recording of Puccini's *Tosca* on her rudimentary stereo system, which drowned the distant clamouring of voices they could hear coming from outside.

Finally he took up the courage to ask. "Bettina, I have the impression there's something else on your mind that you're not telling me. Some other impact of what's happening that disturbs you. Has it got something to do with the Stasi, or your dad, is it something you can't talk about?"

"You're becoming more perceptive every time I talk to you, Thomas." She smiled at him. "The first time I met you I thought you'd have hardly noticed a dead body in the street, you were so focused on yourself, what you wanted. Yes, you're right, there is something else. It's about my brother and it's connected with the Stasi but that's all I'm going to tell you. Another time perhaps. I don't want to talk about it right now. Why don't you tell me exactly what it is they're singing? I don't understand Italian."

Thomas translated roughly the words of the painter Cavaradossi to her. It was the aria in the church, when a jealous Tosca inquires about the painting of the blonde woman.

"How did you learn Italian, by the way?"

"It's because of my father. He was stationed in Italy during the war, and he learned the language. And he loved opera, so he kept putting it on all the time at home. One day, I must have been four or five years old, I started singing along. My dad laughed, and asked me if I wanted to learn it. I said yes, so he started teaching it to me."

"Does your mother speak it as well?"

"No. She hated it, and told dad various times to stop." He laughed. "She said it was a slithery, messy language with nothing of the crispness and certainty of German. She insisted that as Germans, living here in Germany, we should use our own language. But we continued regardless. It became our own private language."

She took a long sip from her glass. "You miss him very much, I think?"

"More than I can say. I miss having someone I can confide with. You're the only person I can talk to now. And to be honest, Bettina, I never really know if what you're saying is really what you think or just what you feel you should tell me."

"You might find it hard to believe, Thomas, but I never lie. At least, not about anything important. I think I know how you feel. I felt the same way when I decided to take up Dieter's offer about working for the Stasi. It's difficult not to be able to confide with anyone."

Thomas shared the last remnants of the bottle between them as she watched silently. Her expression had changed to one he'd never seen before.

"Would you mind staying? I really don't feel like being alone tonight."

Chapter 18
Friday 10 November 1989

After the drama and emotional stress of the previous day Bettina, exhausted, slept on, not waking until well past eight. It was another bright, cold day. The window was uncurtained and the sun warmed her face as she lay on her side drowsily watching the dust motes dance in the shafts of light. She turned over and then noticed the dishevelled state of the other side of her bed. She frowned and stared uncertainly over, then raised herself on an elbow, leant over and sniffed at the pillow. She couldn't be sure, she decided. She lay back, struggling to piece together her fragmented memories of the recent past. She rarely drank much and perhaps the Hungarian wine had been stronger than she'd expected, she thought.

The news of the Wall's opening had distressed her greatly, she remembered, and she'd wanted to hide herself away, wanted only to come to terms privately with what had happened and to nurse her own distress. Then Thomas had appeared at her door, she'd let him in, reluctantly at first, and as they'd ended up listening to *Tosca* she'd been able to banish the harsh sounds of joy and excitement outside and lose herself in the music of a language she didn't understand, the unfamiliar rhythms and cadences complementing the voices of the singers and the instruments and her mood changing and lightening until she'd become calmer and happier. She remembered then that she'd felt very alone and had asked Thomas to stay - but surely he hadn't misunderstood her. She had also been very tired, certainly, and had fallen asleep almost as soon as she'd got into bed.

As she lay in bed, the smell of fresh coffee tantalising her from the kitchen, she suddenly recollected with a flush of embarrassment that as Thomas had been explaining to her the sense of the aria *Non la sospiri, la nostra casetta* she had found herself drifting off dreamily to explore the life of the two of them in just such a building. He'd been too intent on turning Italian into German to notice her absence, however, or even her unconscious experimental sigh, and in a moment she'd crossly repaired the breached shell around her.

The smell of coffee, now overlaid with that of warm bread and of eggs, became too strong to resist. Bettina stretched and yawned, scrabbled quickly out of bed, shucked her feet into slippers, and pulling a dressing gown together, her long rumpled blonde hair making a vivid contrast with the green silk of the garment, wandered to the kitchen where Thomas was preparing breakfast. She smiled as she looked at the preparations, the table set for two, and then frowned at the small bunch of freesias in a thin tumbler by what she took to be her place.

"Good morning!" Thomas waved a wooden spoon from by the cooker where he'd begun scrambling eggs. "You looked dead to the world so I thought you could use the sleep. How do you feel? Did you sleep OK?"

Bettina wrinkled her eyes, yawned and stretched again, nodded, then asked, suddenly wary, "Uhhhu, and what about you? Did you, um, sleep OK as well? Were you, were you comfortable enough?" Thomas, intent on the eggs, nodded slowly and let the smile broaden on his face while he looked at her. She waited, apprehensive.

Looking up from checking the eggs he smiled again. "I was OK. Your sofa was pretty short for me but it was fine. I managed, thank you."

In truth he'd passed a very uncomfortable night. From time to time, fed up with turning and wriggling unsuccessfully to get comfortable, he'd wandered through the apartment, nosing around here and there and looking at

Bettina's collection of miscellaneous objects and souvenirs, indicative of her curiosity and eclectic outlook. Her bedroom door was ajar and twice he'd sneaked silently into her room and stood looking at her perhaps hoping, if he were honest with himself, that she'd waken and drowsily invite him to stay. Seeing her lying on her side, well tucked in under her *Federbett*, her back to the door and curled slightly in a posture just made for spooning weakened him with feelings of desire. On his second visit he'd reached out to lift and caress her hair but had left hastily when she'd sighed and started to turn towards him.

When daylight had begun entering the small living room, he'd abandoned the attempts to sleep and had got up. Once dressed, he'd walked downstairs to look for fresh bread leaving a small wedge of paper inserted in the front door so that it would look shut but let him re-enter. Guided by the smells of baking he'd found a shop a few streets away and bought fresh warm rolls as well as eggs, butter and milk. He'd paid in DM at the official exchange rate bringing a smile of delight to the face of the woman behind the counter. On the way back he'd passed a small park and stolen a few flowers from one of its borders.

Thomas poured coffee and passed Bettina a plate of scrambled eggs, indicating the warm rolls and fresh butter. Bettina began eating, looking at her plate and saying nothing. Thomas had hoped for, expected even, some compliments on his preparations and thoughtfulness, perhaps an expression of pleasure from her, but it was clear there were going to be none. He felt the barriers had again gone up but he acted as if nothing had changed. He was glad he hadn't taken advantage of her fragile state the previous evening.

The phone rang and Bettina answered it quickly in the living room. All Thomas could hear were a series of "yes, yes" and once an "understood" and then Bettina returned.

"That was Dieter. He wants to see both of us immediately, as soon as we can get there." She frowned. "He seemed to know that you'd stayed here. We're to go to the Alexanderstrasse office – apparently the Normanenstrasse one is under siege from protesters."

She glanced at her watch and went to her bedroom to change. When she returned she wore a dark brown leather jacket and a long skirt matching in colour, the outfit giving her a rigid, almost military, look.

Just under thirty minutes later Thomas and Bettina were shown into Dieter's Alexanderstrasse office, two floors above where they usually met for their briefings. It was small and stuffy, much more cramped and nondescript than Dieter's main office in the Stasi HQ. There was a tall, dark-haired man of roughly Thomas's age sitting on one of the chairs in front of the bare desk who glanced over as they entered and smiled briefly at Bettina. Dieter seemed agitated and looked exhausted, as if he'd hardly slept.

"Hanno, you know what needs to be done. Thank you for coming. Report to me tomorrow and we'll talk further then."

He waved his hand towards the young man who then unwound himself from the chair, looming a good ten centimetres above Thomas. He moved to the door ignoring everyone.

There was a long silence after Hanno had left the room. Dieter kept walking back and forth in the small space left between his desk and the window overlooking Alexanderplatz, occasionally rubbing his eyes and at other times standing looking out apparently aimlessly at the scene on the street below him.

"Who was that?" Thomas whispered.

"Hanno Wornletz, another agent. We were quite friendly a while ago but I hardly see him now. He's very ambitious, very pushy, good at networking, clever too, I think. People seem to rate him, but, well, there's something ... "

Dieter turned abruptly from the window and sat down again at his desk.

"I called you here because of what occurred yesterday. It wasn't really a surprise, at least not to us. We knew that something of this kind would happen and probably happen sooner rather than later. Russia is in a desperate situation economically and Gorbachev is taking a desperate gamble to try to correct, or at least contain, this. His policies of *glasnost* and *perestroika* – and for the times I believe they're the correct ones although very dangerous to the Marxist ideal if not controlled and managed properly – have stimulated discontent among our citizens and those of our sister republics. In Hungary and in Czechoslovakia there has been dialogue. In Romania and Bulgaria in contrast there has been none but that will not save their leaders. I'm sorry to say that here in the DDR there are few with the foresight and vision necessary to give the greater freedom that our citizens want while at the same time securing and strengthening our socialist model. Modrow, I suppose, Wolf maybe, although he's supposedly retired, but precious few others if any."

Dieter sighed heavily and looked out of the window, deep in his own thoughts. Thomas and Bettina glanced at each other but said nothing. A clock ticked in the background.

"Now preserving our beliefs and way of life will get even harder. Effectively Gorbachev has sold us to try to buy his way out of economic collapse. In another era he might have sold other smaller states, Kazakhstan to Iran, for instance. Or like Kruschev in February 1954 who simply handed over the Crimea to Ukraine, although that was of course to a sister republic, part of the USSR." He paused and again looked towards and out of the window.

"But those days are over. Nowadays modern states can't be bought and sold against the will of their people. But, if you can change that then anything becomes possible." He glanced at the door and spoke more quietly. "These are strange and difficult times. The judgement of our leaders has been flawed and they have lacked that necessary vision and foresight. They have missed the opportunity to show the people the benefits of a more open society but one still governed by important socialist principles of fairness and freedom. Now the people see freedom as purely a Western philosophy and associate that with German unification and so under that banner we are to be sold off. In return Russia will receive considerable economic support."

"But what happened yesterday was clearly spontaneous." Thomas said, seeking to provoke Dieter. "I doubt the Russians were directly involved."

"They didn't need to be. All they needed to do was to order our politicians not to shoot if someone tried to cross the border. The rest would take care of itself. Revolutions are hardly ever spontaneous, Thomas. There's always someone hidden in the shadows with a match. There's always plenty of brushwood ready to burn."

He reflected for an instant. "This is only the beginning. General Secretary Krenz thinks he has the situation under control but he too will disappear, like Honecker before him. Revolutions, once they really get going, become almost impossible to stop. It takes a lot of dead bodies to halt the wheels of a runaway train."

Dieter looked through some papers on his desk and again there was silence for some minutes.

"The agreement made between the Soviet Union and West Germany is money in return for unification. Perhaps you will say, Thomas, that I should be glad that the two parts of Germany will become one country again. But to say that is to forget our history, to forget that the German state, at least as many now consider it, did not exist before 1871 and indeed that after 1945 large areas of what earlier would have been part of that German territory were lost. To seek to unite two sovereign countries which have existed apart almost two thirds as long as they were ever together is misplaced romanticism. Worse, it is a betrayal of our socialist ideals. We have made mistakes, perhaps, and our leaders have been wanting, perhaps letting power corrupt them and not trusting the people sufficiently. But this last betrayal will bring misery to our citizens as consumerism takes hold. We're going to disappear in ignominy. It will be an annexation, not a unification. Nothing of our system will survive. We will vanish like a joke of history." He sighed heavily.

There were several minutes of silence. Dieter again left his desk and stood staring out of the window, leaning heavily with both sets of knuckles on the sill. Bettina was looking at him, her hands gripping the frame of the chair, her knuckles white. She looked away, caught Thomas's eye, bent her head and suddenly drew her thumb and fingers together over her eyes, cupped her hand on her mouth and refused to look at him. He noticed that her shoulders were trembling.

"But I didn't call you here to discuss politics." Dieter said, turning abruptly towards them and once more sitting down. "Let's understand what this means. Yesterday, late afternoon, a group tried to storm and occupy our headquarters. They were pushed back, though with some difficulty since the guards were ordered not to shoot. I am certain there will be more such attacks in the future. That incident caused a panic, however, and even some people I'd held in esteem lost control and went running around like frightened sheep. They began to burn and destroy files. I was insistent they stop but even with the support of my superiors it took a couple of hours to calm things down."

He looked from one to the other. "I can understand that maybe some of the younger people here may try to recycle themselves and blend into whatever new system will emerge. I can even understand leaders who have made mistakes trying to protect themselves. But it is morally wrong for the leaders to wash their hands of their own doings. Even Hitler stayed in a bunker in Berlin and killed himself only at the very end, only when it was obvious that nothing more could be done. He was crazy perhaps but at least he was consistent and at least he took responsibility for what he'd been trying to do, however misguided."

"I have connived in actions which I now regret." he went on "Some of these actions had the effect of causing harm to certain citizens without even the proper justification of serving the greater good. Of course the needs of the state must take priority but perhaps we should not necessarily be as rigid about this ... " He looked at the ceiling for a moment or two. "As I've got older I've learned that sometimes one may even need to question what one has been taught. Nevertheless I take full responsibility for my actions, even if some of them are ones I now believe to be mistaken. It's the only honourable thing to do. And I shall remain at my post until I'm removed by official order. What's more" and here he smiled thinly and looked hard at each in turn "I expect each of you to do exactly the same until I formally release you from your duty and from your obligations to me and to the Firm."

Bettina looked at Thomas and as she did he felt his heart sink. Dieter had indicated that it was just a matter of time until the Stasi disappeared and yet he wanted everything to remain the same. Surely with the dramatic changes taking place he had no need of what Thomas could bring him? And how could he talk of honour and responsibility when he was forcing Thomas to continue to spy for what was still an enemy state? But with the hold Dieter had over him, and over Bettina too for all he knew, they would be forced to stay in active service until the West German agents entered the building and found their files. They were doomed. They would be tried in the West and jailed as spies. Dieter was crazy.

"Now, I require that you both remain at my disposal until the service is disbanded. This doesn't mean that I want to ruin your lives." he said, as if reading Thomas's mind. "You're young, and both of you deserve better. All my files are to be moved to this office from the HQ and yesterday, during all that chaos, I erased your files and all references to you from the central computer system. Your written records will stay here, under lock and key in my personal safe or in some other secure location and so available to me alone. They will not be handed over to anyone from the BND, you have my word on that. I will destroy them personally before I leave the Service."

He walked to the window and stood watching the sun disappear behind grey clouds. He turned to them. "There's very little time to lose and I now need to rely on you two more heavily than I've done in the past. I trust Hanno enough, but no one else within the Firm needs to know of your existence. You're no longer in the Stasi's computer files, only in the ones in my safe keeping, and apart from your own safety you can be a lot more useful to me this way. But never forget that you have nowhere to run and if you do not continue to follow my instructions, Thomas, I *shall* send your file to the BND. However, the game is about to become much rougher. From now on, consider yourself an agent, not an informant."

He pulled out a small black box from inside the desk and handed it to Thomas. "You're going to need to learn how to use this. Bettina will show you. She's one of the best sharpshooters in our section."

Inside the box was a Walther P38. The serial number had been erased, Thomas noted. His throat suddenly went dry and he shut the box hurriedly as if to forget what he'd just seen.

Dieter looked at Bettina. "I have decided to discontinue Project Cargo. I've got bigger things for you to look after. But you and I will discuss them separately, later. They relate to internal matters. Come to this office tomorrow at noon."

He again turned to look out of the window and he spoke in a more sombre tone, not looking at either. "A final word. From what I saw yesterday, it's only a matter of time before everything will start to crumble. Not just the Stasi, but the whole country. Anyone with any authority will either follow what I believe is the only honourable approach or will try to cover his tracks and so evade responsibility. Some, however, will seek to take advantage of the chaos, perhaps to reinvent themselves and rewrite the past in ways more favourable to them, some no doubt to enrich themselves. More and more it will be every man for himself. From now on, you must be very wary of what you say and of whom you confide in, even within the organisation itself ..." He lost himself in thought for a long moment, then sighed. " ... even within the organisation," he repeated slowly, as if he were now entirely alone " ... even here."

Chapter 19
Saturday 13 January 1990

John looked up from the desk as a key scraped in the lock. There was a scrabbling outside, the apartment door swung open, and Thomas stumbled into the room, kicking the door shut behind him. He rapidly lowered something bulky and heavy in his arms towards the floor, losing his grip and letting it fall the last few centimetres with a heavy thud.

He stretched his arms, pulling at each wrist as if his joints had seized up, and took several deep breaths, leaning against the door.

John stared at the massive, ancient TEAC 4-track tape recorder on the floor, its two large tape reels like owl's eyes staring him down. "What in God's name is that? Why? Are we going into the disco business or something? Do we have to feed it? And just where do you plan to keep it?"

Thomas laughed. "Don't worry. We don't have space here. I'm going to use Kai's apartment for a bit. It can go there."

"What, in East Berlin? Why there? Are you planning to move?"

"Listen. It makes sense. We need to concentrate on our theses and that's hard if we're both always around in this tiny space."

"True enough." John nodded.

"I've got Kai's keys, remember, and when I was over there a bit ago I found this note chasing him for rent. I guess they don't realise he's escaped and that's when it struck it me how useful the flat could be. The rent's not much so I stuck it in an envelope and pushed it under the door of the caretaker's flat. There's a man looks after things while the old woman's in hospital, picks up letters and stuff, does a bit of cleaning. He doesn't know much about what's going on though. The flat's empty, no phone, no distractions, perfect for working in. You work here. I'll work there."

"Fine by me, just so long as you don't expect me to meet all this rent."

"Don't worry, John, I'll pay my share. Just so long as I can sleep here every so often. Could we use your car, maybe shift my stuff over just now?"

By mid-afternoon Thomas was installed in Kai's apartment and ready to assemble the equipment he'd brought over. The building seemed deserted and he was certain no one had seen him or John carrying stuff upstairs.

He'd wanted to inspect the tunnel, both to get an idea of what Kai had been up to and also to satisfy his curiosity about the phantom station. But time was getting short and so he'd merely run down to the basement to check if there was any evidence of investigation. As far as he could see no one had visited the basement room – everything there looked in a state of chaos, unchanged from how Kai and the others had said they'd left thing when they fled.

Back upstairs Thomas worked out what he needed to do, making notes on a scrap of old paper. As he worked he thought about Bettina and the effects the political changes were having on her. He could see that she was uneasy, unsure about the future and sometimes almost out of her depth, it seemed. At the shooting range the day before she'd told him Dieter wanted to see them both that afternoon at four in his private office.

He soldered a couple of wires to the antenna of a radio receiver he'd recently bought and then ran them carefully outside the main window, first using the sill to shield them from view and then running them neatly up the side of the window to as high as he could reach. He stepped back on the tiny balcony and looked at his work, reassured that his additions didn't look in the least out of place among the jumble of other wires and pipes which festooned that side of the building. He was confident no one would notice them from the courtyard or from the apartments opposite.

It was now just after three thirty and he thought again of what Bettina had been able to tell him, really very little beyond Dieter's own uneasiness and uncertainty about developments and that he wanted to talk urgently with them both. He'd sensed that she had a premonition of growing danger and this worried him both on account of the uncertainty and because of the effect it was having on her.

Ten minutes later he'd tidied up, hurried downstairs, walked round the corner into Alexanderstrasse and entered the unmarked building housing Dieter's private office. He felt nervous as he entered and, glancing at his watch, saw that he was gong to be slightly late. Handing his Walther P38 to the guard at the entrance he hurried up the stairs and along the corridors, thinking that there were many fewer people wandering around than usual. The walls were patchy, darker rectangles showing up on the drab paint and showing that pictures of many prominent party members had been removed.

Bettina was already in the office and looked relieved to see him. She was wearing a light brown linen shirt, open at the neck, and a dark green sweater which toned with her simple shoes and trousers. Its colour brought back to him the sight of her that morning in November after the fall of the Wall, still slightly sleepy, her blonde hair tousled, half smiling to herself as she gazed at the breakfast he had made for her.

He'd felt very close to her both then and the evening before but after the phone call things had again changed and barriers had once more gone up. Time and again Bettina and he would move closer to a point where he felt she was within reach and at that precise moment there would be an unexpected coldness, leaving him wondering what had gone wrong. It was frustrating and upsetting but he consoled himself with thinking that perhaps she recognised where her feelings were leading her, how strong they were becoming, but for the moment didn't dare to act on them.

"Whenever you're ready to join us, Mr Wundart ... " Dieter's deep voice, with a hint of mockery, interrupted his daydream. Embarrassed, Thomas sat down quickly in a chair beside Bettina. She looked at him and smiled.

"I'll get straight to the point. Things are moving much faster than I anticipated. First they changed our name to the Office of National Security. Now, apparently to appease the public, we've been officially disbanded as a separate unit as of today. However, much as the politicians might like us to vanish from the face of the earth, it's not that easy to dismantle an atomic weapon. And that's what we are. Some pieces are just too hard to break. Our division has been moved to form part of the Ministry of Internal Affairs. They are dismembering the network of informers although I know that for many months now people have already been leaving steadily, rightly confident that they can get away with doing that. However, old habits linger and I'm hearing that a lot of the people being laid off are regrouping on a private basis and setting up their own intelligence networks. That's highly dangerous to the state for all sorts of reasons. Highly dangerous."

"So it's official? We no longer exist as we were?" Bettina asked.

"It was announced half an hour ago. Thirteenth January will go down as the day the biggest mistake in East German history was made. Let's get rid of the controllers just before the state implodes and a huge wave of crimes begins. But nobody will study our history any more, so it doesn't matter. Anyway, it's not my problem and it's the West who'll foot the bill."

"What do you mean by that?" Thomas asked.

"Elections will bring a landslide victory for Western parties, for the CDU particularly, and annexation will follow. The SED is in a shambles. There is no date set for uunification, but it's likely to happen quickly. What that means for you, Thomas, as I promised, is that you'll be free to forget us in a short while."

Thomas was surprised about his mixed feelings. There was relief that soon everything would be forgotten and he could get on with his life. But there was something else as well, something which pushed in the opposite direction. Over the past two months he'd changed. He enjoyed the daily shooting practice with Bettina, basked in her compliments as he'd steadily improved over the week. He felt that he'd moved beyond just being a student. It was as if familiarity with the pistol had changed him further, made him more responsible, more mature. He was even prepared now to put his own life at risk if necessary, even welcomed the idea. He'd seen how others like Kai had risked their lives for something important to them. He'd taken the easy way out. He'd become a collaborator. He needed redemption if he was going to be able to look at himself in a mirror with pride, he thought to himself.

"I have two important projects, one for each of you." Dieter re-lit a half-smoked cigar. He moved to the window and opening it waved his hand about to clear the smoke. "Let's start with you, Bettina." He stared into the street for a minute or more, his hands on the sill, not moving, then turned back into the room.

"As you'll know, the Stasi was one of the few organisations in the country permitted to hold foreign currency. Each regional head office was provided with the funds it needed direct from the central bank. A detailed reference note was then sent to head office for updating information records."

Bettina nodded. Although she had never been involved in the funding side, she was aware of the financial autonomy of the regional offices.

"On 31 December, Gerd Henkel, the Treasurer of the Dresden operation, requested currency valued at around ten million Ost marks. The majority was in Ost marks, a portion in Deutsche marks and the remainder in French francs. It was sent from Berlin a week later, this Monday past, and apparently deposited as usual in the special custody vault within the local branch of the bank. Three days later Henkel informed us that when he next checked there was no trace of the currency in that vault."

He inhaled deeply, then let out a thick plume of smoke. Thomas coughed as the cloud hit him and, admiration and horror mixing, tried to imagine how Dieter's lungs must have felt.

"Who signed the documentation for receipt?" Bettina asked.

"As is customary, an officer of the central bank and the director of the branch. For security reasons the agents escorting the van are not let into the special vault. Funds of this kind are taken by them to the outer vault, checked there, and then moved into the special vault by a bank employee under the close watch and control of the director or someone nominated by him."

"Could it have been stolen afterwards? Who else besides the director is aware of the security measures protecting the vault? And how do these work anyway? Who has keys, for instance?"

"There were no signs of burglary. Apart from Henkel, half a dozen people have limited access, meaning they can execute written orders on the account. But Henkel, the Treasurer of the Dresden operation, Modrow nominally, of course, Roehrberg, his Deputy Spitze, and possibly one other have unlimited access ..."

"Unlimited ... ?" Bettina interjected.

"I'm waiting to learn the exact security details but I understand that these four, possibly five, each have a set of keys and separately know different parts of the combination. The entry keys are all the same and so anyone with a set can get as far as the outer vault. However, to enter the special vault itself two separate combination locks need to be opened and this then needs two of that highest level group to attend the opening."

"Or for one person to learn a second combination element from another ... ?"

"Yes, that's probably true. There could be collusion or pressure, threats perhaps. As far as I know, however, although the combination part is sophisticated so that any two parts will work together to open the lock there's no record of which parts are used on any one occasion."

Thomas and Bettina remained silent, watching as Dieter stretched out his legs and puffed on his cigar.

"There are several possibilities. Two people might have acted together or just one, as we considered. It's unlikely, but there might even have been further collusion quite outside any of the inner circle. Perhaps the money was never even deposited in the first place. However, that's not very likely, I think, as it has to be checked and signed for by senior officials. The security measures to enter the bank are not particularly sophisticated, especially for someone working for the organization. The special vault itself really is supposed to another matter. But perhaps the security there is not as good as we thought."

"Any suspicions?"

"No. The only thing which I find improbable is that an ordinary bank officer would try to steal money from the Stasi. If he wanted to steal money he could have found easier and less dangerous clients to steal from."

"So you think it's an inside job?"

"Yes. That's the reason I've been charged with the investigation. I want you to go down and find out what happened, Bettina. You know your way around Dresden, and hopefully the fact that you're a young, attractive girl with, they'll imagine, very little experience will disarm them, maybe make them overconfident that they're getting away with it. This also depends on how you decide to play it, Bettina."

He gave her a sideways glance. Thomas felt suddenly nervous at the thought of Bettina getting friendly with dangerous men.

"If you find out something, don't take any action, but report direct to me, and to me alone. You have to be extremely careful. Whoever stole the money could be acting with others, even people really high up in the organisation. This file contains all the documentation I have. You will leave immediately and return within a week. Don't forget, we have very little time left before we lose our jurisdiction completely, before chaos ensues. That's probably what the criminals are counting on. Once we become a single nation and every last trace of the Stasi disappears, it will become almost impossible for anyone to find out exactly what happened or trace the culprits."

"Thomas, your role will be twofold. You will travel with Bettina to Dresden. She will be acting in the open and her mission could be very dangerous. You will be her shadow and follow her whenever and wherever possible. No one knows you within the organisation and so provided you don't acknowledge her in public no one will realise your role as protector. That could be very useful." He again drew deeply on his cigar and waved away the cloud of smoke round his head. "And I've heard very complimentary remarks about your growing ability to handle a gun."

Bettina looked the other way, a little embarrassed.

"Now, to the second matter. I want you, Thomas, to find out everything you can about an organisation called Phoenix Securities. There seems to be someting of a focus on Dresden though I'm unclear about details. Phoenix is promoting loans and a number of our informers all over the country have been contacted. It's very strange. Western banks don't use untrained personnel and are very selective about who they grant loans to. This company isn't properly registered, seems to promise loans to anyone who wants them, and uses unskilled staff, all of it local. I'm pretty sure it's a pyramid scheme. I want to avoid having thousands of people here deprived of their savings."

Thomas wasn't quite sure he'd understood. He knew the principle of pyramid schemes, scams where the pyramid base needed to grow constantly larger to meet commission obligations further up the chain. But what Dieter was telling him didn't make sense. "But you said these people offer loans, not take people's savings. They're the only ones who have something to lose if things collapse, surely?"

"Maybe. That's what I don't understand. I'm certain there's some kind of currency fraud going on but I'm unclear about the mechanism. Maybe they're promoting loans in Ost marks which will be repaid in DMs once unity happens. Maybe their interest rates are exorbitant. It's impossible to tell since to our knowledge they still haven't yet completed a single transaction. They seem only to be getting things ready, but their network is expanding very rapidly. We've had over fifty reports in the last week. Word is spreading fast. We're getting reports from even the tiniest towns, even from a few villages."

"Are there any charges you could stick on them?"

"Not yet, not until we find out exactly what they are up to – and that's what I need you to do. They're based in Frankfurt, which is why I thought you were well placed to look into it. I also thought it could be to your advantage should the BND find out about you in the future. If there is effectively some element of fraud, they might be interested, assuming unification happens. Maybe your friend Stephan can help you out too?"

"I'll try calling him. He's travelling often in the East now, helping set up Deutsche Bank's branch network."

"Well, he can surely be of help anyway. I'm sure he travels back and forth, and maybe he can find something out through his connections. Act as if one of your Eastern friends had asked you about it. He's met Bettina, right?" He glanced through the file, handing it over to Thomas after a brief moment.

The phone started ringing. Dieter sighed. "Call me up as soon as you have discovered something. And don't talk to anyone else ... no one but me, not even to my superiors."

He picked up the receiver and waved them out of the room.

Chapter 20
Sunday 14 January 1990

It was late morning and Bettina was driving her Trabant at full tilt to Dresden. Running at close to the speed limit of sixty-two miles per hour, the engine was raging and juddering as if it would fall off any moment. The road, like most East German roads, was made of prefabricated concrete slabs and as the car raced and leaped down it the rhythmic clunking of the wheels hitting the ends of the slabs turned the vehicle into an ominous metronome. This had droned on for over an hour, as the landscape changed from sparse forest to rolling countryside and back again.

Thomas, unused to Bettina's exuberant driving and to the unfamiliar road surface, had passed the first part of the journey anxiously expecting the Trabant to roll into the ditch on a corner or to break an axle with one jar too many. The steady thud of the wheels eventually relaxed him, his nervous grip on the door handle relaxed, and he passed into a comatose state, his mind wandering here and there erratically but always returning to Bettina and whether he'd ever be able to be with her as he wanted. He was drowsily enjoying an increasingly passionate and loving embrace with her when she raised her head from his lap and he found himself staring at Frau Schwinewitz smiling grotesquely up at him. A particularly severe bump jolted him fully awake and to banish the vision he scrabbled for something to say, anything to bring him back to reality.

"Bettina, what are you going to do if unification really happens? Any plans? Will you travel, perhaps? Are you worried at all?"

They travelled at least a further kilometre without response and Thomas thought at first she hadn't heard.

"Of course I'm fucking worried! Yes! Yes, I've been thinking about it a great deal, about lots of things. Like Dieter, I'm pretty sure now that unification's likely. So I'm worried about how I'll manage for money. Between the museum job and my Stasi stipend I was OK, just. But with unification they'll both go. It's the victors that write history, isn't that what they say, and the version we give in the museum won't suit the West."

They were both silent as the car thumped monotonously over the slabs.

"But I'm more worried about how we're going to manage when we're dragged into joining a country that's so different from ours. People keep saying how good it will be but that's bullshit, self deluding bullshit. Prices will rise. We'll be the poor relations. Things are difficult here but at least people have jobs and houses and get enough to eat. I just don't like the way the West is saying that what matters is buying, buying, buying things, buying things all the time, supermarkets with tins of this and packets of that. That's not what life should be about. You're not a proper citizen unless you spend money all the time it seems."

"Oh, come on, Bettina. I live in the West and it's not like that at all. That's just more lies from the Party to keep people from trying to leave. You've been brainwashed. Sure, we make more money in the West than people do here but we have choices. You have none."

"What the hell has choice got to do with anything worthwhile, with living? Choice! That's a capitalist marketing slogan. I don't want to be able to choose between 57 different kinds of baked beans. Who the hell wants to eat rubbishy food anyway? You talk about the Party and the Stasi controlling people's lives but I'll tell you this, in the West it's big business that controls people's lives and the people have been so mesmerised by this fucking choice you say is so good, this buying of stuff all the time, that they just lie down and let big business piss all over them and then they say, Oh, thank you, sir, thank you very much sir, please piss on me a bit more, sir. They don't have lives any more, they're just drones. Give me the honesty of a socialist approach any time even if we sometimes do have problems with supplies."

Right on cue the engine coughed and died and Bettina steered the slowing car on to the verge. She sat for a moment leaning forward, her hands covering her face then threw open the door, pulled hard on the bonnet release, marched to the front and with a noisy clatter hauled the bonnet up and jammed it on the support. Thomas struggled out of the car to join her.

"Do you know about engines?" He shook his head. "No, I thought not! Well, just get the hell out of it. Piss off! Go away!"

Thomas scurried back to the passenger seat thinking that Bettina was probably quite capable of pulling the engine off its mounting and hurling at him if he got in her way. He sat watching her through the half moon of the opened bonnet, her mouth working and her face scowling as she explored the engine components. Finally she reached down, apparently wriggling some hidden pipe back into place, slammed the bonnet down, returned to her seat and turned the key. The starter groaned, turning the engine ineffectually until it suddenly coughed, died, caught again, roared into life, and died, the starter motor now groaning slower, and slower, then giving up completely.

"Aaaaarghhh. These bastard batteries that can never hold a charge."

She caught Thomas's eye and laughed. "They're from the West." she lied. "We had a choice!"

"Out!" she shouted and with Thomas behind and Bettina pushing on the frame of the open driver's door they got the Trabant rolling until she scrambled in, threw the car into gear and shuddered it into life, hiding Thomas in a pall of blue, oily smoke as he staggered up to where she was now waiting, racing the engine, and slumped into his seat, almost tumbling out again as she bumped off the verge and roared away, high-revving without a glance behind her, making an obscene gesture out of the window to the angry scream of a horn from a now sharply swerving Zil, and showing not the slightest hint of contrition that Thomas could see. He stared at her, his emotions flickering between horror and admiration, and settled himself deeply into his seat.

Several kilometres passed. Thomas experimented silently with several phrases but said nothing.

The soporific thunk of the mobile metronome continued.

"I've been thinking a lot about things." Her tone was quieter, more relaxed, as if taming the engine and giving the finger to a Zil-driving apparatchik had put her in a better mood.

"If unification comes about then they're going to push for Berlin becoming the new capital of a united Germany. That's going to mean prices going up. That's not just food and clothing but particularly rents. Dieter thinks they're going to increase dramatically, get more in line with levels in the West. My rent agreement is just about up and so if they increase rents like we think they might I'm going to be out on the street, particularly if I have no job. Maybe Dieter will be able to pull a few string for me though, perhaps get it renewed on good terms."

She was silent. He looked sideways at her, wondering if there was more than a professional interest behind Dieter's concern and her apparent reliance on him. They spent a lot of time together and he could see she found him attractive, despite the differences in their positions and the age gap which clearly existed.

"Dieter seems to worry a lot about you. Looks after you, I suppose. What about, umm, his wife? Ummm, he is married, I suppose. Man like that. Or, or, ummm, has he a girlfriend? Maybe."

He turned and stared out of the window, wondering again at why he so often ended up wrong-footed, why she had this capacity to turn him into a babbling schoolboy unable to handle his feelings.

The sparse forests came and went.

"Where are we going to stay in Dresden? At your family's place? Are your brother and mother both there now? Oh, no, I remember, your mother moved, didn't she? But you still have it, don't you? I think you said you had an aunt living there. How big is it? Is it in the centre or ... "

"You don't even wait for my answers! I've known Dieter for a long time. I won't give you details but I was kind of forced into working with him and I really resented that. But what I've learned is that he's got integrity and he's loyal but also that he's stubborn and awkward although he comes out right more often than not. I think he'd like to be more sociable but people don't really understand him well enough and he won't compromise, even for the Party, if he thinks something's wrong. He's made enemies but he doesn't seem to care about that. I guess that's why he's not as senior as he could be."

Again there was silence for several minutes, broken only by the rhythmic drumming of the wheels on the slabs.

"You said your brother was living between Dresden and Berlin. If you want we could stop by for a little while. What does he do?"

"No, I'd rather not stop. He does nothing much." She laughed shortly. "Sits around in his room most of the day. I'll see him another time."

She grinned suddenly, glanced across and patted his leg with her hand, then left it lying there for a few beats of the wheels. "And no, Dieter and me, we're not lovers! I've learned the hard way to make a distinction between work and my personal life, Thomas. It might have been different if we hadn't been working together, although I guess if we hadn't then I wouldn't have got to know him as well as I do. But mixing the two leads to all sorts of complications and I made that mistake shortly after I was recruited. Not with Dieter though – I was furious with him at that time – but there was another young guy working closely with Dieter, we got thrown together a lot, he was sympathetic and, well, things happened. You saw him. Hanno."

She spoke quietly after another short silence. "Until I found out what he was really like."

He glanced over but it was clear there would nothing more. "And Dresden?" he asked. "Any ideas about lodgings?"

"Well, as I told you, my family used to live here but they've all moved. I've got an old friend on the outskirts of the city we could maybe ask for leads but now that the border's open there are lots of people lodging visitors in their homes to make a bit of money and we might be best doing that. Let's ask around. But we need to be discreet, say we've known about Dresden and decided to visit, if anyone asks - news travels, even in a city like this."

Once they'd reached the city Bettina drove towards Meissen, avoiding Dresden city centre. Parking in front of a large industrial complex, she told Thomas to wait in the car while she went to see if her friend was around and doing the Sunday afternoon shift. "Best if nobody sees that we're together."

Thomas watched Bettina cross the road and approach a forbidding white gate over which was mounted a substantial "no trespassing" sign. He was too far away to be able to overhear the conversation but it was clear it had taken a wrong turn. The guard was gesturing violently and looked threatening. Just as Thomas was about to go to her help Bettina wheeled and returned rapidly. She got into the car and slammed the door violently, gripped and shook the steering wheel and then beat her fist hard on it.

"Nnnnnrrrrrr! What an arsehole! Said I couldn't go in because the mill is being restructured. Said that no one was there and, anyway, it was private ground. Private ground?! What nonsense! This is a co-operative, always has been. Let's find somewhere to stay before it gets too late."

She started the engine and took off at speed, brushing an ambling dog which yelped out of the way and causing Thomas to hold on grimly as they cornered until finally her mad fury again abated.

They stopped at several farmhouses on or close to the Meissen road but it wasn't until the fourth or fifth that they found a room. This farmhouse was slightly larger than the others they had seen, although more damaged. The back of the pigsty had been blown off, presumably during the war, and a rough roof of metal sheets constructed as a temporary measure, something which had now lasted over forty years, rusting badly in the interim. The plaster and the paint which had earlier covered the walls had almost completely worn away leaving the original reddish brick. As they crossed the yard a motley collection of chickens and ducks scattered and then waddled and strutted behind them while a small flock of geese stood to one side honking fiercely and making hissing, flapping rushes at the intruders on their territory.

"I have one room only" said Frau Gisela Dornbusch "but it's quite a big one. I hope you won't mind the noise. The animals stir early, of course, but guests get used to it quite quickly."

"Sure, that's fine." said Thomas. "It'll be good to hear something other than cars for a change. We'd like to take the room for the week and please, if you could, don't let the authorities know we're staying. It's just that we've come away together against her parent's wishes ... "

He put his arm round Bettina's shoulders, feeling her stiffen as he did so, and smiled at their host as he handed her the week's rent, rounding it up to encourage her agreement.

Frau Dornbusch led them through the large kitchen, which also served as dining and living room, and through a long corridor with doors on the left. Inside, the house belied its desolate outer appearance and felt warm and comfortable, being decorated with utmost simplicity and with only a few household objects, woven baskets, wooden artefacts and the like, lining the walls. They passed a tall solid oak armoire at the end of the corridor before climbing the stairs.

The room was pleasant and there was a large sleeping space in the middle of the floor, made up of two mattresses pushed together without any frame and covered with a couple of large duvets. The only furniture was a mid-sized chest of drawers and a worn desk with a red chair set by it. There was a full length mirror on one wall and beside it a window overlooked the courtyard through which they'd come.

Frau Dornbusch handed them keys. "You can come downstairs and have breakfast with us in the morning if you like. We eat between eight and eight-thirty." she said.

"I'll sleep on the left side, OK?" Bettina put her pyjamas under the pillow. "I know that you'll behave like a gentleman and keep to your own side."

She gave him a seductive smile, arching her eyebrows, and began putting her things away in the chest of drawers. Her blonde hair was tied back in a ponytail and she was looking particularly beautiful, Thomas thought, as he admired the curve of her waist, the subtle directional shifts in the seat of her jeans and the way the material clung elegantly to the backs of her thighs as she moved. He controlled his desire to walk over, to hold her waist and nuzzle and kiss her neck, remembering her earlier mood swings, and instead began to sort out his own clothes.

He had learned that her verbal come-ons were usually immediately followed by almost aseptic coolness. In this, her mood swings reminded him a little of Olga although with his old girlfriend he'd learned that it was just a way to check if she could still control his emotions. Olga had kept it up right until the end, even after she'd started double dating the sculptor with whom she was now living, whereas with Bettina there seemed to be a real concern that something might start which she couldn't control. Work and pleasure don't mix, she'd said. "Maybe the only way to really find a place in Bettina's heart is to stop being so obviously interested." he thought.

"Look." she said, turning round and holding up against her a scooped neck black silk blouse through the double thickness of which Thomas fancied he could still just make out the green of the jersey she was wearing. He imagined what it would look like on her. "Henkel's known as a bit of a skirt chaser so I thought this might work well to get him talking. What do you think?"

She ignored his grunt, laughed and carefully laid the blouse over the back of the chair, covering it with a tailored jacket and placing on the seat a matching skirt and some sheer stockings. She lifted out from the drawer a pair of thin black panties edged with red lace, spread them out at arms length in front of her for a moment and dropped them on the pile, adding to it a matching black bra.

She lay down on her side of the bed, smiled at Thomas, stretched and nuzzled down into the pillow, then stretched again and as Thomas surreptitiously wriggled towards her swung round to grab the file Dieter had given her and again faced Thomas, leaning on her elbow "Let's review the material. There are three likely suspects, assuming the bank director and the central bank officer are clean - and the police are working on these in any case."

She pulled out a typewritten sheet of paper with a photograph attached to it and continued in a low voice, so as not to be overheard outside the room. "Gerd Henkel, Treasurer. Forty-five years old. Single. 1.7 metres. Green eyes. Dark brown hair, balding. Clean shaven. Smoker. Moderate drinker. Leads a reserved lifestyle, although has been seen occasionally in the last two years with younger girls, possibly prostitutes. Last stable relationship with Angelica Dietz, born June 1961 in Weimar, interrupted in September 1987 after almost two years. No children."

She continued with the professional curriculum. "Completed technical studies and joined the Party at the age of sixteen. Enlisted in the Organisation at the age of twenty, first as an informer and two years later as agent. Stays in Bonn, London and Paris. Held post as ... "

"Why are you reading all this to me?" Thomas snapped, resenting the glimpse she'd given him of what he now recognised he desperately wanted but was convinced would elude him. "I won't be meeting them. I'm just here to back you up and make sure nothing happens - but I'm sure you've plenty of experience with men and don't want a chaperone."

Bettina looked up from her files and stared coldly at him..

"You're right. Sometimes I forget that you're not really an agent, that you're being forced to do this. I'd foolishly thought that this time we'd be able to really work together, maybe discuss developments, talk and explore ideas about what was happening. But, yes, you're right. I'll be meeting each of them alone. In private. On my own. Maybe the best use of your time is to study the maps of their homes, in case you need to break in."

She handed him a file with several large sheets of paper showing plans, elevations and detailed notes on various large villas. "Henkel's house, where we'll be going tonight, is in there. He's expecting me at nine-thirty. I'm sure you don't care to learn whether or not he has a pack of Rottweilers so I'll keep on reading on my own."

Stung, Thomas snatched the papers from her, wishing he'd kept quiet. He was angry and frustrated by her changing moods towards him, at how he was constantly being wrong footed by following her where she seemed to lead, opening himself up and then hitting a barrier when he got too close. This was becoming a ridiculous obsession, he thought. He'd best just forget it. And yet, and yet ... Maybe through working together things could change. He saw her in danger and he, Thomas, being the one saving her. He laughed to himself. "And if I then just ignore her ... "

He spread out the house plans on the small table and looked at the notes on the current uses of the rooms, measurements and other useful details. There were similar detailed maps for Roehrberg's and Spitze's villas. His head hurt.

"We'd better head out soon." Bettina said after a while, tidying away her papers and gathering up her clothes to change in the bathroom. "Almost time to meet our Herr Henkel."

Chapter 21
Sunday 14 January, evening

Bettina and Thomas were silent as they drove to the appointment with Henkel, each immersed in their own thoughts. Bettina was nervous, mulling over how best to approach Henkel and get information from him. On one occasion she nearly clipped a parked car as she turned a corner. Thomas was tense and distracted because they'd finally agreed that he'd enter the house secretly while Bettina kept Henkel occupied in the living room. Their argument about this approach an hour earlier had been fierce although the absurdity of sitting on the mattresses on the floor whispering and hissing at each other to avoid being overheard by the Dornbusches had struck them simultaneously and released some of the anger and tension between them.

She parked the car some distance from Henkel's house. This was a stately villa set in a large walled garden and situated in the Prussian quarter, a favoured locality with the Dresdener Party hierarchy and one of the most elegant residential areas of the city. This was less than a kilometre from the Stasi office complex in the Bautzner Strasse and close to the houses of the other two officials, Roehrberg and Spitze.

"Once I'm confident Henkel's alone in the house" she had said "I'll send you a signal that it's safe to come in. Look, we'll be in the living room, here. I'll excuse myself to go to the bathroom. The nearest one's on the ground floor, here, so that's where Henkel will direct me. I'll switch the light on and off three times then leave it on for a few moments – you'll see that easily from the garden. I'll unlatch the window so you can squeeze through into the house that way."

"I don't like it at all." he'd objected. "You can't know who's in the house and he won't tell you. There could be a dog. He might have a housekeeper, maybe a girlfriend keeping out of sight."

"Trust me, I know how to find out, and I shall. Once you're inside go to the study, here, and check what documents you can find. Photograph anything interesting but, anyway, take as many pictures as you can, including of the room itself. Check whether there's any money hidden or any pointers to it anywhere. Look behind the pictures for wall safes. Photograph anything of that kind you discover. If you've time check under the carpets and floorboards."

"You're mad! I can't do all that while you're nearly next door chatting to Henkel. Much better if we break in while he's away. What if I drop something, scrape a chair maybe? Any noise like that and he'll be on to me and we'll both be in the shit. What if a drawer squeaks? Why don't I open up the roof while I'm at it; there's bound to be a secret room in there?"

"The only squeaking I can hear is this frightened mouse talking to me." she'd said. "But I'm not giving you a choice. All these houses have sophisticated alarm systems linked to the Bautzner Strasse complex and five minutes after we broke in they'd be here with the building surrounded. We wouldn't stand a chance. The only realistic time is when the alarm's off and that's only when he's at home. Just do it."

Thomas stood in shadow some distance away and watched as Bettina walked into the circle of light by the gate and pressed the intercom button, glancing up at the point of the brilliant cone of light in which she now stood, shielding her eyes from the glare of the security lamp. She pressed the button again and waited, then angrily pressed it a third time before shortly walking back to where Thomas was waiting.

"He's not answering."

"Yes. Strange. Judging by the lights he's at home. Maybe the intercom isn't working."

"Seems OK. I heard a buzz when I pressed it and, anyway, if it was broken he'd have warned me when we spoke on the phone."

A dark blue Zil cruised slowly past, moving down Böhmerstrasse, its lights chasing the shadows and illuminating the pair briefly. Instinctively Thomas had turned his back to the street and embraced and hid Bettina as the car approached, lingering until it had well gone.

"Maybe he's in the garden and can't hear the intercom. I'll try it another couple of times and if there's still no reply we'll find somewhere and phone him. If we don't get him here we'll try the office – maybe he had to go there and is just running a little late. Anyway, we can't hang about, people are going to notice."

She returned a few minutes later.

"Still nothing. Let's go. There's a restaurant not far from here, the Weisser Hirsch, just down the hill. They'll let me use the phone. You'd better wait in the car for me."

Thomas drove, dropped Bettina and parked some distance from the entrance and well away from street lamps. The street was empty but Thomas stiffened as he saw in the mirror a thickset man in a raincoat, a hat low over his eyes and with a small dog on a lead, approaching on his side of the road. It was too late to hide but as the man reached the car Thomas turned, leaned away from the pavement, and busied himself looking in the glove compartment until he saw the man safely in front and about to round a corner. Moments later Bettina strode out of the restaurant towards him, entered the car and slammed the door shut.

"Goddamn it!" she snapped. "No reply. Maybe Henkel is doing this on purpose to see how I react. Maybe he's just sitting at home in front of the TV waiting to see what I'll do next."

Thomas glanceid at his watch. "It's half an hour after you arranged to meet him here. I'd say you'd be fully justified in climbing into the garden to see if he's at home. You're on a mission from HQ. You've got a formal appointment and he's late. If you're found in the garden you can easily justify it, explain what's happened, say why you're there."

"Whereas your presence couldn't be justified, right?"

Thomas sighed, irritated by the implication that he was letting her take all the risk.

"That's not what I meant. Of course my presence could be justified as much as yours. You could confirm that. But what if Henkel's at home and sees two strangers prowling round in his garden or climbing through a window? Who knows how he'd react and, anyway, if that happens I'm hardly going to be invisible am I? I can't waltz in behind you going 'Don't mind me Mr Henkel, I just need to root through your stuff while you're with Bettina; this is the way to the study, isn't it?' But, OK, if we're careful enough we'll be able to see if he really is around without his seeing us."

Thomas drove a few metres away from the gate towards the side of the house, choosing that part of the road least lit by street lamps. The solid stone-built garden wall, topped with metal spikes, was approaching three metres in height and he parked as close to it as he could manage.

"You're not exactly dressed for this kind of thing are you?" He laughed and his glance lingered on the stylish light grey silk dress which clung to her body, a dress chosen to distract Henkel and imply that she posed little threat.

Stepping on the bumper Thomas jumped lightly on to the boot then stepped on to the Trabant's roof before she could say anything. Reaching up he grasped a spike in each hand and reverse abseiled up the wall till he could swing his left leg up into a space between a couple of spikes, twist his body and lever himself fully on to the wall. That the wall was convex and the coping stones of smoothly polished marble made balancing difficult. He anchored himself and squatted carefully between two spikes, stretching out a hand and pulling her until she could similarly grasp the spikes and haul herself up beside him. The momentum of her arrival caused them both to teeter wildly for a moment before clinging together, balancing and recovering their positions.

"Careful Bettina! These spikes are sharp. If we slip and fall on them, well ... let's say I prefer the tone of my voice as it is."

Thomas looked into the garden, scanning the borders and bushes as well as he could from their precarious position. He froze as he saw a slight movement by a tree then realised it was the breeze swaying a small hanging branch.

"Dogs? You mentioned rottweilers. What did the file say about that?"

Bettina ignored him and, sensing her embarrassment, he realised that, irritated earlier with his attitude, she'd made up the story of guard dogs, needling and testing him further.

Edging round carefully Thomas bent down, firmly grasped a spike in each hand, shuffled his feet backwards to the garden edge of the wall, lowered himself on his stretched arms and dropped almost silently into a flower bed. Bettina threw down her shoes and followed and for a few moments they stood absolutely still, hardly breathing, little fingers unconsciously linked, listening to the night sounds and letting their eyes get accustomed to the darkness so that they could start to see better the outline of the garden and the bushes and shrubs between them and the dark bulk of the house with a single window – the kitchen, Thomas realised – spilling a shaft of brightness towards them.

As they moved carefully towards the house there was a rustle of leaves in a dark part of the shrubbery to their right. They froze and Thomas could feel his heart hammering as they listened. Suddenly Bettina squealed, farted involuntarily, then laughed softly and picked up the cat which had begun making figures of eight by her feet, rubbing itself on her bare legs and purring.

"Not much of a guard tiger are you?" she said, dangling the cat in front of her and rubbing her nose affectionately to its own, then putting it down. The cat miaowed and made little scampering rushes ahead of them as they moved to the house.

They peered in through the kitchen window. The remains of a meal, complete with emptied bottle of wine and a used glass, stood by the sink but the room was empty and there was no one in the corridor which was partly visible through the open door.

They moved along the wall to the living room. The blinds on the windows looking to the front of the house were down but those on the side window were not. The room was dark but they could see outlines of the furniture, wooden cabinets and a large sofa, in the light coming through the open door from the kitchen. There appeared to be no one around.

"Let's see if any of the windows are open." Thomas whispered. "If we can find a way in, you go first and call out loudly to him. If he doesn't respond I'll follow you in. If the alarm system starts, well, we'll just have to get the hell out of it and back to the car as fast as we can."

This side window to the living room was firmly shut as were the large, white framed windows facing the front. They felt their way carefully to the far side, walking on the strips of grass by the house walls to avoid the gravel path in front. Behind them as they rounded the next corner was the main stretch of the garden, filled with ornamental flowers and long established trees. There was a French window in this wall leading into what looked like a smaller living room and when Bettina turned the handle and pushed the door it swung open silently into the room. She stepped inside and the cat scampered after her.

"Mr Henkel. Mr Henkel! It's Bettina List. We're due to meet and you didn't answer the phone. Mr Henkel. Are you there?"

She giggled to herself and whispered "So me and my hired gun, we jest nipped over your spikes, and broke into your house, overpowering your guard cat on the way. A girl's gotta do what a girl's gotta do when the intercom don't work!"

Racked with nervous laughter she stuffed the edge of a cushion into her mouth and collapsed, shaking and snorting, on to a sofa with its scarlet silk cushions. The cat twined round her legs. Thomas peered round the door and she waved her gun, gesturing to him to come in.

The house muffled the garden's night sounds and the sudden silence felt oppressive, growing and looming more obtrusive. Even the noise of the scant traffic on the street hardly reached them but that there was no sound from the alarm system was disturbing. She could feel her heart pounding in the quietness. She wondered if the alarm was a silent one, alerting security staff at the Stasi offices without warning an intruder. They'd find that out soon enough and she'd have to talk fast to explain about her meeting with Henkel. The files described Henkel as meticulous and obsessive, almost paranoid in his approach to security. His alarm system was the most sophisticated of the three and it made no sense that they could enter so easily without anything happening.

Bettina felt cold and hot at the same time. Pearls of sweat formed on her forehead and her armpits felt damp. She could even hear her heart now, she thought. She stopped for a moment, supporting herself on the back of the sofa and breathed slowly and deeply to try to calm herself. She was about to mention the alarm but moved instead to the door as Thomas cautiously flashed his torch around the room. There was a whisky glass on an occasional table set beside a dark leather easy chair next to the sofa. The bottle beside it was almost empty.

"He probably just came home. There's some whisky in the glass." he said softly. Bettina nodded and breathed deeply again, this time getting it over the barrier in her lungs and relaxing a little. He led the way into the corridor. "Let's check out the front living room, then the study down there. No fingerprints." He pulled on his black leather gloves.

The *tic tic* of their slow and careful steps sounded extravagantly loud on the polished wooden floor although they tried, but without success, to walk in time with each other towards the hallway and the front door. He could remember the layout of the house exactly. The main living room with its locked windows opened off the hall to their right and on the opposite side there was an elegant staircase to the upper floors, curving away from the front. Beside the staircase was a short spur of corridor leading to the kitchen, a lavatory and some small utility rooms. A shaded lamp with a bulbous base of oriental porcelain which looked quite modern and which stood on an occasional table just inside the hallway lit the corridor faintly.

Thomas opened the door of the front room and flashed his torch over the furniture and then the rest of the area. The room gave the impression of being little used and everything looked in order, an under drawer of a rather solid chest incongruously standing open and empty, however. They searched the room thoroughly, moving softly from place to place.

As they were about to leave a sudden bell startled them and Bettina gripped Thomas hard on his arm, relaxing when she recognised it as a phone on a side table. They stood silently, holding each other, hardly breathing, listening for

Henkel's voice answering but there was nothing, and after nine rings it stopped and the silence weighed heavily on them again.

As they moved back down the corridor towards the study they noticed a faint light spilling from under the door and they stopped to listen. The silence was complete. Bettina gestured to Thomas to move back then knocked and again called out to Henkel twice. The silence thrummed on. She beckoned Thomas, opened the door, and peered in.

Henkel, dressed in a dark brown well-tailored suit with a surprisingly exuberant tie and matching silk handkerchief in his breast pocket, was sitting leaning back in his chair at the study desk. He'd slid forward and down a little, legs stretched out in front. His head was sideways to the door and was slumped forward not quite hiding the mouth's twisted rictus of grinning welcome overlaid with a hint of surprise. The light from the green shaded lamp on the desk on the angled head made dark shadows of the eye sockets and under the man's chin.

"He's drunk, passed out." thought Thomas and then took in the neat hole ringed with blackened marks on Henkel's temple, his hand languid on the arm of the chair and a small service revolver lying on the floor under it and by his feet. There were a few spots of blood on the chair and a larger, coagulating patch on the floor. Bettina stood in the doorway and Thomas turned to her, gathering her in his arms and standing in front to shield her. His body felt numb, his stomach churned and he felt sick. As they clung to each other the cat arrived in the room and wound itself round their feet causing Thomas to shriek in surprised terror and kick out blindly.

"Jesus! Jesus Christ! We've got to get out here. Someone might be around. Someone could come, find us."

He turned to look at Henkel, looked away quickly then moved away from Bettina and looked again at Henkel's body. He breathed hard, pressed his hand hard to his mouth, swallowed, and again clung to Bettina who gently kissed him on the forehead and disengaged herself to examine Henkel more closely and pick up in her gloved hands an unsealed envelope lying on the far edge of the table. She took out the single typewritten sheet and scanned it carefully.

"Listen. It's a confession: 'I, Gerd Henkel, have stolen money from the Firm in order to repay accumulated personal debts. My shame in having betrayed the faith of my colleagues has led to this, my final decision. I hope that my colleagues and friends will be able to forgive me and that they will spare my memory from ignominy.' He's signed it at the foot, scribbled another comment which I can't quite read, something about 'testament', I think, and it's dated today."

"That explains a lot of things, I suppose, at least if everything is as it seems. Poor man." She glanced over at Henkel for a moment. "We've got to leave soon but there's stuff to do first." She spread the document on the table for Thomas to photograph then returned it to its envelope and replaced it on the table. "Take Henkel from different angles and get some general shots of the room plus anything else we find interesting. Then we can work through things and get out of here quickly."

Thomas, now calmer, photographed Henkel and the surroundings carefully then looked round the room and began opening desk drawers. All were empty other than one holding typing paper of the kind used for the letter. He glanced at the half-empty bookshelves with a few scattered volumes, mainly classic communist titles, took more shots from different angles, then looked closely at the shelves and beckoned Bettina.

"Look at this. Look at the dust traces. Look at the variations on the shelves – here and then here, there and there, here, and now over there. Someone's cleared out a lot of material pretty recently. Looking at the smudges and the traces I'd say they were probably box files rather than ordinary books. What do you think?"

The phone rang again, the study extension quieter and more pleasant than the one which had startled them earlier. Again they stood immobile while it rang then instinctively they both looked at their watches. It was just past ten o'clock.

"Let's get out of here before anything happens." Bettina said. "And we'll leave by the front door. If anyone see us we can say we had this appointment, arrived, found the door open but with no sign of Henkel so we shouted, waited a bit and then left. If we're seen climbing over the wall and a dead body found in the house there's no saying what might happen. And tomorrow, if anyone asks about my meeting, I'll say there was no answer."

Chapter 22
Sunday 14 January 1990, evening

Sunday evenings were always quiet at the Churrasco restaurant, situated as it was in Frankfurt's financial district. As the five young men, mostly dressed in expensive casual wear and with an exuberance of gold cuff-links and luxury watches - a couple of the timepieces not quite what they superficially seemed - variously arrived and made their way between the tables to the private room at the back there was hardly anyone present to pay them attention. Most of the arrivals immediately helped themselves to vodkatinis from the private bar in the corner before sitting down at the long dining table in the middle of the room.

"What a dim cunt that Patrick is." remarked Klaus to no one in particular, looking at the youngest member who had been rooting around the bottles before returning with a tall glass of fizzy red liquid he'd carefully decorated with a slice of orange, a cherry, a lurid bendy straw and a small plastic umbrella. "Got your cherryade, then?" he added loudly as Patrick reached the table, then dug Ralph in the ribs and guffawed, "Not lost his cherry either, I'd guess!"

Patrick coloured, sat down almost on his own and took a long sip of Campari. Roughly opposite him at the head of the table Erwin Hammer was working through figures on a typed sheet he'd taken from a loose leaf file and was writing notes on a pad. Hammer was the public face of Phoenix Securities, second in command to the reclusive figure who was the driving force of the organisation, the brains behind it and unknown to everyone else.

The door opened and Günther Pilsern wandered in, helped himself to a drink and slumped down opposite Klaus. He pushed his legs under the table, leaned back and stretched, then took a long drink before setting the glass down hurriedly. He looked at Erwin who was resting his chin on the edge of his fist and staring silently at him. "Sorry Boss. Phones were frantic tonight and I couldn't get away. At least news of Phoenix is spreading and there's lots of people wanting to sign up."

"Okay, we're all here now. Finally! Except Brains, obviously. He's elsewhere sorting things out for us. Let's get things going. Günther, now that you've finally turned up, let us know how … "

"Before we start I want to know something." Rainer interrupted. "You keep talking about Brains. Brains this, Brains that. But no one ever sees him. He never comes to any meetings. I've never even heard his voice. Does he really exist?" He stared at Erwin then leant his pursed mouth on his newly steepled fingers for a moment. "Or perhaps it's a way that you get a bigger slice of cake?"

Erwin stared him out and as Rainer's gaze dropped he said very carefully, "Oh, he exists all right. Damn right, he exists. All this set-up was his idea. He's a finance hotshot, knows where the gaps and the opportunities are, and he's the one who thought it all up." He looked round the table. "Don't ever, ever, make any mistake about that."

He was silent, looking down at the scribblings on his pad and adjusting some figures. No one moved.

Suddenly he smashed the heavy bottomed glass which had held his drink so hard on the table that a crack spread through it. He again looked coldly at each member in turn. A piece of glass fell off under his hand and tinkled on the table.

"Brains is the one we can thank for what we're each going to get out of this. But that's OK. If you don't like the slice you're getting … " He paused and again outstared Rainer. "If you don't like the slice you're getting, just fuck off out of Phoenix. We don't want you. We don't need you. We're better off without you. I'm not holding anyone against their will. And I absolutely don't want any passengers. Go on, just piss off. Now." He pointed theatrically at the door.

Erwin looked round the immobile group, staring at each person in turn, all of whom looked down at the table or otherwise glanced away as soon as he caught their eye.

"Rainer! Vodkatini." He swept the remains of his glass with the back of his hand towards his colleague without a glance, returned to his scribblings on the pad in silence while the others waited, then accepted his drink without thanks or comment.

"So, if you've all finished wasting our time with stupid questions, and if everyone realises just what a good deal this is for them, maybe we can finally get on with why we're here."

He turned to Ralph, a fat red-haired man on his left, at 34 the oldest of the group and a highly successful forex trader with Raiffeisenbank. "Let's start with the raw stuff, the money. Where do we stand. How is account 5409 doing?" He waved his hand round the table. "Give a little background to these guys while you're at it."

"We're doing great!" Ralph said in his thick Hamburg accent and trader growl. "No one seems to have noticed that this account is usually on the right side of the trade, and that the losers, and the occasional winners, are always the same three, four accounts - ones we also happen to control through proxies, of course. We take the money we gain on one hand …" he said while taking the salt cellar from in front of him, "and we move it to cover the losses on the other accounts." He moved the shaker close to Klaus's beer glass. "It's a zero sum game, sure, but what have you created in the process? A reputation. The bank loves Phoenix Securities now. The credit limit on 5409 was upped from one million to five last week. That should be enough for what we'll need, according to our latest projections. Right?"

"We'll get to that in a moment," Erwin said. "Let's finish with the money first. At what average rate have we bought the Ost Marks futures?"

"We have five million DM's nominal worth of contracts at an average of just over twelve to one. We bought the first million at a rate of eighteen to one just after the Wall came down, when all the Easterners kept pouring in and selling, then the next at ... "

"Spare us the details, Ralph," Erwin interrupted. "We've got a lot to cover. Twelve to one is all I need to know. When do the contracts expire?"

"They're nine-month contracts, so they expire between August and November. But we can renew them if we need ... "

"Yeah, we know finance as well as you do, Ralph. We could renew the contracts, but the exchange rate has moved to less than eight to one in the meantime. Which means the terms on new contracts will be very different. It also means we're already earning a lot of money on the contracts we have if we sold them on the open market. How much are we making?"

"We'd be making more than two million marks ... in a perfect market. Instead, according to the bank's quote, we're in the money only to the tune of around eight hundred thousand. That's mainly because the market is illiquid, but also because of fears that the Bundesbank will limit the amount of Ost Marks they'll let in when they're eventually converted to DMs. And because the traders at Salomon are fucking greedy. They know they're the market. No one else trades the stuff."

The faces around the room were grim. Eight hundred thousand was roughly twice what most of them got as bonuses each year. Split between them, it was peanuts.

Erwin laughed. "Let's not worry about the market value. We're not chasing money from futures. We'll get the real currency and exchange it at whatever official exchange the government sets. I promise you, we'll get each pfennig of our theoretical value. Two million marks could start being worth the effort, but I think we're all convinced the exchange rate will move further down. I heard the government is under a lot of pressure, especially to set up a fixed exchange rate for Eastern travellers."

He turned to Rainer, tall and balding, who looked considerably older than his thirty-three years. Working at the Bundesbank seemed to have this effect on people.

"Anything new on the exchange rate and the ceiling?"

"The situation keeps changing every day." Rainer said. "The politicians are arguing with the Bundesbank for a very low exchange rate, assuming unification happens. They want to create consensus in the East, worry that too punitive an exchange rate could cost them votes. On the other hand, the Bundesbank is scared stiff of the consequences that uniting the currencies will have on the DM. Too high an exchange rate could lead to devaluation of the DM and hyperinflation. And inflation is what the BuBa has been fighting against all these years. It depends on who gets the upper hand."

"Let's hope it's our politicians, then. Any rumours on what kind of rates are being discussed?" Erwin asked.

"I've heard the Governor say he wouldn't sign anything lower than four to one. But other people I've spoken to talk about conversations with the government where even a one to one exchange was discussed."

Klaus stared at Rainier. "One to one? The old official exchange in the East!"

"Exactly. The point seems to be that the large majority of East Germans never had any reason to exchange their Ost Marks into DMs, or anything else, for that matter. But everyone knew that the exchange with the DM was one to one. If, all of a sudden, unity comes along and the exchange is actually eight to one, they'll all be feeling a helluva lot poorer, and probably pretty angry as well. That doesn't make for a great electoral base ... so in all likelihood, the exchange rate is set to move lower."

The door opened and the young waitress, slim and pretty, Saxon-blonde and with her hair gathered in a pigtail thrown over her shoulder and nearly to her waist, looked in. "Can I bring the food in now, sir?"

Erwin grunted and beckoned with his hand while Klaus stared at her, nakedly appraising her, so that she coloured and hurriedly left. "Mmmm!" he said "What an aperitif! Very tasty! I can see she really fancies me too." He reached into his pocket and slapped his wallet on the table, daring the others. "A thousand DM says she's knickerless! Or if she's not she will be before dinner's over."

"And what about the ceiling?" asked Erwin.

"That's the other side of the same old Ost Mark." Rainer continued, smiling smugly at his own joke. "Heads we win, tails we don't lose. It's possible the Bundesbank may be forced to accept the government's argument that a lower exchange is necessary. But at that point they'll pull the brake elsewhere. The only lever they have left is the ceiling."

The waitress returned wheeling a trolley laden with plates of lobster and steak and steaming tureens of vegetables. As she bent over to collect a plate for Klaus from the lower shelf he ran his fingers quickly up an inner thigh then pulled her by her pigtail on to his lap to kiss her. One hand still up her skirt, he used his other to acknowledge the frenzied hooting, table slapping and whistling of his colleagues, noise which turned to laughter as the waitress struggled free, turned and slapped Klaus hard across the cheek and ran from the room leaving him smiling broadly, closing his eyes in feigned ecstasy and passing his fingers ostentatiously back and forth under his nose. "You'd have lost, guys! You'd have lost!"

"What do you mean by ceiling?" Patrick asked after everyone had calmed down and begun eating. His was the only non-finance background of the group and he'd been sweating to understand some of what had been said. His role was to help cover their contacts in the East.

"By ceiling he means that the Bundesbank will set a preferential rate of exchange, establishing a maximum amount of money that each individual resident in East Germany will be allowed to change into DMs at that rate. It's the whole reason we've created this network of people in the East, spinning them the story of consumer financing." Klaus said with annoyance. He had only met Patrick once before and had taken an instant dislike to him. "Thick as pigshit!" he'd thought to himself at the time.

"The grid is likely to be set according to the age of the individual." he added. "Older people will get to exchange more. That's because they've had more time to save and so should have more money. The good news is that it should be a per-head allocation − even babies and small children will count. We'll give our contacts the money and all they need to do is go to the bank and exchange it into DMs at the preferential exchange rate. We pay them a small commission and we keep all the rest."

"But why don't we just exchange the money ourselves?" Patrick asked, his fork raised. "Isn't that a lot easier, and safer?" Seeing the look of contempt on every face made him wish he hadn't asked. The seconds passing felt like hours until Rainier lifted his head from where he'd dropped it on his arm resting on the table, sighed noisily, and answered.

"Westerners won't have access to the preferential rate. And the maximum amount for the preferential exchange will be very low, probably three to six thousand marks range."

Patrick looked blank. The intricacies of exchange rates were clearly well beyond his capacity to understand. Klaus sighed, swivelled his eyes to the ceiling, then sighed again more loudly.

"The most anyone can change at the preferential rate will be what Rainer said, maybe three to six thousand. We're trading millions! Do you know what a million is? It's a thousand thousand. Work it out! At those limits and with the cash we have you'll need thousands of people to get the preferential rate, the highest possible return for the Ost Mark."

Patrick's face still hadn't registered understanding. "Jesus, Patrick, just take our word for it! This way is how we make a lot of money." Patrick stared at the table, aware of the subdued sniggering and conscious of the prickling in his eyes. He blinked hard and pushed fingers over each lid hurriedly.

"When will they decide the terms?" Erwin asked Rainier.

"It's unclear. Sometime after the elections."

"How about the network, Klaus? How's that developing?" Erwin dug into his surf'n'turf.

"We're on a roll - in the hay!" He grunted a couple of times, jerking his clenched fist upwards in time to the noises. "We've got over a thousand direct contacts all over the country. That means we could have anywhere between seven and ten thousand people to be financed. At let's say four thousand marks each that would get us to thirty or forty million Ost Marks to exchange. We still have a few months to go and the phone keeps ringing and ringing." Klaus bragged. "By the way, a few people in the network are starting to ask intelligent, difficult questions. We need to plan a meeting to present the details."

"Good job there, Klaus. A final point." Erwin added. "We still need to finalise how we keep control of the money once it's exchanged. The government will set a fairly short window in which to exchange and, anyway, people in one town or village just aren't all going to go to the banks on the same day. So there's no way we can be present in a hundred different cities to check in person that the exchange gets done as we want and then get our hands on our DMs by the next day. That's why we needed help from some organisation which is everywhere in the DDR, including the smallest towns. There's only two of them, the SED and the Stasi. How are we doing on that front, Patrick?"

"It's not easy." Patrick replied. "We need high level people involved to ensure we have the right backing. And the country is melting," he hesitated, thought of his earlier humiliation, then went for it, "the country is melting like chocolate on a, onawhore'stwat." He reddened and blinked. "The SED's power base will vanish right after the elections." He leant back, blew out his cheeks, looked at the ceiling and crossed his arms.

"They're walking zombies." Klaus said. "All those damned communists are." he said, emphasizing the "all" and looking at Patrick.

"Anyway," Patrick added, ignoring his tormentor, "we're making better progress with the other group. They're more street-wise, and more ready to act. But they want a major slice of the cake."

"How much?" Erwin asked.

"The first meeting I had, the guy made no commitment and asked a lot of questions. After a couple of weeks I decided to contact someone else. But the other contact said half a million − and that's Deutsche Marks − was the minimum to even start discussions. That's when I told him I would have to talk directly with the people in charge. Then yesterday I heard that the Stasi, it's called the ANFS as of last month, is being disbanded. In fact, maybe that's already happened and it's become part of the Ministry of the

Interior. I called him again this morning and he says that for the deal to work it's now a million. DM. That's because he's got to keep the network going on a private basis and that costs, he says. And he wants at least a third of it upfront, and with no guarantees. Trouble is, there's not much we can do to shift him and he's probably the best person to sort things out anyway."

"Actually, if our information's correct the exchange rate should move further down. If it does we can give them their million and still have a boatful for ourselves. But you'd better act fast to get it agreed before things get obvious. And we need to make sure we retain control or else this whole thing falls apart. Make sure you understand that Patrick and get back to me immediately if you have any doubt."

Erwin smacked his hand hard on the table and, standing, raised his glass in a toast. "To the common Fatherland!"

"And to pretty little knickerless waitresses!" smirked Klaus, as everyone murmured and drank.

Chapter 23
Sunday 14 January 1990, evening and on to early morning

Bettina had driven back slowly and carefully from Henkel's house, the nervousness of the earlier drive subdued. Again, neither she nor Thomas had said much, spending the time instead mulling over what had happened, trying to sort out in their minds what Henkel's death might mean. Grabbing sandwiches and drinks in the Dornbusch kitchen, lit only by a small lamp standing by the kitchen range, they'd sat in companionable silence long after they'd finished eating as if the idea of lying in full darkness and ending this fraught day had to be delayed, as if sleeping and waking would make Henkel's death certain, make it more absolute. Once she'd stretched her hand across the table and with the tips of her fingers stroked the back of Thomas's hand lightly for a moment. He looked at her and smiled complicitly but when he rotated his hand to take hers she rose abruptly and stood at the window looking out into the solid darkness of the yard.

They'd trudged upstairs. When Bettina returned from the bathroom Thomas was lying staring at the ceiling and as she approached he turned on his far side and curled tightly into himself. In bed she propped herself on her elbow for some moments looking at him, then switched off the light and lay down well away on her own side of the mattresses listening to his breathing soften and become more regular. She lay on her back, as Thomas had first done, staring upwards as if the meaning of Henkel's suicide would suddenly loom out of the darkness, bringing understanding to her racing mind.

"He was just sitting there, looking at us. Just, just staring. And smiling, almost smiling." The voice had cracked and there was a catch to it.

She was nearly asleep but his voice jerked her awake.

"Thomas, I thought you were asleep. Yes, it was awful, wasn't it? You never really get used to it, I suppose, but the first time is always pretty bad."

The sob, turned quickly into an extended cough, made her turn and stretch out her hand to Thomas's waist. He said nothing further and continued to present his back but edged closer so that her forearm was now across his belly and chest, her covered breasts just brushing his back until she angled slightly away. He freed and moved his arm, trapping hers on his waist in turn and letting his forearm rest along her thigh, his fingers light round the curve of her leg above her knee, bare where her nightdress had rucked up. She did nothing to stop him, changing her own position slightly to better fit the curve of his buttocks in her lap. He could feel on his skin there a slight springiness under the fabric and he pressed back. Again they lay silently in their mutual warmth, more comfortable in each other than for a long time.

"Was it really suicide?" Thomas asked.

"No, I don't think so."

Again there was silence.

"There was nothing in the files about his living wildly." she said. "He didn't gamble, maybe the odd small bet on a horse or something, but nothing regular or serious. He dressed well and lived well, liked good food and wines, ate out quite a bit but well inside his income levels and, anyway, he'd have wangled a lot of that as expenses on Party business."

"What about women? Girlfriend in a fancy flat somewhere, prostitutes, nightclubs, trips to the West?"

"There was a wife earlier but they'd divorced, oh, '67 or so, and there seems to have been no more contact. She's remarried and lives in Bonn, apparently. There were no children. There's no record of any regular visits to brothels or of prostitutes visiting him. There have been a few girlfriends but just very ordinary relationships which seemed to just run their course and peter out. Last one finished a year or so back after a couple of years, Angela, an informer and a waitress in one of the restaurants he'd go to. He may have showed off, taking her to the odd lavish weekend in Berlin but that's probably as far as it went."

She laughed. "Pretty boring guy really! Unimaginative. Not my type at all, for all his Party status."

Thomas sensed her head turning slightly towards him.

"He joined the Party's youth wing and later became an informer, trained as an accountant, apparently met Mielke somewhere and so got more involved. Kept his nose clean, learned quickly how the system worked, enjoyed the things his position brought him, became recognised as reliable and someone able to keep his mouth shut. Moved around a bit between offices, small places first then Leipzig, Berlin and seven years ago became Treasurer here and moved straight into his smart house in the Prussian quarter."

"Enemies?" asked Thomas. "Treasurers probably get to know all sorts of things people sometimes want to keep hidden. And if they're on the make as nearly everyone in this fucking Party seems to be now, he's probably covered up quite a lot of dodgy stuff."

There was a pause.

"Blackmail." said Bettina. "Maybe he was blackmailing somebody for money, or maybe for power. I remember there was talk of his taking over the Berlin Treasurer's job. Maybe that's what he was after and he pushed things just too far."

"Or maybe he was being blackmailed."

"Maybe, but why kill him? Why kill the golden goose?"

"Perhaps he'd had enough. Perhaps it really was suicide. He'd run up debts and was being hassled to clear them and when the money came in he just took it, like he said. Afterwards he was ashamed, got drunk and put the gun to his head. It's what people do sometimes if they're in too deep."

Thomas turned towards Bettina, reached over and switched on the bedside lamp. He leant on one elbow and looked down at her. She raised an eyebrow and shook her head slowly a fraction.

"No." he said "You're right. It just doesn't fit, does it? He was killed, that's for sure. But who did it? Who wanted him that badly out of the way?"

A lock of hair had fallen over Bettina's cheek and Thomas reached over and gently moved it behind her ear. He lowered his head slightly to kiss her but felt her stiffen and turned the move into a clumsy nod. "Who could have wanted him dead? And why?"

"There was something Dieter said to me recently ... it was about unification, something he'd heard about hiring the Firm to keep tabs on people being funded to change money into Deutsche Marks. Seems the top guys are looking at fixing pensions for themselves when everything changes. Maybe the money was something to do with that."

"You didn't mention this before." Thomas looked at her and wondered what else she was keeping back.

"Dieter doesn't know the details, it was just something he'd heard and then he started joining up the dots. I think he thinks that it's maybe that organisation from Frankfurt that's involved somehow, the one he wants you to find out about, Phoenix something, isn't it?"

"Phoenix Securities. Phoenix was what they called the currency when the modern Greek state was founded last century. Meant to signify rebirth, apparently, but then it became the drachma." He frowned as she yawned and glanced up. "What else do you know about this Phoenix and what else has Dieter told you but not me?"

She shrugged. "It didn't seem important right then. I've told you now anyway."

"Did Dieter tell you why he's looking into Phoenix, why he wants me to check up on them?" He looked straight into her eyes. "It would help me know what to ask. I have the impression he didn't tell me the whole story."

"You're probably right. Same with me. But Dieter never does tell anyone the whole story. It's not because he doesn't trust you, or me — it's just too dangerous. If one of us gets caught and talks, the whole project could fail."

"Hmm, the classic cell demarcation strategy. Makes sense, I suppose." He lay back and folded his arms behind his head and they were silent for a bit. "OK. I'll call Stephan tomorrow, maybe, as Dieter suggested. He's travelling all over East Germany now, looking for possible bank branches for Deutsche's new network. Maybe he knows something, come across Phoenix or something. I guess Dieter will be following through what you've just told me about the Stasi."

"If you find out anything useful about Phoenix and just what it's up to we might end up having to do some more work on it ourselves, find out if and how the Stasi's involved with them, perhaps. That's if they are."

"They're going to be involved, somehow, somewhere anyway. It's all starting to make some kind of sense. The Stasi network's still in place and they're not going to pass up the chance to make money. They get the money into Dresden supposedly to pay agents or operational costs or whatever, all legitimate and signed by Henkel. But it's not really for that at all, it's for, it's for, well, maybe something to do with this Phoenix, though we don't now yet what that is, maybe something else entirely ... Anyway, maybe Roehrberg or someone like that's behind it. Henkel finds out and threatens them for a cut but doesn't realise the extent of it and the power behind it and so wakes up dead."

"Hmm. Maybe, but I don't really think that holds together very well. That's a lot money that's gone. What are they going to do with it? They can't just change it into DM and lose it, even with the resources open to them. And they must know that even with the upheaval and confusion going on it's not just going to be forgotten. Not that amount. It's much too big."

"Well, maybe they'll buy up stuff, you know, houses, companies, factories ..."

"Mills! The mill!" She sat up and smacked a fist into one palm. "Mills, factories, all those things are cheap now but won't stay cheap. That's it! Anyone buying now will make a killing. Maybe that's what the money was really for. Doesn't explain Henkel's death, though. He was an ambitious apparatchik, basically, and I don't suppose he had that much integrity. He wouldn't shop anyone if he found something out, he'd cut himself in if he could. Hmm. Maybe your blackmail idea has something in it."

She smiled at him, snuggled down under the huge meringue of an eiderdown, then turned on her side, her back against his chest. With the back of his fingers he idly stroked her hair, sometimes lifting strands free and letting them trail through his fingers. Half asleep, she murmured and settled closer obliging him to move his hips away so as not to press his arousal against her.

Now more awake Thomas slid his lower arm through the gap by her shoulder, settling her neck in his elbow, then brought his forearm round to rest the tips of his fingers on her upper shoulder before letting his arm slide with slow, disingenuous intent back down as if his muscles had relaxed in sleep so that his wrist and then, as he settled into a more comfortable position for them both, his palm naturally rested where he could cradle her lower breast. She murmured again, settled herself slightly and as he swirled his fingers as if trailing the faintest of arpeggios he felt through the cotton the stiffening of a nipple. She murmured again and nestled in closer as they both fell asleep.

The alarm jangled, marking seven thirty and wrenching them awake. Bettina shot upright in bed, yawning, rubbing her eyes and shaking the sleep out of her head. She looked down at Thomas and her eyes softened.

"I had the strangest dream." she said. "Can't remember details but you were in it, I think." She nodded. "You were." She paused and smiled slowly. "Safe. I felt safe and warm and at home and I wanted to stay there and we'd forgotten all this shitty Henkel stuff we've now got to deal with."

As Bettina showered Thomas lay with his arms behind his head, thinking about her rapid changes of mood, particularly as she moved into operations mode as now. "But it is developing." he thought. "It's moving. That fucking alarm clock! If only, if only ... "

He reached out to the files Bettina had left on the table and began reading about Henkel, searching for some clue in his background as to why he'd apparently killed himself. Bettina returned, wrapped in large towel, a smaller one turbanning her head.

"Anything interesting?"

"Nah, boring stuff so far." He looked up and smiled at her. "But of course if your towel drops ... "

"C'mon Thomas. Get up!" She clapped her hands imperiously and then shrieked as the large towel started to unwind. Securing it and trapping the end with one arm she grabbed the eiderdown and partially flicked it off Thomas's body. She giggled and pulled harder but Thomas easily overcame her grip and pulled the eiderdown back over himself.

"OK, if you're going to laze around there just look away, please, while I get dressed."

Thomas turned to face the wall. He knew how marvellously lean and fit she was, both from being with her so often and from lying close the night before and it was with difficulty that he stopped himself glancing in her direction. "Maybe by accident?", he thought.

"Dieter. Umm, I expect Dieter said whether he thought Henkel, no, I mean Roehrberg don't I, whether Roehrberg was behind all this. How long has Roehrberg been there? Henkel's going on holiday soon, isn't he? No, I mean Dieter. Roehrberg, that is. Does he go to expensive places too? A lot depends on a person's character, and there's very little on that in the files." He eased his hip from the slightly sticky patch on the sheet and forced his thoughts back to their mission.

"Holiday? Dieter? Expensive places? What are you on about? Dieter knows Roehrberg from his time in Berlin and was impressed with him, and that's rare. The files are compiled by bureaucrats who simply talk to informers and note everything that's been reported, and that's why they only have limited use. No, Dieter made no comments, except that I should be very careful whatever I do."

"I know he thinks a lot of you but I found it very surprising that he asked you to handle such a delicate and dangerous affair single-handedly."

"Ah, but he didn't, did he? He asked both of us. You can turn round now, guardian angel. What do you think I should wear tonight, this white dress or this shirt and trouser suit?"

Thomas looked frankly at her, at the clothes she held up, and then back again. "Nothing!" he thought. "Absolutely nothing at all would be just fine for me."

"The dress would be good." he said.

Chapter 24
Monday 15 January 1990, morning onwards

There was a squat brick chimney stack at the north end of the Stasi's Dresden HQ, the only clue to the building's earlier life as a factory. On one side it overlooked the Elbe, less than a mile away, with the city, now partially hidden by the morning fog, sprawling in the background. Behind the building there was a large car park and it was here that Bettina left her car. The lowering threat of the building and the clammy feel of the fog affected her mood and made her think nostalgically for a moment of being back warm and safe in bed, luxuriating in her dream before the alarm clock shattered it.

As she walked towards the entrance Bettina remembered how she'd taken a dislike to the building when she'd first seen it as a little girl and before she even knew anything about its function. Clearly designed to contain secrets and prevent casual curiosity about what went on behind the heavily barred sashes and the rows of tiny windows, barred in turn, it was ugly and intimidating. In the middle of the building there was a tall rectangular frame holding many minute glazed openings, the whole covered with yet another of the ubiquitous metal gratings. As it loomed out of the fog as she approached she saw that its grubby white surface was stained and soiled, the paint damaged in places with water dripping down from the roof.

The security guard at the entrance glanced at her identity card without enthusiasm or interest and sent her up the stairs to the first floor. There she met Gina Schmidt, Roehrberg's secretary, who led her down the corridor and into Roehrberg's spacious office. He got up from behind his desk, walked over smiling and shook her hand warmly.

"Good morning, Miss List, good morning. How good of you to come. I hope you found your way easily to our offices." Here he waved his hand in a vague gesture as if apologising for the fact that they weren't as grand as she was no doubt used to. And taking full personal responsibility for the weather, added "I'm so sorry about this dull and rather dreary day but it's what we often have at this time of year, I'm afraid. Do sit down Miss List. Coffee?"

She shivered involuntarily in response then sat down at one end of the large leather sofa indicated and placed her briefcase on the low glass-topped table in front. "Thank you. That would be very welcome, particularly after the fog outside."

She judged his height at around 1.8m and thought that his file picture didn't do him justice, couldn't bring out except faintly his charisma and air of confident authority. He was handsome, with well groomed hair, clean shaven, regular, chiselled features, and was wearing an understated but clearly expensive suit which looked as if it had been tailored for him, and a pair of hand-made black shoes. His voice was firm, almost without regional accent, and well modulated and she caught herself listening to as a series of sounds and so missing the sense of what he was saying. "He could be an actor" she thought "and probably a highly successful one at that." She caught a hint in the air of some musky scent.

She shook her head slightly and consciously made herself more alert. "I must be very careful." she thought, remembering how his manner when she entered his office had almost disarmed her, instinctively made her feel friendly towards him, privileged that he was paying her attention.

She looked away, took out a file and busied herself with the papers it held. When she looked up again she saw that Roehrberg was in a large leather armchair at an angle to her and which he appeared to dominate, despite its size. He was looking at her, playing to perfection the role of the courteous host giving his guest all the time necessary to settle down yet now, alert, she noticed the line of his mouth and the hardness in his steady gaze. Annoyed with herself as soon as it happened she found herself unable to hold his gaze and again had to look away.

"How very good of you to come." he repeated. She looked sharply at him but he appeared to be sincere. "We're really appreciative of that, of the help that you, as a representative of central office, will be able to give us to solve this mystery. It would be a difficult situation at any time, of course, but it's a bigger mess than usual, now that we've officially been disbanded."

She noticed a slight smile flicker across his face as he laced his fingers together and leaned forward, apparently to confide something to her. Crossly she reminded herself that they were not partners working together to solve a mystery but antagonists. Her role was to suspect Roehrberg and his colleagues, to find out exactly how and why the money had been stolen - and now the further puzzle of why Henkel had died. "I must be very, very careful and keep alert" she reminded herself. She pulled a pen and pad from her briefcase, breathed deeply, and interrupted firmly." Have you had many changes since the announcement?" she asked.

"Well, we've had to clear our prison, here in this building. We had twelve prisoners. Nine are now with the police in normal cells, three we've discharged. The Interior Ministry still hasn't told us which personnel are to be transferred to them and which aren't, and what's more people are resigning every day. I'm unsure if we'll even receive in time the money to pay the salaries at the end of the month. It's difficult to keep things running properly in these conditions. Very difficult."

Roehrberg's secretary entered with a tray and transferred china cups and saucers and jugs of hot milk and coffee to the glass table. Roehrberg waited and smiled encouragingly at Bettina who found herself pouring coffee for each of them. With irritation she took a biscuit without offering him the plate. She leaned back, disappeared awkwardly into the sofa, a diminished figure, and struggled back to an upright position.

"So Mr Roehrberg, I've been told ... "

"Rudolf, please. It's from my days in the United States and I rather prefer it." Again there was the urbane tone, the sense of privileged inclusion being offered to her. Again she picked up the slight undertow of menace.

"Fine. Rudolf. OK, fine. Please go through what happened with this financing, this money that's got lost. Please could you tell me when it disappeared and anything else of relevance. I really need to know this." She didn't like the way she had formulated the request. It was stupid and unprofessional, the words and phrasing of a supplicant, she thought. But Roehrberg was effortlessly dominating and had taken control of the meeting, subtly implying that her role as a woman was to deal with domestic matters but he would graciously allow her some of his valuable time. She found it difficult to articulate her thoughts clearly, censoring her comments in case she displeased him.

"There's not a great deal of detail I can give you on that. You will know, I'm sure, that it's Henkel who, as Treasurer, deals with all that side of it and has responsibility for most things to do with the financing of the Dresden operation."

"You've not had a chance to meet Henkel yet, I suppose?" he added. He raised his eyebrows briefly and paused, looking at her. "When exactly was it you arrived in Dresden?"

Bettina felt a sudden chill as she remembered Henkel lounging in his chair, blood on his temple and the floor, looking at them with his lop-sided smile as they carefully opened the door. Just how much did Roehrberg know? Had Henkel told him that he and Bettina were to meet? If he knew that and already knew of Henkel's killing he was astute enough to work out that she probably knew about it as well and would probe to find out how much more she knew. This was going to be far more difficult than she'd imagined. At least he didn't know about Thomas. Well, she hoped not. She swallowed and drank some coffee.

"Yes, I knew that Henkel was, is, Treasurer. I hope to talk with him shortly." She swallowed again. "I appreciate you may not concern yourself with the detail but don't you have overall responsibility? You manage at a high level what the funds are requisitioned for and what they're used for."

"Yes, that's true. In both respects. You'll have to ask Henkel about the detail but, at least within the limits of what I have to keep confidential, I can tell you some things from that higher level. These particular funds were to be used for three international missions in France, England and West Germany. I'd prefer not to mention the specifics – unless, of course, you feel that knowing is of vital importance to you. They are classed at the highest security levels."

"'Don't get any ideas about probing too deeply, my girl', that's what you mean." she thought, and again she felt a shiver run down her spine.

"No, I don't think that's going to be particularly relevant, not right now at any rate." she said. "If there's something there that we might need to follow up then we can perhaps discuss that with you later."

"We?"

Bettina looked at him.

"You said 'we'. I thought you'd come to Dresden alone." He rested his chin on his hands stared impassively at her. Again she had to drop her gaze.

"We? Ah, yes. Me and my colleagues in the office in Berlin, I mean."

There was silence. Roehrberg drank some coffee and looked again at her, waiting politely, head very slightly cocked.

"Because of the reorganisation Dieter couldn't spare anyone to come, ah, to work on this so he asked me to take on the investigation of the missing funds myself." She felt sick. "He said I could count on help from your office if I needed it."

"Of course." said Roehrberg. "That goes without saying. We'll be very happy, within our currently limited staff means of course, to give you all the help you need. I'll instruct Henkel and Spitze, that's my deputy, that that's the case." He looked at her for a moment. "And I'll let Modrow know that we've promised to keep a close eye on you. You can be confident of that."

He glanced at the antique clock standing on a small table at the back of the room.

"Would you forgive me, Miss List. I have an important telephone call to take in a few minutes but as Henkel should be in now you might it useful to talk with him and then the three of us, or four, Spitze as well, could meet later - for lunch perhaps, if you'll permit me."

He returned to his desk without waiting for any response, lifted the telephone receiver, dialled a short code, waited, then put the phone down and pressed a white button; moments later his secretary appeared.

"Gina, do you know where Mr Henkel is? I've just tried his office but there's no reply."

"He's not arrived yet, Mr Roehrberg. Mr Spitze was also asking for him just now. I'll give him a call at home, see if he's been delayed for some reason, and I'll let you know."

Roehrberg looked at the clock again before deciding. It was five to ten.

"Thank you. Yes, give him a call. He may have forgotten that our colleague from head office, Miss List, was due today. It's important that he talk with her. Tell Spitze to keep himself free as well. We'll all go out to lunch together later. Please make reservations at the usual place. 12 noon." He sat down again in the leather armchair and beamed at Bettina.

"Do you know Dresden at all Miss List. It's a beautiful city. *Was* a really beautiful city and is becoming one again. I'd be pleased to show you round some of the historic sights this evening or perhaps tomorrow if that interests you."

"I know Dresden well, as it happens, but thank you. Now, when the money arrived ... "

"Ah, but perhaps only the well known public places, Miss List. It's the hidden Dresden that's so fascinating. For instance, when the Semper Oper was being reconstructed workmen discovered a small, bricked-up room in the cellars and in that they came across ... "

The phone on the desk rang, suddenly and harshly, making Bettina jump.

"Excuse me. This will be the call I mentioned. I must answer it but I'll put him on hold for a moment while you leave. We can meet later and discuss things with the others." Roehrberg stood and lifted the receiver on the sixth ring.

"Roehrberg! ... Yes? ... What?! ... I can't believe that. When did this happen?" He listened for some moments and Bettina could hear an excited squawking coming from the instrument.

"Thank you." He said and replaced the receiver slowly in its cradle. His face had gone grey and the former authoritative expression had disappeared. The skin edging his eyes and his mouth drooped slightly and for a moment or two he looked shrunken and much older before recovering something of his earlier manner. He sat there in silence at his desk looking at but apparently not registering Bettina. He blinked, then screwed up his eyes and passed a hand over them, holding it in place for a moment before drawing it down to hold his pursed mouth. He took a deep breath and addressed the room without looking directly at Bettina.

"That was the police." There was a long silence. "A woman called them and said she had found Henkel dead. His cleaning lady. It seems he may have committed suicide in his study." He stood up, leaning on his desk as if to gather strength. "Please excuse me but I should go and see what's happened. Miss Schmidt will look after you." He crossed the office, opened the door but then turned back to Bettina. "I apologise, I should have asked if you wanted to join me. It's just that it's probably not a pleasant sight, and instinctively ... But I do understand that you might want to come. It could be important."

Bettina rose, gathering her things and trying to bring the right note of surprise and dismay to her voice. "Dead?! Henkel? And suicide?! That's dreadful. I'm so sorry. How terrible."

"It is terrible, isn't it? Yes. Terrible." he repeated. "He was a good man and a great colleague. I don't understand. I just don't understand what could have led him to this."

As they walked to Roehrberg's car, the latest model of Lada, Bettina watched him carefully. As far as she could tell, he looked and acted genuinely shocked and distressed. His remarks to her seemed sincere and she began to wonder about her earlier suspicions.

In two or three minutes they were Henkel's home where a pair of agents were waiting for them. Bettina glanced at the garden, noting its beauty and serenity and contrasting that with her feelings of the previous evening. She was tense, fearful that they might have left traces of their visit in Henkel's house or in the garden, even expecting Thomas to stroll out of one of the rooms as they arrived. She wondered suddenly if the cat was about. As they entered she looked around carefully to see if anything was out of place but could see no suspicious marks of an earlier visit to the house.

"He's in the study." the first agent said. "This way. It happened yesterday, apparently between six and eight in the evening. A single shot through the head."

Bettina followed Roehrberg and the agent, flinching as the familiar scene she had revisited mentally so often appeared. Two policemen were standing in front of the desk taking pictures. The more senior one, a tall and skinny man of around forty, shook Roehrberg's hand then gave him the letter she'd read earlier.

"We've taken prints." he said. "It doesn't matter if you handle it."

Roehrberg read carefully then handed the letter to Bettina who took it in her fingers and immediately regretted holding it.

"I guess this clears up the mystery. I still can't believe it, though. Henkel ... ending up like this. We had lunch together yesterday."

Bettina stared at the letter for the time it might have taken to read it, glanced at the sentences, then handed it back. As she was doing so another man entered the room. From his picture in the files, Bettina recognised him as Spitze.

He nodded to Bettina and turned to Roehrberg. "I can't believe it. I just heard and immediately ... "

"Such a tragedy. A tragedy." Roehrberg said. "If he'd spoken to us, maybe we could have helped in some way. He's confessed to having taken the money, Heinz. That's why he committed suicide. He said it was to pay off debts he'd run up."

Spitze's face was impossible to read. Bettina noticed he had kept the same expression from the moment he had stepped in to the room. He hadn't flinched even when he first saw the gaping hole in Henkel's head or the blood on the floor but had stared coolly at each in turn.

"Can I have everyone's attention please?" There was silence in the room as Roehrberg spoke. "The final wish of our colleague, Gerd Henkel, is to be respected. His memory must not be soiled by this tragic death. I want to see no mention of the word suicide anywhere, in the press or in any reports on the incident. There must be no mention of a violent death. I'm sure I can count on the full cooperation of all of you in referring to his death as a result of ... as a result of a sudden and fatal illness. A heart attack, perhaps, something of that kind. The full details will become known after the autopsy. Our resident doctor will conduct that privately, of course." He glanced over at Spitze, held his gaze briefly.

He looked at everyone in turn while he spoke. "I shall speak with Modrow. I know he will also understand that it's in nobody's interest to wash dirty linen in public just before unification."

He flicked a finger at Bettina to follow, turned on his heel and strode from the room.

Chapter 25
Monday 15 January 1990, morning onwards

The bedroom was chilly and Thomas lay and dozed for half an hour or more after Bettina had left before finally forcing himself to get up. The bathroom was even colder, the window partially open at the top, and as Thomas glanced out into the yard he could see tendrils of fog curling round the trees and in the distance some street lamps giving out a patchy, ghostly light in places. He shivered, splashed water on his face and neck and shaved quickly, then rushed back into the bedroom and dressed in warm clothing.

There was no sign of Frau Dornbusch in the kitchen but a note told him that she'd gone to visit her sister and would return in the afternoon, reminding him to lock the door carefully when he left and adding he should borrow the bicycle in the shed if he needed it. He made coffee and breakfasted on warmed rolls, spread with local farm butter and Frau Dornbusch's apricot jam, and some ham and cheese he discovered in the pantry. It was now just after ten and as he drank the last of the coffee he knew that he could no longer put off going out into the dreary day to follow Dieter's instructions to find out what he could about Phoenix. He must phone Stephan as well, he thought, to ask if he'd come across Phoenix and to check out when he was going to be in Dresden so that they could all meet for dinner.

The fog seemed to penetrate everywhere and despite his layers of clothing Thomas felt chilled as he wheeled the old and somewhat rattley bike from the shed and started pedalling up the road away from the house. When he got to the area of small shops he'd been seeking the fog was almost gone, dispersed by a gusty, cold wind from the north-east bringing slight flurries of snow. He found a phone sheltered by two buildings and began trawling through the list of informants' numbers which Dieter had given him, a pile of coins ready on the shelf.

It was frustrating work. Several of the numbers appeared to have been discontinued and from number after number there was no reply. "Probably escaped to the West when the Wall came down." thought Thomas with irritation as yet another number gave the unobtainable tone.

Finally a number connected. No one spoke but Thomas could hear harsh breathing at the other end and then a hacking cough which crackled on and on. He waited and then just as he was about to speak the phone was put down. He dialled the number again, speaking as soon as it connected.

"Herr Pomberg?" There was a long silence over which he could hear some strained breathing. "Herr Pomberg?" he asked again, firmly.

"Moight be." said a woman's voice, rasping and stifling a cough. "'Oo wants 'im?

"Heinz Schmidt. I just want to talk to him about a company called Phoenix."

Again there was silence, followed by a faint scuffling sound, and then more silence. Thomas was about to hang up when a man's voice growled in.

"Don't know nuttin' about any Fee-nucks." it said. "Wossit anyways? And 'ow'd you get my name? 'Oo are you?" The accent was strong and Thomas had difficulty understanding what was being said.

"It's a company making loans to people in the East. I was told you might be able to help me, Mr Pomberg ... "

"Domburg! Hans Domburg. I knows your gyme, mister, you wi' your fancy Wessie voice. We doan' need no loans 'ere so just you stop botherin' we. Go'way." And the phone was put down.

The next two numbers Thomas tried were discontinued and that this was followed by another wrong number added to his growing irritation. Finally he made contact with someone who seemed genuinely to be connected with Phoenix and got an invitation to visit immediately once Thomas agreed that some money might be forthcoming for help.

Tracing the address on his map Thomas found that it was right on the other side of Dresden. Given the hills it would probably take him half an hour to get there, he thought, and that the fog had now given way to a light sleety drizzle with the chilly wind showing no sign of letting up made him feel greatly dispirited as he pedalled off.

The man who answered the door, Hans Treufel, was around fifty, seriously overweight, unshaven and dressed in soiled brown trousers held up with a pair of braces under which showed what appeared to be a pyjama jacket loosely buttoned over a grubby vest. A splash of old egg yolk decorated the man's front, stopped on its way to the floor by the uplands of his belly. According to the file Treufel had been a medium ranking Stasi officer but had been demoted for some misdemeanour which the file didn't specify. It appeared that he'd been more than merely an informant although again the file said nothing about this or about his actual role.

Treufel led the way down a narrow corridor into a small living room, stiflingly hot and noxious with the smell of stale tobacco smoke mixed with rancid fat. A dirty plate, some half eaten bread and a frying pan lay in the hearth. His manner was unctuous and sly and Thomas instinctively took an immediate dislike to him.

The man pointed to a small rexine-covered settee and sat down in a matching armchair which had been a long time away from any showroom. He took a cold cigar from the mantelpiece, held it to the blazing gas fire at his feet till it started to smoulder, drew on it and puffed till it was going to his satisfaction, tapped the ash on to the thin carpet in front of him, and turned to Thomas.

"Let's see the money first and then we can get started. I can tell you all you want know about Phoenix. It'll cost you, mind. But I can tell you're a man what's clear what he's after, wants the secret stuff, the best bits." He took a puff on his cigar and blew the smoke in failed rings towards the browned ceiling. "You've come to the right place. It's not many that knows what I knows."

Resisting an urge to leave immediately Thomas pulled out his wallet, riffled ostentatiously through the contents and chose a fifty Ost Mark note, laying it on the table between them. "Let's start with that and if what you say's any use to me there'll be more." Treufel snatched it and folded it into his pyjama pocket.

"It'll have to be DMs" said Treufel. "Ost Marks is no good to me now. I'm just taking this one to save you having to get rid of it somewhere else. OK. Phoenix. Yes. I know pretty much everything about Phoenix. You just ask me what you want to know."

They looked at each other. "Tell me what it does, then. And what's your part in it? Who are the people behind it?"

"Ah, yes, Phoenix. What do you know about it already?" asked Treufel slyly. "I can tell you a lot. You've come to the right place."

Thomas waited, set his jaw and then broke the silence. "Are you part of Phoenix? What do you have to do with it?"

"Well, it's not like I actually *do* anything yet." said Treufel carefully "But me and Fritz, we're ready just as soon as we're needed. They're relyin' on us, see. And that's going to be very soon. It's about loans, see, making loans to people that needs 'em. People here in this street and in other streets round the corner. Fritz keeps a book about who needs money and then later we'll go and give it to 'em, see."

"And who's behind it?"

"Oh, they're big. Very big. Yes, they're very big, see. We've not actually met 'em yet but that's going to be very soon."

Thomas stared at him.

Treufel tapped the side of his nose and leaned forward. "It's a man called Brains is behind it." He looked around the room carefully as if expecting Brains himself suddenly to appear and silence him for saying too much. He lowered his voice. "Yes, he's behind it, see. Worked it all out how we Ossies would need money once we joined wi' you lot and so that's why they're making all these free loans, see."

"Have you met him?"

For a moment it seemed as if Treufel would claim that distinction but then he shook his head slightly and sat back in the chair. "Not yet." he said "Not yet. But me and Fritz we'll do that soon enough. They're relyin' on us, see. Nobody ever really sees Brains. Nobody. Works high up in the Finance Ministry he does, has the ear of the Chancellor he does, and so he's got to be careful, see. Once everything's fixed then the Chancellor will explain the plans publicly, see, and we start helping the Ossies with these loans and this Brains can come clean about how he got it all started. But Fritz and me, we're an important part of the whole thing, here in Dresden anyway. They're relyin' on us, see."

He fingered the note in his pocket then leaned forward again. "There's more I could say but, well, it's secret and I've been trained to forget." He coughed and hugged himself. "Maybe another note, a bigger one, would help my memory."

Thomas rose, bit back the words that came to mind, exhaled abruptly, and said "Thank you Mr Treufel. You've been most helpful." He walked rapidly to the door, let himself out, started to close it and then left it swinging, mounted his bike and pedalled off at speed before realising he was riding out of town and turned back towards the centre. In a short while he came to more shops and pulled up beside another public telephone. This time his first call was successful, another informer ready to talk if there was cash to help him remember things. The address wasn't far and ten minutes later Thomas was in the Neustadt, on the corner of Obergraben and Königstrasse.

He rang the doorbell and after a moment heard a bolt being drawn back and the door grinding slowly open to reveal a young man only slightly older than Thomas. Looking at his unkempt reddish hair and square glasses, the effect finished with sandals, a pair of faded jeans and a torn red tee shirt, Thomas was reminded of some left wing intellectuals he'd met in West Berlin. He had always imagined that informers would look inconspicuous, something like human moles whereas Alfred Gertner was exactly the opposite, someone immediately conspicuous in a crowd of hundreds.

Alfred took Thomas to the living room and indicated the sofa while he pulled up a chair for himself. The apartment was very small but decorated with considerable taste and style. It was pleasantly warm and a marked contrast to Treufel's.

"So, you're interested in knowing more about Phoenix Securities. Before we start, just a quick warning. I am an informer, but I don't provide access to the sources. So don't ask me names or phone numbers. You understand, I need to protect myself. If someone found out I'm squealing, I wouldn't have a bright future ahead." Alfred spoke in a high-pitched voice which grated on Thomas' ears.

Thomas nodded and waited for him to continue.

"I was contacted around a month and a half ago by a friend who went over to the West, to Frankfurt to be precise, who called me up and said there was a fantastic opportunity to make money. This company, Phoenix, was looking to provide financing to Ossies and wanted names and addresses. The poorer the people the better, he said. All I needed to do was to talk to people and fill out forms for as many as I could think of and I'd earn a lot of money. He would too, since he'd contacted me and so was one level up. As you can imagine, I know a lot of people. What I do for a living needs that."

"Do you have one of these forms?" Thomas asked, trying to decide whether "the poorer the better" was Gertner's joke or whether there was some meaning behind the phrase, something which for the moment escaped him.

"Sure." Gertner pulled out a paper from the pile of documents by his chair. Thomas glanced over it quickly and saw that it was extremely simple and sought minimal information.

"Last week my friend calls me up again." Gertner added. "He says there's been a big meeting, a convention he called it, and that we need to start moving quickly. He wants me to tell all my contacts that they would be receiving their "welcome money" even if they hadn't made it over to the West. They would get a one hundred marks bonus just for taking out the loans. We'd earn five percent of the actual loan amount. With the number of people I could bring to this, I could earn significant money."

Thomas looked at the form again.

"I can understand that you and your friend could get commission but why *pay* your contacts for taking out a loan? And look at this form - there's nothing asking about income or realisable assets, things the bank can use as security if the borrower doesn't pay back the loan. That makes no sense at all."

"Maybe, but that's exactly how it works." Gernter said. "Don't ask me what it means. I understand as much about finance as I do about nuclear science. I studied Russian literature. But I checked with contacts high up in the organisation and they tell me it's all perfectly legal." Thomas sensed that Gertner was sneering at him.

"Who's your contact within the organisation?"

"What do you mean, head office or here? I know a lot of people."

"Here. Who's in charge of these aspects?"

"Oh, here." Gertner made a slight off-hand gesture with his left hand. "Anything vaguely practical is handled by Henkel - no, sorry, that's changed. It was Henkel but Spitze has now taken that on. Roehrberg's there too but is too occupied making himself attractive to Berlin and to women." He laughed. "One day he'll become a politician, I'd guess. Oh, and Putin too, I think, he's into anything that smells of power or money."

Thomas's mind flickered to Bettina who was probably with Roehrberg even as they spoke.

After some more questions, not all of which Gertner could answer, he thanked him, gave him some money, and left. He searched for a public phone, finally finding one which was secluded enough for him not to be overheard and dialled Stephan's number. As usual, Stephan's secretary answered and in her cold but courteous manner told him that Stephan was at an important meeting all day and would then be away all week. After a little prying, he got out of her that Stephan was leaving for Berlin that evening and from there was due to travel to various cities in the East for about a week. No, she said, she didn't have a number that she could pass on to Thomas. Yes, she added, the cities included Dresden but Mr Peetzen hadn't yet decided on what day he'd visit. Thomas left Frau Dornbush's number for her to pass on to Stephan, adding that he was likely to be there for only a few more days and hoped to see Stephan before he left.

It was now well into the afternoon and what was left of the day was spent tediously chasing up the remaining informants, working through more unanswered telephone calls and the inevitable disconnected numbers. He visited a couple of other informers nearby and talked to another briefly on the phone but got frustratingly little information anywhere. They all wanted money up front and then repeated the same few inconsequential matters or simply exaggerated and lied like Treufel had. Nobody knew any of the details or understood the overall scheme. Gertner at least had given him an application form and some useful information. The only thing that was clear was that the reach and range of the organisation was considerable. There had been meetings all over West Germany with hundreds of participants at each. Each informant could point to at least ten other persons who had been contacted or were building their own pyramid.

The lack of information and the ignorance of his contacts was thoroughly frustrating. It was now dark, there were no lights on the bike, the wind was rising and as he realised it would take him a good twenty minutes or more to reach the Dornbusch farm he decided to give up although he was hardly wiser about Phoenix than when he'd started in the morning. He had at least got important confirmation of the involvement of the local Stasi, he thought. As he pedalled back, tired and with the gusts of wind and flurries of snow snapping at his face and chilling him further, cars suddenly looming up uncomfortably close to him before they braked suddenly and swerved past, hooting at his lack of lights, he wondered how Bettina was getting on. He hoped she at least was making some progress.

Still irritated with his day he slammed the farm door behind him, shutting it more brusquely than he had intended. The crack resonated throughout the house and Frau Dornbush, alarmed, rushed out of the kitchen.

"Oh, it's you, Mr Wundart. Thank God the children aren't sleeping yet."

"I'm sorry. The door slipped in my hand, I think." He stamped his feet and shook himself like a dog coming in, the snowflakes melting off his clothes and puddling the entrance floor.

"There was a phone call for you. From a Mr Peetzen, if I got the name right. He gave me a number where you might sometimes get him in Berlin and said he hoped to see you around the end of the week. He'll call again, he said, maybe on Wednesday if you've not spoken by then. I've written it all down to make sure I got everything for you."

Chapter 26
Monday 15 January 1990, morning onwards

The governor of the Bundesbank, Buba as it was familiarly known, prided himself on his specialist economic understanding but found himself increasingly having to turn politician in order to salvage his professional recommendations, arguing variously that there was insufficient economic data available from East Germany or that where there was information it was unreliable. As far as Buba was concerned what mattered was economic stability, a tight lid on inflation, and sound money and decisions therefore needed to be delayed and delayed until good information emerged.

Kohl, astute politician that he was, would have none of it. He and his advisers were seeking to wear down the bank's caution by holding frequent meetings and deliberately setting short time-scales for producing complex reports. Today's meeting, in Kohl's view, was primarily to hear the arguments for different ranges of exchange values before settling on the most advantageous political one. Stephan looked forward with interest to the inevitable scrap and mentally put his money on Kohl to win with little difficulty.

Kohl glanced crossly at his watch. "Herren, find out for me please just what's going on. We're running late and I can't waste time sitting around here - it's intolerable. I have far too much to do."

As Herren turned to Stephan the door opened and the governor of the Bundesbank, followed by four senior colleagues, came in. He took the head of the long rectangular table and his colleagues sat on either side. He made no attempt to apologize for the delay.

"Chancellor, gentlemen, thank you for coming. Let me present our views on monetary unification with the German Democratic Republic. Here are our findings." He nodded to the younger colleague to his left, who got up and turned on the projector.

"As you'll know, we have very little information on how the economic system of the DDR works. There are no reliable statistics on any of the key monetary masses, multipliers, or anything of that sort. We decided it was essential, therefore, to create our own models. We took some time to do this carefully and duly input a range of possible variables to verify the potential outcomes." He looked with approval at the screen. "This is similar to a Monte-Carlo simulation for option values, if you'll permit me the comparison."

Kohl looked annoyed. "Go on, please." he growled "We're here to learn what you've established, not to be lectured on fanciful comparisons or subjected to jargon."

The governor pursed his mouth, breathed out audibly, and resumed. "We've had a little more luck in getting information on industry production levels, and we hired some experts to provide views on comparative costs and product competitiveness in key industrial sectors."

The first set of slides, which showed cost-competitive charts for various industrial sectors, were projected in rapid succession. "Apart from a few exceptional situations, mainly in the precision mechanics sector, the DDR's production is high-cost and low-quality compared to its western counterparts. Output is significantly down and the events of the recent months are bringing about near-paralysis in the production economy. The following slides show the picture from the individual/family side in terms of purchasing parity and wealth, assuming different levels of savings rates. Then there's a third element, the fact that a number of goods are currently heavily subsidized in the

DDR: bringing their factory-gate prices to Western levels would cause an immediate shock to the system."

Dry though the information presented was Stephan listened carefully, mentally translating the generalised data into information about how the people of East Germany lived day to day, trying to put a human face on to the statistics presented. Since he'd been given the job of scouting for potential business opportunities for Deutsche Bank in East Germany he'd come to see the country in a new way. The presentation ended and there was silence. Kohl leaned over and spoke quietly for a few moment with his advisers. He turned to the governor. "I didn't see slides on realistic values for conversion. What's the conclusion?"

"I thought those were best discussed rather than presented. We're having to take a decision largely groping in the dark. And within limits we can decide how we want the future to shape up: that is, do we want to add 16 million consumers or do we want to improve our competitive positioning by creating our own low-cost production centre in Germany? The choice of the exchange level of the currencies hinges largely on this."

"The exchange rate we settle on has to be fair. It can't be a shock to the East German population otherwise their anger against their own government will switch to us and we'll have riots on our hands. That's not a great start for a newly reunited country and I won't allow that to happen." Kohl said. "I also accept, of course, your arguments that it has to be sustainable economically - we can't risk the future of a united Germany and so we've got to find a rate that will make people in the East happy without raising eyebrows in the West."

Kohl, clearly irritated, looked hard at the governor. "Your job is to put forward the economic arguments, derived from your analyses, relevant to different rates; mine is to evaluate the political dimensions. What I cannot understand is why this process is taking such an absurd length of time. If we were as slow as this in the Bundesregierung we'd never achieve anything."

"We've made progress but analysis takes time. We're finding statistics about two years ago, yet we hear rumours that the East German bank has been printing currency at twice the historic levels and that Shalck-Godowlsky is agreeing contracts for huge levels of imports of foreign goods - some of these may be completely fictitious of course. We have no information whatsoever on the reserves of cash held by the Stasi or the SED, and those could be substantial. Any estimates we make could be completely wrong. I would err on the side of caution and opt for a relatively high exchange rate."

"Yet you still haven't come up with a range of possible values. What do you mean by high?"

The governor paused and took a deep breath. "All our models suggest that a sustainable exchange rate is somewhere between five to seven Ost Marks to the Deutsche Mark."

There was immediate stillness in the room, something going beyond merely absence of sound as if everyone present had stopped breathing while they digested the implications of this extraordinary figure. Kohl rose as if to leave then thought better of it and sat down again, suppressing his obvious fury.

"Don't be ridiculous! Numbers of that sort are completely out of the question. The only exchange rate anyone in the East has heard about is the official one, at parity with the Deutsche Mark. We can't get too far away from that - the people in the DDR simply wouldn't understand it."

"You worry about the electoral implications, I have to worry about the economic ones. We're talking two different languages." The governor motioned his colleague to put on another slide. "Here's the chart showing the black market valuation of the Ost Mark. It's gone from over twelve to one to roughly eight, and that's purely on the basis of political speculation on unity. The markets, being rational, aren't betting on anything higher than that."

"Markets don't vote. People do. Markets don't govern. I do."

"We're making a historic experiment here. We can't get it wrong for short-term motivations. History will judge how we've handled this. The future shape of Germany depends on our choices today."

"May I make a suggestion?" Herren's strong voice broke in. "I can see the reasons behind both arguments. In an ideal scenario, we'd like to add 16 millions of happy voters and consumers with a good level of spending power. On the other hand, we want to ensure that the country's productive base remains competitive whilst it integrates in the West. The two objectives are diametrically opposed, so there's only one clear solution."

Kohl turned his great bulk towards Herren and slapped his hand hard on the table in front of him, smiling broadly as he did so. "That's why I need external experts like you to be here, Alfred. Some people simply pose problems, you offer solutions."

"We should look at applying two different exchange rates." said Herren. "A lower one for individuals, and a higher one for corporations. If we strike the right balance we could ideally get the best of all worlds."

"And what would stop a massive movement of funds from one sector to another?" the governor replied. "When you create artificial differences you're loading the guns of speculators. A parallel market would flourish almost immediately to try to reposition the cash to where the highest value was."

"There's no other way around it. You could put a maximum limit on the amount of cash each private individual could trade at preferential levels, with any excess having to be traded at the industrial level. That would be a crude but effective way to ensure that your approximate calculations turn out to be broadly correct. And it would go in the direction of social equality, which is something people on each side of the border would understand and support."

"My job isn't that of pleasing the electorate, it's safeguarding our economy! May I remind you our main objective at the Bundesbank is containment of inflation. What you're proposing to do will fuel inflation in Germany for at least a decade."

"We need to pay for this in one way or another." Herren said. "Inflation can be an acceptable way of funding growth and helping smooth out the differences, if it's limited in time. Runaway inflation is clearly unacceptable but controlled inflation in pursuit of improved output is acceptable and can be managed."

"Alfred, I appreciate your input." Kohl intervened, "But having two different exchange rates seems overly complex in my view. The exchange rate needs to be set somewhere close to parity. Maybe two to one could still be acceptable, but nothing more."

"Two to one? Two to one!" The governor looked at Kohl in horror. "That number is simply unreachable. Unless you plan to subsidize their economy forever, their industries will fold in a matter of months. You'll have record unemployment levels in the East after just a few years."

"My belief is that jobs lost in the East will roughly equate to jobs created in the West. Many easterners are just waiting for a chance to move over to the West anyway. We're just accelerating that process. I've spoken to a number of industry board members who are eager to create new plants in the East. The workforce is quite numerate, if a little lazy from what we hear."

"So what you're expecting is a rapid colonisation by Western firms of the current production base?" the chairman of Commerzbank butted in.

"I don't like the term you used, Herr Obermeier. I prefer to consider it the best way for the East to wake up to reality. We all know the best way of taking a bandage away is to pull it off quickly. Otherwise it will become an excruciatingly long agony."

Kohl gathered his papers together and stood up.

"Thank you all for attending, gentlemen. We'll finalise details next week. I'll tell you then what I decide."

Chapter 27
Monday 15 January 1990, afternoon

"Thank you, Fritz. I thought we should introduce our visiting colleague, Miss List, to some fine Dresden cuisine." said Spitze jovially as the proprietor of the small restaurant made a point of coming out from his office and showing them personally to their table. Roehrberg had excused himelf from the lunch but insisted that Spitze take Bettina as planned.

"We like it here." he added as they settled themselves. "Fritz is discreet, the food and wine is good and so Roehrberg, Henkel and I often eat," He made a wry face. "*ate*, here, Modrow too on occasion. And it's where we usually bring important visitors, at least for lunch."

He glanced at Bettina, checking her response, but she had anticipated this and was looking closely at the menu.

"Veal, I think - but perhaps scallopini rather than schnitzel. Will they do that well here, do you think?"

"You'll find it excellent, I'm sure. I believe Fritz's mother was Italian and perhaps that's why there's a few Italian dishes offered." He paused for a moment. "You must have Dieter's full confidence to be entrusted with what's really quite a perplexing and an important mission, Miss List. But then no doubt you've been in the service for some time and earned that trust."

"Oh, I think it was more a matter of availability. Following the reorganisation it's all a bit chaotic but I'd just finished another project so I was free." She broke a bit of bread in half on her plate. "And, of course, with a level of experience appropriate to, as you say, an important mission."

"I'm sure you're being too modest." he continued "I know Berlin keeps a tight rein on regional activities so they'd have wanted to get to the bottom of this promptly and efficiently. No doubt you had discussed it all in some detail at a fairly high level?"

"Pillow talk!" she thought. "I wonder what he'd say if gave that answer." She spread some butter on her bread and took a bite before answering. "I really don't know, I'm afraid, that's beyond my level. But I have worked closely with Dieter for some time and, well," she looked down and played with her bread for a moment "I think we get on well together and we do discuss things, privately, and so ... " She looked away from Spitze and then turned to look at him. "But tell me, what are your thoughts about the matter. Do you suspect anyone particularly?"

"It's very perplexing, very perplexing indeed. Let me say that we want to give you all the help and information we can to solve the mystery. I know Rosenberg's already told you that but I want to underline it. You have our full confidence, of course."

There was silence as they ate, each occasionally sparring with the other but gaining no particular insight, and the meal eventually dribbled to an end. As they drank coffee Spitze lit a cheroot, waving away the smoke between them.

"Forgive me, Miss List, but I have meetings scheduled for this afternoon and with this recent incident, of course ... " Spitze's voice trailed off and Bettina gladly took the chance to escape, inventing meetings of her own to attend.

She decided to try to meet Georg. Through his work and his personal connections Georg often picked up interesting snippets of information on what was going on in Dresden. Whether he'd want to discuss it with her was another matter, she thought, remembering how things had changed.

Georg had been a close friend of her father's and had helped the family financially and continued to support them in other ways after her father had disappeared to the West. Her mother and Georg had become close and begun a relationship but although this was only short lived they remained good friends and kept in touch regularly afterwards.

Georg and Bettina had always been very fond of each other but something had interfered with this and at their last meeting his attitude towards her had suddenly changed and he'd become very detached, short and almost irritated with her. She'd caught him looking at her with a mix of sadness and anger and she knew then that he'd discovered her Stasi involvement. With his background as a political radical he was bound to take badly what he'd see as her betrayal of ideals he'd thought she shared.

Georg's office wasn't far and the day, although still chilly, had produced a weak sun so she moved her car first to a convenient location then walked along the west bank of the Elbe and as it made one of its southern loops she turned left at the Art School and made for the old city centre. Georg's office was one of the detachments of the Court, responsible for the administration of the appeals and the registering of the definitive sentences. It was close to the ruins of the Frauenkirche, the opulent baroque church that had once been the symbol of the city.

She entered the modern, nondescript building and let her memory guide her through the seemingly endless corridors to where Georg "sifted paper," as he sardonically said. Georg's office seemed identical in appearance to the first time she had been there, - almost ten years earlier on a visit with her mother − a complete chaos of files, law books and chewed pencils. She'd thought then that it hardly fitted with the image of the blind goddess dispensing justice rationally and without favour or emotion.

Georg was sitting at a worn-out desk, his head deep in a pile of documents and looking the same as ever. With his wide ears, seraphic expression and double chin he could have been a Buddha had he been sitting in the lotus position rather than conventionally on a chair.

Bettina stood in the doorway looking at the engrossed figure, remembering with a rush of recognition how fond she'd been of him. She shuffled slightly, then coughed experimentally but got no response and it took a very loud "hmmmm" to get Georg to acknowledge that someone was present. He recognized her, smiled, and got up from his chair. They hugged for a long moment in genuine affection.

"Hello Bettina. It's good to see you again. How's your mother? I haven't heard from her for a few months now."

"She's fine. You look in good shape, Georg." She'd first met Georg when he was forty-one and he'd always looked identical since although was little was left of his always thin blondish hair now was showing some grey. "How's the photography going? Any exhibitions lately?"

"No galleries, I'm afraid, just small things amongst friends. But I still enjoy it immensely - I'm experimenting now with some new chemicals for sepia colouring."

There was silence for some moments, each wondering how to broach the subject they knew they had to talk about eventually. Bettina looked down at her feet and then back at Georg.

"I've heard about a strange situation you might know about, a privatisation ... "

"Best we talk outside." Georg interrupted. He turned off his desk lamp, closed and locked his door then poked his head into a neighbouring office to tell his colleague he'd be away for an hour or so. Outside, he led Bettina through back streets to a small café bar entirely lacking in quaintness or charm but which was almost completely empty. They took a table deep into the small room and once they'd ordered Georg turned and looked at her.

"You were going to ask me something. But I need to say something to you first. I know who you work for, Bettina.

You must know, particularly after what they did to me, that I can have no sympathy with that. When they tracked down who was behind that newspaper, who had helped fund it, who the 'Hans Frei' who wrote all those critical articles really was, I was lucky to escape a long jail term but they still ruined my life as it was."

"You weren't lucky, Georg. I know how good you were as a senior judge in Leipzig, how well people thought of you there, and it was that and your integrity which had got you some powerful friends."

"Not powerful enough, though, were they? I was good in that work and I could use my position as a judge to stand up against injustice. Now look at me, a clerk in a Dresden administrative office of no importance, a person with no power and no way of helping people as I used to be able to do. If I try anything now I'm facing a long jail term, with anyone who could help me long gone."

Bettina looked away, uncomfortably, and then Georg spoke again. "But I need you to tell me whether you've ever written anything about me, during the time I was with your mother or at any other time, before or subsequently. I need the truth, Bettina. I can understand if you did, although I confess it would hurt me deeply."

Bettina looked him straight in the eyes. "No, never, I swear. Your relationship with mum was some years before my joining and even that apart I wouldn't have informed on you."

"Why did you do this? Why have you got involved with these people? You're such an honest, straightforward girl. I just don't see you in that context, joining those rats spying on people's lives to try to nail them for being who they are. Is it anything to do with what happened to your brother?"

"Please just take my word for it that I've always acted properly. Not all people in the organisation are as bad as you think. And anything you can tell me will stay between us. I promise you that."

"All right then, I'll trust you for old time's sake. It must be hard for you now, I imagine. The boat is sinking and all the rats are trying to grab whatever's left and hiding their past."

The waitress had finally brought the beers and the two clinked their glasses. "I can only talk about my own little world." Georg continued. "For the past three months, we've been ordered to go through all the political trials of the last five years and eliminate any page which makes reference to prominent communist party members' depositions against the suspects. I'm sure that in small towns, where the new political parties can't check, they're cutting the process short and just throwing whole files away." His disgust at this behaviour was evident. "This way, they're hoping not to get prosecuted. I suspect, gut feeling only, that the same thing is happening in every field. The Party and the Stasi controlled everything, did what they wanted. They're not simply going to hand all the evidence over to Kohl, are they?"

"Did you hear about the privatisation of the flour mill?" she said, trying to keep any sense of importance out of her tone.

Georg seemed lost in thought, as if he'd not registered what Bettina was asking. He took a long draught of his beer. "Why would the communists privatise something without being forced to? Find out the date and I'll try to fish out the file. All public acts need to be registered in the Court. The only problem is that in my department we only have the acts registered in the last year. The rest is in the archives."

"This must certainly have happened in the last year." Bettina said. "I'll find out the exact date, or at least the month, and let you know."

"Without the date, it's going to be difficult. There are so many acts registered every day that it would take me ages, certainly more than a day, to look through them all. How long are you staying?"

"I don't know. It depends how some things develop."

"I'll ask some of my colleagues. Where can I reach you if I find anything?"

"I'm staying in a farm on the road to Meissen, maybe a couple of kilometres beyond the mill. The woman is called Dornbush." She gave him the telephone number.

Georg left money for the beers on the table and they got up to leave. They hugged closely then Georg, waving goodbye, headed back to his office block.

"Perhaps on my way back I should stop over at Jacob's." she thought as she returned to her car. "Almost everyone there works at the mill so they should be able to tell me what happened, and when."

When she finally reached the low wooden fence around the garden of the farmhouse Jacob's two terriers, Trap and Chupa, came over to greet her, barking madly, whining and leaping up towards her, alerting the family. Jacob's father, Herbert, peered out. He was around fifty-five but looked much younger as he kept in excellent shape doing most of the work on the farm.

"Bettina, how are you? Such a long time since we've seen you." he said warmly, shaking her hand and passing his left one through his long silver hair. The squeeze felt like iron.

"Yes, probably a couple of years." Bettina said. "Everyone fine?" She knew them well, Jacob having been her first boyfriend. They'd been inseparable until she'd moved to Berlin, aged nineteen, and they'd gradually drifted apart, finishing a few months later.

Jacob came out running and hugged her warmly then leading her into the kitchen where Herbert opened beers and poured out three glasses.

"How are things going at the mill?" Bettina asked Jacob. "I stopped by and they told me it was being restructured."

"Happened a couple of months back. That's the good news" said Herbert. "Now I can use these lazy sons of mine here at the farm for a change."

"Can I say something or is this a private conversation?" Jacob interrupted. "You weren't even there when they told us. You were here planting beans."

"It happened exactly a month and a half ago," Jacob went on. "The Party officer called a workers' assembly and told us that the committee had finally approved the restructuring of the mill. Production levels had dropped, he told us, while at the same time there was increased demand from the city. They'd decided to buy new machines, do some renovation work as well, and all that meant that the mill needed to be closed for a period, probably around six months. However, in order to guarantee the workers' livelihoods the committee had decided to pay a full six months' salary in advance. They shut down a week later. Everyone was extremely happy, as you can imagine."

"Did they say anything else?" Bettina asked.

"Something about changing the name from Dresdener Mehl Kooperative to align it with the more modern image of the country today. I believe Omega Mills was what he said. No one really cared about the name anyway. We all called it 'the pastry', as you'll remember."

"Nothing about it being sold, or privatised?"

"Sold?" Herbert looked worried and moved his chair closer to Bettina. "Privatised?"

Jacob looked shocked. "Sold? Are you sure?"

"The guard at the mill told me that it had been privatised. But maybe it's all a mistake and it simply changed names. I wouldn't worry too much about it." she said. She didn't know for certain what had happened and didn't want to worry the Klimas with rumours. The farm was struggling and the family depended on their mill wages to survive.

"I'm sorry. I shouldn't have even mentioned it." she added. "The guard probably didn't know the difference between just changing a name and privatising something. I'm sure it's nothing."

She drained her beer and got up. "I'm afraid I've got to run now. Say hello to Anja and the rest of the gang."

Chapter 28
Tuesday 16 January 1990

"I'm so sorry to have kept you waiting but I had to finish checking these urgent reports. Today is really hectic. I've got a thousand things to finish before I leave." Roehrberg glanced at his watch and made a brief note on the pad in front of him.

He leaned back in his chair and smiled at her and although he'd reverted to his earlier urbane and charming manner Bettina felt patronised and wrong-footed. "My own fault, I suppose." she'd thought "I shouldn't have just turned up at HQ and expected to waltz straight in to see Roehrberg without an appointment. So much for his being at my disposal."

She'd been given coffee when she'd turned up but that had long been drunk and no refills had been offered. She spent her time going over what she knew of the recent events, trying to identify patterns and make some sense of the remaining mysteries. Eventually his secretary had led her into the inner office where Roehrberg was working through and occasionally signing documents piled on his desk. Barely looking up he waved her to the sofa and continued his work for two or three minutes. She noticed that today he was wearing horn-rimmed reading glasses, finally removing them and placing them carefully on the desk. They made him look even more interesting, she thought, and then for a moment found herself musing on how Thomas would look in glasses.

"You're leaving?" She tried to keep the surprise out of her voice. He nodded.

"Yes, early tomorrow morning. It's the mission I told you about, the one for which we needed the funds. The unexpected lack of the money is causing problems with some of our key informants in France. I have to go over and talk to them and make sure things continue as planned." He moved a document from one pile to another and made a further note on his pad. "But Spitze will remain here - please speak to him if you need any more help. I assume that you've come to tell me that now that matters have been cleared up replacement funds will be sent shortly, right?"

"Well, I can't promise that. I'm not sure how … "

"Yes, I understand it's not your decision but you all do need to understand in turn that our work here continues. Berlin can't just sit around doing nothing and have us wait until it gets round to sorting things out. Did you give Dieter the update on Henkel?"

"Yes, I spoke to him briefly yesterday. He was glad to learn that the solution was apparently so straightforward, if distressing for everyone who knew Henkel." She decided to try to assert some authority of her own, took a file out of her bag and made a show of looking for something there before answering. "But there are a couple of things he asked about and so I still need to check these before I can complete my report. Forgive me, but, as I'm sure you understand, it's a very delicate matter. One crucial aspect is whether you've asked a specialist to verify the handwriting of Henkel's letter and whether he'd confirmed that it was Henkel's."

There was a long silence as Roehrberg stared at her. She noticed with dismay that his eyes narrowed and hardened and his face became livid, relieved only by spots of colour on his high cheekbones. His nostrils flared and he breathed in heavily. She watched as his shoulder started to rise, the right arm tensing and the palm of his hand ready to smash down. With a visible effort he controlled his movement, shut his eyes for a moment, then breathed out and lowered his arm slowly to rest on the desk.

"You're implying that you, that Dieter, thinks that someone murdered Henkel and falsified his handwriting?

You think I don't recognise the handwriting of my subordinates almost as well as my own? I see these people's handwriting on scores of documents each month. It's preposterous. The idea that the note wasn't written by Henkel is just ridiculous. Quite ridiculous."

"Of course!" she said. "Naturally I see that. But you know how people sometimes get odd ideas into their heads even if they're ridiculous. Sometimes it's just box ticking, excessive bureaucracy. Left to myself ... "

"Dammit!" she thought "Why did I have to add that last bit rather than hold my nerve."

"Unfortunately Dieter won't authorise the release of replacement funding until he has my report." She breathed slowly and deeply to calm herself again. "He's made it clear that it's got to include a certificate of handwriting verification before it can be accepted." The silence continued.

"I'm sorry." Roehrberg said smoothly. "Forgive me. Of course you're right. It's routine to do such checks but in this case I just didn't think about it. Gerd was a friend and we've worked together a long time. I know his handwriting intimately and the idea of a forgery never occurred to me. But of course you're right and we should have run standard checks. I'll order them immediately and stress the urgency and we should have the results by early evening. Anything to get this story over and done with. Anything else?"

"Yes, there's one thing I don't quite understand." Bettina shifted in her chair. "You told me that the funds were ordered for three missions - in France, England and West Germany. What I don't understand is why the foreign money that was ordered was a combination of Deutsche Marks and French Francs only; there were no English pounds whatsoever."

"I'm afraid I can't answer that question. It was Gerd who handled all the practical aspects like that. I just checked that the projects were progressing as scheduled, told him broadly what we'd need and when and he just got on with it. The project in the UK is certainly not as far forward as the others and so possibly the funding there wasn't going to be needed until later on, assuming we're all still here, that is. You could ask Spitze later. He might have a better idea."

He looked at his watch.

"Now I hate to do this, but I really need to get some more work done today. Why don't you talk to Spitze, ask him about the English money gap and anything else you need to know, and you'll probably get answers to all your questions. If there are any issues outstanding, you can ask me at dinner, if you'd be so kind as to accept this as my invitation for tonight. And I'll bring a copy of the forensic report on Henkel's suicide note with me for you to take away."

"Thank you. I'd be delighted to have dinner with you." she said.

"Shall I come to pick you up? Where ... "

"Don't worry. I'm from Dresden and I have my own car here. I just need the address."

"We call it Heinrich's" he said smoothly "and it's the just down the hill from my house. If you came there we could walk down together."

"Oh, I know it well. Best if I just go direct, I think."

He jotted down his address and that of the restaurant and handed the note to her.

"Eight o'clock at Heinrich's then, if that's fine with you."

"Perfect. I'll see you later."

Bettina walked down the corridor to Spitze's office, knocked and entered without waiting for a response, just as Spitze was putting down his receiver. He gestured her to sit in the chair near his desk.

"Hello again Miss List. That was Roehrberg. He told me you were coming and asked me to put myself at your disposal, for the day if necessary. He said you had some questions I might be able to help you with."

He smiled, but she remembered her meeting at lunch the day before and far from reassuring her she knew that she'd need to be cautious in what she said and in how much reliance she should place on his answers.

"I'll do my best but as you might imagine we're all a little frazzled today." he added.

"Thank you for making time for me Mr Spitze. Yes, I imagine that today must be difficult. It must have been a terrible shock to all of you."

"Yes it was. It's not something I would ever have thought possible." The both sat in silence for a while, then Spitze leaned back in his leather chair and steepled his fingers. "Now, what can I help you with?"

"The first point, I guess, is the organisational structure. How exactly were the responsibilities divided between your, Roehrberg and Henkel? And was anyone else particularly involved? I didn't get an organisational chart from HQ and I'm a little confused." She ripped out a piece of paper from her pad and started outlining a scheme. "So if this is the structure ... "

Spitze looked at her sketch with disapproval at its messiness. "Permit me." he said, taking a sheet of blank paper from a drawer and creating his own version. Underneath each perfect box with their three names were further squares in which were written out the functions and the number of agents directly depending on each of them. A larger box with Modrow's name headed the paper. He drew boxes, entered names and added comments about responsibilities so that in a short time the sheet was covered with a clear organisational chart all annotated in Spitze's neat script.

"It's quite easy really. Roehrberg heads the whole department, directly under Modrow as overall head, and therefore has no direct functions but through Henkel and me is responsible overall for our various areas and personnel. Of course now that Modrow is Prime Minister Roerhrberg is *de facto* head." he added, pointing to the various lower levels of the organisational chart. "Is it clear?"

"Absolutely clear." she said, taking the piece of paper and folding it back into her pad. "Thank you. This is really helpful. It's kind of difficult to ask Roehrberg these basic questions. He's always so busy and ... "

"I know," Spitze interrupted. "When I first joined the operation two years ago I felt completely out of place. Roehrberg was always too busy to talk to. I even had the feeling initially that he and Henkel were intentionally avoiding telling me about things. Now he's the one complaining, saying he's not told enough!"

He stroked his moustache and as he smiled Bettina could see his tar stained teeth, his habits confirmed by the stale air in the office and the ashtray filled with cigarette butts. "Effectively, I now run most of the office directly. Roehrberg is great for this − he delegates a lot if he trusts you."

"Had he been working long with Henkel before you joined?"

"I think the two had been together about five years before I joined, so altogether now seven years."

"What was Henkel like?" Bettina asked. "Were you surprised to learn that he gambled and had high debts?"

"I was extremely surprised and saddened to hear what happened. No, I can't say I had any clue at all. I don't think Roehrberg did either. He trusted Henkel completely. They were friends as well as colleagues."

"Did they socialise outside work?"

"We all do, from time to time. It's important to keep united. I do it less than others since I have a family, you see, but Roehrberg and Henkel are both single. They could go out together more frequently and quite often did, I believe."

"Could you show me an example of how the internal procedure for authorisation of bank withdrawals worked? Roehrberg told me Henkel and he could authorise others to execute transactions from the bank."

"I could too, technically speaking," Spitze said. "But typically it was always Henkel who did it. He needed to be on top of the finance side more than anyone else." He pulled out a piece of paper from a file behind his desk. "This is an example." It was a note by Henkel, signed at the foot and with some handwritten notes at the head.

"May I have a copy, as a sample?" Bettina asked. "It's one of the things they asked me to verify at head office. I need to show I've covered every detail, you understand … "

"Of course. It's important that the formal procedures are followed, in my view."

Bettina checked her pad to give her time to decide how to frame her final question, the one which had been burning in her mind all along. She looked directly at Spitze as she asked "Who might have had an interest in killing Henkel?"

Spitze's expression didn't change. He pursed his lips, stared at the ceiling, then shook his head. "I can't think of anyone. No one at all. He didn't seem worried. Lots of people are currently worried, especially the older agents, who risk losing their jobs if unification goes ahead. I am too to some extent I suppose. But not Gerd. He was generally in a good mood and almost gave the impression he was looking forward to the changes. Like he was a man with a plan, so to speak."

"But you accept the idea of murder rather than suicide as a possibility? That doesn't surprise you?"

"Oh, I'm certain he killed himself. Just as the note said. Quite certain." He blinked at her.

"What about Roehrberg? Has he seemed to you at all worried?"

He looked startled. "Oh, I see what you mean. No, he doesn't seem at all worried either. But it's practically impossible to work out what he's thinking. Whereas he has the uncanny capability of reading others' thoughts. It's quite extraordinary."

Bettina remembered her coming dinner with Roehrberg, realising she'd have to be particularly careful. And Thomas would be breaking in to Roehrberg's house while they were eating. She would just have to block him out of her mind, she thought.

Chapter 29
Tuesday 16 January 1990, evening

By six-thirty Thomas was in the kneipe Bettina had chosen, sitting at a table with his back to the wall so that he could face the door but also take in the whole room. Bettina was already fifteen minutes late and so, feeling conspicuous without a drink, he ordered a beer. Another ten minutes went by and then she was suddenly in the doorway, looking around. He raised his hand to wave but sensed from her expression that something wasn't right and ran his fingers through his hair instead. She ignored him completely and sat down a couple of tables away, apparently alone and just minding her own business. Bettina's description of the white car which had followed her flashed into his mind. Thomas sipped his beer and looked around. No one could enter or leave without his seeing.

Two or three minutes later a stocky man of around forty came in, unzipping his leather jacket in the warmth of the room. He glanced round and then walked to the small section at right angles to the main run of the bar, just beside the entrance, sat on one of the high stools and leaned back on the end wall so that he could keep the entire room in view. He again glanced round the room at the customers, this time more slowly and with his gaze lingering for a moment on Bettina, then snapped his fingers and pointed at one of the beer taps. The barmaid, who had been watching him from the far end of the counter, reached up to the shelf and selected a specific stein. Cutting off the overflowing foam she carried over the mug and placed it on a mat in front of the man who ignored her and took a long draught. Carefully setting down his drink he again snapped his fingers and when the barmaid turned crooked his index finger imperiously to call her back and then said a few words in a low voice before dismissing her and turning again to survey the room.

"Hmmm." thought Thomas "A regular, but not one who's popular. And he knows what he's doing sitting there, watching everyone." He shivered slightly, drank his beer slowly and waited.

The barmaid took Bettina's order at her table and then pointed to a door marked 'Private', just to the left of where Thomas sat. A moment later Bettina got up, passed by Thomas's table without any hint of recognition, and went through the door. Thomas had been watching the man carefully, noting that although he was again talking with the barmaid he'd followed Bettina's movements closely. He noticed a bulge at the man's waist under the patterned shirt he was wearing." Armed, and someone you clearly don't mess with." thought Thomas. "Roehrberg's?"

As if summoned the man suddenly turned his head and looked straight at Thomas. They locked eyes for a moment and Thomas found it impossible to look away. His heart rate increased and he felt an involuntary shiver at the base of his spine. He managed to look down, shifted in his seat and took a gulp of beer. His stomach clenched and he wondered how he was going to deal with protecting Bettina if anything erupted here. The man was still staring at him, unblinking.

There was a sound of flushing water from behind the door and a few moments later Bettina emerged, glancing towards the entrance as she did so. As she passed Thomas's table she apparently caught her foot on some obstruction and steadied herself with a hand on his table, apologising mechanically and without emotion, before returning to her own seat and sipping her orange juice. She glanced at her watch before pulling out a newspaper from her bag and putting it on the table in front of her.

Hidden briefly from the man's gaze as Bettina had moved to her own table Thomas picked up the scrap of paper she'd dropped on the table and hid it in his left hand. Thomas finished his beer and got up to pay, conscious as he walked to the counter that the man in the corner was again watching him. As he passed Bettina's table he glanced frankly at her, acting the natural response a beautiful young woman might elicit in a passing male. Bettina ignored him.

As he left the kneipe Thomas was conscious of the man's steady gaze. Outside he walked a short distance before suddenly stopping, swinging round and walking back towards the kneipe, patting and feeling his pockets distractedly. There was no sign of the man and Thomas, evidently satisfied that he'd found what he'd thought he'd mislaid, turned and continued his earlier course. Presumably the man's orders were to follow Bettina and if he didn't realise they were together that might be useful later, Thomas thought. He continued walking and in a few minutes ducked into a small alleyway and opened Bettina's hurriedly scrawled message. "Being followed. Stocky, dark hair, grey leather jacket. No attempted contact. Having dinner with R at 8. You need to enter house to find docs. Get out by 9.30. B"

"Shit!" Thomas tore the message into tiny pieces and scattered them in a nearby bin. Last time there had been some tenuous form of justification for breaking in to a senior Stasi official's house but there was nothing like that now. He risked being shot if someone caught him. He gave a wry smile and shrugged away the thought. Bettina and he were by now clearly risking their lives anyway. He wondered about the man following Bettina. If it was Roehrberg, or perhaps Spitze, who had sent him to check on her and what she was doing it was unlikely she'd be attacked, he decided. They needed her alive and out of their hair, able to return to Berlin and say the matter had been cleared up. And had Bettina had found out something about Roehrberg that proved he was involved, he wondered. Why else send him to check out the house?

Thomas returned to his bicycle and started back to the farm. He looked at his watch. By the time he'd got back home he'd have about 40 minutes before leaving for Roehrberg's house, he reckoned, just time to review the maps and the files and devise a plan. Cycling meant that he'd be less conspicuous but if something went wrong it would be harder to escape. Roehrberg, he remembered, was the smartest of the three and would almost certainly notice any small changes in the things in his house. What's more, he had a reputation for being very fond of women and one of his reputedly many girlfriends might be in the house. Thomas realised he had to be extremely careful. This time he was on his own and things were far more dangerous. He couldn't afford any mistakes. He sighed. Berlin and his student life seemed years away, as if that life had been lived by someone else.

Fuelled by the adrenalin pumping through his system, Thomas felt no strain in cycling up the long, steep hill which led to the farm. He let himself in, shouted a greeting to Frau Dornbusch and ran up the staircase and locked himself in the room. He turned the combination of the briefcase lock then opened it quickly and took out one of the files. He turned to the information on Roehrberg's house and began reading.

Some time later Thomas, now dressed in dark clothes, went downstairs and wheeled out the bicycle ready for the ride to Roehrberg's villa, a street or so away from Henkel's. The two were similar in structure although Roehrberg's had an observation turret built into the roof which commanded an excellent view of the surrounding neighbourhood as well as across the city, thanks to the hill on which the villa stood.

Roehrberg's wall seemed somewhat lower than Henkel's, he noticed. It was now approaching five to eight.

There were lights on in several rooms on both floors and Thomas regretted not arriving earlier to watch who came and went. Now he would have to wait to see whether Roehrberg was still at home or if anyone else was around. If Roehrberg had the habit of leaving lights on when away then Thomas would waste valuable time waiting unnecessarily and would probably also have to prowl riskily around the house to check that it really was empty.

"The files aren't detailed enough." Thomas thought as he passed the house on the opposite pavement and searched for a spot far enough away not to be recognized if Roehrberg came out but still close enough to monitor movements through the front door.

Some minutes later he saw a tall shape hurry through the front door, slamming it shut behind him as he went. "Roehrberg." he thought, judging the man from his long stride as he headed off at speed down the hill and in the opposite direction from where Thomas was standing. Thomas locked his bicycle to a street lamp and walked toward the entrance, scanning the building carefully. He walked past the front door and saw to his relief that most of the lights inside were now switched off. He checked that there was no one on the road, walked to the far end of the wall, jumped as high as he could, gripped a spike and fluidly pulled himself up, swinging over and dropping lightly into the garden. Despite Roehrberg's reputation for efficiency he hadn't fortified his garden wall as much as Henkel had done but perhaps that meant that the security measures taken at the house itself were that much more dangerous to intruders.

According to the maps and the files there were only two openings on the ground floor where the alarm wasn't connected, one a tiny bathroom fanlight too small for anyone to get through and the other a barred wooden garden door down to the basement. He hoped that Roehrberg might have left something open, remembering how easy the entrance to Henkel's house had been, but then realised that even if he had it would be impossible to use it without setting off the alarm. In Henkel's case the open window had probably been used by the murderer to escape. It was increasingly obvious that Henkel hadn't committed suicide at all, he thought.

He stayed very close to the garden wall while circling the building, moving to look inside where possible and trying to hear any noise, however small, coming from the interior. Everything was silent. It seemed that Roehrberg had left the house empty. Even for him it was probably embarrassing to confess to a girlfriend that he was off to dinner with a beautiful blonde, business meeting or not.

He found the basement door and examined it closely, finding it as he'd imagined from the plans he'd seen. The door itself was stout and in good condition, held shut by a thick iron bar which was fixed with a ring to the side wall at one end, passed closely across the door and ended in a hinged hasp which passed over the large staple in the door and was secured by a serious looking steel padlock. With the lock opened and removed the bar could be lifted out or up and the door thereby freed but cutting through the padlock was going to be impossible. Shielding his torch he examined and tested the staple and the surrounding wood but could see no weakness. There was none that he could see in the metal bar either but as the light showed up the fixing of the ring in the wall he saw that it was old and that the builder had used concrete rather than lime mortar, thereby damaging the surface of the stone. The wall itself was weathered with softened edges and the concrete was already slightly pulling away; with luck, a few well placed smacks with a stone chisel would complete the task and free the ring.

Although the chisels he'd brought were padded on the handles the noise would still be significant but he realised he had no choice. The small battery operated drill he'd brought might also work but wouldn't really be much quieter and would take several times as long.

He cringed as the sound of chisel on stone rang out absurdly loudly in the still evening. He stopped and listened but there were no footsteps on the pavement, no challenge as to what was going on. In the end it was easy and after only a few blows he freed a lump of stone with the ring and bar still firmly attached. With the lock pushed round the staple there was just enough play at the hasp end to allow him to swing the bar clear of the door and in a moment he clicked the latch and pulled it open with a harsh creak. Again he listened but there were no worrying sounds nearby.

Standing at the top of a narrow staircase Thomas cautiously flashed his torch around, hoping that the report on Roehrberg's house was accurate. He waited for a few moments but there was no sound of an alarm breaking the stillness and so he pulled the door closed behind him and cautiously walked down and into the large basement room, flashing his torch around as he went.

This was clearly a junk or storage room, with objects of all kinds stacked in corners and piled on top of each other. In the far left corner there was a tall wooden construction housing a collection of bottles. On the right hand side a couple of paintings leant against a wall. Further on there were some old cane-bottomed chairs apparently waiting repair but now covered in dust. By the foot of the stairs from the garden were gardening tools. In a far corner there was a female mannequin wearing a battered fedora at a jaunty angle, her right arm angled up and holding a pretend cigar near her mouth.

Thomas moved the torch around a final time before deciding there was nothing of interest. He moved to a door opposite, finding it opened on to a staircase to the house. He climbed carefully, alert to creaks and to any noise from above, opened with infinite slowness the door into the corridor by the kitchen and stood looking for the characteristic red lights of motion sensors. There was nothing that he could see so he moved to the front hall to find and deactivate the alarm system if necessary.

Checking the sheet of the report which showed the system details, he identified and took down from the wall by the front door the painting which concealed the controls. To his surprise it looked as if the system hadn't been activated and he checked his paper several times to make sure that this puzzling discovery was correct. Possibly Roehrberg felt safe since Bettina was having dinner with him. Indeed, maybe that was one reason he'd invited her out, to avoid her poking her nose around elsewhere. But a lot of other people, including foreign agents and burglars looking for pickings from large houses, could have had an interest in breaking in. Thomas had no time to think the matter through. It was very odd but all that mattered was that Roehrberg had left the system off, whether by mistake or intentionally.

At the end of the front hall, opposite the main entrance, was a wide flight of carpeted stairs curving elegantly round to an upper landing. Roehrberg's study was through the third door on the right upstairs, the last room on the corridor, according to the maps. Thomas quickly climbed the stairs and walked along the unlit corridor, feeling in his rucksack for the camera as he went. About to enter the study he saw light coming from under the door. He bent to look through the keyhole but seeing nothing straightened, turned the doorknob cautiously and pushed the door open. It squealed slightly. His heart beat fast as the image of Henkel's body and the blood-stained desk flashed briefly through his mind.

For a moment he stood in the doorway and looked around the large and well proportioned room. In the middle of the short wall opposite the door there was a large fireplace with a marble mantelpiece above. There were still warm ashes in the grate. The long wall to his left had three large windows running almost to the ceiling and looking out over the garden. The facing wall was entirely covered with solid mahogany library bookshelves which then continued along the shorter wall to the door where he stood, most of the shelves filled with books. There was an ornate desk in the corner between the door and the outside wall and on it were a couple of silver framed photographs of a laughing, beautiful dark-haired, tanned woman in her early twenties, taken by the sea. A large Persian carpet lined the floor, its rich blue setting off the dark polished wood surround. Near the far corner between the fireplace and the longer outside wall, balancing the desk and facing the centre of the room, there was a small velvet sofa with a low table in front of it on which were scattered some magazines. In the other corner a wing chair, upholstered in dark red velvet to match the sofa, faced at an angle a fireplace set in the middle of the short outside wall directly opposite the doorway.

Thomas closed the door and looked at the piles of cardboard boxes neatly stacked in the middle of the room by the table. Crouching, he opened the first box and found it held a number of large volumes bound uniformly in light green cloth and dated variously on the spines. The first one he picked up held manuscript accounting records for the period 1980-1982. He skimmed through the pages, glancing at the figures showing weights of raw materials, labour costs and the tonnage of goods sold, then turned to the front to check the name of the company but couldn't find anything relevant. He picked up another volume, finding different information covering the same period but still with nothing to show the company concerned. About to close the box and try another he noticed a slim volume bound in blue and saw that this was a five-year plan setting out the anticipated production of tonnes of relevant products. He flipped to the front page and his heart skipped a beat as he read "Dresdener Mehl Kooperative" 1985-1989.

Chapter 30
Tuesday 16 January 1990, evening

As Thomas propped open the report on the mill and began to take photographs there was the sudden slam of a door from somewhere downstairs. Startled, and with his heart hammering, he listened but there was no further sound. "Wind from an open window somewhere" he thought, but failed to convince himself. He listened again but could hear nothing but his breathing.

After a couple of minutes, his tense muscle starting to ache, he relaxed and lifted the lid on another box. As he was reaching for another blue bound volume he heard the creak of a floorboard somewhere and a moment later the low sound of voices. "Shit!" he thought. "Two. At least." Impossible to sneak out of the room. He jammed the lid crookedly back on the box and looked round frantically for somewhere to hide. In a panic he grabbed the mill report and darted behind the sofa in the far corner, crouching. He pulled out his gun, flicked off the safety catch, and eased himself as low and out of sight as he could manage. He realised he was breathing hoarsely, panting, and forced himself to breathe slowly to clam himself. The voices grew louder.

"Third door on the right, Roehrberg said. The room with the light on." a low-pitched, gruff voice said.

The doorknob rattled and he heard the men enter the room. They were several feet away but Thomas felt as if they were standing next to him and could hardly fail to notice him crouched behind the sofa. "So that's why the alarm system wasn't on!" he thought. He held his gun at the ready and waited for the worst.

"I guess this is it." a younger voice said. "Must be twenty boxes there, by the look of things."

Thomas could hear someone lifting boxes and putting them down again.

"Shit, they're heavy." the deeper voice said. "I think we'll bring them down one by one. We still have a bit of time before the boss returns, no use breaking our backs."

"You're lucky," the younger voice said. "I had to move the things on my own the other evening. And not just down stairs either, out of one place round the corner and then into this one. Not to mention the rest."

"Shut up and move them." the other growled. "I don't want to hear a single word about it, do you understand? Complain again and I swear I'll cut your balls off. Now pick up a box and get your young arse downstairs with it. You should be glad I'm helping you and you're not loading them all in the van by yourself. OK, get the tape and let's get these babies sealed as we move them. You got the scissors?"

Thomas checked the exact time on his watch as they left the room and waited until he heard the steps descending before coming out from his hiding place. The footsteps vanished into the distance. It would take them a couple of minutes, possibly more, he judged, to drop off the boxes in the van and return to the room. The first two boxes contained bound books. The other ones, bigger but lighter, held collections of lever arch files. Thomas opened one file and then another, opening the files randomly and taking several photographs each time. As the footsteps returned, coming back up the stairs, he put the file back in its place and hurried behind the sofa. The two voices kept talking as they came up. Thomas could barely hear them.

" ... at the airport ... this as well ... driving ... "

Their voices became clearer as they approached along the corridor. It was the more senior one talking. " ... been stepping on a little too many toes these days. He could soon become a thing of the past, if the rumours I heard are true.

He's never been able to mind his own business, they tell me. Too bad. Too bad for him anyway, I mean."

The younger one made no comment to this but Thomas heard him again after they'd sealed and lifted a box each and were walking down the corridor, the voice strained with the weight its owner was carrying.

" ... but the girl is quite pretty. Roehrberg is always ... dinners ... "

"Whatever these boxes contain, they're obviously very important if Roehrberg wants them shifted out immediately," Thomas thought "so I'd better work fast." He picked up a file from one of the other boxes. This was marked 'Paula' on the cover and appeared to be a contract. He picked up another, 'Omega', and took more photographs but ran out of film as he heard the footsteps returning. Grabbing the whole file he darted behind the sofa only a split second before the door opened. "I need to be more careful!" he thought. "That was much too close." He crouched behind the sofa trying hard not to breathe too heavily.

They were still talking about the girl, the older one this time.

" ... and did you see those legs? I mean, the first day, when she showed up in that sexy black dress with white dots? Knocked my pants right off." He laughed coarsely. "Bet she'd have liked to have gone somewhere and helped me!" He stopped for a moment as he picked up a box. Thomas realized they were talking about Bettina. This was the dress she'd worn on one of the first times they'd met, and she'd worn it again that first day she had gone over to the Stasi offices. His stomach clenched as he struggled to grasp everything that was being said, understand what he was listening to.

"I still don't understand why Dieter would send down someone so junior ... " the voice continued. "I guess he can't trust anyone these days. Clever bastard." Thomas felt a chill down his spine as he realized they were talking of Dieter as an antagonist. Possibly the earlier reference they'd made was also about him. If so, Roehrberg was obviously dancing to a different fiddle. Not that that was any great surprise from what Bettina had told him.

He heard them leave the room and waited until he was sure they were clear before racing over to the boxes. He took another small file at random, not even looking at the name or contents, then stepped back behind the sofa. This time it was a good twenty seconds before they were in the room again. Thomas could hear they were starting to breathe hard from the exercise.

"OK Thomas, the game's over." the voice boomed, less than a metre away.

Thomas's heart jumped at hearing the name. They'd found him! He gripped the gun tightly, getting ready to step out and shoot.

" ... you do these last ones on your own. My muscles are aching." He heard the heavy footsteps of the older one coming in his direction. Thomas crouched even farther behind the sofa, then felt the back of the sofa hit him as the body fell heavily on to it.

"Did you check out this babe, the pictures on the desk?" the man said as he slumped down. "This is Roehrberg's real girlfriend, the steady one. He's got style, huh? French. A real treat. Now move it, we've got fifteen minutes before the boss gets back."

Thomas held his breath. He could feel the presence of the man as if he could touch him, and was afraid the other felt his too. The minutes went by in a constant agony, Thomas ready to pull the trigger any minute. Maybe this sitting down was just a ruse. Maybe the other was getting ready to act too. His breathing was regular, if still a little strong. A smell of sweat came to him, acrid. Thomas could see the man's hairy left arm lying across the back of the sofa. He kept staring at it, watching as a mouse might look for the tensing muscles of a waiting cat. Still, the arm seemed relaxed and if it remained in that position, it was unlikely he could shoot.

The younger man came and went, descended and mounted the stairs several times. Most of the time the older man relaxed on the sofa, his breathing easing but then during what was to be the last couple of trips got up to nose round the room. Thomas heard him lift volumes from the bookshelves and then move to stand in front of the fireplace. "Please God he doesn't come to the windows." thought Thomas, and gripped his gun tightly. At least he'd have the benefit of surprise on the older man he thought and he wondered briefly what it would feel like to shoot to kill. And then he'd have to deal with his namesake when Thomas came running in to find out what had happened.

The door opened and the older man turned from the fireplace and walked in front of the sofa. "I'll help you bring these last two down. You take the heavier one on the left and turn off the light before you leave." he said. "Will you be flying the plane tomorrow morning?"

"Yes. We're supposed to be taking off at eleven but it won't surprise me if it's later. Roehrberg's going to call me at eight thirty, let me know the plan." He turned off the light and closed the door.

His nerves stretched and now sweating profusely Thomas waited with growing relief as he heard their voices fade and their steps disappear in the distance. He looked at his watch. It was twenty-five past nine. He had to leave the house quickly if he didn't want to risk Roehrberg coming back and finding him there. He hoped Bettina would keep him at the restaurant until nine-thirty, but then Roehrberg was probably an important client and they would be served quickly. He moved from behind the sofa, placed the documents in his rucksack and slowly opened the door. There was silence again. He heard the sound of a nearby van leaving and decided it was now safe to get out. He ran down the stairs two steps at a time. He had just reached the door to the basement stairs by the kitchen when he heard the front door being opened. There were two voices, Roehrberg's deep one and another much quieter one which, he realised with a sickening jolt, was Bettina's. What was she doing here? Why had she come in with him?

Something the older man had said in the room upstairs came back to him, troubling him, the phrase 'a thing of the past'. From what they said later they were almost certainly talking of Dieter, who was clearly at risk, perhaps already even in danger. They had to get out of here. It was obvious why Roehrberg had persuaded Bettina to come in but why was she wasting time coming back with him? And why was she behaving like that anyway?

Bettina's clear laugh from the living room was followed by Roehrberg's deeper voice saying something with a chuckle but it was too indistinct to let Thomas distinguish the words. Then music started to play softly. He went cold, jealousy gnawing at him. He thought for a moment of confronting Roehrberg, rescuing Bettina and carrying her away but that made no sense. Bettina would certainly find it pathetic and Roehrberg would have him arrested and jailed for breaking in. He walked down the basement steps and across the room, lashing out incautiously with his foot as he passed an old sideboard, rattling the dishes on it dangerously and forcing him to catch one as it nearly smashed. His earlier triumph now felt like defeat. As he trudged into the garden and walked past the living room window he saw the blinds were down and the lights dimmed. He could hear nothing but soft music playing and he tried not to think of what might be going on in the room. He felt sick and very alone.

Chapter 31
Tuesday 16 January 1990, evening

At six-thirty on a Tuesday evening in min-January 1990 Erwin Hammer was sipping a piña colada at Frankfurt's Café Hauptwache while waiting for two of his Phoenix colleagues to show up. Klaus joined him a couple of minutes later followed shortly by a sweaty Patrick.

"I had a hard time finding my way here." Patrick grumbled as he sat down. "None of the taxi drivers had heard of it or seemed to know the alley by name. The guy I got drove for hours and then dropped me off miles away. What made you choose this place?"

"Bloody foreigners!" sneered Klaus. "Think everything has to be done for their benefit."

"I like it here. It's discreet. The guy who runs it knows how to shut his eyes and his ears." Erwin looked at Patrick and laughed. "As you discovered it's hard to find if you don't know where it is. Get yourselves drinks from the bar. I've told the waiters not to disturb us. "

Patrick grunted and helped himself to a Campari soda which he topped up with couple of vodka shots from the freezer. Klaus looked at him with distaste as he poured himself a generous gin and tonic and added ice and lemon.

"Let's check where we are." said Erwin. "Klaus, you told me the network was continuing to expand well. We'll talk about that and any problems there shortly but first let's get an update from you, Patrick. You told me you'd run into some problems in securing the support we need to keep control of the individual loans once they've been changed into Deutsche Marks. Bring me up to date with the situation."

"There are problems in two areas. As our network expanded more and more areas of the country were brought in and so we now need pretty much total geographic coverage in terms of keeping control. At the beginning we were talking about having agents and borrowers only in the seven main cities but now they're everywhere, even in the smallest towns, even in villages for Chrissakes."

"What's the problem?" Klaus interrupted. "What difference does that make? The Stasi's got its fingers everywhere, right down to the tiniest hamlet. They can keep tabs on everything."

"Makes a big, big difference." Patrick retorted. "Before this the Stasi's cut could be kept small. The cake was being divided into a few slices for the big boys and a few crumbs for their city helpers. Now half the country's involved so they need a great mass of crumbs and those aren't coming from the big boys' slices. So the cake needs to be much bigger because everyone's hungry and there's now so many of them."

"How much bigger?" Erwin asked.

"My contact is talking three or four million DMs to get it done."

Erwin stared at him.

"Shit, that's ridiculous! That's eight times what they first asked for, half a mil. We can't pay that!"

"I know." Patrick said. "But they're not stupid and they know the kind of numbers we're playing with. That the exchange rate has dropped dramatically is no mystery. I obviously didn't give them any figures about borrowers but if I say we now need country wide coverage they can work out why. They know that even paying them this amount, we'll still make enough money to make it worthwhile. I don't see that we have any choice. Sure, we could haggle a bit but they've got our bollocks in the vice and they know just how hard to squeeze. We're stuffed if we don't get an agreement with them and they know that."

"OK, we'll talk about that in detail later. What's the other problem?"

"Our contact is meeting internal resistance."

"What's that supposed to mean?" asked Klaus. "You keep talking in riddles. No one can get sense from you. What the hell is 'internal resistance' and why does that need more of our money?"

Erwin placed a calming hand on Klaus's arm as Klaus and Patrick glared at each other. "Jesus!" he thought "They're like two mad dogs around bitches in heat. I wish to God I'd never brought Patrick into this, the trouble he's causing. And Klaus isn't any better – Brains was right saying that he'd be trouble. "

"Exactly what I say." said Patrick. "Our contact is being pressured by a senior colleague. The Stasi no longer exists, at least not in its old form. It's been turned into the ANFS and everyone's busy covering their tracks from the past, dumping evidence, sanitising everything, that sort of thing. So everything's more difficult and costs more to make it worth the risk. That's the justification anyway."

"He's just getting greedier." Klaus said. "Or maybe you are." he added. "These figures don't add up. Maybe you're splitting the money with them? You can fix things with more money, you say, but how do we know it's not just sticking to you? You said they could work things out but it's not as easy as that so just how do they know how much money we stand to make? For all we know you could be ... "

Patrick stood up and shoved the solid table violently in Klaus's direction, following it with his body and trapping him against the wall of the room. The edge hit Klaus in the solar plexus and he doubled over, the air violently expelled from his lungs and his words cut off in mid sentence. Seeing his advantage Patrick kept pushing on table with all his strength while Klaus kept trying to escape, feebly unable to get the leverage he needed to push the table back and fighting to breathe

The sudden rush of the table had caught Erwin, knocking him off his chair to the floor. He scrambled up and rushed to pull off Patrick, hooking his elbow round Patrick's throat and kneeing him in the back. Despite his strength he had no effect, such was the force of Patrick's rage. Clark Kent had suddenly become his alter ego. Eventually Patrick let go of the table and shook off Erwin casually in turn. He glared at Klaus and shook a finger at him.

"Don't you dare say I'm a thief ever again. You arsehole. I'll have you properly next time. You'll find out just what Ossies are capable of."

"Just stop it. Stop it! Both of you. I didn't get you here to watch a fight between raging dogs. We're trying to get a multimillion deal closed, for Christ's sake. You can kill yourselves afterwards, for all I care, but right now we've got some serious stuff to work out. You're acting like fucking children. Just remember, I control this – pull another stunt like that, either of you, and you're out of Phoenix for good."

"That's not ... " began Klaus, the rest unsaid as Erwin grabbed him by the shirt at the neck, twisted it tight, dragging Klaus's face centimetres from his own, and said with quiet menace, "Shut it! *I* make the decisions. *You* follow them."

Erwin sat down, breathing hard and thinking how things risked falling apart without him.

"Patrick, sort the table. Klaus, get us fresh drinks from the bar. The same as before. Now!"

Erwin sat stiffly, glaring at each in turn until everything was arranged to his satisfaction.

"Patrick. You told us about internal difficulties in the Stasi. Is it a formal investigation? Isn't your contact high enough not to care?"

"He's one of the higher ranking officers in The Firm and directly in charge of all the regional headquarters and of covert operations. Earlier that would have meant that he could do pretty much what he liked. He and his colleagues just made the law to suit them. But things are different now. There's even talk of prosecuting Mielke. Mielke! Mielke *was* the Stasi. So he's got to be more careful and a lot of this is pretty dodgy – utilising the Stasi network for private gain, for instance."

"So is he afraid of someone below him, or of someone from outside? A judge, maybe, or magistrate? Where's the problem?"

"He didn't say, but knowing the system I'd doubt that a magistrate would get involved. They're too busy fixing political trials to be interested in chasing corruption cases. They've always been well trained in minding their own business and doing as they were told. Could be someone getting their own back, now things have changed after all this time, of course."

"Hmmm." Erwin thought out loud. "I guess there's no way we can easily check if our Stasi contact is telling the truth or just trying to screw us. Probably a bit of both. The fact remains, he's asking for a lot more money. Tell him I need to meet him personally, in Berlin. Arrange a meeting for two day's time. I guess it's too late now to try to activate the second group, right?"

Patrick shook his head. "There's no way we could get something set up in such a short time with the SED. And their power and reach is now pretty much non-existent anyway. We're stuck with the Stasi and the problem is they know it. Too many people are in the loop now. They'd make it their business to destroy us if we cut them out. But they're armed and they can be ruthless. Anyone exchanging money will think twice about trying any funny games. We can count on that at least."

"Well, this money will have to come from somewhere. What would a good businessman do in this case?" He waited, a slight smile on his face, but neither Klaus nor Patrick made any comment.

"Well, then, I'll tell you. A good chief executive would cut his incidental costs."

The two others looked at him, puzzled. Costs looked as it they had just gone up by three or four million Deutsche Marks, possibly more, and Erwin was talking about cutting them.

"There are three places where we'll do that." he said, looking at each of them in turn. "I kept telling you to make sure everything was properly tied up, Patrick, and you should have done this earlier. You haven't delivered as I wanted and now even if I can salvage something when I meet this guy we're still going to be out several million from the figure we expected to pay. That's your responsibility and because you haven't delivered fully your percentage will go down from 10% to 7%. However, given the state we're in with the numbers and the new exchange rate that's still pretty reasonable, probably even a bit more than the 10% at the beginning would have brought."

Klaus had been grinning in triumph during this speech as he watched Patrick's discomfiture and irritation with the changed percentage. As Erwin turned to him the grin vanished and he looked wary.

"As for you, Klaus, you've done a good enough job building up the agents but you haven't thought things through, have you? You don't know the difference between turnover and profit. You don't know enough about costs and marginal returns. Sure, there's now lots of agents and that helps with loans and the amount we can convert but there's greatly increased costs, proportionately increased as well, in servicing all those out of the way borrowers and that's going to hit our percentage profits. Wouldn't surprise me if some even came in at a loss. Part of that is this extra millions we've heard about. So I'm cutting your percentage as well, knocking the same proportion off. But as I said to Patrick, you're still going to do pretty well out of it."

It was Patrick's turn to smile slightly but each realised they were in a corner, unable to move. There was nothing either could do about it. There was no document setting out the formal division of profits or the percentages each could expect and so they were ultimately in Erwin's hands. And he'd made it very clear that he'd act fairly but expected a great deal from them.

"That's 6% so far" added Erwin "and if we're talking about 20 to 30 million that's still too little, maybe a million and a bit, approaching two million max."

He drew out from his briefcase a sheet of paper on which he'd earlier drawn a pyramid to explain to an agent how everything worked. With a deliberate motion Erwin drew a big X over the pyramid. He looked at it for a moment. "Bye, bye, agents' commissions." he said. "Bye, bye. That's an expense just too far."

Chapter 32
Wednesday 17 January 1990, early hours of the morning

It was well past midnight when the door opened and Bettina crept into the bedroom, her clothes bringing a whiff of cigar smoke from her evening with Roehrberg. Thomas lay stiffly in bed as he had done for an hour or more since he'd given up in despair waiting for Bettina's return.

He had tried to sleep but his brain churned with thoughts and vivid, painful imaginings of Bettina and Roehrberg together. He'd drifted into a half sleep but then jerked awake as he'd seemed to hear again her laugh through the living room door as he'd moved carefully to escape. Her music had been overlaid with inaudible words in Roehrberg's deep growl and which ended in a chuckle. Then there had been silence, a silence almost impossible to bear. What were they doing? There was soft music playing but otherwise the silence continued. Why had she not made excuses and left? The voices stopped but there were other sounds which repeated and quickened then died away to more silence. He drifted in and out of consciousness.

Then, as on a screen, he watched stubby fingers caress Bettina's neck and saw her stretch and arch her neck then nuzzle like a cat, smiling with pleasure. The fingers undid a button and then a second, ran their backs lightly over the smooth, swelling skin now partly exposed and showing white with veins repeating the deep blue of her shirt, then moved lower and although he looked away the screen followed, lurched into his line of vision even with his eyes shut, though now the picture was shifting and fragmenting, now swirling into nothing, now showing disordered fabric, the hem of a dress or the edge of a shirt and always those stubby fingers moving and lightly stroking. Then a knee appeared at the foot of the screen and moved slowly upwards as it bent and rose, widely separating from its fellow across the whole width and always those stubby fingers, now stroking and caressing with more urgency, a soft moaning returning. He had a flash of pain and with that the screen vanished, leaving him half awake, the taint of cigar smoke in his nostrils and with a feeling of immense sadness.

"Thomas. Are you awake?"

He lay there, still, nursing his feelings, keeping his jealousy and fury warm. After a moment she pulled the curtains a small distance apart and the moonlight streamed in.

Now fully awake he watched as she undressed, her back turned to him, the soft rays highlighting her breasts as she turned and walked to retrieve her nightdress then stretched and raised her arms to slip it on, but shadowing under them and failing to penetrate lower and deeper. The thought that she'd been in Roehrberg's arms filled him with a turmoil of emotion, of sadness and anger and despair.

As he'd escaped from Roehrberg's house and pedalled furiously back to the farm he'd felt resentment towards her and an intense jealously of the older man. This had given way to self-pity and despair and at the bottom of the hill he swung round the corner too fast and wide, for a moment dragging himself intentionally into the path of a fast approaching car until the blare of its horn brought him to his senses and he returned to the proper side.

As Bettina slipped into bed he knew that he wanted her with a passion beyond mere animal lust, a feeling that went beyond what he felt when he'd thought of her with Roehrberg, and he realised that he'd fallen in love with her, something he'd not earlier been prepared to admit. It had taken seeing her with another man, a man he both feared and despised, to make the wall he'd built around his heart crumble. But he had to accept he'd lost her, as he had with

Olga, and then his despair gave way to anger and he hated her.

"How often has she done this before?" he thought. And then "I suppose that's just what she does to get information out of people."

He could feel the warmth of her body next to him, drawing him towards her. He thought back to the different times he'd felt close to her, that first evening when he'd tried to impress at the French restaurant and the night the Wall fell and he stayed in her apartment. There had seemed then to be a growing attachment. He'd felt her close enough to reach her, to develop love between them, but had lacked the courage to try. If he did then that might confirm his worst fears, remove any remaining hope. Maybe his instinct had been correct. It seemed to him now that it was all in his imagination, that she'd been using him, just as she did everyone, playing with his emotions the better to control him. He was her responsibility within the organisation Thomas reminded himself. He had been a fool to think anything true could ever happen between them.

She turned, and was facing him now, her head resting on the pillow. He could feel her breath on his face and the familiar smell of her skin had replaced the cigar smoke of her clothes.

"Are you awake?" she breathed.

He lay for a moment, pretending sleep, but it was too much for him to bear. He opened his eyes and stared at her in the darkness as he might at an unwelcome stranger. He didn't recognise his own voice when he spoke.

"I've not slept. Not properly anyway. Did you enjoy yourself at Roehrberg's? At Rudolf's. Or is there a pet name you use now?"

She turned and reached for the side light, fumbling for a moment then finding the switch and turning it on. She glanced at him but then looked away almost immediately and lay down, turned away from him and burrowed into the bedclothes. He blinked in the light and sat up a little in the bed, leaning on his elbow towards her. Her voice became increasingly muffled.

"You think I went to bed with him, do you? You think I just went out for a good time, and *eine gute Ficke* to complete the evening. ... think I'm a whore ... I'm an easy lay ... you bastard ... "

He grabbed her shoulders and wrenched her round to face him.

"If you've got something to tell me, say it to my face."

"He asked me to give him a lift back up the hill from the restaurant and when I was about to drop him at his gate I noticed your bicycle nearby and realised you were probably still inside. That's why I accepted his invitation in, because I thought maybe you could do with not having him prowling around while you escaped. But I don't have to justify myself!"

She wrenched herself away, turning from him, and they lay in sullen silence for some minutes.

Thomas sighed then stretched out his hand and at his touch on her shoulder she shrugged him off and burrowed deeper away from him. Once more he stretched out, this time cupping his hand on her shoulder, pressing firmly, not forcing her to turn but making it clear what he wanted. Then he removed his hand and lay back and after a moment she turned partly towards him and lay on her back in turn looking at the ceiling, now breathing more calmly. Neither spoke. Shortly afterwards, as she settled, he felt her knuckles brushing his knee in what might have been an accident had it not been for the moment of hesitation in contact. He glanced at her.

"Roehrberg's study was full of documents packed in cartons." he said. "Remember those things we thought had gone missing from Henkel's shelves. Looks like they ended up with Roehrberg. I managed to take some pictures and grab a few documents before a couple of men arrived to remove them and I nearly got caught. Roehrberg's taking them with him, wherever he's going."

"Well, that's good." she said flatly. "That could tie him in to Henkel's death."

He looked at her, wondering why she wasn't giving him more credit for what he'd achieved.

"Yes, but there's more. The two men were talking about stuff as they worked, this and that, not a lot that meant much to me. But they mentioned someone getting just what he deserved, and they were pleased about that. They also mentioned Dieter, with hostility, and it sounded as if someone had been killed or maybe was to be killed. Do you think Dieter ... ?"

Bettina stared at the ceiling for a long moment, then turned to Thomas.

"It's not Dieter. It was Herren. He was on his way to a meeting, perhaps with Kohl although I don't know, and his car was ambushed, blown up. Roehrberg had just learned of it and told me tonight. He was killed instantly and that there wasn't much left of the car."

"Herren? Herren assassinated?!" Thomas's mind flew back to the interrogation at the Stasi HQ in Berlin after his visit to Frankfurt. It made more sense now and he realised how they'd used him and how the information he'd given had led to this. His heart started to race and he could hardly breathe. He stared at Bettina, enraged that it apparently meant little to her.

"Jesus, Bettina. You're a real cunt." He was shouting now, not knowing what he was doing, heedless that it was the middle of the night. He found himself grabbing handfuls of her hair, pulling her down and towards him, shaking her like a terrier with a rat. "You don't give a shit! You and Dieter don't give a shit about what happens to other people.

Just so long as you get the information you want. That's all that matters. I told you what I'd learned. And you killed Herren because of that. I killed Herren! How can you just lie there? It's got everything to do with you. You're in this as well."

Sweat rushed down Thomas's face and he felt chilled then hit by a violent convulsion in his stomach, acid filling his throat and spilling into his mouth. He threw her back, tumbled from the bed and rushed to the bathroom, kneeling by the lavatory pan to retch, the porcelain cold on his face. Returning, his fury had changed to a cold anger at Bettina.

"You and Dieter killed Herren. And I guided you! And now Stephan could be at risk of his life. All because of what you made me do."

"Thomas, I understand your feelings but that's not ... "

"Don't patronise me. You don't understand the tiniest bit of my feelings here. You just play with my feelings to control me. At one point I thought I could trust you but I know now what a goddamn fool I've been."

"It was nothing to do with Dieter. Nothing to do with us. Nothing to do with the information you gave us. Marcus Wolf and Mielke had already learned about Herren. And it was the Red Army Fraktion, the Baader-Meinhof gang as people call them, who did it. Nothing to do with us. Believe me. Nothing to do with the Firm. Herren was hit by a West German terrorist group just as they've hit other capitalists in the past and will again."

The noise of Thomas's open hand slapping Bettina's cheek startled them both. She fell back on the pillow, her cheek violently reddening as tears ran down her face. Thomas raised his hand again and then slowly dropped it, overcome with remorse, with a deep weariness and shame but lost as to what to do next. His anger ebbed but making any gesture of apology or reconciliation was beyond him. He turned away, buried his face in the pillow, his hands clasped on his head, his knees on his chest and his body tightly curled.

As he sobbed desperately he became aware that Bettina had moved close to him, spooned round his back, and was gently stroking the nape of his neck, her other arm lying over his waist and pressing on his knee. He pushed her violently away and then later, as she persisted half turned towards her, straightening his legs, his head pressed to her chest and lay there, his despair and anger draining away.

After some considerable time, each of them drifting in and out of sleep, he settled further on her and feeling a nipple through the thin cotton of her nightdress caught it with his lips and brushed it with his tongue, playing as it stiffened to his touch and as she settled closer round him he felt the touch of bone and hair on his hip. When he nipped her breast lightly with his teeth she yelped and pushed him away and as they smiled at each other settled down more closely, Bettina on her back, Thomas further turned towards her with his upper arm now resting on her belly, the back of his fingers lightly brushing her inner thigh.

"Later." she said, turning the light off. "Later, Thomas. Now we must sleep. We've so much to do tomorrow. Good night." But in the darkness she lay there as before, still.

He moved and kissed her lightly on the chin before brushing his lips over hers then lay back, his arm lying as before, feeling the warmth of her lower thigh on his hand. She clasped her free hand with his and drew it upwards leaving him to curl and uncurl his fingers in slow glissandi, his courting finger now dipping and stroking and easing open the moistened, tumescent surfaces, sliding it gently upwards and curvingly towards him, upwards and back, as her breathing quickened and, moving her hand cupped and grasped and stroked him in turn until with an urgency new to each of them they joined fully together.

Chapter 33
Wednesday 17 January 1990

"Good morning! I hope you both slept well."

"Thank you, yes." said Thomas. "I had a wonderful night. Both of us, I think."

Thomas glanced at Bettina and they smiled complicitly at each other as Frau Dornbusch welcomed them with a jug of steaming coffee and set a large plate of toasted bread on the table.

"There was a call early this morning for you, Fräulein." she added. "He called himself Georg and said he needed to talk with you urgently. He said to come to his office, if possible."

Thomas looked enquiringly at Bettina but she ignored him, giving her attention to the butter and conserve she was spreading on the toast in front of her. They chatted with Frau Dornbusch about trivial matters for a few minutes before quickly finishing breakfast and returning to their room.

"Stop it!" she said, trying to sound severe but spoiling the effect with her smile as Thomas slid his arms round her waist and pulled her towards him. "I have to ... mmmhhh .... get ready .... mmmmmhhhhh ... to see ... " She finally pulled away from his embrace. " ... Georg." It sounded like a command as she skipped out his reach.

"I'll see him on my own and you can stay here and check through those documents you stole from Roehrberg, find out if they're interesting. We'll catch up later on back here."

In half an hour she was at Georg's office finding him again oblivious to interruption, working on a pile of documents. Again she watched him for a few moments before she knocked softly, then more loudly, on the door. He glanced up, shook his head very slightly, waved her away and gestured that they should meet outside in a few minutes. When he appeared round the corner of the building he looked grave and serious and with an air quite different to the one he'd had at the previous meeting.

"What's up, Georg? You look like something terrible has happened."

"Let's take a walk a bit further away, shall we? It's about the mill. Yesterday I asked some of my older colleagues if they knew of any registrations of sales of state-held industrial assets in recent months. A couple of them seem to know everything that goes on here. Let's find somewhere quiet, somewhere no one can hear us, and I'll tell you what I've learned."

He took her arm and they walked in silence for some minutes, crossing the Elbe and making for a small park on the other side of the river. A narrow footpath wandered over the grass and Georg selected an isolated bench set some distance back from the track and away from bushes and trees.

"I managed to find the approximate date yesterday through a friend who used to work at the mill. Apparently the restructuring was announced and approved a month and a half ago. I assume if the mill was sold it must have been at the same time. So yesterday afternoon I started checking the archives within the last couple of months for the sale details. I even went back to three months before, but there was nothing there."

"That's very strange."

"Listen, Bettina. While I was there, Wolfgang, one of the older colleagues I mentioned - we call him the walking archive as he seems to know so much - came in to look for something. So I asked him if he knew of any documents relative to the privatisation of a flour mill. He immediately looked startled, then fearful and turned around to check if there was anyone else in the room. He closed the door, came over to me, put his finger to his lips and whispered, in a tone I'd never heard him use: 'Why are you poking around in this, Georg? Don't get yourself in a mess. Forget about it. Just forget all about it if you care for your life and your family.' He looked seriously worried. I think you've hit on something very suspicious and very ugly."

Bettina sat looking at him, intrigued by this new twist. "But then ... why didn't you find the document? Did you check everywhere?"

"I went through everything, file by file. There was absolutely no sign of it."

"What about Wolfgang? Can you trust him? Maybe he was warning you off because it's something he's involved in."

"Trust?!" he said sharply, and laughed. "I should have thought you would know you can fully trust no one in this place. No one. Nearly everyone's a spy of some sort. Even family members." He glared at Bettina and then after a moment took her hand and patted it. He shook his head slightly and sighed.

"I'm sorry. That was unkind. I do believe what you told me earlier. It's just. This place. It gets to you and you can't think straight. The police and the Stasi watch everybody. Everybody's told it's their duty watch others, to report anything suspicious. It's to reduce crime and anti-social behaviour, they say. They tap telephones, listen to people, photograph people, keep records, note who meets whom and where and for how long." He laughed shortly, without humour. "They say it's for state security, for everyone's security, that if you've nothing to hide you've nothing to fear. And they wonder why people go mad, why they try to escape, why they kill themselves. That's the corrosive effect on society, on any society, of spying on everyone."

They sat in silence, George still holding Bettina's hand then got up and they walked slowly across the grass towards the river.

"Wolfgang is sound. At least, as far as I can tell, and I have no choice but to trust him."

Abruptly Georg stopped walking and stood motionless staring at the distant ruins of the Frauenkirche across the river and just visible through the trees along the banks. Bettina held her breath, waiting.

"Unless, ... unless they forged the dates and the protocols." he said slowly. "That would explain why the matter is so sensitive and dangerous. If Wolfgang knew that had happened that would explain his alarm. It's a serious infraction of Court procedure. Falsification of public documents is a serious crime in law. Sure, the Party just changes the law when it wants to keep tabs on people's communications but this is different. That's it! That's what must have happened."

"But how is that possible? Aren't the documents registered one by one, with all sorts of signatures from different people?"

Georg was again silent, thinking over the issues. He spoke slowly and carefully.

"The various parties involved sign the documents at earlier stages and these are certified by the public notary. Then there are only two signatures required for the registration of all public documents. One is that of a state notary, the other that of the president of the Court. So unless they counterfeited these signature it means the notary or the president, or quite possibly both, are involved. But the documents also need to be assigned a protocol number and registered in the relevant archives. That's the job Wolfgang does. Someone must have told him to add a document to the existing protocol lists. That could only be someone very senior within the Court – well, unless Wolfgang's part of it and did it on his own initiative, and I'd find that very hard to believe."

"But why wouldn't they have just registered it now? Why would they backdate something like this?"

"I guess they'd want to protect themselves in case anyone decided to investigate the sale. Properly done, it would be extremely difficult for anyone to prove that the sale didn't take place a long time ago and that the procedure followed wasn't regular according to the law at the time."

"Could someone other than Wolfgang assign a number and register the document so that he wouldn't know?" asked Bettina.

"Yes, possibly. Particularly if the insertion in the archives was supposedly some years ago." He thought for some moments the shook his head. "No, I'm afraid not. Well, yes, they could, but Wolfgang's meticulous and sooner or later he'd find the cuckoo and wonder why it was there. That's what's happened, I'm sure of it. He's followed it through and been told in no uncertain terms that he'd better forget what he saw. So it must be someone really high up. Poor Wolfgang. He's the one in danger. No wonder he was terrified when I mentioned it."

He paused for a moment, lost in his thoughts and mulling over the problem. Suddenly his expression changed.

"But wait, no, there's an even better reason for backdating things. Sure, it hides malfeasance but more importantly it secures ownership. After five years from when an act of sale is registered it's no longer open to raise objections to that sale. Any rights of creditors or those with title, whatever they happen to be, are automatically annulled. It's as if they never existed."

"You mean the sale becomes irreversible."

"Exactly. Whoever did this is probably understands the law well enough to know this. So when the country is unified they'll be able to avoid any risk of West German politicians investigating, maybe to support past private owners of the property, and getting the sale overturned. No one will be able to do that."

"Not unless they can prove that the sale was fraudulent and the supporting records falsified."

"Sure, but how do you do that? If they filed all the documents correctly, there is no way to tell the fact occurred at a different date. You would have to get someone who signed the document to testify to its falsity. Or persuade Wolfgang to speak out - if he's still alive that is."

"And who would the signatories be?"

"In this case, we have no idea who the buyer is but if you are correct the selling entity must be the state. They would both sign - that's easy here, of course. Then later, as I mentioned, the document gets signed by the President of the Court and by the state notary. We don't know if these have been forged or if those officials are also involved."

"But it looks as if the Party is involved as well. Given the risks it's probably someone high up in the chain." Bettina said. "No wonder Wolfgang told you to stay out of it."

"If they've done everything by the book then even if you found the document - and at this point it could be registered any time prior to now, or before January 1985 if my theory is correct, which means finding it will be almost impossible - then you would have to prove ... "

"At least we'll be able to know who's involved. I think we're too deep into this to simply pull back."

There was a long silence and then Georg sighed.

"Information can be very dangerous Bettina, and you should understand that better than most. I need a little time to think this thing through. Right now I'm not sure I want to risk my life to discover which of the crooks stole some asset from the state."

Bettina stared at him for a moment, her initial shock turning to anger.

"Georg, you're the one who used to rant at home against the injustices of this regime, the hypocrisies, the low-level dealings. You started a newspaper to expose them, for God's sake! When I was a kid, I was scared but secretly I really admired your courage." She stopped for breath. "Just the other day, you get on your high horse and tear strips off me for being in the Stasi. But I'm ready to take risks for the sake of justice, in defence of our laws and country. What's happened to you?"

There was a long, awkward silence. Georg looked at the ground, unable to hold her gaze.

"I'm sorry." he said finally. "It was a long time ago and there were different reasons. And now, after all these years, I'm tired. I want to help, I know I should help, but that's what a surveillance state does to you, I'm tired. I thought I could fight the state. I don't think I can. I'm very sorry."

"At least tell me where I'd need to search for the document."

"It would have to be in the Archive building, in Lothringerallee, assuming they've backdated it."

"Do you go there often? Couldn't you try to find the document while officially doing something else?"

"I used to go there a lot, but these days hardly ever. So if I went now, after having mentioned this to my colleagues, it would look very suspicious. Who knows who's in on the scheme. You know how the Stasi works - little bits of information here and there fitting together and making a bigger picture. I'd be arrested. And anyway, it's going to be almost impossible to find. We don't know the false date and there's thousands of documents. Each archive room holds only a few months of each given year and I couldn't just wander around the place. I would need lots of time to do this properly."

"We don't have time. The state is about to collapse and that's what these crooks are counting on. Georg, we've got to do what we can to stop them."

She moved close to him, put her arms around his shoulders and laid her head on his chest.

"Georg. Please. Please help me." As she looked up at him he looked away, unable to meet her gaze. "Remember the paper Georg. Remember what you thought was so important to fight. This is important. Remember what you fought for. Please Georg."

Gently he opened her arms and stepped back out of them. "I'm so sorry Bettina but that will has gone. I'm tired of being watched. Tired of always being careful about what I do. I've done nothing wrong and I've nothing to hide but knowing the state's watching you just makes you fearful. You always start to wonder. What's it going to be like if I really do do something illegal? I can't face that. I'm just too tired. Too tired. I've got to look after myself."

He turned, not looking at her, and walked away and as he did she watched his stooped shoulders and dragging walk feeling a wave of immense pity for him and anger at how her country had so damaged the man she'd known and admired for his ferocious integrity.

Chapter 34
Wednesday 17 January 1990, afternoon

Sitting alone in his office, his colleague Ussolzev then away briefly in Leipzig, KGB agent Putin reflected on the recording he had first listened to the day before. The *kneipe* known simply as Egon's, just a few streets away from the KGB office in Angelikastrasse, was favoured by senior officers of both the SED-PDS, as the East German Party had now become, and of the Stasi as a discreet location in which to discuss sensitive matters.

With the Stasi now officially disbanded on the previous Saturday and with the DDR in a state of near-anarchy places like Egon's had grown in importance. Trust between colleagues had become fragile and taking care not to be overhead had become even more of a priority than usual. Böhm was still nominally in charge of whatever was left of the Dresden Stasi though in practice Herbert Kohler had taken over. Dresden's Party secretary, Hans Modrow, had become Prime Minister in December and although nominally retaining his position had conceded authority to Roehrberg.

Although the Stasi and the KGB had worked closely together Böhm had become increasingly irritated with Putin's activities. Seeking to build a network of spies for his own use in targeting students and foreigners in East Germany Putin had successfully turned several who had already been active as Stasi informers. A complaint to Mielke had led to a reprimand to Putin but although Putin promised to scale back his activities, at least where existing Stasi agents were concerned, he had in fact ramped them up as the political turmoil increased and the dissolution of the East German state became imminent. "My loyalty is to Russia and Russia's interest," he'd said "not to the DDR."

No one realised, however, that Egon - sound, reliable Egon who had been loyal to the Stasi for many years - was now also one of Putin's and that there was built into the fabric of the *kneipe* a sophisticated and highly sensitive directional and noise cancelling recording system that meant that everything said there was always fully open to Putin. Every morning one of three assistants would collect the previous days recordings. Then between them they would copy the tape for security, listen to everything and mark for Putin's attention items of interest, typically delivering a tape and notes to him the following morning, but occasionally rushing urgent matters over. A planned assassination didn't really fit into the urgent category unless Russia's interests seemed to be affected.

Putin glanced at the notes on Sunday's recording, saw the reference to Roehrberg, moved to the marked point on the tape, and pressed play.

"Where is the money now?" he heard Roehrberg asking and then Henkel explaining that he'd moved it initially to his office in small batches and then discreetly to a deposit private section in a local storage facility as they had earlier discussed and agreed. He'd passed the key over to Roehrberg as he spoke.

"The problem now" he added "is this investigation. We'd counted on longer, a couple of weeks or so, to muddy the trail, lose the cash through these foreign trips, but when Dieter called Böhm and had him check with me on some pretext or other I had to call him back and say the money had mysteriously vanished."

"Did Böhm believe you at the time? And what about Dieter?" asked Spitze.

"I don't know for sure. I think Böhm swallowed it or in any case decided he'd no choice but to go along with it. Maybe we ned to pay him off. Dieter's something different.

You know what he's like, keeps digging at things till he gets the answer, won't be bribed or threatened so he's difficult."

"I spoke with Dieter yesterday" said Roehrberg "and he told me he's sending down an assistant of his to look around and check things out, Bettina, Bettina something, List, I think. We're meeting tomorrow though how Dieter thinks someone junior like that can find out answers I don't know."

"Sounds like we shouldn't have much to worry about, then." said Henkel. "You can work your famous charm on her, Rudi, you'll have her lapping it up, tell her anything she wants to hear and she'll swallow it!"

"Maybe." said Spitze. "But my guess is not. Dieter's no fool and I'd doubt his assistants are either. She'll be talking with you Gerd and you need to be careful. What's our story going to be? Well, *your* story Gerd. You signed for it and it's your responsibility. You can't just say, Duh, it's vanished, must have been the tooth fairy took it. You, we, need a proper, watertight story that's going to convince Dieter, or at least hold him off for a few weeks. We need to work that out."

"OK, OK. You're right. Look, I've got to go. I'm meeting someone. But I should be home by seven - give me a ring just after that, Rudi, or call round if you want, and we can finalise things then and sort any minor loose ends out in the office tomorrow. Don't worry. We're not going to trip up now. That money's ours. We've got it and we can hang on it, whatever Dieter think or tries."

Putin fast forwarded over the sounds of Henkel leaving, of the remaining two collecting beers from Egon, and of a short discussion with one of Roehberg's junior staff who had called in with some papers to sign. Reaching the next trigger point he pressed *Play* and leant back, listening intently.

"Damn right we're not going to trip up now!" The voice was Roehrberg's. "Sponden can lean on Dieter but you know what's Dieter's like. He'll just go his own way irrespective. He's like a fucking dachshund after a badger once he's picked up the scent, and he'll just keep at it - unless someone kills him first."

The tape went quiet and Putin imagined the two men, alone in the café, looking at each other.

"Unless someone kills him first." said Spitze slowly. "Unless someone kills *Gerd* first."

"Think about it." he added. "Gerd kills himself. Leaves a note admitting his theft. Money's gone. No one knows where. We're clear."

"Yeah, sure. But Gerd's an old friend. I like Gerd. Why not you? Why don't we have you steal it, you confess, you commit suicide. Same result. I could fix that."

Spitze laughed. "I'm sure you could! And the same goes for you, Rudolf. You could have done it, better than me given your position. But Gerd, as Treasurer, is the most obvious candidate. He had the opportunity. All we need to do is construct a plausible motive."

"And get someone reliable to do it. Don't forget that bit. Or are you offering?"

There was another silence and then Roerhrberg spoke again. "I don't know. It's a good suggestion, but Gerd? I don't think so." He sighed heavily.

"Ten million's a lot of money." said Spitze softly. "The expenses may go up a little, sure, but it'll now be shared two ways, not three. Think about it." There was the sound of a chair being scraped back and then further silence for several minutes until there were the sound of returning footsteps and of Spitze sitting down again. "Well?" he said.

"I've thought of someone." said Roehrberg. "And at least Gerd hasn't any family, not like you, not even girlfriends like I have. God, I can't do that to him, though."

"He brought it on himself." said Spitze, suddenly and harshly. "You don't know this but it wasn't really a proper investigative visit from Böhm at all. Gerd freaked out. I know because we talked, he was really nervous after he'd moved the money, said he was going to call Dieter and report it stolen. He said Böhm was suspicious, asking questions, and it would be better that way. I thought I'd calmed him, persuaded him just to hang on till the foreign trips when we'd be clear. Obviously not."

Again there was silence broken again by a heavy sigh.

"There's someone people call der Schlächter, the Butcher." said Roehrberg. "He does this and that for cover but he does other, well, specialist work as well, specialist contract work. He's discreet and efficient." He sighed again. "I don't like this but, OK, I'll call him. There's a safe phone outside."

Again there was the sound of a chair being scraped, this time followed by the *kneipe's* outside door slamming shut. In a few minutes Roehrberg was back.

"7.30." he said. "He comes to my house first and gets the letter and we finalise some details. I'll ring Gerd, say we've worked out a plan, that I'll send a friend over to explain how he can help and that I'll follow. But I can't go to see him. I can't. Not Gerd."

The chair scraped back. "Fuck you, Spitze." he said fiercely, and strode rapidly out, slamming the door hard.

Putin took off the headphones and looked at his watch. He picked up the desk telephone and dialled a number.

"Herr Roehrberg, please. Major Putin."

"Roehrberg!"

"Rudi. It's Volodya. Look, something has come up and we need to talk about it. Spitze needs to be there too. It's about der Schlächter. And Henkel." He listened as the handset squawked.

"I think you do, Rudi." he went on. "I think you know exactly what I'm talking about. I know about your talk with Spitze. We all know about what happened to Henkel later on Sunday. You see, I've got a copy of some interesting recordings and although I could get these to Berlin it would be better for both of us to hear my proposal."

He listened again for a short while.

"Yes, exactly. And of course I know about the money and the mill and all the other stuff that's going on. I just want my fair share of it, that's all, and maybe a bit extra to remember Henkel by. I'm sure you'll want to be generous when you hear what I have to say. Shall we say Egon's again in what, twenty minutes? Excellent! See you both at five, then. Oh, and Rudi. Remember I said a *copy* of interesting recordings - the original's quite safe. Quite safe and quite inaccessible to you, believe me."

Chapter 35
Wednesday 17 January 1990, afternoon, evening and night

"If Georg won't help us then we'll do it ourselves! We can't risk asking around. We have to break in and just search the place."

Bettina had returned to the farmhouse after her meeting with Georg, alternating between disappointment and fury with what she saw as his weakness in not being prepared to help. This wasn't the Georg she remembered, the friend she'd idolised as a child for the way he stood up for the rights which were being trampled on, the fearless journalist whose clandestine writings had enraged the authorities by pointing up their many faults. 'Truth to power!' That's what he'd said then was the only course a concerned and committed citizen could honestly take. Look at him now!

They lay on the bed and Thomas had tried to calm her but over an hour later she was still despondent and crossly upset at what she called Georg's betrayal.

"OK!" agreed Thomas. "I'm with you on that, but how do we do it? Do you think our master keys will work or will they have special locks there? What if people are working late? How do we find where the forged document is anyway? We don't even know the date and it could be anywhere, according to what Georg told you."

For another hour they picked over the difficulties and how to overcome them. Bettina had learned from Georg that the cleaners came in at seven in the morning and that there was usually someone working late although rarely beyond about ten thirty in the evening. For safety they decided to break in shortly after midnight giving them, they hoped, about six hours to search. It wasn't much but it was all they could risk. They'd have to make do and hope to strike lucky.

By now it was late afternoon and winter dark and for a while they lay on the bed dozing lightly, newly comfortable in each other's presence and watching the moon rise over the countryside beyond the window. At six they rose, washed the sleepiness out of their eyes and went downstairs to eat with Frau Dornbusch and her family.

"Maybe our own last supper!" Thomas said, then winced as Bettina kicked him under the table. They smiled at each other and when the meal was finished went out for a short walk before returning to their room.

"Let's get our sleep in first – we'll be pretty tired by the morning if it all works out."

Again they lay on the bed, fully dressed, entwined, and dozed fitfully until startled awake by the alarm. It was approaching midnight and time to set off. Grabbing the rucksack Thomas headed quietly downstairs followed by Bettina, each remembering to step over the third step from the top which creaked when anyone stood on it. They walked in silence to the car which they'd parked a little distance from the farmhouse.

The archives building on Lothringerallee was a long rectangle of solid stone on four floors which dominated the street. The façade was imposing and loured ominously in the moonlight, the wide steps leading up to the solid front doors throwing deep shadows. Rough-cut blocks of limestone jutted out from the façade, separated by gaps looking just wide enough to take a toe hold. Thomas and Bettina circled the building, trying to identify the best way to enter. On the second floor, on the corner with Ziegelstrasse, each side had a window opening on to a small balcony, which looked promising. Across the road there was a long wall with the Elias cemetery behind it.

"If anything goes wrong and we can't get back to the car, we'll hide over there, behind the wall." Bettina said quietly, pointing.

They continued walking round the building, turning at the next corner into a narrow side street, Schulgutstrasse, and then along the full length of Geyerstrasse before turning back into Lothringerallee. On two of the building's corners there were small towers, built higher than elsewhere and presumably providing exits from the interior to the flat roof. Although they'd walked slowly, searching the structure carefully, it had still taken them a good ten minutes to circle the archives building.

"God, it's huge!" Thomas said. "We'd easier find a virgin in a brothel as find the document here. And look, there's still some lights on – not good."

Rather than go boldly up the main steps they continued round to the secondary entrance on Ziegelstrasse where the risk of being observed was much less. Although the late night streets were deserted and the building had now become dark Thomas's heart was hammering and he could feel the adrenaline surging, giving his body a strange, jittery warmth. He pulled out the set of master keys from the rucksack and began trying them in sequence. After a few fruitless attempts one slid into the lock and half turned but then stuck, unable to engage with the wards to open the lock. He moved it carefully backwards and forwards by fractions of a millimetre, willing his fingers to understand by extension the intimate nuzzling of the framework of the key seeking passage.

The key rotated a fraction further but as he concentrated they heard ragged footsteps approaching along Lothringerallee, getting louder and then drifting into Ziegelstrasse itself. They embraced, Bettina burying her head in his shoulder and Thomas turning to face the building, a courting couple finding privacy in the shadows.

"Thash the way, mate! You give it 'er good'n'proper." the drunken voice encouraged as a hand waved vaguely in their direction and the erratic footsteps zig-zagged away. Their silent laughter broke the tension.

"Just wanted to make sure he'd really gone." said Thomas as they eventually disengaged reluctantly and he tried once more to open the door. None of the other keys worked and although they again circled the building carefully it became obvious that the locks were all of the same type and that the master set of keys was of no help.

"What now?"

"We could try with another set of keys now that we know which type enters the lock." Bettina suggested. "But that's going to mean another day and night lost and Dieter wants us back as soon as possible."

"Let me try something. Look, these lower windows are barred but the upper ones aren't. I used to do mountain climbing and free-climbing with my dad. I'm sure I could get to that window there on the second floor, on the corner by the balcony. It's only about, what, six metres I guess, maybe seven."

"I don't think that's a good …"

"Just help me up this first bit. Lace your hands in front of you and I can use that as a first step and then get to that first ledge."

Swinging smoothly on from Bettina's cupped hands and lightly stepping on her shoulder Thomas grasped one of the blocks of stone above his head and stood on the top of the decorative facing running round the foot of the building. He placed a toe in the narrow gap between two higher stone blocks then pulled himself up, rested for a moment, then stretched up and grasped the next block to haul himself further. He'd reached the first floor window, about half way to the balcony, when there was the sound of a car in the distance and in a moment he saw a pair of headlights turn into Ziegelstrasse and come towards them. Bettina walked briskly down the street in the direction the car was travelling and he flattened himself against the building, immobile, barely breathing, hoping that the driver would be concentrating on the road or might be distracted by the sight of Bettina ahead of him. The car continued past without stopping and without changing its speed and as it disappeared round the corner at the end of Ziegelstrasse he hauled himself up another block.

But by now he was beginning to tire and his arms hurt. He was more out of condition than he'd thought. He hauled himself up by another block and was now almost in reach of the balcony, just to one side and a little recessed from it. The edges of the blocks sloped slightly to the outside, however, and although that hadn't mattered much before his fingers were now starting to lose their feeling in the cold and he was beginning to despair of retaining his grip for the time he still needed.

He stuck his toes into the gap as deeply as he could wriggle them, relaxed his arms for a moment, and then turned for the final push to the balcony. He could feel the weight of his body dragging him downwards and he wondered briefly how much it would hurt if he fell. He might well kill himself, he realised. He stretched for the edge of the balcony and although he just touched it with his fingertips it was too far for him to get a good grip on either the parapet or the protective railing above it. He was hit with a sudden bout of panic, the fear of losing his grip and falling almost paralysing him and he stood there for what seemed an age, unable to move up or down and with his arms growing increasingly tired. He willed himself consciously to relax and hang there till he felt calmer.

He breathed deeply and slowly, willing strength back into his arms and fingers, then carefully edged sideways as close as he could to the balcony, hampered by damage to the block which limited where he could grip, and prepared to make a last desperate attempt to grip the parapet above him and to his right. Matters were complicated both by the wide decorative cladding at each floor level and by the wide and sturdy square stone pillars, topped with an acorn finial, which closed off each end of the balcony and which were too big to grasp securely.

There were footsteps coming along Geyerstrasse and the fear of being seen acted as a catalyst. Summoning all his strength he exploded upwards, lunging at the edge of the balcony, scrabbling with his fingers and managing to grab one of the thinner vertical stone railings in from the square pillar at the end. Praying that it wouldn't break with the extra force and so dump him on to the pavement he used all the strength of his tired limbs to haul himself up, forcing one foot to waist level and placing it on the decorative cladding separating the floors. At first, precariously balanced and with huge tension in his arms and back, unable to get leverage, it seemed as if he could move no further. Then, slowly, again summoning all his remaining strength he straightened his bent leg and forced himself further upwards just enough to grasp the top rail of the balcony with his free hand, bring up the other to join it and pull himself over, tumbling on to the balcony and lying there exhausted, his face pressed to the stone floor as the footsteps passed underneath him on the pavement, stopping briefly but then continuing as if reassured.

In a few moments he roused himself to his knees then stood up, looked over and hissed to Bettina: "Sorry! I was whacked after that, maybe even passed out for a moment. Everything's fine now, though. I'm going to try the window."

He rooted around in his rucksack and took out a thin metal ruler which he slid into the gap between the frame of the casement and its surround. He worked it upwards till it pressed against a catch then tapped it from below with another tool he'd brought, the small hammer with the muffled face. With a few light taps the catch sprung up, freeing the window, and he stepped over the sill and into the room beyond.

Switching on his torch he cursed on discovering that the batteries were very low so that he could hardly see where he was going. Too late he remembered the set of new batteries he'd left on their dressing table to make sure they weren't forgotten. As he moved further into the room and out into the corridor the moonlight faded and although the torch gave hardly any light his eyes had acclimatised and he was able to move reasonably well although he banged his shin hard on a low table in his way and hopped in pain for some seconds.

He opened another door and found himself at the top of stairs leading to the lower floors. The building was designed with a large rectangular atrium roofed with glass through which moonlight now streamed making his descent easy. On the ground floor he stopped, looked around to orientate himself and to work out where the exit to Ziegelstrasse was likely to be.

As he left the atrium by a nearby corridor the light from the moon again faded and half way along his torch gave up completely forcing him to feel his way. At the end the corridor became a T-junction and the direction he tried first became a dead end lined with nothing but locked doors. Frustrated and angry at the loss of time, cursing himself again for his stupidity in forgetting the batteries he retraced his steps and now saw, as his eyes had again become accustomed to the darkness, a faint glow ahead of him growing brighter and which turned out to be moonlight coming through a fanlight above what had to be the outside door.

Running his hands down the edge of the door he found what felt like a cylinder deadlock with a doorknob further down but no sign of a mortice lock as well. He turned both knobs and pulled at the door without success. He tried again, first ensuring that the lock was caught open and then twisting the doorknob with both hands and tugging hard.

Perplexed and frustrated, the moonlight little help as it cast light behind him and left the door in shadowy darkness, he looked at the door and then, realising, ran his hands round the frame until he found the bolts securing it further, one at the top and the other near the foot. They were stiff but slid back without too great an effort and as he turned the door knob and pulled the door it began to open with a slight creak. At the noise a man, dressed in a long sludgy green, belted greatcoat, standing a few metres away on the edge of the pavement, entirely along and looking into the street, threw down his cigarette and turned towards the opening door.

Chapter 36
Thursday 18 January 1990, early hours

"So, what kept you Thomas? Had a bit of a sleep on the way, did we? Let me in – it's fucking freezing out here." She punched him lightly on the shoulder as she stepped past him then turned and threw her arms around him. "Actually, that was pretty amazing. Except you scared the hell out of me on that last bit. I thought you weren't going to reach the balcony, maybe even come crashing down."

She hugged him again, hard, and held her face against his for a moment. "Don't ever, ever, do anything like that to me again. Just don't. Please." They stood together for a moment.

"That man," he asked "who was he? That's what scared the hell out me - seeing him there and no sign of you. I thought he was Vopo. And then when you knocked just now I couldn't be sure that it was you. What happened?"

"Him? Oh, that's Heinz." She bent her fingers and studied her nails. "I've a date with him tomorrow evening, well, half past midnight. Here. Just outside."

He stared at her.

"He works night shift round the corner, making uniforms, things like that." She smiled at his confusion. "His wife's just run away with someone to the West and he was pretty fed up so he'd come out for a smoke on his long break and to think about things. I knew where his factory was so I asked for directions to a street near there and he walked part of the way with me and then I doubled back. He said he saw the door opening but I said it was probably just the cleaners and he accepted that." She smiled again. "He was sweet. Shame I have to stand him up tomorrow. Maybe, though, I could just ... a quickie ... you wouldn't mind would you?" She laughed and skipped out of the way as Thomas growled and lunged at her.

"Don't you dare! OK. Let's get moving, though I'm not sure how we can even start. This place is a maze, it could take us forever just to find the right room, and all the doors seem to be locked as well. We'll need your torch, mine's given up."

As they walked along the corridor and turned to return to the atrium they flashed Bettina's torch on the doors, trying them randomly. On each door there was a brass casing holding a light yellow card with a single name – A Altdorfer, H Burgkmair, H Bosch, I Calvino, A Merkel, name after name but with no indication of the sex or status of the employees working behind the doors.

"This is hopeless! These are just private offices, I think. Maybe the archives are upstairs." It was now just after one in the morning and Thomas's tone was gloomy as he could see things becoming a complete failure. They went to the stairs leading up from the atrium floor and lit by moonlight they climbed to the top of the building. At first this looked identical to the area they'd just left but as soon as Thomas checked a door their excitement returned. Instead of names on the doors the cards now had dates.

"Jan-Mar 1967, Apr-May, 1967 ... " he read out then moved rapidly along the corridor. "Jun-Jul 1968 ... Apr-May 1970 ... "

The last entry on the corridor, at the end furthest from the atrium, was Nov-Dec 1971. They tried the neighbouring corridor but the dates there were earlier. In the other direction they found 1972, then 1974 and as they moved round the edge of the atrium and into the corridors finally hit 1979 before the door cards changed again, now marked with titles like 'Stationery', 'Cleaning supplies', "Men", "Women", 'Interview 1', 'Interview 2', and with several claiming assertively to be private. They went down the stairs one level and after further false starts again picked up the date trail.

"OK, we've got dates again. 1980! Looks like we're on the right floor at least." Thomas laughed, his earlier brush with death forgotten in the excitement of tracking down the document. "And only thirty or forty locked offices to search in, what is it now, a little over four hours, five if we push it!" He laughed again. He'd just have to try using his master keys to open the various doors and then use the keys that Bettina had persuaded Georg to lend her to try the filing cabinets.

"I should have asked Georg the date in which the current President of the Court was named – they've probably not backdated it beyond that." Bettina apologised.

In the distance, towards Lothringerstrasse, there was a noise of a key being turned and then a door scraping open. Thomas stopped and held his breath, listening to the noise which was now certainly that of the main door being pushed shut and locked. The faint sound of footsteps was gradually becoming more distinct, moving towards them.

"Shit! It must be the guard doing a patrol, coming to check all's OK." Thomas peered over the balcony but could see nothing in the shadows.

There was nowhere to hide and all the doors were locked. Breaking into an office would be impossible without being heard. They took off their shoes, knotted the laces together and hung them round their necks. By now the noise from the hard leather shoes of the intruder had grown louder and was mixed with speech, indistinct but clearly speech. "Shit! There must be two of them. Jesus! Let's hope they stick together or at least stay downstairs."

Then there was the sound of a door opening followed by a silence which was more unnerving than the footsteps had been. A long minute passed, then a second which stretched on and on and well into the third again the sound of a door opening with, faintly in the background before it banged shut the noise of a cistern flushing. The footsteps started again and and they strained to distinguish the number. Now it was clear that the steps were coming up the stairs towards them.

They had already established that all the side corridors running off the main perimeter corridor were dead ends. All they could do was stick to the main perimeter corridor, keeping ahead and hoping that the guard or guards would do one circuit only and then leave. They set off, moving as rapidly as they dared, away from the moonlit staircase to the relative darkness of the perimeter corridor but it seemed that as the following footsteps reached the the top they turned towards them and increased in speed. Thomas and Bettina moved as fast as they dared and again the footsteps moved faster in turn. Now they were almost running but hampered by the need to keep as quiet as possible. At the corner of Schulgutstrasse and Ziegelstrasse, they paused to catch their breath, wondering how long they could survive this chase in the darkness without giving themselves away.

Suddenly, from the direction of the following footsteps, the beam of a powerful torch cut them out of the blackness, blinding them, turning them into perfect targets. There was nothing they could do, no chance of escape. There was a clink of metal and Thomas braced himself for a shot. He moved to Bettina and held her, turning to shield her with his body. He felt in his pocket and eased out his pistol, hiding it for the moment.

The figure moved nearer, breathing hard, saying nothing, the torch still trained on them but wavering as if it was too heavy to hold still. Suddenly the figure stopped and sank to the floor in front of them.

"Bettina!" it croaked. "Bettina! You can't do this to an old man."

"Georg!" she shouted. "Damn it, Georg, you scared the shit out of us."

"Jesus!" said Thomas crossly. "Forget this old man stuff. You can't do that to us. We were pissing ourselves not knowing what was happening. We could have been shot. I nearly shot you. If you're a friend why didn't you say who you were?"

Bettina patted him on the arm, laughed softly in relief, then reached out to help Georg to his feet and hugged him. The large bunch of keys at Georg's waist clinked as he moved.

"I told the custodian there was an emergency hearing and I needed the keys to access documents urgently for a court case tomorrow." He stopped and panted for some moments, leaning forward with his hands on his knees. "I was sure you'd be here and that you could do with some help." Georg said. "He lives out of town, some distance away, but I'd hoped to get here by midnight only there was an accident on the road back and that delayed me seriously."

"Georg, this is Thomas. He's a friend." The two shook hands.

"Georg, when did the current Court president get nominated?" Thomas asked.

Georg thought for a moment. "It must have been just over seven years ago, in 1982," he said finally. "Ah, I see. If his signature's on the document then it has to be after he was appointed. So we only need to look between 1982 and 1985. Well, maybe till 1989 if I'm wrong about why they did it but let's start with those four years."

"And if a new document was to be added to an existing list it would have to be placed as the last one of the year because of the numbering, wouldn't it. So we only need to check the December files of the various years." Thomas added.

"That's good thinking. So that's only four sets of files to check. Or maybe eight maximum. Let's go!" Georg was smiling now, caught up in their enthusiasm.

The door marked "Nov-Dec 1982" was two side corridors away and opened easily when Georg selected a key from his bunch and fitted it into the lock. The room was approximately four metres square painted in the standard grey of the DDR as if using a bright colour would show a lack of serious purpose in the important task of building socialism in the country. The walls were lined with three-drawer filing cabinets in an identical shade to the walls, each drawer neatly labelled with numbers which meant nothing to Thomas or Bettina.

"Don't worry!" Georg said, noticing their dismay. "Sifting paper is now my speciality. Look, they're all ordered by date and protocol number. There's probably only one drawer which has the files of the thirty-first of December. The later the date, the farther back in the room it is. Then it moves from left to right." He moved to the right side of the room. "Here it is. Bring your torch over." He pulled out another key and opened the bottom drawer of the file cabinet. "It should be somewhere in here." He pulled out a couple of files and laid them out. "Protocol 82/9227. No, this isn't it. A sentence on a petty theft. Protocol 82/9228. Nothing."

Thomas and Bettina glanced at each other, marvelling at the speed with which Georg checked through the files, realising it would have probably taken them an hour merely to find the right cabinet. Finally Georg stood up. "No." he said, locking the cabinet and getting up, "It's not here. Let's try another year."

They moved down the corridor and into the "December 1983" room. It took fifteen minutes for Georg to sift through the cabinet, but again he found nothing.

Thomas's euphoria had left him and he was beginning to feel discouraged. "Georg, how can we be sure they didn't substitute the file with another one?"

"We can't be sure, but that would be a more risky approach because of the protocol numbers. If you replace one file with another then the original file would have to disappear entirely, to become as if it had never existed. The problem then is that references elsewhere to that case with that number wouldn't match the new one and so inconvenient questions could get asked. But yes, it's possible and if that's what they did then our chance of finding it is immensely difficult, impossible even. It could be anywhere in this building and it could take us a year just checking the possibilities."

They moved to the room holding December 1984. Georg opened the last filing cabinet on the right and began looking through the drawer at the top and then moving on to the second drawer. In that year there had been a large number of records and there had obviously been a rush to get them all entered in time before 1985. Bettina looked anxiously over Georg's should as he worked while Thomas paced up and down, stopping occasionally to gaze out of the small window at the street lights and the silhouettes of the nearby buildings.

Georg yawned and stretched, then rubbed his eyes, scrunching them up and blinking. He pulled out half the files from the lowest drawer and placed them on the table in the centre to check carefully, anxious to be sure that his tiredness wasn't leading him to miss anything obvious. He glanced at the first and turned it over, face down. The second and the third followed and he moved steadily through the pile, discarding the files in turn until he came to the last one. He began turning the pages carefully and then went through the complete document a second time. He stopped and rubbed his hand across his eyes and looked at them.

"We've found it!" he said, matter of factly. "Look ... " He pointed to the preamble and began to read "Sale of Dresdner Mehl Kooperative to Omega Mills. The parties hereby convened ... " He began flipping through the pages roughly until he reached the end. "There's the signature of Gerd Henkel, representing the purchasers. He's the one you told me died recently, isn't he?"

Bettina looked at Thomas and took his hand.

"Yes. That's the one. Thomas, let's get a good photograph of every page."

"OK, but why don't we just take the document itself? That's the proof!"

"It is, but suppose someone gets suspicious. Suppose Roehrberg comes and checks, or sends someone to check, and the document isn't there. What's that going to say? I'd love to take it but we just can't."

Once on the pavement outside the archives they hugged, elated with their success and feeling a new sense of purpose which drove out any tiredness. Bettina looked at Georg and touched him lightly on his cheek.

"Georg, thank you. We couldn't have done it without your help. But Georg, I've got another favour to ask."

"Figures. At this point, I'm in so deep it doesn't make any difference. Just give me a day, I'll have to do it after work." He held out his hand and took the film that Bettina had removed from Thomas's camera.

"We've got another couple of rolls we took in Henkel's house. Maybe Thomas could bring them over to you tomorrow?"

Chapter 37
Thursday 18 January 1990

Bettina was again on her way to the Dresden Stasi HQ, this time for her meeting with Spitze. The excitement of the previous night and particularly the lack of sleep had made her nervous and edgy and as she approached the centre she became certain she was again being followed, this time by a nondescript dark blue Lada. It was being done very professionally and because the driver hung well back and periodically changed places with other traffic she'd been unable to see his face clearly, only that he appeared to be wearing heavy, square glasses, almost hidden by the brim of his hat. She wondered how Thomas was getting on handing over the films to Georg. They'd decided that Thomas would wait for half an hour or so after Bettina had left and would apparently just be cycling into town as anyone might, in order to allay suspicion. Sooner or later their connection would become known, however, and she knew that when that happened they'd both be in even greater danger. All the more reason for completing what they could and returning to Berlin as soon as possible, by the weekend at the very latest she hoped.

She turned into the car park and saw the Lada roll to a stop, discreetly pulling up behind a parked van, allowing the driver to see Bettina's movements without being conspicuous. She thought of suddenly driving out at speed and doubling back later but decided the game was boring and these people were too professional to be ditched easily. In any case she had to visit Spitze and as soon as she stepped inside others in the organisation would monitor her movements and set another tail on her when she left if they chose to. She might as well get it over with and work out later how to ditch anyone following her then.

As she opened the car door to make for the building the sky darkened rapidly. She heard distant thunder and as she got out got caught in rain which now fell heavily, the drops bouncing off the parking spaces and cars and beginning to form deep pools at the edges of the roads and paths. The few people in the street were scurrying along, bent against the downpour, some scampering and using briefcases or bags to shield their heads while others sheltered in doorways. She dashed back into the car, pulled the car door shut and waited for the downpour to stop, cursing herself for forgetting to bring an umbrella. The torrent of rain increased, if anything, and as it showed no signs of stopping she made a dash for the entrance to the building, round the corner and some distance from where she had to park. The raindrops stung her face and made it hard to see her way so that at one point she missed the edge of the pavement and ploughed through a small lake before she could stop herself. By the time she reached the door she was drenched. She thought for a moment of returning to the Dornbusches to change then realized doing so would make her absurdly late for her meeting. She felt cold and miserable.

As she came upstairs Roehrberg's secretary stepped out of the photocopy room and stood in front of her, blocking her way.

"Miss List?" she said, smiling tightly, pleased with herself as the bearer of discomforting news. "Mr Roehrberg needs to see you. This way please."

"I thought he was travelling today. I'm sorry, but I need to dry myself a little before anything else. You can see I'm drenched." She looked down at the puddle by her feet. "And I'm already late for my meeting with Mr Spitze. I'll be happy to see Mr Roehrberg after that, though."

The older woman ignored her, knocked on Roehrberg's office door and then immediately opened it and stood aside, ushering Bettina in. Roehrberg was standing in front of the window, his back turned to her, staring out into the pouring rain falling into the Elbe and beyond, and splashing on the city roofs and domes. She assumed she'd been seen from the window.

"Miss List, sit down." His tone was glacial and his coldness, matching the temperature of the room, and her wet clothing made her shiver as she sat in the leather chair opposite his desk. Looking down she saw that she dripped water on to his carpet and that her trousers had made a serious damp patch which would later show up as a stain on the leather. The realisation gave her a childish pleasure and, taking small victory to herself in the unpleasant encounter, she squirmed to spread the water around as far as she could.

"My patience is at an end. I've had to postpone my travel plans because of everyone's inefficiency, yours and that of other colleagues. I'm surrounded by people who either lose documents or are unable to produce them – it seems as if only by doing things myself will they be done properly."

"I expect to finish my work today." She considered adding his first name to attempt to initiate a friendlier conversation but couldn't bring herself to do so and decided that in any case the attempt would be lame and counterproductive. "I'll be seeing Spitze shortly and clearing the last details. I expect to leave for Berlin tomorrow and so my report will be delivered and considered later that day, certainly by Monday at the latest."

"Your excuses don't interest me. I'll be travelling to Berlin myself in a couple of hours and I'll meet there with my superiors. That should ensure that the replacement funds will immediately be made available and so short-circuit this ridiculous snail's pace of activity. And while I'm at it I shall stop by and give Dieter a piece of my mind. I wanted to let you know that. That's all, you can leave now."

As she left his office Bettina came close to swinging round and letting Roehrberg know what she thought of his arrogance and discourtesy. After her father had left she'd got casual work in theatres and vaudeville. Honed in heckling exchanges and in fighting off lascivious directors she'd developed a considerable ability to give as good as she got. Her skill in making vulgar and wounding comments on an assailant's parentage and sexual proclivities was considerable and she was more than a match for anyone in trading insults in Saxon demotic. She knew she could humiliate Roehrberg as soundly as he'd just humiliated her. Seething with fury though she was her training kicked in and she forced herself to leave calmly and make her way to the lavatories.

"Fuck Roehrberg! Fuck Spitze, too! He can wait till I get dried and sorted."

She took her time, part of it simply sitting in one of the stalls mulling over recent events and in particular her meetings with Roehrberg. Where exactly did he and the others fit it and how high did it go? That was something she would need Dieter's help to unravel. She was sick of Dresden now and longed to get back to Berlin. Thomas was meeting Stephan for dinner this evening - inconvenient perhaps but it was Stephan's only time free. In any case she had to collect the photographs later from Georg and she could spend that time examining them and looking more closely at the material Thomas had stolen from Roehrberg's house. Then later, she thought, and smiled to herself at the prospect, she would collect Thomas, return to the farmhouse and they would go straight to bed. They could leave first thing in the morning. Or at least whenever they could tear themselves away.

Her meeting with Spitze was perfunctory and formal. He was cold, distant and unhelpful in contrast to his somewhat obsequious manner when they'd last met. She realised that the Dresden office, or at least the senior elements of it, now saw her – and presumably Dieter too – as the enemy. Perhaps they'd become suspicious of what she'd found out, what she knew and wasn't revealing.

After a frustrating half hour during which she learned little more and was totally unable to get substantive answers to her questions she gave up. The rain had lessened but she still got wet running to her car. She turned the heater on full and sat there trying to complete her drying out, irritated and still cross with Roehrberg and Spitze.

As she pulled out into the traffic she watched carefully for followers but could detect nothing unusual. Perhaps they already knew enough about her movements not to bother or perhaps they reckoned they'd frightened her enough and didn't need to try again their common trick of letting someone know they were being followed. Or, more worryingly, they now knew the danger she presented and were actually following her discreetly and professionally to find out all they could. Whatever the situation she would have to be very careful when visiting Georg later to collect the prints. She thought again of Thomas and hoped there had been no problems with his visit.

She returned to the farmhouse, rested for an hour, and in a calmer frame of mind began to compile her report. This was more difficult than she'd anticipated because she needed to stick to the known facts and whatever she'd learned from her visit to the Dresden Stasi offices in order to avoid alerting any of those she now thought as suspects by revealing any hints of the ideas churning in her mind. That information was for Dieter only, to be delivered in private, and the sooner she could talk openly with him the sooner she'd be able to relax.

So engrossed was she in her work that she barely heard the bedroom door open or Thomas cross the room to stand beside her.

"What's this then? Had enough of me already?" As he kissed her lightly on the head she dropped her pen and threw herself into his arms. They stayed still for several minutes, enjoying the feel of the other's body, Thomas gently stroking her hair.

"Thomas, I've had such a shitty morning. How about you with Georg? But, look, I'll soon have finished the report for Dieter and we can be out of here tomorrow, back to Berlin."

"I spoke to Stephan again. He's fine for tonight as we'd planned but wants to meet earlier and get away by 9 at the latest. Seems he's got a really early start tomorrow, 4.30 or 5 he said, as he's got an 8.30 meeting in Leipzig, or something. We agreed to meet at the Semper Oper at 6.30 and walk round to the Italienisches Dörfchen. Is that OK? And no problems with Georg. He said he'd have the prints ready at half past six or so."

"Perfect! I can drop you near the Hofkirche, maybe twenty past. It's only a short walk from there and I can go on to Georg's. It's busy so no one's likely to notice us. And then I'll come and pick you up at the Dörfchen, what, nine maybe, or a bit before?"

"Come earlier, 8.30, twenty to, and you can have a drink with Stephan. He really likes you, remember, and it would be good to meet up with him again."

By five the report was finished and checked and they spent some time sorting and packing their things ready for an early start in the morning. They went to the kitchen, settled their bill with Frau Dornbusch and drank some coffee while she prepared supper for her family and then went upstairs and got ready to go out. After the storm earlier in the day the evening was quiet and still and the moon was a little smaller and less bright than it had been the night before. Bettina dropped Thomas by the Hofkirche, barely stopping, almost bundling him out of the car, and around six forty, after following a deliberately circuitous route and confident that she hadn't been followed, she walked the last few hundred metres and rang Georg's door bell.

Georg was tired and sweaty from working in the small, airless darkroom and was busy drying with a small, antiquated hair dryer a batch of prints pegged up on the line. A pile of contact sheets and selected enlargements were scattered on the table. The heat from the hair dryer made the room unpleasantly stuffy, heightening the smell of the chemicals and the acrid odour of the stop bath, and she immediately felt claustrophobic and uncomfortable. She took a clutch of prints into the hallway and as she waited glanced through them. Thomas had taken very clear pictures and all the minor details were sharp. She examined particularly closely the ones of Henkel's letter and decided that a calligraphy expert would be able to make a judgement based on the prints rather than needing to see the original.

This was useful information to pass on to Dieter and she remembered that she needed to update him anyway. For a brief moment she considered using Georg's phone then realised that with his background it was certain that his private phone would be tapped. Later, once Georg had finished his work on the prints, she would call from the public phone a few streets away which Georg used when he needed to keep his conversations private.

Of course the probability that the Stasi had tapped this public phone as well was very high, she thought, but it couldn't be helped and at least anything she said there wouldn't directly incriminate Georg. She would nevertheless have to be very careful in what she said to Dieter.

She turned and knocked on the door to see how Georg was getting on.

"Turn off the hall light and come in. Nearly finished. Sorry I've been longer than I'd thought."

In the dull red light she could see Georg fixing the last of the enlargements he'd made. He fished the two sheets out of the tray, rinsed them in another bath, let them drain for a few seconds and hung them up with perspex clips on the line above his head. He switched on the white light, yawned and then stretched.

"All done. I thought you might like some really large prints of the handwritten note so I've added these. Thomas did a good job with focus and exposure. They've all come out pretty well."

He picked up the hair dryer, set it going on low and waved it around in the general direction of the wet sheets, gradually bringing it closer as he noticed Bettina glance at her watch. He rubbed his fingers over the surface, gave the prints a further few wafts of warm air then took them down and put everything into a large envelope and handed it to Bettina.

"Georg. That's wonderful. Thank you so much. You've no idea how much this has helped us but I'll tell you the whole story later when I'm able to."

She held him for a moment then left the house and walked back to her car. It was later than she'd expected but it didn't really matter as she'd plenty of time in hand before collecting Thomas from the restaurant. She sat in the car for a short while, thinking things over, and then drove to the telephone box, waiting discreetly about 50 metres away until it became empty.

An unfamiliar male voice answered. She gave her code name and asked for Dieter and in a moment he picked up the receiver.

"Hello Hyena. Anything urgent to report?" Dieter's voice was very controlled, almost bored, and she was immediately alert. "He's got someone with him." she thought. She chose her words carefully.

"The matter I was investigating seems clear in its implications. I have very good copies of Henkel's suicide letter and from those you'll be able to establish his hand in writing it. There's also some documents about that and about related matters involving other parties which I have, as well as other very good copies of more materials which are interesting and relevant. However, there's one additional issue I've come across. It's probably nothing but a little puzzling. Are you aware of any privatisation activity in East Germany, specifically in Dresden, in the last few months?"

There was a silence before Dieter answered. "No." he said slowly."No. Not directly."

"Well, we seem to have ... "

"We can examine your report and discuss matters in more detail later. Henkel has confessed and committed suicide. That seems all clear and straightforward and so your mission is over." Dieter's voice was firm and brusque. "However, I need you for another urgent matter which has only just come up. Return to base immediately, tonight. We'll meet in the office in which we discussed the Prokov case."

He hung up before Bettina could say anything. He hadn't even asked how Thomas's investigation into Phoenix was proceeding, she realised. She thought over the exchange, now convinced that someone was in the office or perhaps even listening on the line. She put down the receiver with a strong sense of unease, wishing Dieter had told them openly whom they were playing against. They'd discussed the Prokov case at Dieter's house, she remembered, so he probably now trusted no one at all. Just what was going on here?

She hurried to her car, returned to the Dornbusch farm where the older boy helped her load the car with their things. She took a last look round the room, said her goodbyes and hurried off to collect Thomas. At least he wouldn't be hungry on the drive, she thought.

Chapter 38
Thursday 18 January 1990, evening

Thomas arrived at the Semper Oper a few minutes after the half hour to find Stephan already waiting, punctual as always. As he approached he saw that Stephan was looking preoccupied and wondered if meeting so soon after Herren's assassination was really such a good idea. "We've known each other for ever, though," he thought "so I guess we can talk about things in ways that Stephan might find difficult with his colleagues."

They greeted each other warmly and hugged, Stephan seeming to prolong the contact a little longer than usual. They separated and Thomas held Stephan by the shoulders at arms' length, looking him over.

"You look well, Stephan, older but more authoritative and mature. And tired, you look tired." They looked at each other for a moment and then Thomas dropped his arms. "And Herren. I guess, are you, have you, that was a huge shock to me so I can't think what it must have been like for you, so close to him."

Stephan nodded without speaking and they turned and walked in silence towards the nearby restaurant in the Theaterplatz where they intended eating.

"It was a huge shock to me, to everyone." said Stephan after a while. "You know how sometimes things happen and although you know they've happened part of you doesn't believe it. Maybe that's because it's just too big to take in. Even though I knew what had happened I expected to see Herren yesterday. There were things we had to talk about, important things, and I was kind of waiting to be summoned to his office but of course that never happened. I can't believe I shan't see him again." He turned away and passed his hand quickly over his eyes and shook his head slightly.

Thomas touched him lightly on the shoulder and they continued walking in silence for some minutes.

"I had a call from that guy I'd got to know at university, Richard Köpp, you remember? I found out later he'd gone into the BNG but we've not seen each other for a while. We talked on the phone. I know he was after information that I could give him, anything that might give a lead, but he was so sympathetic, Thomas. And that really helped, you know, like he cared and I could say things to him, like how much Herren meant to me. You know. Just that. It really helped. Just ... "

He shrugged and they walked on, saying nothing.

"BNG?"

"BNG? Did I say that? Sorry, I meant BND, of course."

They stopped for a moment and stood looking out over the river, saying nothing.

"But things are otherwise going well, Thomas. I'm frantically busy travelling all over the place, analysing potential joint ventures between Deutsche Bank and the local Eastern ones, the project that Herren asked me to take on earlier. It was dreadful when he was killed and there was chaos, still is chaos obviously and I guess that will continue for a bit. Of course the bank had backup structures in place but because of Herren's position and the fact that so much of his work was secret, commercially and politically, things have got pretty awkward and confused. Now there are people jockeying for position, pushing their own agendas, that sort of thing. No one's asked me about what I'm doing so I decided to just keep quiet, get on with everything, make sure that it's only me that knows in full detail what's going on with the project. In any case it's too far advanced and too good for us to pull out and if things work out I'll be in a pretty good position now."

There was an odd note in Stephan's voice, almost of pleasure and of satisfaction with events, Thomas thought, and he glanced sharply at his friend. They stopped for a moment on the river bank to admire the baroque façade and colonnaded front of the Italienisches Dörfchen Restaurant ahead of them, before climbing the wide steps into the foyer, now ablaze with light. Neither had visited before.

"Bettina comes from Dresden, as you know I think, and so she recommended this place. It's apparently quite special not only for its food and atmosphere but also its history. It's mid-eighteenth century. The Elector of Saxony, I think she said it was, was offered the Polish crown but first had to convert to Catholicism. The Pope asked the Elector to seal the deal by building an outstandingly beautiful church in the heart of the city - that's the Hofkirche, right here in front - which had to be designed by an Italian architect and built by specialist Italian workers. They all lived here, hence the name of the building, the little Italian village. Now it's a restaurant specialising in both Italian cooking, as you might expect, but also local Saxon food."

"So what's the speciality, Polish pizza with potato dumplings?"

Thomas laughed, and followed Stephan as the waiter led them to their table in the baroque and somewhat stuffy grandeur of the main dining area.

"How are things going with Bettina? She seemed a great girl, very bright, I thought. What are you doing here, other than maybe going to museums?"

"Oh, just that I'd never been to Dresden, I had some time free and Bettina thought she'd show me around. Her mother doesn't live here any longer but Bettina expected some of her old friends might be about. She's seen one or two and I've really just wandered around looking at things both with her and on my own. We're going back tomorrow or Saturday. She'll be along later to pick me up so you'll see her then."

"And what about Berlin? You're still there and still studying, right? How's that going?"

"I'm working on my thesis at the moment. I wasn't quite sure what direction to take but I've now selected 'The calculation of the monetary mass in East Germany' as the topic. My supervisor is quite excited by that because of all the political changes. If monetary union does go ahead I'll work in something on the effects of unification on the DM." He looked at Stephan. "That's your area isn't it? You probably know more about what is being discussed right now than anybody else."

"Well, maybe. I was in some of the early meetings with the Bundesbank but as things heated up the numbers became much smaller and Herren decided I needn't attend. But I do know a lot of people in high places, of course, and I keep myself informed. I'll be glad to help if I can."

"So what's the latest on unification?"

Before Stephan could answer the waiter appeared with their beers, setting a brimming mug clumsily in front of Stephan so that the liquid slopped out on the table and over the trousers of Stephan's dark Alpaca wool suit.

"Damn it!" he said, moving back hurriedly, and staring at the waiter who was now dabbing casually at the beer on the table cloth after a perfunctory apology.

"The bugger was smirking at me!" he said as the man left. "He did that deliberately."

"Perhaps he resents Wessies turning up, looking stylish in well-cut suits!" Thomas said, laughing. "We'll have to watch out that we don't get served rat instead of pork."

Stephan took a long draught of his beer. "Mmm, good. Wish I hadn't lost so much on my trousers, though." He glanced round the restaurant, taking in the mixing of flat colour on the walls with the Art Deco influenced lighting and the rather staid oil paintings scattered around in display. He turned back to Thomas.

"So, the latest on unification and money ... Well, it's all pretty incredible, isn't it, even though there's still a lot of uncertainty? The market exchange rate is now down to five to one and that's broadly correct from a purchasing parity point of view. But I hear some people talking about a unification rate of two to one, maybe even parity. That would be pretty incredible if it happened. The Bundesbank doesn't like that talk one bit but of course it's under a lot of political pressure. The real problem is that there's really no reliable hard data around on which to base decisions. No clue about what cash in circulation plus deposits amounts to, monetary mass, as you know.." He laughed. "If you hurry and finish your thesis you'll be able to give them the answers! We need to wait for the elections in March but if Kohl wins - and even now a landslide looks pretty likely - it'll be parity and the Bundesbank will just have to lump it."

The waiter arrived with their dishes. Stephan eyed him warily, moving his chair well back from the table, but this time there was no incident. He served them carefully, commented briefly on the dishes and asked them courteously if they needed anything. They glanced at each other and began eating.

"Damned good rat." said Stephan. "I expect the ones by the river wharves are the biggest and juiciest so maybe I should take a few back to Camille, ask for the recipe and get her to cook them for us."

"Damn it, Stephan, I'm eating!" Thomas grabbed his water glass and drank, tears streaming down his face as he coughed repeatedly and tried to banish the image of the notoriously elegant and fastidious Camille skinning and cooking rats for supper.

"Anyway, BuBa has been sending staff over in order to do its own estimates. Apparently the East German central bank keeps on printing money at full tilt. BuBa wants to impose some controls on that, of course, given the possibility of unification, but they're not having much luck. Basically they're probably being fooled."

"What about the financial metrics, though, you know, things like cash, M1, the wider definitions. Wouldn't that give the information that the bank needs?"

"Ordinarily yes, but that's not how East Germany works. It's a command economy, remember, and so it doesn't see the relevance of distinguishing such metrics as you'd need to in a market one. I can see their point."

"And when West German banks began moving east" Stephan continued "the first thing BuBa did was to take regulatory action to ensure that when Ost Marks were converted to DM any inflationary effect would be minimised. That's good for the country, of course, but it limits hugely what banks can do and so basically they're just sitting there waiting for people to open accounts and deposit money. Bo-ring!"

"Yes, I can see that. Fascinating." said Thomas slowly. He was beginning to get a glimmer of what Phoenix might be up to.

"Now, here's the other snag. The Bundesbank wants to impose an upper limit on the amount that each individual can exchange into Deutsche Marks at the preferential exchange rate. That's another way, although a crude one, to try to control monetary mass. They can't tell how much money is really out there in the East so they're using a proxy which is based on a calculation of the only figure they can be certain of, the East German population."

"But maybe the population figures all wrong now, given so many have come over the West!"

"You're probably right but even if they're in the West most will still want to change their money and get the benefit of the good exchange rate. Remember that everyone counts, children and even babies as well, so that's around sixteen million people. Let's say they put the ceiling at

3,000 Ost Marks. If the exchange rate is set at one to one then that means 48 billion Ost Marks could turn into the same number of Deutsche Marks. But what they're counting on is imperfect wealth distribution. Many people, particularly families with kids, won't have anything like 3,000 Ost Marks a head available while those who are wealthier are going to get hit by the 3,000 ceiling. That's why BuBa expects the total Ost Mark exchange at the preferential exchange rate to be much lower than the theoretical maximum, maybe only 30 million instead of 48 million. Any other conversions will be at less favourable rates, maybe two or three to one. That limits the inflation impact and possible damage considerably."

"So those with more than three thousand Ost Marks will come out of it badly, having to make do with a poor exchange rate for anything over the ceiling?"

"Yes and no. There may be some differential terms allowed. Older people might be given a higher ceiling, for instance. And what a lot of wealthier people are already doing is investing their money, buying land and houses for instance. And although BuBa won't admit it I'm certain a lot of wealthy individuals will get their poorer relatives to exchange the money for them, probably paying them a commission to do that."

Thomas sat staring into space, thinking about what Stephan had just said. You could do this on a national scale through a network of local agents, paying them small commissions for everyone they got to exchange money up to the limits. And if you'd already bought up Ost Marks at good rates you'd make a killing. So that's what Phoenix was up to. That's why they wanted to know family numbers. That's why they didn't care about credit worthiness. It all made sense now. It wasn't a loan service at all. It was a money laundering scheme.

"What's up? Everything all right?" Stephan asked, looking at Thomas curiously.

"Uh, sure." he said, as he picked up his fork and again began eating. "But can't the Bundesbank do anything to stop this illicit lending?"

"BuBa has regulatory power over banks but no control over individuals. Any person can lend money to someone else. There's nothing illegal about that so unless they draft a specific law against lending it to convert there's nothing can be done."

"What if someone was doing it on a large scale? A financial services company, maybe."

"Most of them are regulated by BuBa and so the main risk there is losing their licence. Also I don't know that BuBa could regulate activity occurring abroad and right now the DDR is a foreign country. They might, might, be able to impose sanctions but they're going to be pretty minimal. It would be pretty low risk."

They sat in silence for some minutes.

"The people at Phoenix have planned this very, very well." thought Thomas. "They're set to make millions and there's nothing anyone can do about it. It's the West German public that's going to pick up the bill because of all that extra money in circulation and hence the higher inflation and reduced value of the Deutsche Mark."

"Have you heard of a company called Phoenix, Phoenix Securities?" he asked.

There was a moment's silence and Thomas thought he caught a fleeting wariness in Stephan's expression before he resumed his usually impassivity.

"What Securities? Phoenix, did you say? Like the bird, or maybe the US city? ... no, I don't think so. Who are they? East Germans from Arizona?" He laughed but seemed to be watching Thomas intently. "How did you come across them? And what do they do?"

"I forget. Just something I read about, I think. Or maybe Bettina mentioned them - she was talking about new financial service companies springing up. Would companies have ways of exchanging more money at the preferential rate, shareholders or something like that?"

"Well, yes, that's another big issue. What to do about the money held by corporations and organisations throughout the country, things like government departments, the SED, whatever it's called now, state-held corporations and, I suspect, others like the secret services. That's pretty important given the sums involved. The East German politicians argue that there can't be limits imposed on these amounts. BuBa insists there have to be limits. That's where the biggest surprises could come from in terms of overall numbers."

Yet another piece of the jigsaw fitted, Thomas thought. And he could see why Stephan looked a little uncomfortable, even with him. This was high level, secret even, and Stephan was probably close to the limit of what he could reveal. Yet at the same time it was obvious, particularly now that Stephan had spelled some things out. The mill privatisation and the loss of the Stasi millions must be connected. Accounting standards in the East were primitive and it would have been trivially easy to cook the books to show that the mill had had a huge cash balance which could be exchanged for DM. And with the forged document showing the transfer some years earlier the nominal owners, Roehrberg and whoever else was involved, owned it all. It was a perfect loophole in the system. And this time it was the East Germans who would be paying.

He felt uncomfortable in half lying to Stephan about Phoenix. He wished he could take him into his confidence more fully about both matters but it was impossible at the moment. Yet he knew that Stephan would have been fascinated by what he'd discovered and would have had some interesting comments to make. Oh, well, time enough for that later.

A movement caught his eye and he glanced towards the entrance. "Oh, here's Bettina. She's early!" he said and stood as she approached.

Stephan followed in turn. "Bettina! Great to see you again. You're looking well. I hear you've been showing Thomas the sights." They embraced and he pulled out a chair for her. "We've almost finished, just some coffee maybe. What will you have to drink? Or would you like coffee too?"

"Great to see you too, Stephan, but nothing to drink, thanks." She sat down. "Thomas, I'm so sorry but I've got a splitting headache. It's just been growing over the past hour and I'd like to go straight back to the farm if you don't mind." She turned to Stephan. "I'm sorry. I'd really have liked to have chatted but I'm not very good company. I hope we can meet properly soon, though."

"I'm sorry too but of course you need to get back. Let's do that though. We were talking earlier about making a social date soon. I want Camille to try a gourmet recipe, a Dresden speciality that I have in mind." He winked at Thomas. "Let's just get the bill. I can have coffee back at the hotel. I've some work to do and a really early train to catch tomorrow so leaving now suits me too."

Chapter 39
Thursday 18 January 1990, evening and on past midnight

Thomas was driving at full speed down the two-lane concrete road, the numerous ruts and holes, coupled with the imperfect fit between the slabs, making the journey pretty uncomfortable. It was very late and they were practically alone on the road but the gibbous moon, declining and now approaching a semicircle, was shining brightly and gave the landscape a silvery beauty and a sense of mystery. He thought of how differently it felt from when they had come to Dresden only a few days ago, much of that trip having been passed in awkward silence. Now, returning to Berlin, they had spent the first half hour without speaking, but it was a companionable silence, each of them happy in the other's presence. Every so often Bettina would caress Thomas's hand or reach over to kiss his neck, on the first such occasion causing him to swerve violently on the road.

As the few lights of Ortrand disappeared behind them Bettina, drawing back from another caress, laid her hand on Thomas's thigh. At first they linked fingers but when Thomas returned his right hand to the wheel Bettina leaned closer on his shoulder and began - it seemed by mutual intuition - lightly and slowly, almost absent-mindedly, stroking his thigh with the tips of her fingers. Initially this was just above his knee but her hand almost imperceptibly made longer sweeps, moving higher and deeper. He glanced at her, saw her mischievous grin and caught the sparkle in her eyes. A finger, now probing behind buttons and meeting stiffened flesh made Thomas swerve bumpily on to the verge and bring the car to a shuddering halt, turn, press her hand strongly against him and kiss passionately. Each longed to be back in their bed in Dresden, away from Dieter and his missions, back in the only world that now seemed to them to matter. For longer than was sensible but for far less than they each desperately wanted they clung to and explored each other's bodies as the freezing night air seeped into the car, the chill wind urging itself through the old rubber seals. Eventually, with much procrastination and regret, they again set off down the highway.

Around an hour later they stopped again, this time by a public phone to call Dieter at home once more. Nobody answered.

"Where else could he be? Does he have a woman friend?" Thomas asked as Bettina returned.

"Not that I know of. His wife died a couple of years ago, and I'm pretty sure he hasn't had a relationship since. He focuses all his energies on work."

They set off again and again drove in silence for some time.

"I'm sorry, this is a very personal question, but I wondered if Dieter had ever made any advances towards you? You've been working closely together for, what, seven years now and you're so attractive ... " He trailed off, aware of inappropriate layers in the question.

"Never. That's one of the reasons I respect him so much. When we first met, he could have taken advantage of the situation. I was desperate. Hadn't had a shag for months and the batteries on my Rabbit had run down. I was desperate, I tell you, desperate." She sensed Thomas staring at her in astonishment. "Oops! Sorry, wrong script. Kind of segued into Bad Mark, singular, without thinking. Right. Ah, yes, here we go. As you were."

She glanced out of the window at the rain now streaming down, beating rhythmically on the glass. "In reality he offered to help me in all sorts of ways, all clearly disinterestedly. He's been the closest I've ever come to a father figure." She turned to look at him, her eyes glistening. "You really are something special. We've only started making love and you're already jealous?"

"Damn right!" Thomas smiled. "That's the Italian influence."

"Well, I'm getting a little worried that we can't get hold of him."

"Dieter? Come on, he'd outsmart anyone. He's out, maybe called away to a meeting or something. He'll know from when you called him in Dresden the earliest we'd be back would be after midnight. We'll try again later. Did you have time to check the pictures? Are the documents legible?"

"Yes, I looked through a few of them. Georg printed out those with text on large sheets and they're all pretty clear."

He felt around in the back seat for his rucksack, hauled it over and passed it to her.

"Can you read in the car without feeling sick? We need to find something in there that will compromise Roehrberg. We still don't have any proof of a link between him and Henkel, unfortunately, or just where the mill fits in, and the clearer the detail the easier it's going be for Dieter to act."

Bettina fished out the cardboard box with the pictures, around fifty or sixty in all. "Let's see what we've got." she said, turning on the interior light. "Hmmm. This is just a whole lot of numbers. Looks like an accounting report of some kind."

"Any names written anywhere that you can see?"

Bettina flipped through the pictures. "Here's one. It says Dresdner Mehl Kooperative. Looks like some form of business plan."

"I remember finding that. The book itself should be there too - it's got a blue cover I think. That might help establish a link. Roehrberg's got to be involved in the privatisation, surely. Why else would he have had these documents at home, particularly if they were taken from Henkel's house as looks likely. What about the others?"

"There's a couple of pages in French." Bettina continued. "Contrât d'acquisition ... first few pages of a contract to buy a house in France by the look of it. In Nice. Roehrberg seems to have had a lot of money to invest. Hang on, there's a scribble here - can't quite read it, something about this being personal, not a joint venture. What does that mean?"

"I think his girlfriend is French. I saw pictures in his study and the people moving the boxes were talking about it. One of them was taken by the sea, looked Mediterranean and so could have been Nice. Maybe that's where the documents are going, somewhere they can't easily be found."

"He was supposed to fly to France yesterday but cancelled to go to Berlin in the morning. I told you he was furious and mentioned that some documents had gone astray." She laughed. "I guess that's your fault!"

"Do you think he stole the money himself and then killed Henkel to shift blame?"

"Not sure. Possibly. More likely they were in it together and then Roehrberg got rid of Henkel. Maybe Spitze's also involved, although I think he's possibly clean. But Roehrberg had me followed the whole time I was in Dresden and I think the only reason he invited me to dinner was to be sure I wouldn't be around when he moved his files." She smiled and caressed Thomas's neck softly. "Except that Dieter was smarter and had sent you too."

"We make a good team!" He smiled at her, resisting the urge to stop the car again.

"There's quite a few more." Bettina said, resuming her working tone of voice. "This one is ... wait, it's hard to understand, it's the middle of a contract of some sort ... oh, another house purchase. In Munich this time."

"Seems our friend had a fair bit of money to invest, didn't he? How much do you think someone like him earns, more or less?"

"No idea. I would guess no more than seventy thousand Ost Marks a year, though."

"There's no way he could buy a house in Munich earning that kind of money, or Nice for that matter. The Ost Mark was worth hardly anything out of the country so that's equivalent to a salary of, what, maybe five or six thousand DM. That wouldn't even get him the front door, let alone a whole house or two. You read something about a joint venture earlier. Maybe Roehrberg is the treasurer and it goes a lot higher, a high level Stasi syndicate doing deals and creaming off funds for themselves, putting that into houses and the like. Remember what Georg said about Wolfgang's warning him not to meddle. But what about the Omega Mills contract from the archives? Are the pictures OK?"

Bettina leafed through the pictures and pulled a few out.

"Yes, here it is. Let's see ... the sale price is set at 35,000 Ost Marks."

"That's ridiculous! Maybe half what you said Roehrberg might earn in a year and even if it was supposedly five year ago. I bet if we got hold of the balance sheet we'd find the net worth a whole lot higher, the building itself for a start let alone what the nominal cash balance probably shows. Just reinforces the case that the whole transaction was rigged."

"We still have the problem that Roehrberg doesn't appear in this document."

"Probably because he's too smart to sign documents himself unless he really has to, like the contracts for the houses." Thomas said. "He could be involved in Omega Mills but not appear as a signatory, particularly if this is a syndicate venture. We need to find who owns that company and who the shareholders are. If it's registered in West Germany that shouldn't be that hard to do."

"What if he doesn't show up?"

"We'd need to find a link between the shareholders and Roehrberg. He could be using proxies. They all could be. Or we'd need to show that Roehrberg was involved in Henkel's murder. And to do that proving that the documents I photographed in Roehrberg's study came from Henkel's house would really help. Henkel's study certainly contained a lot more files than were there when we came in. The dust tracks showed that. Two days later we find boxes of incriminating documents in Roehrberg's home, including the Omega stuff. The coroner estimated the death at around six in the evening, you said, so probably an hour after Henkel left the office. We were there from nine thirty. This would mean Roehrberg or someone he sent was in Henkel's house between those times and took the material. How would they know that was a suitable time? Unless they casually happened to assist in a suicide, I think it's pretty obvious they killed him, or at least arranged the killing."

"We don't have proof and we don't really have the motive either."

"Roehrberg knew you needed a culprit for the investigation. Maybe he had Henkel steal the money for both of them, perhaps telling him they would somehow lay the blame on Spitze. Then, once the money was theirs he killed Henkel instead."

"Why not use Spitze as a culprit then?"

"Roehrberg is clever. We now know Henkel was compromised and that he was much more dangerous for Roehrberg than Spitze could ever be. Once unification occurs, a lot of Stasi top brass will get interrogated. The West German services will try to nail them any way they can to make them pay for what they've done for the last forty years. Henkel would have been a weak link in the chain of Roehrberg's defence. He would probably have cracked. And maybe Spitze was involved in the killing anyway."

"How do we prove it?"

"What about the confession? Was it authenticated?" Thomas asked.

"Roehrberg said they'd done a handwriting analysis and it proved positive. But he would say that wouldn't he! Dieter has a couple of people he normally uses for such things so by tomorrow we should know if the confession is authentic. If it turns out that Henkel didn't write it, then that's another things against Roehrberg. He would have to prove that the test was actually done and that no pressure was exerted on the expert. I wouldn't think that these guys generally make mistakes."

It was almost 12.30, early morning, when they reached East Berlin. The city was deserted and looked eerily beautiful, wreathed in wisps of fog from the Spree. Bettina took the wheel as they crossed a large part of the city before entering one of the residential areas in the north east, Niederschönhausen.

"Dieter lives in one of these houses here." she said as she swerved left into a winding road. "I had to bring him some urgent documents once. It was a breach of protocol but he trusted me enough and we always met there when there was something particularly secretive to discuss. The house is hard to recognize as they all look pretty much alike but it should be farther along and to the left, toward the end of the road, in Wolffstrasse ..." she said, wiping the fogged up window with the back of her hand. She opened the window slightly, letting in the chilly night air. "I guess it's just about ... What are all those cars doing there?"

Two police cars were in front of one of the houses, their red lights flashing, painting the façade of the white house with regular splashes of a dark red hue. Another one, its lights turned off, stood a few metres further on.

"Keep driving. Don't stop here. Are you sure it's Dieter's house they're in?"

"Yes, it's his. I'm certain."

"Shit!"

Bettina swerved into the next side street and found a parking spot. As they hurried back Thomas took Bettina's hand and slowed her down as they approached the house.

"We have to be careful. Casual passers-by. Let me speak, OK?"

They opened the small gate and walked up the path towards the front door which was standing open. Thomas, ahead of Bettina, saw the policemen clustered inside, one of them kneeling and examining a body crumpled on the floor. Part of the face, by the left temple and forehead, was badly damaged, blown away by a large calibre bullet from short range Thomas guessed. Blood matted the hall carpet and pooled on the floor boards. It lay stickily in the body's hair and had run down and congealed over much of the face. Despite the distortion to the features Thomas was certain it was Dieter, killed as he answered the door by the look of things. He stopped in the doorway and turned, taking Bettina in his arms to try to block her view.

"We need to get away from here. Fast."

Despite his efforts she glanced over his shoulder, became rigid then shuddered and screamed in anguish, thrusting him aside to look. "Oh no! NO!" She clung to Thomas, burying her face in his shoulder, sobbing. A senior policemen turned and moved swiftly towards them.

"Who are you? Why are you here? Do you know the victim?"

Thomas staggered slightly, affecting inebriation. "My fiancée and I were at a dinner party down the road and saw the door open. What's happened? Is anything wrong? Can we help."

"What does it look like? Get out of here or you'll be arrested. Go home."

Thomas nodded, glancing round as best he could. Everything seemed orderly and with no sign of a struggle. Dieter had probably known who killed him, he thought.

"Let's go." he said to Bettina softly as he turned and guided her, still sobbing convulsively, to the gate. "We've no time to lose. They got Dieter. We're probably next on the list. We have to disappear."

Chapter 40
Friday 19 January 1990, early hours of the morning

Back in the car they sat thinking, mulling over the recent developments. Bettina had stopped sobbing but kept suddenly breaking down as grief overwhelmed her without warning. Thomas sat in the driving seat, one arm round her, holding her close, and the other stroking her hair but all the while alert and wary in case of any danger outside.

He could feel fear prickling his skin. It was midnight-quiet, still and silent, and whenever leaves rustled beside the car shivers ran down his spine. His heartbeat seemed all over the place and at times he had difficulty breathing but he continued stroking Bettina's hair and calming her.

"We must go. We really must go. It's dangerous here." he whispered.

She nodded, moved away from him and sat back in her seat, now calmer but gulping occasionally, her eyes still wet.

"Drive over to my place. We need to rest. There's no way now we'll be able to do anything about Roehrberg."

"Whoever killed Dieter will be looking for us as well. Could be Roehrberg but whoever it is they'll know about you. Your apartment is the first place they'll look. This is the Firm we're talking about, the people who make it their business to know what everyone's doing, remember. We need to avoid all your usual hangouts at least until we understand what's going on."

They drove across the city and as they neared the centre, approaching the police station and the former Stasi's operative offices in the Alexanderplatz, Bettina became increasingly agitated. Surely if they were hiding from agents they were in exactly the wrong area, she thought. It was late, but anyone could be around, a car out at this hour could be noted and she knew that her car's make and registration would be in her file.

Sensing her concern Thomas reached out, took her hand and pressed it. "Not far now. We'll be safe once we're inside."

He turned into a small dog-leg back street with a few run-down houses and which ended in a patch of rough ground frequented by prostitutes and their clients. Although the police made high profile visits every month or so the area was generally undisturbed and a car left round the corner was unlikely to attract attention. Gathering their things they set off for Kai's apartment, less than a kilometre away.

As Thomas pushed open the solid wooden street door and they climbed the four flights to the apartment he prayed silently that John had visited daily to do what Thomas had asked. Thomas had arranged matters initially to give him leverage against Dieter and the difficult situation in which he'd found himself but now, as things had turned out, their lives might depend on matters having worked as he'd planned.

When they entered the apartment Thomas saw that the stereo was still on but the TEAC four track wasn't moving. He walked over, put the headphones on and pressed the rewind button, hoping it was a temporary problem. The large reel started turning slowly. Bettina was still standing at the entrance, staring at him and the equipment.

"Where are we? What's all this equipment?"

"We're in a friend's apartment. As for this," he said indicating the TEAC, "you should know better than anyone else. Isn't half the country being listened to?" He sat down on the battered sofa and patted it to have her sit beside him.

"I was a little slow in realising what you two had done. Once I'd recovered a bit from the battering Dieter's goons had given me I spent a little time trying to figure out just how Dieter knew I'd been lying about my Frankfurt visit. You were tense when I came into the room and I saw how you reacted to my answers but why didn't really strike me at the time. Then that came back to me later and that made me realise you'd already known everything. Dieter's questioning was just a farce. It was a chance for me to tell the truth, to be seen as reliable, and to hide the fact that you'd been listening to me somehow. Right?"

"Yes." She stared at the old carpet, swallowed and then forced herself to look at Thomas. "I willed you to tell the truth. You don't know how much I willed you to do that. I knew what would happen if you didn't but I ... but I ... " She looked away again and once more grief for Dieter's death welled up, mixed with her earlier betrayal of Thomas, and she again sobbed bitterly as he held her.

"Nobody at the canteen could have overheard our conversation. Stephan wasn't a spy, otherwise you wouldn't have needed me." He got up and opened the fridge. John had almost finished the beers but there was still most of the UHT milk he'd brought over. He reached for the Bialetti moka machine and began preparing coffee for them both. The reel had now rewound completely and had stopped with a snapping, cracking sound. Bettina was watching him, following his movements, waiting in silence for him to continue.

"There were only two plausible explanations. One was that you'd been able to place microphones inside the Deutsche Bank canteen. But it was impossible for you to know where we would sit and not realistic to wire the whole canteen. The other reason was that you also seemed very much aware of what had happened during my interviews. You couldn't have miked the whole building. Or again, if you had, you wouldn't have needed me."

Bettina nodded as he continued his analysis.

"Oh, by the way," he continued. "I've been wondering all this time, but couldn't really ask you, if the person listening to my conversations was a young man lying on the grass of the Taunusanlage."

"With a Walkman?"

"Exactly. I saw him from the interview window and envied him, lying there in the sunshine. It was only much later that I realised it was probably he who had nailed me."

"His name is Sylvan Battenmeier." she said. "He likes to travel, so Dieter sends him on the easy missions. The Walkman idea is his, his trademark approach. He hates sitting in a car the whole time, so he miniaturised the radio receiver system and put it inside an old Walkman he picked up on one his trips."

"Wiring the building was impossible so you must have planted the mic on me somehow. At first I thought of my clothes. But I hadn't changed before I went to dinner and you seemed to have lost contact then. And you couldn't be certain of what I'd be wearing anyway so it had to be something I'd definitely have with me. There was only one explanation - the briefcase. It was a classic, the Trojan horse! A nice present just before the first mission."

"When did you find out?"

"No more than a week or so after I got beaten up. From then on, I let you hear only what I wanted you to hear. I always had the briefcase with me in meetings with you or Dieter but otherwise only when it suited me. It was all carefully crafted."

The coffee made its characteristic gurgling sound as it filled the upper chamber and Thomas poured it into two cups, adding milk to one and then continuing his explanation.

"Now, when the Wall came down I realized there was a big risk that I'd be prosecuted as a spy in the West. I needed to have some evidence, something to hand over to the

Western agents in case I was put on trial. The only hope I had of saving myself was to prove I was a double agent, or at least was trying to be. Even if Dieter didn't give my file to the BND, I had no way of knowing my name hadn't already been recorded somewhere."

"So that's when you bought this?" she said, indicating the TEAC 4 track recorder.

"Yes. Rudimentary, but very efficient. I had a limited budget and this worked fine for my purposes. Although I had to spend a fortune on the miniaturised microphone and the signal amplifier. Those really are state of the art. I was lucky enough that this flat was available and that it was so close to the Stasi offices, suitably within wireless range with a decent antenna here."

She sat up and stared at him. "You planted a microphone in our offices?" Her hand jerked, spilling coffee over her hand and the floor. "Damn! That's hot. You're joking!" she said, looking intently at him, and then "Aren't you?" He laughed at her surprise, enjoying the release of tension from their situation.

"In Dieter's office, to be precise. During that last meeting, while Dieter was talking and you were both looking out of the window at something across the street."

She stood looking at him, wrinkling her forehead and shaking her head slowly, her slightly amused expression flitting between incredulity and admiration.

"When we left for Dresden, I'd arranged for a friend to come over and change the tapes every day. It should have recorded everything from about ten each morning to maybe eight in the evening. I'd have done it for longer but it was a case of balancing the recording time on a reel against when something might be happening."

"Dieter gets in early and usually works late. You could have missed something vital."

"He does, yes, but not many others do and it's the interaction, the meetings and conversations, that I was interested in. You can't tape people's thoughts. And anything particularly secret is more likely to be discussed when the office is pretty empty, particularly later at night. I had to make a judgement, balance the time I could run the thing against when things might be happening. As I explained I initially set it up for entirely different reasons but now it should help us understand what happened to Dieter and who may have wanted him dead, fill in the background to what led to that perhaps."

"Can you find my last conversation with him?" Bettina asked. "He behaved very strangely, just as if he couldn't talk freely."

Thomas started looking through the reels piled on the table, each of them with John's neatly written date and start time in black marker. "Shit!" he said finally. "Yesterday's seems to be missing. Why the hell did he overlook that one?"

Bettina looked at him in dismay. Then she started laughing and pointed at the machine with the tape he'd just rewound. Thomas began laughing as well, shook his head slowly and tapped his temple, then put on the headphones and began listening, fast forwarding periodically for long bursts. He smiled at her, stuck a thumb up in the air, and then switched the output through the speakers.

"You're right. That was yesterday so of course it was the tape in the machine." He breathed a sigh of relief. "What time was your call?"

"7.30 anyway, probably nearer 8, I think."

"Hmmm. Let's hope it's there." He fast forwarded slightly then set the tape playing again. "... so there's been no reaction yet." It was Dieter's voice, loud and clear. A long pause followed his words as if he were talking on the phone.

Thomas moved the fast forward button again. He fast forwarded the tape then, pressing play periodically and listening for a second or two each time.

"Hello Hyena. Anything urgent to report?" It was Dieter's voice, followed by a long pause. "Yessss ..." Thomas said, punching the air, happy that the system had worked and that the quality was good though he wished he'd been able to put the microphone inside the telephone instead of underneath the table. They listened to the conversation, then Thomas rewound the tape again.

"It's as if he wants someone to hear that he's calling the investigation off. Probably the person who was in the office with him then. Listen to it again." He pressed the play button once more.

" ... seems all clear and straightforward ... your mission is over ... another urgent matter ... "

Bettina's lip trembled as Dieter's familiar voice reached them. "You're right. Dieter would never have called the investigation off until he'd heard what we had to say."

"Let's try to see what happened before you rang." Thomas said.

He rewound the tape, listening to the helium-gabbling until there was a sharp crack and then silence. He fast forwarded to the crack, backtracked a few seconds and then set the machine to play. The speakers gave the sound of a door being slammed shut, heavy footsteps and an angry voice becoming louder and clearer as it approached the area of the hidden microphone under Dieter's desk. They listened, silently holding their breaths as if they would otherwise give themselves away, as the tape played on slowly and the angry voice berated Dieter. The words were hard to make out, coming and going, as if the person were walking around the room and only occasionally talking in the direction of Dieter or approaching the desk.

Thomas pressed the stop button and turned to Bettina. "Do you recognize the voice?"

"No," Bettina said. "I don't think I've ever heard it before."

Thomas rewound for a second or two then pressed the play button again. He started jotting down the words he could make, hoping to fill in the gaps later.

" ... an investigation going on of which I'm not aware. Since when do you have the authority to conduct missions without my ... understand what and who ... " There was a sudden bang as if the unknown man had slammed his fist on to the desk to vent his fury.

Thomas pressed the pause button. "Damn it, there's huge gaps. But it must be someone superior to Dieter, complaining that he's not been informed. Who else is above him in the chain of command?"

"I've no idea now that we've been moved under the Interior Ministry. Dieter used to be one of seven heads of department. They all reported to the Director of Operations, Markonberg. Above him are the Leiter of the whole Secret Service, Mielke, and the Vice-Leiter, Sponden. I've never met any of them, I'm afraid. But the most likely should be Markonberg. He's Dieter's direct superior."

Thomas pressed the button again and the tape continued.

"... about financial services. We have other priorities. The ... is over. ... an order. I don't want to hear another ... Securities."

Thomas stopped the tape and wound it back. "Did you hear the last words? It seemed to me like he was saying Phoenix Securities." He pressed play again.

"... an order. I don't want to hear another ...eenix Securities."

"It's definitely Phoenix he's saying."

Bettina nodded. "He's being ordered to halt the mission on Phoenix. That's why he told us to come back immediately. Of course, and that's why he mentioned Henkel! I'd told him of the suicide letter copies we had and I'm sure he picked up my doubts. That's why he said so firmly it was clear and straightforward, finished, when it obviously wasn't."

Thomas let the tape run on.

"I believe there may be a case of fraud on a vast scale. They have built a network all over the country." It was Dieter's voice now, perfectly audible. He was talking vehemently, but with the respect due to his superior. "The ..."

There was another loud bang as if the second man had again slammed his fist on to the desk. The voice continued gaining and losing volume as Dieter's visitor strode around in his fury, sometimes shouting, sometimes talking quietly and coldly.

"... has been investigated fully ... Wornletz ... you appointed ... nothing to explain. Do you not understand? That is an order. You are to take no further action in this area."

"Hanno?" Bettina looked at Thomas. "That means Hanno's in danger too. I need to warn him."

From the tape there was the sound of the phone ringing, a pause, a click, and then Dieter's bored voice repeating "Hello Hyena. Anything urgent to report?"

"That's when you called." Thomas pressed the pause button. "No wonder he reacted the way he did. You couldn't have chosen a worse moment." The tape continued, and they listened, waiting for the phone conversation to end. When it did, the other voice resumed, perfectly clear as if he was now standing next to Dieter.

"Thank you, Colonel Dieter. I'm glad to see you have understood. Don't let me ever hear about you taking up this investigation again or you'll find yourself in extremely serious trouble."

The door again slammed. There was a pause, then…"Yessir, Herr Sponden, sir." Dieter's voice said as if to himself, as the tape ran out.

Chapter 41
Friday 19 January 1990, early morning

"So that's who was trying to stop the investigation." They looked at each other, now seriously concerned that the corruption triggered by imminent unification reached almost to the top.

He sighed. "Looks like every single former Stasi high ranker's got his snout in the trough. Who the hell can we talk to about Phoenix and what we've discovered in Dresden? Dieter was maybe an exception to this grubbing around for personal gain and look where that got him. And why was he interested in Phoenix anyway? Was it just because he didn't like what he suspected others were getting up to? Maybe. There's got to be more to this than we know."

"Thomas, Phoenix is the least of our concerns right now. We're in serious danger and we need to work out what to do. If people of Sponden's rank are involved and this is linked to Dresden that's why Dieter was killed. I'm sure of it. And I'm next in line - you too because even if they didn't know before what Dieter was up to they sure as hell know now and they'll be looking for both of us."

"Maybe they killed Dieter because they discovered he'd evidence of their links with Phoenix. Maybe it was something else entirely. Maybe the money disappearing in Dresden and the sale of the mill are nothing to do with Phoenix, just coincidence. Maybe it's just simple theft and fraud." He indicated the small stack of tapes on the table. "We should try to listen to all these tapes. They may well have clues to ... "

"Thomas! You have no idea, do you? Jesus! How can I get it into your fucking thick head that these people don't play games when they're threatened. They're probably already looking for us, guns ready, and you want to listen to *tapes*?"

"It could help us to work out why Dieter was killed and learn who might be trying to kill us and why."

"To do what? There's no way we can stop people like Roehrberg or Sponden now that Dieter is gone. They still control thousands of people inside the country and outside. Listen! Dieter had integrity. He had intellectual honesty. And so although he was committed to this country and its ideals, like me, he also saw how things could get bent, how people could justify things, how the Stasi grabbed more and more power to itself."

She look straight at him. "Look how they justify spying on people in the name of state security. Look how they get ordinary people to spy and report on others. Look how they bend the laws to hide what they're doing. All that shit is just to frighten people about things they don't really understand. It can seem plausible enough but really only has one aim and that's to ensure the powerful retain power. They've seen how things are going now, they intend to benefit and if people get in their way they'll be eliminated. That includes us."

Thomas had rarely seen Bettina simultaneously so angry and so despairing. She sat with her face in her hands and for a minute or two there was silence. She looked up at Thomas and spoke more quietly.

"We have to get away. We have to disappear. But even that won't be easy. Dieter promised to deal with our files but we don't know what that meant – now that he's dead they could be going through them right now."

Thomas had forgotten about the files. Even if Dieter had managed to hide them somewhere in his office where the murderers wouldn't find them, it was likely that the files would shortly fall into the hands of BND agents. Either way he was doomed. He had no idea about what they contained but the documents he had signed, and which would certainly be there, were sufficient proof that he had been a Stasi agent.

"Where would Dieter keep them?"

"They could be anywhere. He said on a couple of occasions that he would keep them with him at all times. So they were probably in his house when he got killed. Maybe he secured them well, maybe he didn't."

Thomas thought to himself for a moment. He could see only one opportunity. If he couldn't find his file and destroy it then he needed to prove that he'd been trying to collaborate with the West German services. If the BND found his files and pulled him in then even the tapes wouldn't be much use.

"Is there anyone within the organisation that you can absolutely trust to help us?"

Bettina sat silently for a long moment, biting her closed fist. Then she shook her head.

"I've always worked for Dieter, and mostly on my own. I've never been involved with the political aspect of things. I met a lot of colleagues but most of them I know only superficially."

She coloured, looked away from Thomas, then added.

"There's Hanno, of course. Remember, you met him briefly that day in Dieter's office. He's OK but he's still junior, although he was always pretty ambitious. And from what the tape said he's at risk too as he seems to have been asked to make some report about what we were investigating. I really don't know anyone strong enough to go against Sponden or Roehrberg, like Dieter could have done. Dieter was very different from the others. He did whatever he felt was right, regardless of the consequences. That's why he never made it to the top, despite his intelligence and capability. He wasn't controllable."

"OK, so we need to vanish. But how do we do that? Trying to hide from the Stasi, ex-Stasi I guess though it doesn't really matter, is going to be pretty much impossible wherever we go in Europe if the likes of Roehrberg or Sponden really want to find us. And we can't hide forever, particularly as we need to find out more. Trouble is finding out more, getting the proofs we need to nail them and free ourselves, makes us even more dangerous to them short term."

Thomas took a deep breath. He knew what had to be done but he also knew there would be fierce resistance from Bettina and he wanted to explain and justify his plan to minimise that. Though as with all unwelcome news, he thought, maybe the best thing was to come straight out with it. Pull the plaster straight off in a swift jerk.

"The Firm is finished. What's more it looks as if it was responsible for killing the one person there you valued most. I know your loyalty to it and particularly to your country. But the Firm's become your enemy, our enemy, and if there's a link with Phoenix or with the kind of financial scam we saw with the mill then it's your country's enemy as well. We're not strong enough to stop it or halt people like Roehrberg or Sponden on our own so we've got to get somebody as strong as them, even stronger, to help us."

They looked warily at each other. Thomas could see that Bettina was already ahead of him. He took another deep breath and rushed on.

"We need outside help to find and prosecute Dieter's murderers. We need help against Roehrberg and his comrades and we urgently need protection. We need to contact the BND. We need to tell them everything we know. With unification they'll control everything ... "

He reeled back as Bettina slapped him hard across the cheek. He felt her fists striking wildly at his chest, his shoulders, his arms and his head in a flurry he could do nothing to control. He'd expected a strong reaction but this was something else entirely, its violence well beyond anything he'd anticipated. Suddenly, the onslaught stopped and Bettina threw her arms round him, sobbing bitterly into his chest as he held her.

"You can do what you like, Thomas, but don't ask me to betray my country. To me the BND is no different from the CIA or MI5, worse even, the number one enemy of my country for as long as I can remember."

"If it comes to unification it will be because the majority of your fellow citizens just as much as mine want it. It'll no longer be us and them, the DDR against the West, Stasi against the BND. We'll be the same country, one nation."

He stroked her hair gently, talking softly and trying to calm her.

"No, we won't be. West Germany is one nation. The DDR will be a colony, an appendix, a poor relation, nothing more." She gulped convulsively.

It was as if he were hearing Dieter himself as he looked out of his office on the last occasion they'd met, his thoughts clearly having influenced Bettina greatly. Thomas decided to approach the matter from a different angle. The information he knew personally was too limited to be of much interest to the West German services, the tapes perhaps excepted, and he desperately needed Bettina's cooperation and support. In any case, there was no way Thomas could craft a credible story without mentioning her or Dieter, and they both needed to flee Berlin to have a chance of surviving.

"Bettina, do you want Dieter's killers caught and prosecuted? Or would you be happy to see them escape, go unpunished for what they did?" he asked. "This is what it boils down to."

Bettina remained silent, trying to think of something to say, some other way out of her nightmare. Thomas could see the tension in her features, the conflicting thoughts flitting over her face, her desperate efforts to avoid accepting the inevitable. She was like a caged lioness, pacing up and down the room, torn between remaining faithful to her principles and her will to survive. Finally her gaze sank and Thomas knew she was about to give in.

"Do as you wish." she said, in a whisper. "Now I must sleep." She lay down on the bed which served also as sofa in the room, turned to the wall, curled up tightly and drew the covers over her head. He watched as they jerked and shook and then settled as her breathing grew calmer.

It was now approaching five in the morning and still dark outside. He was tired too but reluctant to lose connection with the events just past, to draw a line under Dieter's death and their flight. He put a fresh tape in the machine. "I'll keep on listening while I work in case anything is going on in Dieter's office. Then we can listen to the earlier tapes at night when nothing should be happening there."

He pulled out a pad from his briefcase and started jotting down the things they needed to do immediately. He had to call home to Frankfurt and contact John here in Berlin, telling them he was travelling outside the country and wouldn't be reachable for another month, just in case someone found his file and started enquiring for him. They were probably safe here in Kai's flat for a while but Bettina would have to stay inside and avoid being seen. And he would need to be especially careful at border crossings. Although now people could move freely there were still a series of formal checkpoints where he would be easy to spot.

Thomas pressed the record function, put on the headphones and then lay back on the easy chair and quickly fell into a fractured doze. The sound of a key turning in a lock woke him suddenly and for a moment he lay back confused as to where he was but certain that someone was entering Dieter's office. It was only when the door swung open suddenly in front of him that he realized the noise was right here, that someone was entering the apartment.

Chapter 42
Friday 19 January 1990

The slam of the door startled Bettina awake and for a moment she was lost, groggy and unsure of herself in the unfamiliar surroundings. Instinctively, still half asleep, she rolled on her back sliding her hand beneath the pillow for her pistol as she did so. That there was nothing there brought her to full consciousness and she looked towards the noise, fearing that whatever had made it might be the last thing she would see. It came back to her that in this supposedly safe location, dog tired and distressed with all that had happened, she'd dropped her gun on the floor by the bed as she crawled under the duvet. She could see the gun now, just out of easy reach and with its safety catch on.

At the same sound Thomas had jerked upright, fully awake, and was raising himself from the chair and dipping into the rucksack beside him for his own gun. As his hand closed on the butt and he moved it round, ready to fire through the canvas, the figure turned towards him and beamed with delight.

"Thomas!" John exclaimed. "Hey! I didn't know you were here. When did you get back?"

Thomas removed his hand from the rucksack and lay back in the easy chair, his heart pumping furiously and the adrenalin tenseness slowly ebbing. He thought John's dramatic entrance had probably shortened his life by a couple of years but he was nevertheless delighted to see his friend. He rested his forehead in his palm for some moments, breathed slowly and deeply, and waved a hand in laconic greeting in John's direction.

"God, John! You have no idea how close you came ... " He broke off and looked at his friend, dispelling the image of John collapsing on the floor, blood staining the carpet, which had flashed through his mind. "Hey, man, it's really great to see you. How are things? Thanks for dealing with the tapes – that was really, really helpful."

"Well, if I'd known you were back I wouldn't have come all this way to make the change today – you owe there me there, pal! Anyway, what's all this about? You need to fill me in with what's been going on, what's so interesting to need all this stuff. What've you been up to?"

As he spoke Bettina rolled off the bed, yawned and stretched and as the movement caught the edge of his vision and John turned to look at her with frank admiration she smiled at him, her foot nudging her pistol out of sight under the bed.

"Bettina, this is John. I've told you about him and how helpful he's been - despite being a citizen of the evil Empire. There are a few good ones around, you know." He laughed as Bettina pulled a face at him. "John, meet Bettina!"

She stretched out a hand and shook his warmly as she looked him over, noting his build, fair hair and frank expression. "Hi Bettina. I'm sure glad to meet you at last after all that Thomas has told me." He appraised her in turn, adding "I'm from Minneapolis but my granddad's from Berlin, that's my mom's dad, and my other grandparents were from Heidelberg so I'm kinda back home studying here." They smiled at each other. She could imagine him filling out a purple football shirt, a huge white number on the front.

"Hey, can I join the party too?" Thomas stood with arms akimbo, looking at each in turn. "We've been away for a few days, only got back in the early hours this morning, really zonked. I'd have called you shortly to let you know we were here – sorry it wasn't soon enough to save you the trip. But, really, thanks again for changing the tapes, that's been so helpful. Coffee?"

"Had some already, thanks, but I'll take another. Glad it's helped but I'm just not used to getting up early like this every morning. Now that my PhD's over I can go home, become a boss and not an employee, work when it suits me." He laughed and waved his hand round the room. "So what have you been up to with all this? Going to tell me anything yet?"

"I'm sorry, John, but, look, it's complicated and this is just a bad time. I'll fill you in with the details soon when we're both a bit less frazzled and with less on our minds. Promise. There's another thing, though ... I, I need to get away for a bit. There could be some people looking for me because I, well, I couldn't pay some debts in time and they're a bit pissed off. I need time to sort things out. Don't tell anyone about this place. Absolutely no one. And if you hear of anyone asking for me tell them I've gone on a trip abroad and won't be back for a month or so and, no, you don't know where. These people are hard so it's really, really important that no one knows about this place, about me or where I am."

"Look, Thomas, I have some money. If you're in trouble I can ... "

"Thanks John, you're a real friend." Thomas interrupted. "But this is something I need to solve on my own."

John looked at him intently. He'd come to realise that Thomas was deep in something strange but also very important to Thomas. He'd listened to some of the tapes from time to time but they told him nothing other than Thomas had apparently hidden a microphone in someone's office or house nearby. What was that about?

They shook hands and embraced and as John reached the door he turned back and laughed, punching Thomas lightly on the shoulder and then again looking at him closely.

"Do you know, when I was checking the tapes, making sure they were working, recording properly, I heard some odd stuff, like someone was talking about Mielke as if they knew him. He's the head of the Stasi, right? Or was, anyway. And for a ridiculous moment I thought, Hey, maybe he's listening to what's going on in some Stasi office or other. Strange times, mad thoughts. Ain't that crazy!" He chuckled, raised an eyebrow, punched Thomas lightly again, adding "Remember, if you're in trouble ... " and the door clicked shut behind him.

Thomas walked over to where Bettina stood looking out of the window and put his arms round her waist, leaning his head on her shoulder. She covered his hands with her own, leant back on him and they stood for several minutes without speaking.

"What is it, Bettina?" He turned her to face him, stroked the hair out of her eyes and kissed her lightly before holding her close. "What is it? Are you thinking about Dieter again?" He caressed her cheek with the back of his fingers and again kissed her lightly, this time with a small response, followed by her suddenly throwing her arms round him and holding him tightly, her head pressed to his chest.

"Yes, it's Dieter. I can't stop thinking of him lying there. And that's mixed up with how we get out of this. I'm trying to think through this and I'm getting really afraid, Thomas. I know these people. I know what they can do. They're about the worst enemies we could have and they won't stop. And there's also Paul, my brother. Oh, Thomas, Thomas."

There was a long silence and then she pulled back, turned slightly and stared at Thomas, her eyes welling until her face crumpled and she threw herself back against him, her cheek again on his chest. He stroked her hair.

"But where does Paul fit it? Is he in danger too? You've never mentioned Paul, other than saying he lived somewhere between Berlin and Dresden and didn't do much of anything. I don't understand."

"Paul wasn't an agent. In fact he'd just finished technical university in Leipzig and started a job with Zeiss where he was doing really well. Then one night he got caught up in a fight. He was meeting some friends in a bar he didn't know and confused the name. He's homosexual and the place he went to, the wrong one, turned out to be a hangout for closet Nazis and queer-bashers. He wasn't known so one of them challenged him and I guess then taunted him, slapped him around a bit and it all got out of hand. Wrong place, wrong time, no one to help him. Someone pulled a knife but in the fight the guy got stabbed instead and later died. In the fuss Paul managed to escape but of course got picked up later. At the trial everyone there in the bar said it was his fault, said he'd started it, and so he got fifteen years, no chance of parole. Nothing we could do."

"God, that's really tough. But what has this got to do with you. Or the Stasi?"

"A couple of weeks after the court case I got a letter summoning me to the Stasi offices. That's not the kind of invitation you can ignore. Dieter met me, introduced himself, said he was sorry to hear about what had happened to Paul, could see what had gone wrong and was I prepared to do something to help. Of course I was! So Dieter made me an offer I really couldn't refuse – every year I helped the Stasi would bring two years off Paul's sentence, maybe even more if I was really good, really helpful. I was 16 then, four years younger than Paul. That was 1982, autumn, so now less than a year left for Paul if the deal is honoured."

Now she was no longer holding back her tears. Thomas let her rest her head against his shoulder and continued stroking her hair, reassuring her, willing her to feel safe with him.

"I started with Dieter pretty much straight away, little things at first, watching this person or reporting on that one, but then it quickly became more serious and almost before I knew it I was a full-scale agent, an undercover one. And Dieter was good to me, as I said. He was absolutely punctilious in dealing with me and I know that he came to trust me. He helped me a lot too, in various ways. Trouble is that he too often went his own way, took decisions that he thought were best for the country even if they went against the rules. Despite the mania for collecting and noting every bit of potentially useful information Dieter would never tell me what was in my file and I had a suspicion maybe he'd even kept quiet about this deal. I just don't know but as I trusted him it didn't really matter. At least until now."

"I'll talk to the BND agents in West Germany. It's got to be a package deal. Either they help your brother out as well, or we won't collaborate. But I need to have all the details." He was trying to sound confident, but had no idea whether they would accept such a proposal or whether they had the power to interfere with a judicial sentence. It was already a stretch to save himself and Bettina but there might be value to the BND in getting trustworthy information about the Stasi from one of their agents and he'd just have to talk that up. There might be a small window of opportunity before a mass of ex-Stasi agents changed sides and flooded the BND with information.

"Do you really think there's a chance ... ?"

"I don't know. I really don't know. But it's the best chance we have. And the more valuable the information we can give them the better for us and the more chance we have of getting Paul out. They're going to find out about Paul and about you anyway once they start combing through the archives but they won't necessarily know about the deal. And they'll find out about me. Our information's valuable now so we need to use it now. Six months down the line it could be too late."

She pulled away and again looked steadily at Thomas, then nodded slightly. "It doesn't seem I've much choice. Who are you going to call?"

"Stephan mentioned someone he was friendly with at university who was apparently recruited to the BND, Richard Köpp, his name was. Anyway, Stephan learned in a roundabout way what he was doing now, although it was secret. Apparently he also rang up following Herren's death and Stephan said he was really sympathetic then, although he was clearly also chasing information. I never met him but Stephan said he was pretty bright but could be a bit distant. Maybe not senior enough, I guess, but it's a start. Look, will you listen to what's happening while I'm out?"

When Thomas closed the front door behind him and stepped on to the pavement the sun was shining brightly, lighting up the grey exterior behind him and giving it a slightly rosy hue. The pavements were crowded with people going to work and the streets were filled with vehicles jostling for space, many of them emitting bursts of exhaust fumes which stung his throat. It was still the capital of a sizeable industrial country and one of the busiest cities of the Warsaw Pact, he reflected as he walked. He wondered how many of these ordinary citizens going about their business had been, perhaps even still were, Stasi informers and the thought took away some of the pleasure he felt in the bustle and the warming sun.

Finding a suitable public telephone was difficult but he eventually came across one in Jacobystrasse, isolated enough to make it difficult for someone to overhear him without being spotted. He sorted through a handful of coins, thought about what he was going to say to the BND and what excuse he'd make to Stephan but then decided first to call his family in Frankfurt. To his relief it was the answering machine rather than his mother and he left a message explaining that he'd be travelling for a bit.

There was now no putting off the critical call. He knew he had to handle it well, develop enough interest but not give anything much away. He spent some more time planning his approach and then pulled out a piece of paper and dialled the number on it. Almost immediately the phone was answered.

"Richard Köpp, please."

In a moment the phone was again answered, this time by a young but authoritative voice.

"Köpp!"

"Hello, is this Richard Köpp?"

"Speaking."

"A mutual acquaintance gave me your name." There was a short pause.

"Yes. Go on. Where are you calling from?"

Thomas recognised the secret service style, its immediate instinct being to control the conversation and to try to gather as much information about an unknown caller as possible.

"East Berlin. We need to talk. I have information useful to you."

"Yes. Go on."

"No. It's not safe here. I'll come to Frankfurt. Can we meet tomorrow?"

"Yes. I'm here. But can you tell me at least ... "

"I'll call you again from Frankfurt as soon as I get in."

Next he rang Stephan but learned from his secretary that he was not yet back in Frankfurt as planned but had further meetings East Germany. She promised to contact Stephan immediately. Moments later the phone rang.

"Thomas, I'm really sorry. I'm in Berlin tonight but as soon as I land I've got meetings with the senior Berlin-based management over dinner and until really late so I shan't even be free to meet you after that. Damn! I thought you were still in Dresden or I might have wangled things differently but I'm committed now. You're going to be in Frankfurt tomorrow I hear but tomorrow afternoon I'm off to Leipzig. Damn! Damn! At least you can stay at my place. I'll warn the porter to expect you and he can let you have a key. Oh, well, see you next time. Got to rush."

Thomas hung up, managed to book a seat on the last flight that evening to Frankfurt, and left the area immediately. Remembering there was almost no food in the apartment he bought some black bread and some tinned food and other items in a small grocery shop. On his way back he passed a tiny confectioner's, tucked between two larger shops and proudly displaying in its window some of the extravagant tarts and chocolates which had begun to appear in the city, and spent more money than he would otherwise have thought sensible on getting something he knew would appeal to Bettina and perhaps soften her isolation. As he arrived at the apartment block, now uniformly grey and again desolate as the sun had moved round, he checked that there was nobody following or watching him, strolling beyond the door and then doubling back. He opened the door swiftly and raced up the four flights of stairs, knocking first on the apartment door in their agreed manner and then opening it with his key.

Bettina put down the headphones. "She looks worn out!" Thomas thought as he pulled up a chair beside her and put his arms round her. She rested her head on his shoulder, closed her eyes and nestled closer.

"How did it go?"

"I'm meeting with one of their agents tomorrow. I've booked a flight to Frankfurt this evening. I can stay at Stephan's but he won't be there."

She sat up, distancing herself from him so that she could see his face.

"What do you mean, I? Aren't we both going?"

"Better if you wait for me here. I'll negotiate a deal for both of us, and then we'll get them to work out how to bring you over. It's too dangerous for you to leave the city now in the ordinary way. The more I think about it the more certain I am that it whoever had Dieter killed was someone with influence and authority. They've probably passed your name and picture to all the border crossings, to the train stations and the airports as well. They could arrest you on any pretext and just hold you. With luck, at least if they haven't found the files yet, I'm relatively unknown. I'm sorry. But it's really the best way. Heard anything useful?"

"No, nothing. Nobody has come into Dieter's office yet. I expect it won't take long before someone does though."

"Before I go, I need to know what I can tell them. I can't risk writing anything down and I'll explain that the detail has to come from you but at least I can give them a good idea of the sorts of things you know about."

It started as a trickle but rapidly grew in scope and volume. Thomas was surprised at the amount Bettina knew about events ranging from the attempted murder of the Pope by Ali Agca and the Bulgarian services a decade earlier, through various quite diverse matters including about the Red Army Faction training camps and the military support provided by the East German services. As what she knew flooded out, some of her information first hand, some of it clearly from other agents or perhaps through Dieter, he became more and more convinced of its value to the BND. There was plenty they could offer and he became increasingly confident they could use it to save themselves.

"Now, tell me all you know about Herren's assassination." He had waited to ask this question until the end. He wasn't sure he wanted to have it confirmed that the Stasi had actually been involved and that the information he'd delivered had in fact been used to help the terrorists plan and complete the attack. Rather, he still hoped Bettina had earlier told him the truth. She held his gaze without speaking and he sensed that she was thinking the same, asking herself whether he really wanted an answer to that same question. "Do you really want to know?"

He nodded slowly. "Yes, I have to know about that. Without some credible information then the other stuff is going to be discounted. But if we can tell the BND things they perhaps don't actually know that will make them listen to us and help us."

"Herren was on our list of priorities for a long while. He had enormous political influence. He had control of much of Germany's industry, and particularly the defence industry, through Deutsche Bank's participation in Daimler-Benz. And he enjoyed a special relationship with the Chancellor."

"Do you mean that you'd intended to assassinate him?"

"No, we needed to, as we called it, source him. He was a perfect source of valuable information. That's why Dieter was so pleased when he learned of Stephan's role. Maybe in time we could have found out something about Herren, something compromising, a bit of evidence that could have helped us blackmail him, get him gradually under our control. But in the beginning it was the value of the information we could get about West German industry, about secret areas of West German politics and policies, about all sorts of little things as well, that was important to us."

"So why kill him?"

"Exactly. That's the last thing we wanted. We needed him alive. But we had to share the information you gave us. For instance, it was the twenty-second department that dealt with terrorists, not us. And they were among those who had to be kept informed of what we knew."

"So you're saying it's possible that the information I provided on Herren was leaked to the Baader-Meinhof gang even if the Stasi didn't order his assassination? Nods and winks, maybe?"

"I know for a fact Dieter didn't want Herren dead and would never have ordered or requested that. He was furious when he heard the news. Absolutely furious. Storming around and office and talking of going direct to Mielke. But you're right in saying our politicians wanted Herren dead. Dieter had to file and report your conversations immediately and so among the others the political spheres were updated, and their reaction was extremely violent."

"So the Party found out too. And they were the ones who were most directly affected, since they would be losing their position and influence." Thomas said. "Unification was at stake and the SED and the Stasi were the sacrifices to help achieve that and of course they didn't like it."

"Yes, killing Herren was a simplistic attempt to halt the negotiations, or at least delay them. Dieter only found out after the assassination that a Major Gudenberg of the twenty-second division had been the one who leaked the information - and he was rapidly promoted to Colonel."

"They attacked the West Germans because they couldn't lift their hands against the Soviets."

"The SED tried to get the Soviet generals to overturn Gorbachev but failed. Then we learned that 50 billion DM will be paid by West Germany to the USSR." Bettina said. "Officially, it's for the replacement of the military bases and the repatriation of the Soviet military. Then, there's the amount to be paid to their allies in Europe."

"What do you mean?"

"You remember the initial reactions after the fall of the Wall? The French and the British kept insisting that unification was out of the question and that an enlarged Germany would pose a threat to European equilibrium."

"Yes, I remember. Thatcher had spoken quite clearly against the idea."

"Then Kohl made his speech on the ten points to unification and things really got going. We heard through our contacts in London that the deal to get agreement was that Germany should pay a larger share of the European Community's bill for the next ten years."

Thomas thought back to his first meeting with Dieter and Dieter's comment then: "Most of real history is never written down."

It was now early evening and much as Thomas ached to stay with Bettina he knew he had to leave shortly for Tegel airport in order to catch his flight.

He hated the idea of leaving Bettina and was worried about her. He had never seen her so tired and so lost, so disheartened and apparently lacking in spirit, following Dieter's death. She was almost unrecognisable compared to the carefree and self-confident girl he'd met at the party in the youth centre. But then he too had changed, he knew.

They lay on the bed and he caressed her body which then arched toward him in response. They kissed deeply. "I'll be back in a couple of days. I've brought enough food for three or four. Don't go out for any reason. They're out there looking for you. Try to listen to the back tapes and see if there's anything useful there for us. When I come back, hopefully we'll get straight out of here with the help of the BND." He handed her a small sheet of paper. "I'll be staying in Stephan's flat in Frankfurt. This is his number in case of an emergency. Try to memorise it or else conceal it somehow, mixed up with another number you recognise maybe. And this is the BND number here."

"Don't go, not yet. I need to feel you next to me."

Thomas held her tightly and gently kissed her face and neck. He wished for time to stand still so they could make love and forget about everything around them.

"Bettina, I hate to leave you but I really have to go now."

"Take me with you. Please. I'll go crazy here on my own."

"I'll be back soon. I promise."

He gave her a last lingering kiss and held her tightly in his arms for several minutes then eased free, kissed her lightly again, and walked to the apartment door without daring to look back. He descended the stairs silently, lost in thought. He had almost reached the ground floor when the small black door on the right opened, the corridor light snapped on and an old lady in black, carrying a stick and walking with a heavy limp, emerged and turned to shut the door carefully. Thomas headed hastily to the front door, glancing in her direction, but before he reached it she turned again, saying nothing but staring at him in a way that made him shiver despite himself as he recognised Frau Schwinewitz. He closed the front door behind him, feeling deeply uneasy, and headed to the Friedrichstrasse crossing.

Chapter 43
Friday 19 January 1990, evening, then Saturday 20 January

Thomas had become concerned about catching the last British Airways flight out of Tegel airport to Frankfurt but it had been straightforward enough. The border crossing had been easy. There was huge chaos as hundreds of people kept streaming in from all directions, paying little attention to queues or order but just milling around and pressing forwards. The border officer only had time to look at his face and check that he had a valid document before the surge of people behind Thomas pushed him towards the Western side.

Maybe I should have brought Bettina along as well, he thought, as he found his seat. Dieter's murderers could still be looking for her in Dresden and might not yet have switched the search to Berlin. In a couple of days' time everything would become more difficult. But they'd have needed to bring all the tapes and the documents over as well in order to find out what was in them. And anyone moving around with a couple of large suitcases would seem suspicious and likely to be detained and inspected more carefully when leaving.

"She really safer back at the apartment." he decided and then he remembered his last minute glimpse of the sinister figure of Frau Schwinewitz. "She's deteriorated badly since my first visit there." he thought, not unsympathetically, although he shivered. "Maybe that smack on the head and the long coma she was in has permanently damaged her."

He made himself comfortable on the seat. He had hardly slept in the last thirty-six hours, and his head was starting to ache. He closed his eyes for a moment and waited for the plane to take off and level into its flight path.

"I must be careful not to give too much away before I know we've definitely got a deal." he thought, jotting down a few notes on a piece of paper loosened from his pad. "Does Richard Köpp have sufficient authority to agree a deal, I wonder? Probably not. So I need to make sure that I only say enough to reassure him that I'm for real and can provide useful intelligence. Then I can ask for a meeting with his superior or with whoever it is that handles this sort of stuff."

The issue of Bettina's brother was particularly tricky, he realised. But most importantly, he needed to avoid being identified and to minimize his own involvement. There was still a remote chance that he could find his file in the East and eliminate all proof of his collaboration. If he confessed his role to the BND agents and they then reached no agreement, he would have condemned himself with his own hands. He needed to be very careful. He dozed off and the biro slipped from his hand.

It was a hard landing. The plane bounced once and Thomas jerked awake from his sleep filled with visions of Dieter's assassination. Three men had entered through the front door as Thomas stood watching from the garden window. They had started searching the house as Thomas desperately looked for the gun that Dieter had given him. Then Dieter had come in the room, and two of the men immediately drew their guns and shot him. He saw the body falling heavily to the floor, face first. Thomas shouted, and the other man looked over at him, hatred suffusing his face. He tried desperately to escape but as he ran his feet would only move slowly and he felt as if he were wading through treacle. He had his hand on the gate, almost escaping, when he felt a hand grasping his shirt and holding him back. He turned, and over his shoulder saw that it was Bettina, smiling slowly, turning her head and leaning closer, her mouth gaping to bite, traces of blood on her hair and teeth.

He shuddered, shook the image away, passed his hand behind his neck and noticed he'd been sweating profusely. He felt so washed out he was tempted to make straight for Stephan's flat and immediate bed, leaving it till the next day to call Richard to confirm their meeting, then thought of the risks to Bettina back in Berlin and realised that he had no time to waste. Although late, Richard suggested meeting immediately but Thomas, conscious that he had to be at his most alert, refused and they settled for 10.00 the next morning. Within the half hour he'd reached Stephan's flat by taxi, collected the key, strewn his clothes on the floor, set an alarm clock, stumbled into the large and comfortable double bed, thought again how he would have liked Bettina with him, and immediately fell into a deep sleep.

The alarm dragged him awake, this time from an apparently dreamless sleep. He felt refreshed and capable of beating the BND at whatever game they chose to play with him. He'd still need to be careful and very much always on his guard, he thought, but he felt much more confident and while lying there for a few minutes updated the approach he planned to follow.

He'd travelled light from Berlin and as he and Stephan were roughly the same size, Thomas a little better built, perhaps, and had frequently worn each other's clothes during the many holidays they'd spent together he decided to raid Stephan's wardrobe. He needed to look as impressive as he could for the meeting, he decided, and selected an Armani suit of navy blue lightweight wool the severity offset with thin pin stripes of light grey, which fitted him perfectly. He added a light cream linen shirt, very slightly starched, and a fairly sober silk tie with, nevertheless, a riot of subdued colours seen when looked at more closely. He added casually to his top pocket a matching handkerchief and saw, looking at himself in the mirror, a confident young man, reliable and sober but with clear sparks of intelligence and individuality showing through. He twirled a point of an imaginary moustache, winked at his reflection and left the flat, eager for the meeting.

As he reached the towering building in the city centre which housed the BND headquarters, Thomas could feel his heart beating faster while a prickly edginess made him realise how much of their futures were at stake. He stood on the pavement some metres from the main entrance, breathed deeply and slowly several times, then walked through the sliding glass doors into the main vestibule. It was approaching 10.00am.

"Richard Köpp, please. He's expecting me." The young man at the desk looked through the computer directory, dialled a number and had a brief, discreet conversation. He wrote out a pass, led Thomas across the entrance hall and through a metal detector, then accompanied him into the lift. At the eleventh floor the metal doors opened of themselves and Thomas stepped out into a small reception area walled on all sides with reflecting dark brown glass. On the right an open panel revealed a small meeting room with two men present. Thomas guessed that the younger of these, a tall man of about his own age with dark, slicked-back hair was the man he'd arranged to meet.

"Richard Köpp. How do you do?" the young man said, holding out his hand as he walked over. "I didn't catch your name when you called ... "

"Wilhelm Schultz." Thomas said, holding Richard's gaze and noting the fleeting smile which acknowledged that it would be useless to insist on Thomas's disclosing his real name. "How do you do?"

"OK, Wilhelm." He turned and indicated the other man. "This is Ulrich Bockmann, responsible for the anti-terrorist department here. I thought it would be useful to have someone senior present at the meeting so we can cut right to the chase if necessary."

Thomas nodded and shook hands with Bockmann. He realised this was primarily a tactic to intimidate him and so better extract information, but in any case Richard was probably too junior to be able to strike a deal without authorisation from someone more senior. Bockmann was shorter than Köpp, about 50 Thomas judged, had neatly groomed short, white hair, and was dressed formally in a dark suit with a deep blue tie. He had very cold grey eyes, a tanned complexion and a muscular face with a particularly bulky neck. "He looks like an old sailor," Thomas thought "the kind that hunts sharks in the Caribbean."

Bockmann led Thomas into the small meeting room and Köpp closed the glass door behind him. The room was rectangular with the wall opposite the door almost a complete picture window giving a spectacular view over the Frankfurt's west end. On the side of the table facing the winter glare from the window there was a single chair and as Bockmann laid a hand on the back to pull it out and invite Thomas to sit Thomas deliberately moved to the head of the table instead, taking a position where he would now be able to watch the expressions of the other two while more easily hiding his own. Köpp glanced at Bockmann but neither man said anything.

Bockmann's voice was dark and deep and he spoke slowly. "So, Mr Schlitz, how long is it that ... "

"Schultz." Thomas said. "My name is Schultz."

"I'm so sorry! I must have misheard you. It's such a common name, of course. How long is it that you've been in the service? I mean the Stasi. You look so very young."

Thomas glanced at Köpp and saw that he was looking firmly towards Bockmann. It was clear that the older man was in charge and that Köpp had no intention of interrupting.

"Wait a minute." Thomas said. "This is not an interrogation. I came here of my own accord to discuss ... "

"We know why you came, Mr Schultz. You're not the first Stasi agent to knock on our door, and you certainly won't be the last. In fact, there's so many of you I think we should set up a special division. We could call it the Rapture Division, something commemorating the end of your world." He stared at Thomas and smiled thinly. "Realise that you're in a buyer's market, not a seller's. You really have very little to offer. We already know most of what you have to say and as for the rest, well, we'll find that out on our own in a couple of months." He took a few strands of tobacco from a leather pouch, put them in his mouth and chewed, staring reflectively at Thomas.

"Definitely an old shark hunter!" Thomas thought. He waited for the man to say more but the silence, and the steady chewing, continued. Finally Bockmann spat the tobacco into a small ashtray without taking his eyes off Thomas, leant back and vaguely waved his hand in a gesture which seemed to suggest that it was Thomas's turn to speak, that he, Bockmann, was waiting and that Thomas had better not waste their time.

"Then I guess it was a waste of time coming over." Thomas said as he got up from his chair. "I'd thought stuff like, oh, the real story of why Herren was assassinated the other day and who actually did it might have interested you but I guess if you know all that stuff already ... Thanks for the coffee anyway." He gestured to the Thermos flasks and the three clean cups at the end of the table and made to leave.

He reached the glass door, pulling at it and finding it locked, before Bockmann spoke. "Not so quick, Mr Schulz. I'll decide whether what you have to say is worth listening to."

Thomas turned slowly and they looked at each other for a couple of seconds without speaking, Bockmann smiling in the way Thomas imagined a cat smiles with pleasure at a mouse about to be played with and duly eaten. "I've got him!" he thought, and walked back to his chair and sat down. He had to control the conversation, he realised, and to do that he had to attack from the start.

"Let's lay our cards on the table, shall we?" Thomas said matter-of-factly. "I'm here on behalf of an agent who's been in the service for nine years and was privy to high-level detail. We can provide privileged information about a lot of events - terrorist attacks in West Germany, Herren's assassination as I mentioned, criminal behaviour on the part of senior Stasi officers, and a great deal more. We have hard evidence which will allow you to nail many of the people responsible, including for other stuff you don't even know about yet." He looked around the table to see the effect his words had produced. Each man was listening attentively.

Bockmann grunted. "Go on."

"You'll find this is all valuable stuff, not even suspected in the West in some cases. We have three requirements in return: one, the agent needs a new identity and a suitable new job; two, the file of an informer who was coerced through blackmail into helping the Stasi needs to be cleared; and thirdly, an unjust prison sentence passed on a relative of the agent needs to be reviewed and quashed or, at least, reduced considerably to time already served."

"What is your role in all this, Mr Schultz? An innocent bystander, perhaps – or something more? Why would you be negotiating on this other person's behalf?" Bockmann's voice rose and he slapped the table in front of him fiercely and suddenly. "You talk about putting your cards on the table but I don't see any real cards there, merely hints about what they might be. You must think we're gullible fools, eager to buy anything trivial! We'll decide what the information is worth and therefore what we'll pay for it. And as far as this prison sentence is concerned, we have no power to ... "

"It's a package deal. All or nothing. This person was given fifteen years for killing an attacker in a fight in a bar. Here in West Germany he would likely not have been convicted or at most would have got maybe five to seven years for inadvertent manslaughter. It was a miscarriage ... "

"What would you know about the West German legal system?" Bockmann interrupted. Then he looked at Thomas and smiled slightly. "Ah, but going by your accent I'd say you're from somewhere close to here, close to Frankfurt. Well, this makes matters possibly more interesting ... Go on."

"I, this informer was blackmailed, as I said. If he hadn't cooperated he would have been jailed for an indeterminate period. He really had no choice but what he then did do was spy on the Stasi in turn. He accumulated information he knew would be of value to the West and he did this to prove what side he really was on. That, added to what the agent knows through day to day activity, is material you will certainly be interested in."

"What do you mean, 'spy on the Stasi'?" Bockmann asked. The deep voice was languid but the doubt and the amusement were clear. He glanced at his watch in a staged gesture of impatience.

"He bugged Colonel Dieter's private office in the Stasi operational building. He placed a microphone in a hidden corner of Dieter's desk and captured the conversations wirelessly in a nearby location."

The two men started, almost got up from their chairs. "Dieter? The head of ... "

"Exactly!" Thomas interrupted Köpp. He was glad he had finally managed to get the two out in the open and he now knew that they would all close the deal. After the initial exclamation Bockmann took control again and looked at Thomas through narrowed eyes which expressed his astonishment and incredulity and, Thomas thought, a grudging respect.

"And I assume that we will be able to verify that the voice really is that of Colonel Dieter? Or is he the other agent you keep referring to, by any chance?" He raised his eyebrows and Thomas flushed at the mockery.

"So you don't yet know that Dieter is dead?"

There was no reply. The news had clearly surprised Bockmann, who kept his eyes on Thomas, trying to guess whether the young man was lying.

"I guess then you don't know everything after all." Thomas continued, a slight smile raising the left side of his mouth. "He was murdered two days ago in his own house. You will, I think, find it particularly interesting to learn who had probably arranged that and why."

Bockmann and Köpp glanced at each other and then Bockmann pursed his mouth, rested his chin on his clasped fists and stared at the table. There was a long silence.

"Tell me this, Mr Shultz. We know Dieter to be someone who trusted very few people, even among his colleagues. However, there were two people, not obvious people, he appeared to trust and, we believe, may have confided in from time to time. Who were they?"

"Perhaps you mean Bettina List as one. The other is probably Hanno Wornletz."

"Hmmm. Perhaps we may be able to come to some arrangement after all, including on the matter of what you call the unjust prison sentence. That's provided you can deliver what you claim and provided it all hangs together and meshes properly with what we already know. But if you're bullshitting, and particularly if you're lying, I guarantee we'll put you behind bars for longer than you ever thought possible. Am I clear?"

Thomas nodded and they shook hands.

"Köpp. Give Mr Schultz something to eat and then get started checking the detail. If it stacks up he can go back tomorrow and we'll make arrangements to get the agent and any material brought safely over here in a day or two."

Chapter 44
Sunday 21 January 1990

"I miss lying with him curled round me," she thought "warm, safe. Dammit! I need him back. I need him now."

It was a couple of days since Thomas had left for Frankfurt and so a couple of nights that Bettina had been on her own. At first she'd coped well enough, self reliant, absorbed in her monitoring of the tapes. The worst times were when she listened to Dieter speaking and it had taken all her professional self-control to put to one side her memories of the person and instead focus on the content. Every so often she'd catch her memory drifting back to the sight of Dieter lying bloodied and lifeless on the floor and she felt a fury towards his killers that surprised her. Then the fear started to take over, mixing with her anger and leading her to question whether she, whether Thomas and she, could escape this danger.

On the second day she even found herself doubting Thomas. Perhaps now that he was in Frankfurt he'd find it too difficult to return. He'd find some justification for not coming back. "Absurd!" she thought as she pushed the thought away firmly "He'd never desert me like that." But later it returned and with it an image of her father and his abandonment of his family. She stared out of the window for long periods, carefully standing back so as not to be noticed, watching the people on the street, coming and going, carrying out their voyages and visits, doing their mundane daily tasks, unconcerned, and she envied them.

She prowled around the small apartment and then threw herself into the easy chair. Lying back, she drifted in and out of sleep, imagining Thomas and her together, their caresses exploding into urgent lovemaking with the world of spying and sudden death utterly forgotten. She smiled and wriggled into a more comfortable position, hugging herself.

Sometime later she was instantly awake, listening to light dragging steps outside the door accompanied by a soft, stifled cough. The door knob turned very slowly and quietly and the door creaked slightly as someone pushed against it. There was a scratching of metal at the lock and although she knew she'd secured it well after Thomas left she pushed back the safety catch and pointed her gun at the door, intensely alert. The door handle slowly reverted to its original position and she heard the same dragging steps moving away, descending.

She shivered, let out her breath pent up since the first hint of a possible intruder, pushed on the safety catch, and lay back in the chair, then laughed as a scene from a foreign jailbreak film she'd watched in a small art house cinema with her brother Paul just before he was arrested flashed into her mind. "Stir crazy! That's me. I'm going stir crazy. God, where's Thomas? Why isn't he back yet?"

She'd worked late into the evening listening to the tapes, reluctant to go to bed and knowing that sleep would be hard to come. On that second night, lying awake, her mind churning, thinking over everything that happened and trying to make connections, she'd abandoned her attempt to sleep and got up at four in the morning, sitting down soon afterwards to eavesdrop on what had been happening in Dieter's office. Now she was up to date and had made records of the tapes' contents and the positions where anything of interest had happened.

Most of the conversations were about the situation in Dresden and it had taken time for Bettina to piece things together and begin to understand something of the interlinked events. She'd come to realise that Thomas and she had seen only hints of what had been going on and that the issue was much bigger than they'd thought.

Dieter kept asking someone about how Roehrberg and Spitze were reacting and had earlier talked also about Henkel and what was being said about his death.

"Putin?" Dieter had said on one of these occasions. "You mean the major in the KGB office?" There had been a long silence as he'd listened. "You did well." he'd said "I'm not surprised Roehrberg was angry if Putin was muscling in. I know he detests Putin anyway, thinks he's a thug. Well he is, of course, but he's a dangerous one too and he's clever, not someone to underestimate." There was another long silence.

"It's what I'd thought." he said. "The money vanishing just didn't make sense, given the security. It had to be someone inside and Roehrberg and Henkel were the obvious people. I suppose Böhm could have been part of it but, again, he and Roehrberg only just tolerate each other. Putting the blame on a dead Henkel gets rid of the problem. No one's going to investigate too deeply given the state we're in now." He'd laughed. "And then Putin turns up! I'd have given anything to see Roehrberg's face when he realised what was happening, that he was stuck." He laughed again, one of the few times Bettina had heard him. "Get that evidence back to me and any more you can find and we'll nail them all. And maybe even some here in Berlin."

He'd also asked what Bettina was doing, where she'd been and whom she'd met with. Thomas had only called Dieter once so it was clear that this was someone else who had been watching her movements.

Then she recalled Thomas's comment that it was strange that Dieter would have sent Bettina on her own in such a difficult and possibly dangerous mission. Suddenly it all made sense. "There was another agent there in Dresden" she thought "and Dieter sent me as bait, to try to push Roehrberg, Henkel, or Spitze into making a mistake."

The other agent was hidden, conducting his investigation in the shadows, probably from within the Dresden office she now understood. She wished desperately that she could hear the other side of the telephone conversations, perhaps learn what the agent was telling Dieter or even recognise his or her voice.

"That's who it must have been," she realised suddenly "that man in the grey leather jacket who was in the kneipe that evening and who trailed me in the white car." Her eyes filled as she thought about it. "Oh, Dieter, Dieter," she thought "you might have exposed me to danger but you made as sure as you could that I was protected. And I thought that guy was Roehrberg's man."

From a couple of comments made by Dieter later it seemed that the other agent had found more of the missing pieces of the puzzle. Henkel's will had been deposited two weeks earlier at a notary's, apparently the same Manfred Dornbush who had signed the fake privatisation document, and left everything to his close friend Rudolf Roehrberg. "Well, well!" thought Bettina "I expect the handwriting matches that on the suicide note!"

But it was what she learned about Phoenix Securities which particularly alarmed her. She knew that Dieter had asked Thomas to look into it from Dresden and this was apparently because it was too risky to investigate in Berlin. Apparently there was also a connection of some sort with Dresden although, frustratingly, the details were never specified in the conversations.

A couple of these conversations were with Hanno Wornletz. Dieter had told Hanno that he'd been contacted by a senior agent of Phoenix Securities some three months earlier. Phoenix was looking for help from the Stasi network of agents nationwide in order to provide monitoring assistance for a financing project and was prepared to pay a fee of close to a million DM for support for a week. Dieter had been cagey and tried first to probe for information but the person concerned had cut off all communication and disappeared from Dieter's view.

Then he had learned recently that Phoenix had begun expanding dramatically all over the country and a couple of sources had confirmed to him that the growth was supported by the Stasi network. It was clear that someone within the Firm, someone at a very senior level and so able to deliver the whole network, had accepted the proposal and agreed to work with Phoenix. No doubt, in his typical style and in an attempt to test reactions, Dieter had dropped hints that he was himself looking into Phoenix and had found some interesting connections although nothing yet appeared certain.

As she knew from the earlier meeting Thomas was to find out what he could about the organisation and management of the company, and in particular who headed the scheme in West Germany. Hanno's role, however, was the more delicate one of investigating internally to find the rotten apple in the senior ranks of the Stasi, working closely with Dieter and using misinformation as necessary to trap others into revealing more than they intended.

"You've been placed in Sponden's office, haven't you?" Dieter had said "Keep your eyes and ears open, note anything unusual, let me know who visits, who calls."

"Oh, I don't think Sponden's inv... " Hanno had said and then stopped and as he did so the telephone rang and Dieter got caught up in a tedious administrative discussion, breaking off briefly to say to Hanno that they'd continue the discussion another time, presumably waving him out of the office.

Dieter had also used himself as bait but had had no one to save him when the shark had attacked, she thought. Now she and Thomas were in serious danger because Dieter had brought them in and they now knew too much. Hanno was at risk too, it seemed, and she wondered how she could warn him.

After the incident of the mysterious prowler outside the door she'd grabbed something to eat, levering open a can of lentils with a knife and washing the contents and a couple of slices of pumpernickel down with some fruit juice. She'd listened to the morning's tapes but like all of those following Dieter's death very little had happened. A couple of people whose voices she didn't recognise had entered the office and spent some time searching for documents, found what they were looking for and had then left.

"Perhaps those were our files" she thought "and that makes us the next targets." And then she remembered, although it did little to reassure her, that Dieter had promised to keep their files with him and that therefore they had probably been hidden at his house. Thomas was right − their only hope lay in contacting the BND for help. On their own it was almost impossible for them to oppose Roehrberg and his colleagues.

As the afternoon wore on she paced the apartment, occasionally slumping into the chair and trying to doze but with little success. "Where is he? Where is he? Where is he?" she kept thinking. "His meeting was yesterday and he should have been back last night, this morning at latest." She paced around more, uncomfortable with waiting helplessly inside, somone who needed to act and be active.

Perhaps Thomas had been captured even before leaving and was in serious danger. Maybe he'd been shot and it was only a matter of time before they found her and killed her too. Or maybe he'd made it to Frankfurt but instead of doing a deal had been arrested as a spy and was now in jail. She couldn't stand not knowing.

She made a sudden decision. Towards dusk, around four thirty she calculated, she'd slip out of the apartment, make a quick phone call to the general BND number Thomas had left her, perhaps buy some bread and cheese, and be back in no time. The chances that anyone would mark her, let alone recognise her if she dressed appropriately, were remote. She longed to be outside and she was desperate to find out something of Thomas's movements. She might even manage to speak with him. The decision elated her and she thought with excitement of her coming adventure and temporary escape.

She found a dark brown scarf and, tying back her hair, used it to cover her head completely. She chose an old coat, a slightly shabby one in a sludgy greeny-brown wool, with a belt, which she'd never liked much but which she occasionally wore when it was particularly cold. She looked at herself in the mirror, pushed under the scarf a few stray bits of her distinctive blonde hair and decided that she looked older, a little run down and not someone that anyone would look at twice. Importantly, it would be difficult for anyone to recognise her unless they were very close. She must remember to look down and perhaps shuffle slightly, she thought. A battered leather shopping bag she found in a cupboard completed the illusion of a housewife out for supplies.

Bettina slipped her gun into a coat pocket, listened at the door for some minutes and then opened it cautiously. She looked down the stairs and over the rail into the well and, seeing no one and hearing nothing, pulled the door behind her using the key to prevent the lock clicking into place with a loud snap. She turned the key of the mortice lock carefully and in silence.

Again she looked over the rail and then quickly ran downstairs. It was a wonderful feeling to be able to move freely again. The apartment was so small her legs had almost felt numb and she'd felt heavy and dissatisfied with her lack of exercise. As she reached the bottom of the stairs she heard dragging footsteps but hardly noticed the old lady cleaning behind the staircase with a broom. Quickening her pace, anxious to get out into the open, she reached the front door as she heard a cough and then a voice behind calling out to her. Ignoring the sounds she opened the door and stepped out. Who the woman was she had no idea but she didn't seem particularly friendly and Bettina saw no reason to engage with her.

Chapter 45
Sunday 21 January 1990, evening

It was now dusk and the street lights had come on, some of them not yet warmed up and so still fairly dim. She turned to the right, recalling there was a public phone not too far away. She felt slightly unstable as she made her way down the street, trying to avoid looking into the eyes of the people she passed. Lack of sleep and the constant nervous tension of being hunted had made her feel weak and the familiar streets outside almost seem part of a foreign country.

On the corner of Schillingstrasse, she again turned right. It was an area of Berlin she knew well since it was close to where she'd studied at university and near the Stasi offices. The small coffee shop where she'd brought Thomas on their second meeting was just around the corner, and she felt very tempted to make a detour and stop by. For her, the place was like home.

Then she had a sudden, unexpected vision of Dieter's body lying on the floor in a pool of blood and had to stop, leaning briefly against a wall until the weakness and distress she felt passed. A man walking towards her hesitated as if to ask if she needed help, a movement that shook her and reminded her of how dangerous it could be for her to have left the apartment. She straightened, lowered her head to avoid eye contact, coughed into her hand, and walked on. At least the phone booth was now close by in a small side street and in a moment, turning the corner, she saw it.

Searching in her pockets she at first found nothing but then, a couple of seconds later, crumpled and in a small inner pocket where she'd stowed it for safety, she found the piece of paper which Thomas had left her. She tried Stephan's number first. Nobody answered. Hesitantly, she called the second number and asked to be put through. After four further rings, a firm, young-sounding voice, answered.

"Köpp."

"I'm looking for Mr Schultz." she said, in her most nondescript tone of voice. "He asked me to call through this number." She had no idea of how the discussions between Thomas and the agents had gone.

"There is no one of that name here. Who am I speaking to?"

"A friend. Do you know his movements? Is he on his way back?"

"Ah, I understand. You must be the other person he spoke to us about." Köpp became authoritative. "What is your code name? Where are you calling from?"

She hung up. There was no way she would start a conversation with a West German agent without knowing first what had happened to Thomas. Perhaps he was now in prison and they were trying to get hold of her. She stood in front of the phone unable to decide what to do next. She lifted the receiver to call Stephan again and leave a message but then put it down almost immediately. She knew she should head straight back to the apartment and wait but the sense of freedom kept her outside. Still she waited by the phone, reluctant to move, uncertain of what to do and continuing to relish being out in the open again. At least Thomas had made it to Frankfurt and met with Köpp, it seemed, but if he didn't return by the next afternoon it would suggest that something had gone wrong.

She shook her head slightly to clear her thoughts, and noticed someone walking towards her. She looked down and turned away from the phone. She would buy some food, she thought, and as she and the man passed each other she turned right, heading for a small shop two streets away. The thought that she and her colleagues had often stopped there to buy food when they were working late at the office alarmed her but it was the only shop within a kilometre or more of where she was and also took her back somewhat in the direction of the apartment. It was dangerous to wander around the city, she decided, so she would just have to be careful and make sure to be extremely quick in buying what she wanted.

She passed the small clothes shop and a bank and was heading along the well-known street towards the grocery shop when she noticed a tall, blond-haired man walking towards her on the opposite pavement. He seemed familiar and when they were almost opposite she glanced towards him again. Their eyes met only briefly but it was enough for her to recognise that it was Hanno Wornletz. Overjoyed at seeing one of the few colleagues she considered a friend and anxious to warn him of the danger she thought he was in she started to greet him when a strange gut feeling of something not quite right, of some imminent danger, stopped her. Instinctively she dropped her eyes and turned back in her earlier direction.

"Bettina! It's wonderful to see you." Hanno was now crossing the street, apparently ready to greet her warmly, now bending a little to look at her closely. "We, I, thought you were still in Dresden. When did you get back?"

"How are you Hanno? It's good to see you." It was impossible now to pretend and she smiled at him, taking the hand he held out to her to shake. She noticed as he did so that he'd retained his old habit of slightly clicking his heels and nodding his head as he did so, a telling rigidity of manner in a young man which had always slightly disturbed her, even when they had been close for a period earlier.

"Dresden?" she said and wondered why she felt this prickle of suspicion, why she felt a need now to hide things. He was in as much danger and she was and surely she needed to warn him. Why, then, these guarded responses, this need she felt to test him? "Oh, only just back. I'd finished things on Friday but I couldn't get hold of Dieter so I thought it could wait till Monday and so I took a day meeting old friends."

"And Thomas? Did he come back with you?" The tone had an edge to it and he spoke each word of his next question distinctly. "Where is he now?"

"A friend of his was visiting Dresden so Thomas spent some time with him and then we drove back together this morning. I dropped him near Friedrichstrasse so I guess he's back in the West. We can both report to Dieter tomorrow." She looked up at his handsome face with its open smile, and as she noted again his differently coloured eyes, one brown and the other a greenish grey, remembered their joint mission some years earlier in Poland and how confused but also drawn to him she'd felt when he made it clear how attractive he found her. "How is Dieter? Have you seen him recently?"

Hanno glanced up and down the street and put a hand on her shoulder, drawing her closer and talking softly.

"You hadn't heard? Dieter is dead. Someone killed him."

It took all Bettina's skill to express surprise and horror. "What! God, no! No! When?" She looked at her feet and then at Hanno, wide eyed and with her mouth open and then forced herself to cling to him for a moment. "Oh, dear God! How did that happen?"

"A couple of days ago, at his house. At night. Seems there was a burglary which went wrong. He was shot."

"A burglary? Armed thieves? Are we turning into the United States?"

"I guess so. I don't really know the details. Someone in the office told me about it. I hadn't actually worked for Dieter in quite a while or seen him recently."

Bettina remembered Hanno's discussions with Dieter on the tapes andd disengaged herself from the embrace. Was

Hanno himself involved or he was distancing himself from Dieter as a defence against his murderers? Either way it was now impossible to ask whether his internal investigation around Phoenix had yielded results. Looking at him closely, she saw no trace of nervousness but noted someone fully confident and in control and nothing like a hunted animal trying to shake off predators. Despite herself she shivered, realising she needed to leave immediately but although she did her best to appear normal he clearly sensed that something had changed. He moved closer to her, took her arm and smiled.

"Shall we get some coffee and catch up?"

"I'd love to but not now, thanks, I'm tired and I need to get home once I've bought a couple of things. Another time soon, though. Tomorrow, if you're around."

"Where are you, still living in Prenzlauer?"

"Yes." she said, surprised, and then remembering she had given him her address at the time.

"Let me give you a lift home then. You do look very tired. Tired, but still very beautiful."

She smiled back. "Thanks, that's kind, but I've got my car just round the corner."

"OK, but I'll come with you, help you carry your shopping and we can chat."

She nodded. "Sure, thanks." He was becoming more insistent and she didn't want him to realise how nervous she had become. "It'll be good to catch up."

The shop was small and there was only a pair of double backed shelves, sparsely filled with tins and some packets, subdividing the rectangular room. To their right as they entered was a small counter with a few small loaves next to a large sausage, half sliced. A plump woman with badly dyed hair stood behind it, idly examining her nails. On the near row of shelves were a pile of tins close to where they stood and some scattered packets elsewhere and on the backing shelves more packets and another pile of tins at the far end. Beyond this central island of shelves and on the row at right angles on the back wall were some bottles of beer. She took a tin from the pile beside her, looked at it, and then turned to Wornletz.

"Hanno, could you get me half a dozen bottles of beer, maybe, and two or three tins, please? Chick peas or maybe beans or both. These ones," she said, looking at the tin of lentils in her right hand, "are about the only thing I can't stand. Anything else will do. I'm starving. I'll get the bread and maybe some fruit here as well."

"OK!" He headed down the narrow aisle and picked up six half litre bottles of beer from the far wall, holding them against his chest. As he disappeared round the end of the middle shelves in search of the tins she brusquely swept the pile of tins of lentils from the shelf beside her scattering them between the counter and the door as she rushed out into the street to the cries of outrage from the shop assistant.

Although she ran as fast as she could the street was long and as she turned into Schillingstrasse she caught sight of Hanno loping after her, easily keeping her in sight. For a fraction of a second she thought of trying to reach her car, parked in a nearby lane, before remembering she had left the keys in the apartment. She pushed some pedestrians out of the way and darted across the street, narrowly missing being run over by a car bearing down on her at speed. Hanno was now chasing her openly. The charade was over.

She fingered the pistol in her pocket but realised she couldn't use it - regardless of whether she hit him that would bring the police after her in minutes. As she ran, her heart thudding in her chest, she tried to decide whether to lose him by disappearing somewhere nearby or to run direct to the safety of the apartment and risk Hanno seeing where she was hiding out. After a moment's indecision, she decided on the apartment and although she feinted and cut through a narrow alleyway and then doubled back she was unable to lose him, despite her speed, and she could hear his footsteps growing louder. She could feel her chest tightening and her legs aching and an acrid taste at the back of her throat but fear helped and for a minute or so she even gained some distance till he in turn began to close on her again. As she ran she felt in her pocket for the keys, selecting the large one for the street door and holding it firmly at the ready as she sprinted the last hundred metres to the grey building.

As she reached it and inserted the key her hand shook and in her fear she tried to turn it the wrong way before realising and opening the lock, Hanno's footsteps thundering closer as she pushed open the heavy door and slammed it shut against him. Moments later the door shook as he apparently hurled himself against it, shouting at her to open. She stopped to put her key in the lock and then bent it rapidly from side to side until the metal cracked, leaving the end jammed in the lock, sealing it for the moment against use.

Panting, she ran upstairs wondering if there was some other exit, perhaps by a fire escape, through the attics or over the roofs. As she reached the third floor a door below opened and she heard steps dragging to the front door. Looking over the rail she saw the small woman with grey hair and a pronounced limp. It was only a matter of minutes before Hanno would identify himself and the old woman would try to open the door to him.

Chapter 46

Sunday 21 January 1990, evening

"Hi, there! I'm back!"

Thomas bounded up the stairs to Kai's apartment, knocked in their code to warn her and then unlocked the door, flinging it open and rushing in, slamming it behind him. Two days away from Bettina at this stage of their relationship was too long, he'd thought. Now he was eager to see her again, to tell her that it looked as if everything was going to be fine.

On the flight back he'd drifted into a comfortable doze and indulged in a lucid dream where he played and replayed the coming scene, telling her that the BND agents had agreed to all his demands, including to help Paul, and had been deeply grateful for his help. He roamed around different scenarios, including one where the agents had held out against helping Paul and where he overcame their resistance by deploying irrefutable logical arguments and sheer force of will. "You're a force of nature, Mr Schultz," he'd had Bockmann saying, before deciding to tone things down to more plausible levels. Still, a little heightening of the difficulties was surely permissible and he felt he deserved the gratitude that would show in her eyes and the special extra warmth she would bring to her embrace for saving her brother.

But now there was silence. The bedroom door stood open and the room was empty. It was the same with the bathroom. Bettina seemed to have vanished. The balcony was tiny and there was nowhere in the apartment she could hide, no cupboard large enough, no hidden corner. She'd clearly left. His heart sank and for a moment he wondered if she'd changed her mind about collaborating and had gone into hiding elsewhere. Surely she hadn't risked returning to her own apartment – that would have been madness.

The tape machine was still running, the reel turning slowly and the tapes were neatly piled up. That was reassuring. If someone from the police or the Firm had been there they would certainly have removed what they found of interest. Nor had Frau Schwinewitz been snooping around as there were no signs of disturbance or searching, no signs of any foreign presence, nothing unusual or out of place.

He searched carefully for a note or any clue that Bettina might have left for him but there was nothing. He wondered if she'd found the set of keys to the basement and gone there to explore, perhaps even to hide. Had she explored the tunnel itself and was now in the West? He shook his head. "That's fanciful!" he decided "She knows nothing of the basement or the tunnel and how could she possibly make her way safely along the tracks?" A moment later he discovered the basement key still in the small jar in the kitchen but saw also that the spare set of keys to the apartment weren't in their usual place. That suggested she'd gone out for some reason, but why? And why was she not back?

"Dear God, no." he thought, slumping into the easy chair. "She's been seen and caught." Perhaps even at this moment she was being interrogated by Sponden or Roehrberg or by one of the specialists who had no compunction about what they did to extract information. "Perhaps she's already been killed." His euphoria gave way to despair, his eyes welled up and the emotion hit him hard. He sat still, eyes closed, considering the possibilities and what he should now do. He forced himself to think. "Bettina's a survivor if anyone is." he concluded. "She is, really she is."

He stopped the machine and dropped the newer tapes into his rucksack. He didn't know when, or even if, Köpp would permit him to listen to the material so it was better if he took the tapes now. He set the machine recording again, a fresh tape in place. He slipped the basement key into his pocket, made some coffee and sat on the sofa bed to think things through.

If Bettina had been caught by the Firm it had to be today, and almost certainly not long ago, as otherwise the apartment would have been ransacked and a guard posted. Actually, they'd have posted a guard anyway, he decided, so this place must be still secret. "Well, at least if they haven't traced her here or tortured it out of her." he thought and winced at the memory of his own ordeal in the Stasi cells and the beating he'd been given on Dieter's orders when it was discovered he'd been lying. If Bettina had been caught then remaining in the apartment was dangerous. But so was returning to his flat in West Berlin, where they'd probably be watching and waiting for him. Yet where else could he go?

He looked round the room, saw his gun beside the TV and put it into his jacket pocket, feeling a little reassured at its weight and ready accessibility. He wondered about Bettina's gun but much as he searched it was nowhere to be found. The thought that she was at least armed comforted him.

He drank his coffee and cursed Bockmann. If only that man hadn't insisted that his full confession be taped before he returned to Berlin they wouldn't be in this mess. Thomas had argued he needed to get back urgently but Bockmann had been adamant. The deal had to be done according to the rules and he, Bockmann, was the one making them. That's just how it was. If Thomas preferred time in a West German jail that was an alternative that could be arranged instead. Now Bockmann's rules looked as if they might have killed their chances of surviving.

He checked through his rucksack. The West German passport the BND had prepared for Bettina was there, together with the hair dye preparation and the coloured contact lenses. The striking blonde would become a brunette who attracted no interest. It had all looked so simple when they'd discussed matters in the BND's office. Thomas would leave the tapes in the apartment and agents would go pick them up later, using the copy of Thomas' keys they'd made while he was in Frankfurt. He was ready to leave but there was no sign of Bettina.

Suddenly there was the violent slam of the street door and loud, confused shouting and noise. He ran to the door, opened it quietly and looked down into the hallway where he saw someone was locking the door, twisting the key around in agitation. There was hard banging on the door outside and a man was shouting furiously. He could see little of the figure except the coat, part of a dress, and a headscarf and in a moment it was hurrying upstairs.

"Bettina!" he thought. "That's her! That's how she moves." Then the figure stopped briefly on the floor below to peer over the rail and in a wave of disappointment he thought he must be mistaken but then it started up the last flight to the apartment, taking the steps two at a time. Certain it was Bettina but now confused and knowing that a mistake might cost him his life he moved back out of sight and waited, gun at the ready, until the figure reached the top.

As he moved forward Bettina from the shadows Bettina instinctively brought out her own gun but then recognised him and hurled herself into his arms, kissed him and almost at once disengaged herself.

"We have to get out somehow. I had to go out but I was seen. Hanno! He's with them now. I've jammed the door but he'll break through any time. The roof? Can we escape there?"

"Not possible. But there's another way. Let's go!" He grabbed the rucksack, closed and fully locked the apartment door and hurried her down the stairs, two or three steps at a time, guns ready. At the first floor they could hear the furious commotion below. Hanno was hammering on the door, kicking it wildly and shouting.

"The lock is jammed. I can't open it." Frau Schwinewitz shouted back, trying to assert her position as the building's custodian and long time Stasi monitor. "You must find a locksmith to come here and open it. Then if you show me your documents and can confirm your status and authority, I will let you in."

For a moment there was silence and then the door shook from a further assault and the man standing outside roared with a fury than made Frau Schwinewitz shrink back. There was further silence and then the voice spoke quietly but with clear authority and menace.

"Listen to me carefully, old woman. The girl is dangerous and must not be permitted to leave. If she does, you will answer for it, believe me. Be sure of that, whatever your age or previous party service. I will find some way of getting in but until I do make sure that no one, no one, absolutely no one, leaves. Remember, you will answer personally if they do."

"Wait there by the door while I go to my apartment, just here, to get a weapon. There is no other way out of the building. She can't escape. When I return and guard the door in turn you can find a locksmith."

As Frau Schwinewitz turned from the door Thomas and Bettina heard a muttered "Fuck the locksmith!" and the door shuddered as Hanno threw his weight against it. They looked cautiously out from the shadows on the half landing, listening to the dragging footsteps as the old woman made her slow way back to her apartment and disappeared inside.

"Now!" Thomas hissed and they moved rapidly down the last half flight, crossed the hall and opened the door to the basement, jamming it behind them with the wedge of wood used sometimes to keep it open.

Outside in the street Hanno was pacing up and down, waiting for Frau Schwinewitz to return, relieving his impatience and frustration by periodically kicking hard and charging the door and shouting for her. At least he now had Bettina cornered. He knew these apartment blocks well enough to know that the only way in and out was through the door he was guarding. She was his. That much was certain.

He thought back to his part in Dieter's recent assassination and how his partner there had double crossed him at the last moment although Hanno been the first to shoot immediately after Dieter opened the door. Sponden's orders had been clear – he'd wanted Dieter dead and whoever achieved that would get a bonus of fifty thousand DM on top of the base fee of sixty thousand to each of them. He'd fired twice and as Dieter lay on the floor knelt, put his pistol to the jerking head and fired again, stilling it. As he stood up his companion had fired four times into the now lifeless body, smiled at Hanno and remarked "Guess we'll just have to share the bonus, eh? Let's have a look round and see if there's anything interesting hidden here."

At least this time there was no one to cut him out. He'd had some initial qualms about killing Dieter but it was clear Dieter was on the wrong side and had to go whereas someone like Sponden would certainly survive. This was no time for personal loyalties or for remembering past debts. It was important to be alert and to stake out one's position in the exciting new era which would open up after unification.

Bettina and Thomas were marked too, it seemed. He'd glanced through the files he'd found hidden in Dieter's house, taking the trouble to copy them before passing them on to Sponden. Their contents didn't particularly surprise him although learning why Bettina had become an agent and how Thomas had been blackmailed was interesting information he filed away mentally. He'd had a suspicion of the real reason for their mission in Dresden and the files confirmed what Dieter had asked them to investigate and therefore how dangerous both Bettina and Thomas now were.

He didn't care about Thomas in the least but he'd need to steel himself to despatch Bettina. The trick was removing any friendly connection between them. He'd shown that he could shoot a man as easily as a surplus horse; well then, what was difficult about dealing similarly with a woman? Dieter had been an enemy and Bettina's loyalty to Dieter, as well as what she had now probably discovered, condemned her. That they'd they'd been friendly once, close even, was irrelevant. He mustn't think about earlier friendships; she was worthless, an enemy like Dieter.

There was also that time in Poland when he'd proposed seriously to her and she'd laughed at him, startled, even though she was kind to him as well. That she didn't respond to him rankled and was something he could never forgive. So, yes, he would first take what she'd denied him in Poland and then kill her as her kind deserved. The thought both excited and angered him. He banged hard on the door again then reached inside his belt and eased his underwear as he thought of the coming meeting. "I could shoot her at the very instant!" he thought. "A double climax."

He smiled as he remembered how Dieter had asked him to investigate in the utmost secrecy who within the Stasi was connected with Phoenix. "Interesting." Sponden had said when he'd told him. "Let's give him a few names - you can feed them slowly to him. That'll give him something to think about."

"Bohm", Hanno had said first of all, "and that KGB guy, Putin, too I think. He's playing a very devious game." Dieter had looked hard at him and he'd been tempted to say "Mielke" to see what effect that produced but he'd left it and now, carrying out Sponden's orders, it was too late, which was a shame he thought.

He heard the sound of the old woman dragging herself back to the door, announcing her return with her gun, and immediately raced to his car, several streets away. He opened the boot, scrabbling around until he found the large lump of metal he kept there to smack the bar when undoing tight wheel nuts and from the tool kit he picked out a screwdriver and a tyre lever. He slammed the boot lid shut, grabbed his own gun from the glove compartment, and raced back.

"Stand back from the door!" he shouted, placing the blade of the screwdriver in the gap of the door at the level of the lock and smashed at the haft with the weight, cursing as the wooden handle of the screwdriver split in two and fell off. At least there was now a larger gap into which he was able to fit one end of the tyre lever. With two or three blows the lock was pushed back off the screws holding it and a swift wrench with the lever freed the door completely. He burst in, pointing his gun at Frau Schwinewitz and showing her his badge with his left hand.

"Where is she? What about the roof? Is that a possible escape route here?"

Frau Schwinewitz pointed up the stairs. "There's two of them there. Mr Room ..., Room ... ." She ferreted around, deep in her mind trying to dredge up memories. "Room ... , Rumpel, yes, that's who it is. Rumpel!" She was silent, looking at nothing, blinking her eyes. There was something she knew she should know but couldn't remember. Hanno grabbed her by the arm and shook her hard. "Mr Rumpel. Yes, and his girlfriend. They're both there."

Hanno had bounded to the first half landing before she'd finished speaking, exulting at the thought of a double bounty if he found Thomas as well. And if Thomas wasn't there he would return and so it was just a case of waiting for him. Things were turning out well! He raced up the stairs then crept quietly up the last flight, gun in hand, and listened at the door. There was a very faint whirring noise with an occasional squeak which he couldn't identify but otherwise silence. He listened again then moved back the width of the landing and launched himself hard at the door, planting his boot on the mortice lock which gave with a sharp crack, the lower part of the door splitting away. With his shoulder he smashed open the upper part and stumbled in to the room, gun ready.

A large TEAC recorder, reel still turning, was the first thing he noticed.. He looked for a moment at the three dirty cups by the sink, one of them slightly warm, and wondered what that might mean. Why three? He'd need to remain particularly alert, he thought. But the few rooms and cupboards were empty of anyone and there was no trace of an attic entrance. He stood on the small balcony and looked down. It was clearly impossible for Bettina to have jumped down without killing herself. Climbing down might just have been possible but would have been very difficult and in any case there was no obvious exit from the internal courtyard except back into the building. He leant as far out as he could from the balcony and looked up but the roof was a good five or six metres above it and it looked impossible to reach. It was obvious no one could be there.

In the hallway Frau Schwinewitz was waiting patiently and as she stood there scraps of memory floated into her consciousness. There had been something earlier, something similar which had damaged her, given her this limp, something in this building. There had been a chase. A woman. Rumpel, perhaps, and another man. No, two men and she'd been attacked. There was something else. Something important but she couldn't remember. Darkness and pain.

"The apartment's empty. No one is there. She's hiding in one of the others. We'll search them all. Get your keys."

Obediently Frau Schwinewitz began her dragging shuffle back to her apartment and then stopped, turning slowly to face Hanno, struggling to put scraps of memory into order.

"The basement. They've dug a hole. A tunnel. That bastard. And his girlfriend. She's not always here but I saw her today. Going out. Rumpel. That's the bastard that did this to me." Her face crumpled, she beat with a withered hand at her useless leg and then screamed suddenly and loudly, high and keening, startling Hanno as the echoes reverberated round the hall.

She shuffled over to the grey door leading to the basement, took out her small bunch of keys and tried to open it, then pushed feebly against it. She battered her fists on the door, her fury returning. "That's where they are. I remember now." She screamed again. "I remember. The tunnel."

Again Hanno smashed at the door with his shoulder, this time nearly tumbling down the steps as it suddenly cracked open.

Frau Schwinewitz pointed into the darkness. "Go there, all the steps, right to the bottom. Follow the main corridor. Go right to the end. It's the last door. I remember now. I remember!" She shook her head like a bull, dart-struck in the neck, unable to raise its head, groaning with impotent rage. "Now I remember! The last door. Right at the end." she screamed, flailing her leg with her arm as she turned and dragged her body back to her apartment.

Chapter 47
Sunday 21 January 1990, evening

Hanno ran quickly down the stairs, snapping on lights as he went. Reaching the basement he switched on the corridor light and moved cautiously, gun at the ready, alert for the slightest sound or movement. His heart hammered and he stopped for a moment to breathe deeply and calm himself. There was no trace of Bettina, no sound, no movement of any kind. This wasn't how it was meant to happen. But she had to be there and he would get her. He was certain of that.

When he reached the last door he listened carefully but heard nothing from the other side. He shot three bullets from his silenced gun through the wood at different positions in case she was hiding behind the door but there was still silence after the echoes faded. The door was locked but he dealt easily with that, bursting it open with a couple of well-positioned kicks and stumbling into the room.

He stared in amazement at the scene. Near one wall he saw a large hole, a tunnel leading into darkness. Dirt was piled high, sometimes to the ceiling, and scattered in ridges and piles over the floor. There were tracks around the hole, well defined and some looking new, the footprints revealing slight damp where the earth had been disturbed.

He crouched and looked closely at the marks, confirming his initial glance suggesting that there were two distinct sets of footprints, each a different size. A wave of excitement hit him and he laughed at the realisation that he'd trapped them both. Cautiously he examined the entrance then leant down into the hole, flashing his torch to light up the empty tunnel. Again there was silence but a few moments later he heard a faint, distant rumble and the slight singing sound of metal on metal. He dropped into the hole, bent over and hurried off to track and catch his prey.

At the end of the tunnel he found the hole in the bricks and, looking through, saw the gravel-strewn area below. Flashing his torch in the cavern he caught a glint of rails and picked out the tiles lining the walls opposite and a little distance away. He wriggled through the gap, lowered himself as the others had before him, and dropped lightly on to the gravel, swinging round and instantly ready in case of attack. "Where the hell am I" he wondered "and what's this tunnel? What are these rails?" He shivered in the damp air and tried to make sense of things and work out which way to move. So much for his earlier excitement, he thought, this was going to be harder than he'd expected. Still, if he was careful he would probably take them by surprise.

He stood in the darkness shining his torch around, trying to make sense of the situation and find clues as to the direction in which they might have gone. Then he felt a slight waft of air on his face and heard again that far-off rumble and singing, the noise growing louder until a train appeared round a bend and he realised he'd stumbled into some part of the metro. The brickwork of the tunnel was now lit up and beyond and to his right he picked out the platform of what looked like an abandoned station, its tiled walls now clearly visible. He read the name 'Leinestraße' on the train's illuminated destination indicators as it came towards him, before it roared off and left him again in darkness.

"Of course!" he thought "This is the bit that crosses the border." and he tried to remember what he'd earlier heard about this closed loop and the abandoned stations.

Towards Leinestrasse was going to be the quickest way to West Berlin, he reasoned, and if Bettina and Thomas knew what they were doing they'd almost certainly have gone that way. But what if they hadn't, what if they'd researched this hidden part of the line and knew something he didn't. He dredged up from his memory what he could about the loop, deciding that the other direction definitely went deeper into East Berlin, at least for several stations. So even if they had gone that way and he went the other he could most likely get out at the first station he came to and get colleagues to guard the various exits and arrest the pair when they emerged. He would regret not being able to toy with and enjoy Bettina before killing her but he couldn't risk letting them get away. He set off after the train, running lightly between the steel rails.

As the sound of the approaching train grew behind them Thomas and Bettina were still short of the first station, Jannowitzbrücke. They were running as fast as they could, but they had only one small torch, already in Thomas's rucksack, and the lack of light was a major handicap. He cursed himself for forgetting the bigger and stronger one he'd left on the table in the apartment. At one point he misjudged his footing, stumbled and crashed to the ground, barking his shin badly as he hit a tie securing the rails. Moments later, as they rounded a bend, there was a slight lightening of the gloom and they could see the start of the station looming out of the darkness a few metres ahead. Thomas scrambled up, reached out a hand and helped to pull Bettina on to the platform. Less than thirty seconds later the train passed slowly in front of them, its headlight opening up the station's shadows and its passengers brightly visible, sitting in their seats reading and staring and talking, oblivious to the fugitives lying a metre or two away. Bettina stared around in wonder.

For a moment, Thomas considered shooting to try to stop the train but realised the driver would in all likelihood accelerate and call the police for help. Once the train had passed, they dropped back down on the tracks and again started running. After a few steps, however, Thomas had stopped and caught Bettina by the shoulder, gesturing to her to wait. The sound of the nearby train was still in their ears, dying away in front of them, but from the other direction came the faint, steady pad of footsteps and occasionally a sharp clink, the sounds amplified and sharpened by the hard walls and contained by the tunnel.

"Shh! Someone's coming. Listen!" For a moment they stood, silent and increasingly afraid, then Thomas whispered again.

"Shit! It must be Hanno. At least it sounds like only one person."

Gripping their guns they set off again, moving deeper into the tunnel, trying to juggle speed with silence but realising that it was impossible for Hanno not to hear them while they were moving.

The footsteps behind them were growing louder and a few moments later changed in character and they realised that Hanno had reached the station and was rapidly catching them up although it was difficult to judge just how close he really was. At one point there was a brief flash of light behind them. The sounds echoed down the long tunnels, the echoes changing as the configuration of the tunnels changed, but it seemed likely that he was now no more than maybe four or five hundred metres away. At their respective speeds, and particularly in the faint light they had to rely on, they had no chance of making the next station before he was on to them. It was better to turn and face him, to try to hide their presence, to avoid the noise of running and perhaps take him by surprise. There were, after all, two of them and if they separated Hanno would be unable to deal with them simultaneously.

"There's another bend just ahead. Maybe the tunnel will widen a bit or there might be alcoves. You keep on this side and I'll cross over. Run for two hundred steps and then get as close to the wall as you can. If you see him, or he sees you, shoot. I'll do the same."

Thomas brushed his hand down Bettina's cheek and across her lips, pushed her lightly forward, crossed quickly to the far wall and then ran as silently as he could manage round the corner and along the following straight.

Behind them, and despite their care, Hanno heard their steps and smiled to himself. He'd chosen the right direction and his luck was still with him. There were no witnesses here so he could kill them both and run no risk of a police investigation. He'd kill Thomas first, he thought, and then play with Bettina. Or, no, perhaps he'd incapacitate Thomas, let him watch beyond endurance and then finish him off once he'd finished with Bettina. He'd let Sponden know discreetly of the execution, to be praised and rewarded in turn. He reloaded his gun and set off at a steady pace, fast enough to be certain of catching them up but one which allowed him to move more quietly so that he might take them by surprise.

As Thomas and Bettina stood opposite each other they realised that the sound of the following footsteps had gone. The silence continued and with it their nervousness grew. They didn't dare whisper across the space and in their isolation their fear grew and the sweat broke out on their foreheads as they waited for something to happen.

Then Thomas felt something, a mere sensation, an intuition rather than anything approaching a certainty, as if air were moving through the tunnel towards him but without the force, and certainly without the vibration or noise of an approaching train. Perhaps, he thought, it was an unreliable feeling deriving from the intense tension of their situation but as his nervousness increased and the feeling grew that something was approaching he decided to make the first move.

After they'd rounded the corner the tunnel had run straight and if something was now there it must have come along between the tracks – there was hardly any space to the side and in any case any movement there would have produced inevitable sounds from the gravel and stones which lined the track. He stepped silently out from the wall to the middle of the track, bent on one knee, held his arm as parallel to the ground and to the direction of the rails as he could judge, steadied his arm and fired.

The tunnel was lit up for a brief instant by the flash and noise of the shot hammered off the walls, the echoes repeating and then dying away. Initially startled by the shot, Bettina had noticed in the brief flash a shadowy bulk less than fifty metres away and instinctively shot at it.

There was a low grunt of pain, amplified by the tunnel, followed by the thud of a body collapsing to the ground as Bettina's bullet hit Hanno's right shin and continued its trajectory to skip off the brickwork in turn. A blip of light from their pursuer's location and the muffled sound of a shot barely clearing Thomas's head as he crouched and then singing off the metal cables to the side showed that Hanno was alive and still dangerous.

Thomas reacted automatically, shooting three bullets, none of which hit their target. A moment later Bettina fired from his left, two shots in rapid sequence evoking an almost instant response from Hanno whose three muffled shots were followed by a sharp cry from Bettina and the crunch of gravel as she fell to the ground.

There was silence, the dark weighed in on Thomas and he couldn't tell whether she was even still alive. And now, he realised, he had only two bullets left. He had to get across to her, check her condition and help as necessary, but also get the ammunition he knew she would carry with her as an agent.

He lay flat between the tracks, feet towards his pursuer in case of shots, and tried reaching out for her with his hand but couldn't find her, although he knew she must be close. He eased himself in Bettina's direction, constantly alert to any movement or sound down the track. His anguish now threatened to overcome him completely and he realised he was squeezing the gun so hard his hand hurt and was shaking wildly. He breathed in and out slowly, in and out, seeking to relax. Seconds passed as he waited for the movement of a shadow, a greater solidity in the darkness or some sense, some other clue that Hanno was closing in.

Then there was a soft moaning slightly ahead and he realised that Bettina was regaining consciousness. But as he reached her he became aware of a rush of air and of another sound, a now familiar low rumbling and a singing of metal wheels on metal tracks, growing louder and with the faintest of light just starting to outline the corner. She was almost certainly partly on the track he reckoned and he had to get her out of danger. Careless of danger from Hanno he caught her under her shoulders lifting her and trying to drag her to the tiny space by the tunnel wall, putting her down again to free her foot from where it was awkwardly trapped by the rail as she'd fallen and twisted, the roar of the train reverberating louder and louder in the tunnel.

Then the light brightened as the train approached the final bend and he saw a dim outline of Hanno, perhaps thirty metres away, standing with one leg inside the rail and leaning for support against the tunnel wall, his hand holding the pistol towards them, wavering as he balanced and aimed. There was a flash and he felt the passage of the bullet past him, perhaps only a centimetre away only, and in that same instant Hanno made towards them, stumbling and hopping on his good leg, now suddenly a strong silhouette in the blinding headlight of the train as it rounded the corner. There was a huge hiss of air as the brakes went on, a scream of metal as the wheels locked, and a juddering as the train began to slow, its bulk still sliding towards the man, sliding faster than he could possibly move to escape and with no refuge to the side.

The wild screeching of the locked wheels on the rails reverberated through the tunnel but as the train caught up with Hanno there was a soft crack and something heavy lashed Thomas violently knocking him to the ground with Bettina as the train finally screamed and stopped less than a metre from them. In the sudden silence and with the realisation that they were both alive Thomas felt for the object which had knocked him over and now pressed on his leg. It felt warm and sticky and when he withdrew his hand it was drenched in blood. As his eyes focussed in the brightness of the train's headlamp, moments before he passed out, he found himself staring into Hanno's face, the rest of the man nowhere to be seen.

Chapter 48
Saturday 28 July 1990, evening

In the Frankfurt suburbs the sun was setting in a mackerel sky, the blood red rays streaking the sky's azure and turning the clouds into bunches of candy floss in a variegated salmon hue. It was starting to get cooler. Thomas swithered over whether they should eat on the tiny patio with its view of the rose garden or whether he should set the large dining table in the living room. He decided that it was too good an opportunity not to show off the patio and garden. If anyone felt cold, well, there were sweaters he could lend them.

His left arm still felt a little stiff and he could lift it only halfway. The physiotherapy helped – he did the exercises regularly for over an hour a day – but the improvement was still too slow for his liking. Bettina's operation had been more complex. Two bullets had hit her, one fracturing a kneecap and the other passing through her right thigh but without hitting the bone. As soon as she regained some consciousness she had realised her perilous position and the risk of being run over by a train and with an extraordinary force of will had attempted to move herself out of danger but without success. Swirling in and out of consciousness she'd felt Thomas lifting her under her arms and then putting her down again to try to free her foot, the noise of the train getting steadily louder. When Thomas thought back to how close she'd come to death, indeed how close they'd both come, he shivered. They were so much a part of each others' lives now that the idea of her not being there with him was intolerable.

Thomas knocked on the bathroom door. "Bettina, have you fallen asleep? Stephan and Camille will arrive any moment, and I could do with some help if you don't mind." he shouted, pitching his voice above the noise of the hair-dryer. There was no reply and he walked back to the kitchen to decant the wine. The occasion was nominally a house warming, a dinner to inaugurate their new accommodation in Frankfurt, funded by the BND and furnished with some money he'd negotiated from his mother. The security agency had found Bettina a job teaching history at one of the better high schools in town. They had also offered her a position as an agent, but she had refused. It was too early, she'd said. She needed time to recover and to reflect on what she wanted to do with her life.

The documents Thomas had stolen from Roehrberg's house had given the BND valuable information, including the address of the house in Provence. Working with their French counterparts they'd organised a covert operation to search for other materials. Köpp had refused to tell Thomas anything about what they'd found, confirming only that it was Roehrberg's archive.

Searches had revealed that Omega Mills GmbH was the fully owned subsidiary of a Dutch financing company, Omega NV. Getting through the legal smoke screen had taken longer but after putting pressure on the ABN Amro officer who served as legal representative they'd discovered that the shares were held equally by Henkel, Roehrberg and Sponden and now, with Henkel's death, by the two survivors. The vehicle was an old shell company, incorporated in 1975 but dormant until a year earlier when a West German subsidiary had been incorporated. This helped to confirm that the document of the sale of the mill, dated 1984, had been falsified and that the accounting documentation was also false.

Roehrberg had caved in when he realised that the BND had found incriminating documents. He agreed to collaborate in exchange for a reduced sentence and had provided most of the evidence incriminating the other two. Sponden, in his turn, believed himself relatively safe and had incriminated Roehrberg as the agent of Henkel's murder. He further confirmed the forging of the will in Roehrberg's favour. Thomas laughed as he imagined Bockmann presenting first Roehrberg and then Sponden with offers they'd feel unable to refuse and shuttling urbanely between them encouraging each to bury the other in an even deeper hole with vague hints of leniency for themselves.

Apart from the fifteen million marks which Omega Mills had exchanged at two to one, none of them had confessed to other financial frauds. The investigations were still proceeding.

Putin, who in any case was not named on any of the documents, was now safely back in Russia and beyond easy reach.

The doorbell rang just as Thomas finished the delicate operation of decanting a bottle of Ch. Beychevelle 1986. It had cost a fortune but Thomas had seen how Stephan was developing expensive tastes and knew how much he appreciated good French wine. He was looking forward to pleasing and surprising him. He went to the front door and opened it. A beaming Stephan, dressed in a green polo shirt and blue jeans, greeted him warmly. Camille looked more beautiful than ever in her pearl grey silk with matching earrings and high heeled evening shoes in iridescent magenta satin. It looked as if they were going to different parties. Thomas smiled thinking of all the times Stephan had complained to him about her dress habits, one of the few irreconcilable differences between them. The other had been East Germany.

"Hey, this is a great place." said Stephan as they entered and looked around with interest.

"Isn't it just?" added Camille. "Wow, look at the colours – and the blue and brick in that carpet is lovely, just right for those walls. You are clever!"

"We found it in the flea market last weekend." said Bettina, finally emerging from the bathroom, still limping. "It's a kelim, from eastern Turkey, we think. It's a bit worn and so it was cheap. But we really like it."

Bettina had dressed with care and was wearing a dark red silk shirt, open at the neck, and a black linen skirt which she had bought just that afternoon and which set off her figure to advantage and complemented her hair. Thomas had never seen her looking so beautiful and stood mesmerised for a second, admiring her.

Stephan noticed his expression and laughed. "Come on, Camille, I think we should leave them alone for a bit. And I guess dinner's going to be pretty late!"

A tall white candle flickered behind the decanter, layering the tablecloth with intermittent splashes of dark red. Stephan and the two women settled themselves in bamboo chairs on the patio and admired the still striking sunset. Thomas arrived a moment later, carrying a steaming dish of pasta with one hand and in the other the empty wine bottle wine which he handed over to Stephan with a small, mock serious bow.

"Wow! What a bottle!" Stephan exclaimed. "Do you have an important announcement to make?" he asked, looking slyly towards Bettina.

Thomas smiled to himself. Stephan had been extremely inquisitive ever since he'd heard they were both settling down in Frankfurt about how things with Bettina were proceeding. Stephan poured wine as Thomas served the pasta.

"As a matter of fact I do have announcements, two of them." Thomas said, when everyone had been served. "First, I would like to propose a toast to Stephan in respect of my degree. I learned a couple of days ago that my thesis had got the maximum number of points. That was really thanks to your help, Stephan." he said, turning to his friend and raising his glass. "I don't know what I would have done without your insights into the monetary system of East Germany. Now I've got ten days of doing nothing but relaxing before I start with Deutsche Bank."

"What's the second announcement?" Bettina asked.

"I'm pregnant." he said. "IVF. I've been taking hormones as a guinea pig for the Frankfurter Transgender Institute and they seem to have worked. Isn't that lovely?" He pirouetted on the ball of his left foot, pulling out his shirt as he did and letting the heavy silk swirl round him gracefully. "I'm so excited. I thought we'd call him Dieter."

In the silence that followed he pirouetted a second time, beaming into the faces round him and then wagged his forefinger. "Just kidding!"

"I got a call an hour ago." he went on. "Haven't had a chance to tell you yet ... " he turned to Bettina " ... but I'll be performing my first opera role in September, Tamino in the Magic Flute. It's not the Frankfurt Opera, but still a good producer. I couldn't believe it, I auditioned two months ago but felt I didn't have a chance."

"That's wonderful!" Bettina said. She stretched out a hand and squeezed his and then leant over, pulled his face towards her and kissed him. "Wonderful."

"To Thomas!" said Stephan and the two women raised their glasses with his and echoed his words.

"And to Bettina and to Camille ... " added Thomas, raising his own glass in turn and then clinking it with those of the others.

*

Pretty much at the same time other glasses were being raised less than two miles away to the north west. Three magnums of Dom Perignon Cuvée Speciale had just been opened in Erwin Hammer's new villa in the exclusive spa town of Bad Homburg. The six people standing around the crystal table looking on to the heated swimming pool were in exuberant mood, smiling and laughing excessively at each other's jokes. It took a couple of seconds before the host could quiet them for long enough to be heard.

"Gentlemen. Tonight we celebrate the realisation of a dream." Hammer struck a pose and began to declaim, indulging his weakness for rhetoric now that he had a captive audience. "A year ago, my founding partner and I had a vision, a vision of things to come, a vision which has now materialised, a vision which has turned out probably better than any of us had dared to hope."

He paused and looked round the room, nodding a welcome to each of the guests. "It has taken a lot of work from all of you around this table to make it come true and I thank you for this. There have been many difficult moments, moments in which I sometimes feared, we all sometimes feared, it couldn't be done. But we've done it!" he finished loudly, raising his glass high into the air. "I can tell you tonight, gentlemen, that the proceeds from this operation have exceeded all of our expectations, perhaps even our wildest expectations. It has been a triumph of vision, organisation and execution and although my founding partner and I may have been the ones with vision, and the organisational driving force behind everything, we needed your help and support to execute the project well. We benefited as the preferential exchange rate was set at one to one, with residuals exchanged at up to three to one. Our futures contract entitled us to sixty million Ost Marks. Since we were able to source the poorest of the poor our average exchange rate was one point three!"

The others cheered and clapped. This was fantastic news, since it meant they had almost fully been able to exploit the preferential rate. Only a small fraction had had to be converted at three to one, the rate applicable to West German residents.

"The Eastern connection delivered perfectly, thanks to our friend Patrick and of course to my intervention and no money leaked away where it shouldn't. Our gross profit from the exchange was forty one million. Taking out all costs incurred, we have made over twenty six million Deutsche marks."

There was total silence as each of the guests calculated what this would mean for them, depending on their particular personal stakes. Erwin and "Brains", the two founding partners, held the majority yet even a small stake in the fortune gained was worth more than any of them would have been able to earn in a substantial period as employees.

Erwin pulled out an envelope and took out the first cheque. "This is yours." he said, handing it over to a beaming Patrick. "Pretend it's Christmas today! I've added a little something from my own stake to round up the thousands. Now, who's next?"

*

"My turn to announce something important!" Stephan said as he rose from his bamboo chair, finding it a bit uncomfortable and glad of the chance to ease and stretch his legs. "As you know I've decided to return from East Germany and settle again in Frankfurt. It's such a wonderful part of the country that that wasn't an easy decision but in the end Camille and I decided we were missing the excitement of the city, of Frankfurt."

He looked at Bettina first and then at Camille, his expression conveying more than any words could his true feelings about the decision and about what he'd given up.

"For my part" he added "after the frantic weeks during which the currency exchanges took place there was hardly anything much of interest left to do. I think it will take a while before we are able to offer the same services in the West and in the East." He paused for a second, collecting his thoughts, then smiled broadly at everyone. "But that's not what I wanted to tell you. What I really wanted to announce is that Camille and I have decided to get married. In September, next year."

There was a surge of excited talking, congratulations and laughter as Thomas and Bettina reacted with joy and excitement to Stephan's news. Thomas brought out a bottle of matured Kirsch, proposed a an extravagant toast and everyone clinked glasses again. Camille brought her hand out from underneath the table and showed the huge diamond ring Stephan had given her the night before.

"And how about you?" Stephan asked.

"Give us time." Thomas said, looking at Bettina and stretching out his hand to take hers. "We're still fighting over wardrobe space. And now that Paul – that's her brother - is coming over for a week or so we'll have a real test of our relationship. The flat's so small we might all have to sleep in the same bed!"

*

Erwin finished handing out the cheques and asked the waiter to open another two magnums. Günther took one and started filling up the glasses to the brim.

"I propose a toast to Erwin." he said loudly, lifting his glass.

Erwin had hoped someone would have had that idea and Günther Pilsern, the one who followed Erwin around like a small dog, was the most likely candidate.

"If it hadn't been for his stroke of genius, we'd all still be working for a living! To Erwin!"

The others cheered and shouted. "To Erwin!" Erwin beamed with pleasure and gratification, then raised his hand for silence.

"I forgot to tell you the funniest part. You remember the phone number at Phoenix?"

"Sure." everyone replied. They had all taken turns working the phones in the evenings.

"It turns out they reassigned the number to this old woman when we cancelled the contract. I called last night asking for Phoenix, and she went batshit crazy on me! Told me she'd received hundreds of calls, and threatened me if I ever tried calling again! I swear, you should have heard her … " he laughed and held his stomach, almost in tears at the memory.

*

Thomas and Stephan were standing together near the front door, waiting for Camille who had disappeared into the bathroom with Bettina and was no doubt gossiping about mutual friends and events with no regard for time. The evening had been extremely pleasant and after getting carried away in making numerous toasts they all felt somewhat tipsy.

"What are they doing in there?" Stephan asked. "Are they making out or something?"

Thomas laughed. "I guess they've just got a lot to catch up on."

"How's your friend Kai managing? I'm sorry I couldn't do anything about him in Deutsche Bank but with his studies he just didn't fit in. I tried arguing for him, you know, supporting someone from the East, but it didn't work."

"He's been able to find something through some other friends just the other week, so don't worry."

"I'm glad. He seems a real nice guy. What's he doing?"

"Assistant salesman in a sports shop in Cologne. He was really happy to get that, he's not a career kind of guy. He's making a visit to Frankfurt and he's coming to dinner tomorrow with Bernhard ... and Ulrike, his former girlfriend. They went through a lot digging that tunnel and escaping through the underground system and unfortunately for Kai, those two are now an item. But he's taking it okay I think. At least it appears he is."

"Yeah. Not exactly what he had in mind, I'm sure. But then life tends to be full of surprises, don't you think? And luckily not all of them are negative. Ah, here's the late Camille, escorted by your stunning girlfriend." Stephan sighed theatrically. "If only I wasn't already promised ... "

Stephan grinned at Thomas and the two friends embraced warmly as Bettina opened the door.

*

The full moon hung above the swimming pool, its light reflected in the crystal blue water. Two marble copies of statues from Hadrian's villa, or perhaps more accurately from the sweep up to Caesar's Palace, lit by pink halogen lights stood watching the scene from a distance. The party was more subdued now, the noise reduced, as everyone was beginning to feel tired and sated from all the food and wine they'd consumed.

Erwin tapped on his glass with a knife and lifted his hand for silence, the group now responding easily to his request. He peered at the others, focussing with some difficulty, and began another pompous oration, booming far more loudly than he either realised or needed to do for the small group.

"Now, the last thing I would like is that any of you would complain about my hospitality."

There was a loud murmur as they sounded their approval of the evening. They had expected a dinner and been served a gargantuan feast instead.

"Of course, the evening's not over yet." He smiled at their eager expressions.

"You're probably all too drunk to be able to drive so I've had prepared a bedroom, complete with a little gift, along the corridor there for each of you." He waved his hand in the direction of the door and the house interior. "You'll find your names on the doors and if you hurry you may still find, well, let's say your pleasant surprises, still awake and anxious to please." He laughed with pleasure at their expressions of disbelief and anticipation. "I just hope none of you have especially strange tastes because I must admit I haven't catered for such possibilities." A roar of drunken laughter answered him as the guests jostled each other to get through the doorway and rushed down the corridor looking for their names. "Good night! Good night!" Erwin shouted as they all disappeared.

*

The door closed behind them and Camille leaned her head on Stephan's shoulder. "God, I'm tired. I'm starting to feel the lack of sleep from last night. But I'm glad we came. I think Thomas and Bettina are probably the friends of yours I enjoy the most." she said, yawning. "And about the only ones who know how to cook."

They walked lazily to the car. As Stephan opened the car door the car phone started ringing. It had been installed it only a week earlier and he had given the number only to his very closest friends.

"Hello?"

"Hello, Shtephan." the voice said. "You misshed an exshellent party."

"Hi there, Erwin. I'm sure I did." he replied, leaning back comfortably in the leather seat. "But you know me. I'd rather keep out of the spotlight. I leave all that to you."

"Sure, Brains, I know you can't run any risks. At least with the precautions we took it's probably almost impossible to track us down."

"Unless the others act stupid. Did you warn them about not throwing their new wealth around? And did they like the special presents you brought them? How about the pictures?"

"Video cameras are all in place. I'm sure tomorrow we'll have enough material that none of them will want to talk out of turn once they've seen the film show. I told the girls to be particularly deviant."

"Well done. Let's meet tomorrow for lunch. We need to discuss details of the account movements, make sure they're not traceable."

"Sure, I took care of that already. You come down to the fifth floor and I'll give you the details. Every time I come up, there's those damned security measures in the way."

"Okay. See you at one. I've got some material you might also like to see, some amusing pictures - the originals are safe but I'll bring copies with me. Goodnight Erwin."

Stephan put the phone down and sat for a moment staring out into the night. Camille, tired and sleepy, was starting to get fractious and was anxious to get home.

"Who was that?"

"Oh, just a colleague." he said, starting the engine. "Tonight there was a closing dinner for a deal I put together." As he drove off his mood changed as he thought back on Herren. He missed him, on both a personal and a professional level. He was intellectually a notch above anyone he'd ever met. That he had managed to pull off this deal was all thanks to the information he'd got from working with Herren and being taken into his confidence.

Had Herren been doing all this for the good of the country or did he have his own secret schemes to make millions from unification as well, Stephan wondered. There was no way of telling now but his guess would have been the latter. One thing he had learned was that you don't make it to the top by being a nice guy. Particularly if you're a banker. But then again Herren was rich enough already not to need it. Maybe he was just trying to make history. Now he would forever be part of it.

He glanced at Camille, dozing in the seat beside him, smiled, then pressed the accelerator and set off for home.

Lightning Source UK Ltd.
Milton Keynes UK
UKOW05f1034080615

253079UK00001B/1/P